THE SPY DEVILS

JOE GOLDBERG

NOTE

All statements of fact, opinion, or analysis expressed are those of the author and do not reflect the official positions or views of the Central Intelligence Agency (CIA) or any other U.S. Government agency. Nothing in the contents should be construed as asserting or implying U.S. Government authentication of information or CIA endorsement of the author's views. This material has been reviewed by the CIA to prevent disclosure of classified information. This does not constitute an official release of CIA information.

The Spy Devils

Copyright 2021 by Joe Goldberg

First Electronic Edition: May 2021

13 Digit ISBN: 978-1-7364745-1-8

10 Digit ISBN: 1-7364745-1-0

First Print Edition: May 2021

13 Digit ISBN: 978-1-7364745-0-1

10 Digit ISBN: 1-7364745-0-2

Cover by Damonza.com

Printed in the United States of America

❄ Created with Vellum

To my parents, Gene and Janet.
I wish you were here to read this.

FOREWORD
FROM BRIDGER

Let me get straight to the point. I never thought I would be writing the foreword to a book, be in a book, or allow a book to be written with me and the Spy Devils as the main characters. Never. Not once.

Then Joe approached me about telling the Spy Devils' story in a fictionalized book.

I said, "hell no!"

"You have stories that need to be told," he kept saying.

After many asks, he finally convinced me.

I thought about it. The world is a dangerous place. Why not give people a peek into the world of espionage? Why not shine a little light on topics governments, international organizations, or corporations would rather leave in the shadows?

I did ask for conditions.

Any specific details about our missions had to be changed. Names of all people, companies, dates, and locations had to be changed. We are still active and our enemies would love to find us. There are also regular hard-working people who got caught up in this, and we need to protect them. Some of you reading this will know who you are. Others will think you know, but will be wrong.

I stressed the point that when it comes to the Spy Devils, the old adage 'Truth is stranger than fiction' is, well, true.

Here it is. Truth as fiction.

Bridger
USA
2021

nything of value in a hotel safe is as risky as sticking a loaded gun in our mouth, pulling the trigger, and hoping it misfires.

One man swung the heavy metal door open. Inside was an oddly haped silver briefcase. On a shelf in the safe was a smaller device, imilar to a remote control for a television. The man took a dark fabric araday electronic signal-blocking bag from a backpack.

He stuffed the case inside and zipped up the bag, making the case lectronically invisible. He handed it to his partner, then reached back, icked up the smaller object, and stuck it in his coat pocket.

They left the suite, making certain to close the door. Their total ime inside the room was fifty seconds.

They exited the hotel the same way they entered, through the nguarded employee entrance on the backside of the building. Within ninutes, a sleek BMW 4 Series Coupe maneuvered through the narrow treets of the Kyiv night, taking a zigzagging surveillance detection oute south toward the E40 bridge across the Dnieper River. The men vere following orders to locate and remain hidden in a safe house in he Darnytsia District near Boryspil Airport until a man arrived to take he case.

Once over the bridge into the Darnytsia District, the BMW took the outh exit ramp off the E40 onto Petra Hryhorenka Avenue. As they urned onto the side street that led to their safe house, the windshield hattered as bullets tore through it and into the men. The BMW veered eft, impaling at full speed into a car parked along the side of the road. The exploding sounds of ripping metal and shattering glass were ollowed immediately by the sudden calm and hiss of escaping fluids rom the car.

Inside, the BMW's active safety systems saved the men's lives, who sat dazed among the deployed airbags. A passenger van pulled up beside the smoldering vehicle. The side door slid open, and four men dressed in dark clothes, their heads covered by balaclavas, jumped out. With Sig Sauer 9mm pistols raised to shoulder height, two men silently ook sentry positions at the car's front and rear. One other crept around o the other side of the van.

The final man walked to the car, raised his weapon, and emptied

1

THE STREETS OF KYIV

Kyiv, Ukraine

The instant he was tossed from the balcony of his luxury suite into the cool darkness, he calculated how long it would be before he landed on the crowded sidewalk ten stories below. He couldn't help it. That's how his quantitatively-oriented mind worked. Factoring his considerable weight, distance to the sidewalk, and gravity, he determined he would hit the concrete in roughly four seconds. Give or take.

Only a few seconds had passed since he heard the light taps on the wide, overly ornate door of his executive suite in the InterContinental Hotel Kyiv. He was fresh out of the shower and, in his haste, opened the door without looking through the small peephole.

That, he now realized, was a mistake.

A fist with the force of a sledgehammer crushed his nose. Staggering backward, he grabbed his face with both hands. He felt the warm blood already pooling in his palms. Then he felt powerful hands gripping his arms.

Then came the sensation of weightlessness.

Random thoughts wandered into his consciousness. Accelerating past the eighth floor, he admired the beautifully illuminated exterior of the hotel and the city's gorgeous skyline. His feet were chilly, and he wished his comfy slippers hadn't flown off like balloons in the wind.

A wonderfully plush hotel-supplied bathrobe fluttered at his sides like broken wings, exposing his enormous hairy naked body. He worried his office would be saddled with the expense of a white robe soon to be ruined with his blood and goo.

Tumbling by the fourth floor and through eyes watering from the wind, the cracks in the sidewalk appeared, flooded by soft yellow rays from lamps near the hotel entrance. The air smelled of river water and exhaust fumes.

Then terror-induced depression arrived from deep within his shocked brain. He would never shoot a round of golf under eighty. He would never taste McDonald's fries again. His ex-wives would be despondent, he hoped, and he felt slightly amused by that. Just a few feet above the sidewalk, he felt nothing but guilt as his last mortal thought was any chance to fulfill his fantasy to fuck Scarlett Johansson was officially over.

The sidewalk outside the InterContinental Kyiv was crowded with couples returning from a traditional late evening Ukrainian dinner and sightseeing through the fifteen-hundred-year-old city center.

One young couple from a village in western Ukraine celebrated their honeymoon with a fine meal at Pantagruel consisting of beef carpaccio, bruschetta, tomato bread soup, and pasta with rabbit. Every delicious morsel was washed down with too many bottles of the cheapest Italian wine.

They walked through the wooden door framed by red-and-white striped awnings onto the streets of Kyiv. Crossing the narrow cobblestone street, they strolled by a life-size bronze statue of a cat perched on a rock.

"Nice kitty," they giggled as they patted its cold head worn shiny by thousands of hands.

Their route brought them to the expanse of St. M[...] dominated on the opposite side by the Ukrainian Baro[...] Michael's Golden-Domed Monastery. They didn't spen[...] marveling at the pale-blue walls and half-dozen golde[...] mering in the night. Instead, they bent left around the s[...] InterContinental with nothing but a long night of lover[...] minds.

The body hit the concrete head first at forty miles [...] feet in front of the young couple. Blood and human deb[...] every direction as if someone had dropped a spoon into [...] warm bowl of meaty red Ukrainian borscht soup.

The blood-soaked couple stood staring at the brok[...] human steaming in the night air. Screams and shrieks [...] directions, each sound amplified as they echoed off [...] surrounding buildings. The man pulled his companion [...] spreading pool as she fainted to the ground.

She would spend the rest of their romantic honeym[...] her room.

Ten stories above, two men dressed in black business[...] shirts, and pencil-thin ties had been busy. They located the[...] the master suite bedroom mounted in the walk-in closet. [...] than most average hotel safes, an oversized accommod[...] important guests who would pay for the suite—the kind [...] felt they must secure laptops, passports, jewelry, docume[...] valuable possessions.

A digital display above twelve buttons on the beig[...] glowed green in the dimness of the closet. One man pus[...] button until the display flashed and entered six green zer[...] set, and rarely changed, manufacturer's administrative [...] The safe door clicked open. Within law enforcement, [...] agencies, hotel staff, and thieves, it is an open secret [...]

the entire magazine of ammunition through the passenger window, then through the shattered front windshield. Inside, their bodies shredded and jerked as glass and blood sprayed across the once pristine interior of the luxury car.

He reloaded the Sig Sauer, then secured the weapon in a shoulder holster. He unlocked the door, pushed back the now bullet-riddled airbags, and with gloved hands, reached in and forced the large dark bag out from between the dead man's legs. A white phosphorus grenade was tossed in the BMW as the van pulled away into the darkness of the streets of Kyiv. The grenade exploded with a bright flash—the car filled with flames.

In the passenger seat, the man dialed a mobile phone, waited, listened, and then replied "None" to a question at the other end. He powered off the phone, then removed the battery and SIM card. He tossed the phone out the window, then, after several blocks, he tossed the battery. He stuck the SIM back in his pocket.

They exchanged a nod and smile. The mission was a success. No problems. No witnesses. They had the case. The boss would be pleased. But they were wrong. They had failed to recover the small device from the pocket of the dead man they left in the burning car.

THE STREETS OF TAIPEI

Taipei, Taiwan

"They're chatting and looking around. Checking for surveillance," Bridger announced in a calm voice.

He had been on operations like this so many times over the last half-decade his pulse never wavered. It was the waiting that distracted him, and the fact he allowed it to distract him, even briefly, distracted him even more. Patience is a virtue, says the proverbial phrase. Bridger tried to live by it—but he was willing to adapt to circumstances.

Bridger was ready. His team was ready. The mission was in motion and ready to drop like a sledgehammer on the assassins. He looked at his Shinola watch, which displayed, "it's time to fuck with these guys."

The sky was bright blue. The air was refreshing. The 7-Eleven smelled like mint air freshener and steaming hot noodles.

The ambush was set.

Bridger sat at a short counter by the windows of a 7-Eleven that provided a direct vantage point to observe the corner of Guangfu Road and Wenchang Street in central Taipei. Bridger was amazed at the quantity of 7-Elevens that dotted the Taipei metro landscape. Every

THE STREETS OF KYIV

Kyiv, Ukraine

The instant he was tossed from the balcony of his luxury suite into the cool darkness, he calculated how long it would be before he landed on the crowded sidewalk ten stories below. He couldn't help it. That's how his quantitatively-oriented mind worked. Factoring his considerable weight, distance to the sidewalk, and gravity, he determined he would hit the concrete in roughly four seconds. Give or take.

Only a few seconds had passed since he heard the light taps on the wide, overly ornate door of his executive suite in the InterContinental Hotel Kyiv. He was fresh out of the shower and, in his haste, opened the door without looking through the small peephole.

That, he now realized, was a mistake.

A fist with the force of a sledgehammer crushed his nose. Staggering backward, he grabbed his face with both hands. He felt the warm blood already pooling in his palms. Then he felt powerful hands gripping his arms.

Then came the sensation of weightlessness.

Random thoughts wandered into his consciousness. Accelerating past the eighth floor, he admired the beautifully illuminated exterior of the hotel and the city's gorgeous skyline. His feet were chilly, and he wished his comfy slippers hadn't flown off like balloons in the wind.

A wonderfully plush hotel-supplied bathrobe fluttered at his sides like broken wings, exposing his enormous hairy naked body. He worried his office would be saddled with the expense of a white robe soon to be ruined with his blood and goo.

Tumbling by the fourth floor and through eyes watering from the wind, the cracks in the sidewalk appeared, flooded by soft yellow rays from lamps near the hotel entrance. The air smelled of river water and exhaust fumes.

Then terror-induced depression arrived from deep within his shocked brain. He would never shoot a round of golf under eighty. He would never taste McDonald's fries again. His ex-wives would be despondent, he hoped, and he felt slightly amused by that. Just a few feet above the sidewalk, he felt nothing but guilt as his last mortal thought was any chance to fulfill his fantasy to fuck Scarlett Johansson was officially over.

The sidewalk outside the InterContinental Kyiv was crowded with couples returning from a traditional late evening Ukrainian dinner and sightseeing through the fifteen-hundred-year-old city center.

One young couple from a village in western Ukraine celebrated their honeymoon with a fine meal at Pantagruel consisting of beef carpaccio, bruschetta, tomato bread soup, and pasta with rabbit. Every delicious morsel was washed down with too many bottles of the cheapest Italian wine.

They walked through the wooden door framed by red-and-white striped awnings onto the streets of Kyiv. Crossing the narrow cobble-stone street, they strolled by a life-size bronze statue of a cat perched on a rock.

"Nice kitty," they giggled as they patted its cold head worn shiny by thousands of hands.

Their route brought them to the expanse of St. Michael's Square, dominated on the opposite side by the Ukrainian Baroque style of St. Michael's Golden-Domed Monastery. They didn't spend too much time marveling at the pale-blue walls and half-dozen golden domes glimmering in the night. Instead, they bent left around the street toward the InterContinental with nothing but a long night of lovemaking on their minds.

The body hit the concrete head first at forty miles per hour a few feet in front of the young couple. Blood and human debris exploded in every direction as if someone had dropped a spoon into the middle of a warm bowl of meaty red Ukrainian borscht soup.

The blood-soaked couple stood staring at the broken pieces of a human steaming in the night air. Screams and shrieks came from all directions, each sound amplified as they echoed off the hotel and surrounding buildings. The man pulled his companion away from the spreading pool as she fainted to the ground.

She would spend the rest of their romantic honeymoon sedated in her room.

Ten stories above, two men dressed in black business suits, white shirts, and pencil-thin ties had been busy. They located the hotel safe in the master suite bedroom mounted in the walk-in closet. It was larger than most average hotel safes, an oversized accommodation for the important guests who would pay for the suite—the kind of guests who felt they must secure laptops, passports, jewelry, documents, or other valuable possessions.

A digital display above twelve buttons on the beige metal door glowed green in the dimness of the closet. One man pushed the lock button until the display flashed and entered six green zeros—the preset, and rarely changed, manufacturer's administrative access code. The safe door clicked open. Within law enforcement, intelligence agencies, hotel staff, and thieves, it is an open secret that putting anything of value in a hotel safe is as risky as sticking a loaded gun in your mouth, pulling the trigger, and hoping it misfires.

One man swung the heavy metal door open. Inside was an oddly shaped silver briefcase. On a shelf in the safe was a smaller device, similar to a remote control for a television. The man took a dark fabric Faraday electronic signal-blocking bag from a backpack.

He stuffed the case inside and zipped up the bag, making the case electronically invisible. He handed it to his partner, then reached back, picked up the smaller object, and stuck it in his coat pocket.

They left the suite, making certain to close the door. Their total time inside the room was fifty seconds.

They exited the hotel the same way they entered, through the unguarded employee entrance on the backside of the building. Within minutes, a sleek BMW 4 Series Coupe maneuvered through the narrow streets of the Kyiv night, taking a zigzagging surveillance detection route south toward the E40 bridge across the Dnieper River. The men were following orders to locate and remain hidden in a safe house in the Darnytsia District near Boryspil Airport until a man arrived to take the case.

Once over the bridge into the Darnytsia District, the BMW took the south exit ramp off the E40 onto Petra Hryhorenka Avenue. As they turned onto the side street that led to their safe house, the windshield shattered as bullets tore through it and into the men. The BMW veered left, impaling at full speed into a car parked along the side of the road. The exploding sounds of ripping metal and shattering glass were followed immediately by the sudden calm and hiss of escaping fluids from the car.

Inside, the BMW's active safety systems saved the men's lives, who sat dazed among the deployed airbags. A passenger van pulled up beside the smoldering vehicle. The side door slid open, and four men dressed in dark clothes, their heads covered by balaclavas, jumped out. With Sig Sauer 9mm pistols raised to shoulder height, two men silently took sentry positions at the car's front and rear. One other crept around to the other side of the van.

The final man walked to the car, raised his weapon, and emptied block seemed to have at least one of the popular convenience stores. They were busy all the time, with lots of people standing around eating, reading papers, or just staring into space. This made them perfect locations for static surveillance.

Outside, his covert team, now known worldwide as the Spy Devils, surveilled and waited. His people controlled this area, and only they knew it. Soon, two more members from China's Ministry of State Security (MSS), Bureau X, code named Dragon Fire, would be well aware of the situation.

"Guud mawnin. I teenk we need ah cawplah yuuuuuge egg rolls, right?" Snake said in a bad accent mixed with a thick layer of his linguistically strange New York dialect. He was on a scooter, circling randomly through the nearby streets and neighborhoods. No pattern. No street traversed twice.

A few chuckles squawked in his ear.

"Snake. Concentrate," Bridger said in a serious voice. "No mistakes."

"Ruyz-ah-Roynah," was Snake's reply. More chuckles.

"Beast? Demon?" Bridger queried his men hiding in the garage around the corner from Bridger's position.

"We've got the van covered," Beast's baritone voice reported.

"We were here all night, dumbass," a rock-crusher voice crackled over the secure radio. It sounded older, more traveled than the others. "We ain't sipping a latte. We're still in this concrete shithole."

"Remind you of home, Demon?" Snake asked.

"Fuck you." It was Demon's standard reply.

That reminded Bridger to issue the warning.

"Demon. Please, don't kill them."

"Fuck you."

"Imp?" Bridger asked.

"No signals at all. We are clear."

Imp, a twenty-something with bloodshot eyes behind thick tortoise shell-framed glasses, sat at a corner table near a window of a 7-Eleven two blocks away. He was looking at a series of colored boxes on his laptop screen. With modified commercial software and several micro antennas, Imp was able to monitor police and emergency communications. Another antenna scanned for static in the encrypted frequency bands. Imp made sure the two security cameras screwed to the ceiling of Bridger's 7-Eleven were not functioning this morning.

The two MSS officers, which they had identified as Bai and Peng, were getting closer. Bridger read them like the receipt from last night's noodle dinner.

Bai was just that—at least a foot taller than his colleague. Powerful, with a barrel chest and a confident demeanor. Large and in charge. The more senior intelligence officer. His partner, Peng, was the opposite. Unpretentious. Wimpy. A follower in every respect and not helped by the ill-fitting tan suit that hung off his body like melting skin.

They had yet to kill any of the Dragon Fire team. They did that themselves. Killing violated his Spy Devil Rule Number One: No killing unless there is no other option. Also, there was a small chance he would violate Spy Devils Team Rule Number Two: No mistakes.

Bridger hated mistakes. Treating any operation as routine would get them killed. He sniffed for anything that smelled of routine. Predictability was a death sentence in espionage. It was what she had taught him—year after year after year.

"They are coming in," Bridger informed the team. He expected the assassins to make one last surveillance detection stop on the way to the garage—and they were.

As they approached, Bridger sipped his tea and read his paper. Three other morning loiterers were at the counter. For now, he was simply a businessman enjoying the morning.

Bridger had the kind of looks that allowed him to morph into invisibility. Even at thirty-nine-years-old, he was still Brad Pitt handsome. Five feet eleven. Toned, lean, muscular body. Sandy brownish hair that appeared to alter its tint with the sun, or the angle of his head. His eyes took on the nearest color. Hazel. Not brown. Not green. His complexion was just a permanent shade below a light summer tan. No moles, scars, dimples, or unusual features. His voice was neutral American Midwest, but accents of any kind were not an issue.

He was a clean canvas for disguise kits.

This morning, it was reddish curly hair with thin-rim glasses. An average blue business suit. White shirt. Solid blue tie. The blank jet-lagged stare of an ordinary forty-something American traveler staying in a congested area of Taipei's business district. Boring. Common. Invisible.

Bridger took one glance in their direction. Their strides were a few inches too long and paced too quickly for the small space. Peng was glancing around too much. Bai's neck muscles were tight. Their arms and hands were tense. Tension around their eyes. Their wiggling hands were unnatural. Their rate of breathing was too quick by a few breaths.

Peng will come in first, scan the store, and take a tactical position in the far corner pretending to choose some snacks. Bai will follow in a few seconds. He will go to the coffee station and fill a to-go cup. When he is done, they will rotate positions so Peng can get his beverage.

They did exactly what he predicted.

A bulge in jacket near the small of their backs. Probably a Taiwan manufactured T75. Not a problem.

Bridger knew Chinese Ministry of State Security intelligence officers would typically carry a variant of the Chinese built QSZ-92 semi-automatic pistol. But when on an operation, they would acquire a handgun from the local market.

The MSS men paid the clerk at the bright white counter, exited the store, descended a few small steps, then turned right and right again down Wenchang Street.

Bridger clicked the sensor in his hand, sending the signal to his team that Bai and Peng were on their way. Bridger waited until the men had passed the side window. He stood, folded his paper under his arm, and left the 7-Eleven.

The assassins quickened their pace once they turned down Wenchang Street, now a claustrophobic narrow one-way maze of urban density. Dull apartment buildings were stacked above stores protected by corrugated metal pull-down security doors. Cars and scooters fought to occupy every inch of open sidewalk and road. Red advertising signs and green plants hanging off every apartment's balcony were the only colors besides dirty brown.

The Dragon Fire men turned left onto an arterial lane lined with more balconied apartments, cars, scooters, and trees. Under a square blue "P" parking sign, Bai and Peng stood at a door leading to a parking garage beneath the apartment complex.

"At the door," Bridger announced.

Bai pulled the handle on the dirty white door, shooting sunlight into the darkness and exposing particles of dust swirling thick in the air. They tossed their coffee cups to the ground as they descended five steps. Peng entered first. Bai followed.

Rows of fluorescent lights spaced across the low ceiling illuminated a fifty-by-fifty-square-foot space. Concrete ran from wall to wall. Floor to ceiling. Wide support pillars were spread across the garage. Small cars, scooters, and motorcycles of every kind crowded the rest of the floor. Narrow aisles allowed just enough of a gap for the cars to squeeze their way to the ramp leading to the rusty door and the outside.

The space smelled like mildew, gasoline, and rubber tires.

Bai and Peng's steps echoed as they moved toward a white Toyota passenger van backed against the far wall. A beep from the key fob and click from the van pinged through the air when Bai remotely unlocked the vehicle.

Reaching for the van doors' handles was the last clear thought each would have for many hours. They made the mistake of not seeing Demon and Beast rise from the shadows and extend telescopic batons into the unsuspecting faces.

An enhanced capsaicin neurotoxin concoction simultaneously sprayed from the end of a two-foot-long carbon fiber baton into the men's faces. Momentary gasps and muted gagging followed. The sensory nerve endings in their corneas immediately inflamed, resulting in total blindness. Tear ducts exploded. The automatic reflex to rub stinging eyeballs only worked to spread the chemical and make the pain worse. Their nasal passages and throats became inflamed, as their larynxes became completely paralyzed.

Both men attempted to gulp clean oxygen into their now aggravated lungs but managed only to fill them with more capsaicin-saturated air.

The homemade paralyzing agent overrode their central nervous systems, forcing the muscles in their extremities to spasm. They collapsed to the cold concrete like a rock in free fall. A sickening hollow thud echoed off the walls as scalp and skull dribbled like basketballs against the floor. A few drops of blood mixed with the grime on the dirty garage floor.

Their teammate Milton—a tinkering genius—created the weapon. The Stick was a telescoping multi-threat baton that contained an intensity-controlled electroshock weapon—a stun gun—similar to a cattle prod used by farmers. Depending upon the dial setting, it could cause temporary "neuromuscular incapacitation," as Milton called it. At higher levels, it delivered excruciating pain.

It was also a Taser capable of firing two small dart electrodes attached to wires to shock a person up to a distance of thirty feet. The most potent weapon was the jets that dispersed an array of dial-controlled toxin mixtures. Some settings pacified the victim. Some knocked the victim out. Some caused paralysis. If set at maximum dosage levels, it could cause the heart to stop beating.

Demon stood over Bai, a scowl on his seventy-year-old stubble-covered face. Demon's hair was a short, tangled nest of gray. Deep creases snaked across his face, but there was still a youthful look in his eyes. They also contained the look that told people, *"don't fuck with me if you know what is good for you."*

Turning the black rubber handle on his baton, he jammed it behind the defenseless assassin's ear. For three seconds, thirty thousand volts convulsed Bai into a violent wiggle. The uncontrollable muscle contractions shocked the drug-impaired body like an earthquake. Demon sauntered around the body and repeated his treatment on Peng.

"Shit, you are a badass, Demon," Beast said.

He looked up with a smile. "It's the amps, not the volts."

"Demon. Really?" Bridger said as he came through an interior door to the garage. He had walked down Guangfu Road around to the other side of the building. He slipped into a gap between the structures, then entered through an unlocked, unguarded service entrance hidden between some trash bins.

"You said after Hong Kong I could do what I wanted to the last group," Demon said.

"No. I didn't. Finish the job."

Beast took out rolls of duct tape and rolled it around the unconscious men's feet and arms. Beast was less than half Demon's age, broad-shouldered and tall at a few inches over six feet. His bushy beard needed a trim in contrast to his head of dirty brown hair that was short and neatly combed over. The visible parts of his face wore the tanned skin of a man who spent a life outside. His movements were quick, precise, and surgical. He had the straight-backed posture of someone who got things done.

"Two in the bag," Demon announced thirty seconds later as he and Beast stood over the two men—their wrists and feet now bound with tape.

Beast opened the rear cargo doors of a Mitsubishi SUV parked a few spaces away, then picked up Peng and tossed him inside. Demon looked at Beast and then picked up the limp body of Bai and threw him through the opening like he was stacking wood. The assassin hit the floor with a hard thud.

Beast got behind the steering wheel of the SUV. Bridger took the passenger seat. Bridger liked having Beast in the driver's seat. Besides being the best at offensive and defensive driving, Beast was cool under pressure, reliable, loyal, and deadly.

Demon jumped in back, closed the door with a bang, and jammed his baton into Bai's groin. The man lurched like a fish taken off the hook and tossed into the bottom of a boat.

"Oops, my mistake." He looked at Bridger, who just shook his head.

When Imp gave the all-clear signal, Beast started the SUV.

No Mistakes. So far. So good, Bridger thought.

The man on the roof across Wenchang Street had expected the garage door to open. He was just amazed at how swift it must have happened. He checked his watch. Three minutes.

These Spy Devils are quite impressive. I have to admire their efficiency.

He smiled when the garage door opened and the Mitsubishi SUV pulled out. When his men had gone to check on their van yesterday, he told them to look for any large vehicles in the garage. His men reported that among the scooters and small passenger vehicles, there was one Toyota truck and a Mitsubishi SUV. They had placed tracking sensors on each.

He felt bad about using two of his men as bait. He was getting short of men, but Bai and Peng had stepped up when he asked. Whatever it took to get his revenge against the Spy Devils, he would do. If that meant offering up two of them as bait, *wǎng yáng bǔ láo. Better late than never.*

He looked at his phone. The tracking application was working perfectly. When he knew the exact location of the Spy Devils safe house, then *bào chóu xuě chǐ.* He would get his revenge and erase the humiliation he had suffered at the hands of the Spy Devils and their leader.

The one called Bridger.

3

THE HARD WAY

Taipei, Taiwan

"Helloooo?" Bridger gently tapped his palm on the side of one man's face, then the other. "Wakey, wakey," he said like he was trying to get a child up in the morning on a school day.

Bai and Peng were sitting slumped in barely functional folding chairs. The eyelids of the two drugged Dragon Fire men slowly opened, revealing glassy eyeballs. The tissue surrounding their eyes and under their noses were red with the irritation from the spray and subsequent rubbing. Beast had cut the tape off their wrists and feet. Bridger wanted to allow them the belief they were not prisoners.

They wouldn't run—they couldn't if they wanted to. The gas would not wear off for at least thirty minutes, maybe more. Just in case, Beast stood by the door, dressed in khakis and a polo shirt. He held his Devil Stick in one hand. His preferred weapon of choice, a Sig Sauer P226, was in the other.

Beast was the hairiest guy Bridger had ever met. If he shaved in the morning, he had a full beard by lunch. So he gave up and grew the beard all the time.

Beast wouldn't talk about it, but Bridger had read his military file.

"Sorry about that, guys," Bridger told them in perfect Mandarin—letting the men know he spoke their language—which warned them he understood anything they would say. Bridger knew from previous interrogations of their colleagues that Dragon Fire members all spoke perfect English.

Bridger had morphed during the surveillance route from businessman to punk—blonde spiked hair, red-tinted glasses, jeans, a faded green "Free Ferris" t-shirt, and small fake tattoos on his forearms. *Hellraiser* on the left. *Mother* on the right. He didn't have to; he just liked to.

On closer inspection, Bridger knew Bai was not only a mountain compared to Peng, but he thoroughly wore the skin of the senior man in charge. Experienced. Bone tough. Peng was much younger. Green. It seemed to Bridger that Peng was just one step above bagger at the Piggly Wiggly grocery store.

A rookie. They are so short-handed they are using guys fresh out of the water.

During the year, his Spy Devils had captured, interrogated, and exposed nineteen of them. Twice in Hong Kong and Australia. Once each in the Philippines, Malaysia, and Thailand. A blow to Chinese covert operations in the South China Sea area, and he hoped, a crippling blow to the Dragon Fire program.

Bridger helped them back into their seats and pulled a knee-high bamboo table toward them. On it was a platter of fresh melon and cookies. A pot of tea was warm and ready. Fans hummed in the background, forcing some movement in the dusty, damp air but did little to cool the confined space. A low-light video camera on a tripod pointed at them at an angle to their left. It was on.

"It is the thought that counts, right?" He poured some steaming tea into two small cups and held them out to the men. Neither reached out to take it. "No?" He set the cups down and nodded at Demon again.

The jolt sent the men to the floor. Bridger helped them to their seats again. He took a piece of melon off the tray and ate it. He smiled a satisfying smile and licked his fingers.

"You ever heard of Major Sherwood Moran? The United States

As much as Bridger could tell, Beast was a Special Force
for a combat battalion—Iraq area of operations, who some
into a shitshow involving an undercover operation involv
tribal leaders, Syrians, and smuggling routes. Whatev
Beast found himself on the shelf, then out of the service.

Bridger found him working security on a constructi
ana, of all places.

He was a perfect fit for the Spy Devils.

The SUV carrying the three Spy Devils and tv
Dragon Fire men arrived after a two-hour surveillance
SDR, through the busy Taipei streets and surround
Beast was certain they were clean, he drove to a small
ingly forgotten utility building he had scouted days be
by farmland and buried behind fences and deep fol'
was hidden off a one-lane auxiliary road. The road
ends to Xidong Road, Sanxia District, New Taipei
river ran behind it.

The fifteen-by-fifteen-foot interior was a mess.
like pancakes were large coils of thick red hose. F
and smelled like fertilizer fanned out from along
degree angles. Pipes, broken buckets, and an a
tools Bridger thought were last used to build the
rest of the cinder block walls. The air smelled like

It was an ideal place to talk to the Chines
served and uninterrupted.

"Wake up, damn it!" Bridger shook his head
nodded to Demon, who stood behind the MSS
usual blue jeans and a black pullover jacket.
Stick. Prominently tucked into his belt was
Armory Colt M1911.

"Hey!" Demon shouted. When they still d'
thumb over his Devil Stick to "cattle prod" m
on the shoulder.

Crackles sounded as they jolted off the
dirty concrete floor.

Marine who wrote a seminal paper on interrogation techniques based on his research during World War II?" Bridger looked at them for an answer. Glazed red eyes stared back. Then he picked up and ate another piece of melon.

"I'm trying to lose a few pounds." He smiled a mischievous smile. "Never heard of him. No? Well, his analysis revealed that Japanese prisoners of war who were treated nicely by their interrogators—with respect and understanding—were much more successful than those who used physical threats and torture."

Bridger picked up the tray.

"So, pals, would you like some cookies? Fruit?" Peng slowly raised his watering eyes to look at Bai, who only stared back with an unreceptive blotchy-red face. "No, again?" He set the tray down and slid the table to the side.

Come on, assholes. Take my offer. Have a cookie. Let's be pals. You don't want me to be your enemy.

"The immediate success using torture is the stuff of fiction novels and Hollywood movies. Hey, and it is better than letting Demon here pull your fingernails out with a rusty pair of pliers. Right?" Bridger laughed.

"No, it isn't." Demon's voice was a low growl, like a dog ready to be unleashed.

A look of fear crossed Peng's face, which he tried to hide when he saw Bai sitting as still as death.

"Listen, you have spent months away from home and family. So have we."

Well, I don't have much of a family, but maybe you do, Bridger thought.

"I respect you as members of the same intelligence profession. So, let's get this over—then you can go home. We can go home. And we are all happy. What do you say?"

Bridger showed his white teeth through a sincere and friendly smile. He held it, then his chest rose and fell with a deep sigh.

Bridger knew he would "*get his hands dirty,*" spending a lifetime hunting and destroying foreign intel operations and international criminals. Hell, he knew that decision was made for him a long time ago.

His elevator descent from guiltless-saint level to guilty-devil level began in Honduras. Then came the human traffickers. The so-called warlords of insurgencies and civil wars. Arms dealers. Russian crime bosses. Ukrainian crime bosses. Russian SVR. Chinese Ministry of State Security. The list was endless. The work had been relentless.

Bridger looked at Demon, then he reached into his back pocket and pulled out a rusty pair of pliers. He waved them in front of Peng.

"We may have to do this the hard way."

The right corner of Demon's mouth twitched up and down like he was having a muscle spasm. It was as close to a smile as he ever got.

Li Chu, the leader of MSS Bureau X, the Dragon Fire, crouched in the tall grass fifty yards to the south side of the building.

So far, the trap to locate and kill the Spy Devils was working perfectly. The tracking signal gave away their location. After an excruciatingly long two-hour wait, the SUV finally reached its destination.

Even with his monocular, he couldn't see a thing through the dirty window except that the light was on. Under trees to his right, at the end of the drive and near the door, was the Mitsubishi SUV.

Crouching low to his left was Fuhan, a new man fresh from the Ministry of State Security Academy in the Xiyuan area northwest of Beijing. All of the men with Li Chu about to assault the building were new graduates.

Bai was all he had left of his best men. Bai had been with Li Chu since the beginning of Bureau X. Now he was willing bait, held captive by the cursed Bridger and the Spy Devils inside the one-story white building.

Li Chu knew the resources he had were not optimal, but he had the element of surprise. Li Chu had one other weapon at his disposal—complete, unadulterated hatred.

New strands of duct tape were wrapped around the MSS men's chests, mummifying them to the back of their rickety metal chairs.

Bridger sat in a chair facing them. He expected Bai to hold up to the discomfort caused by the cattle prod setting of the Devil Stick. He did. He was a tough bastard and barely made a sound each time Demon jolted him.

Peng, on the other hand, wasn't doing as well. He was gasping for air. It was already hot in the room, but an unbelievable cascade of sweat was rolling down his face. His clothes were soaked with sweat and urine.

"You know," Bridger said as he leaned forward, "your man Shen, maybe you know him?" Bridger looked from Peng to Bai. "He only made it to setting four. Demon, how many volts is that?"

"It's the amps, *not* the volts. And the answer is not enough. Can we get on with this?"

With his Devil Stick in his right hand, Demon stood behind the MSS men, irritatingly tapping it on the back of Peng's metal chair. *Cling. Cling. Cling.* In his other hand, he was opening and closing the pliers with a metallic *click click click.*

Bridger grinned. He had to admire his devotion to duty. Demon had always been there for him—since he was a kid living in CIA-paid housing in a dozen countries. Teaching. Training. He was always larger than life to a young, fatherless boy. In many ways, to Bridger, he still was. Bridger would always be there for him, too. He loved the man.

"Now, on the other hand, I think Qiang made it all the way to six, but he lost a few fingernails in the process."

He looked at Demon.

"Two. We are only at two," Demon answered without being asked.

Peng whimpered.

"So, back to business." Bridger smiled, leaned over, looked at the cookies, picked one up, and popped it in his mouth. He chewed and swallowed. "So much for that diet. Now, where was I? Yes, Fan, Ye,

Dequan, and the others told us most of what we needed to know about the operation of Bureau X, with your fearsome Dragon Fire name."

Bridger knew that was only partially true. They *had* been extracting some information from the Dragon Fire captives, but May had been sending Bridger real intel since the beginning of the mission. His prisoners didn't need to know that.

"They became quite cooperative, eventually, and provided your mission, how long you have been active, your targets, and base and safe house locations. They also added detail on your leader. Li Chu, is it? Perhaps you can fill in some of the blank spots on this elusive Mr. Li Chu."

Bridger looked from one man to the other. His eyebrows raised as a quizzical look appeared on his face. Peng looked at Bai, eyes wide in desperation. Bai didn't look at him at all. He just returned Bridger's gaze with one of his own.

"Gentlemen, you know how this will eventually end, right? In a day or two, no matter if you talk or not?" Bridger raised his arm to shoulder level. His index finger was out, his thumb was up, and the rest of his fingers were curled back in the universal hand position to look like a gun. He pointed at Bai.

"Bang!" Then swiveled and pointed at Peng, who flinched when Bridger shouted "Bang!" at him.

Bai's expression of defiance dropped in the momentary realization of understanding, then went back to defiance. Peng started to moan.

"Oh well," Bridger sighed and motioned to Demon to continue. Demon increased the setting on the dial, but before he could tap a shoulder, three electronic beeps came from Bridger's phone. He reached in and looked at the caller ID on the Signal secure communication app.

"Are you kidding? Hang on, Demon. I have to get this. Sorry, guys."

"Son of a bitch!" Demon scowled, dropping the Stick to his side and stuffing the pliers in his front pocket.

Bridger stood, hit the answer button, turned his back, and walked away from the men. He knew she didn't call when they were operational in the field unless it was pre-scheduled or life-threatening.

He put the phone to his ear.

"Not a good time to chat, May."

"When I call," said a voice with a slight Western New England accent, "it is always a good time."

4

THE DEVILBOTS

Taipei, Taiwan

"You should be close to the completion of this operation," said May Currier, Senior Advisor, Special Projects, to the Deputy Director of Operations for the CIA.

"Yes, we are, so let us get on with dealing with the Chinese assassins."

"Yes, that is nice to know, but I have two important issues I need to discuss."

"Now? Don't you have some paper clips to requisition or some other staff to terrorize?" Bridger said too loudly for the room.

"I have intel you are about to be ambushed. Did you know that?"

"Thank you, I do know. I am capable of spotting an ambush."

"Well, I hope so, son. I taught you. Then have a nice time. Don't forget to call me."

For a moment, Bridger stood with his phone still at his ear when the line went dead. Then he dropped his arm and stuffed his phone into his pocket.

"Imp. What's the status?" Bridger said, his comm system picking up his question.

"Status? You want the status? The status is I'm hiding in a car blocks away, hovering this toy on overwatch, while the others get to play bang bang."

"Grow up," Milton replied with a hint of Alabama in his voice.

"Be a good boy, Imp," the soft voice of Beatrice contrasted with the hard sarcasm they transmitted. A few anonymous chuckles cut the tension.

"Beatrice, you can—"

"Stop right there," Milton said, cutting Imp off.

Milton and Beatrice. The lovebird couple.

Bridger found Milton—named for the author of *Paradise Lost*—unsuccessfully flailing at pitching beyond comprehension start-up ideas to his alma mater, MIT. Scientific master of everything. He was twenty-nine but looked fourteen. Paper-thin. Red soup bowl-style cut bangs. One hundred fifty-five pounds, max. Wire-rimmed glasses over a freckled, ruddy face. A stereotypical egghead who spent most of his time in high school hiding in the science lab to avoid the daily beating by bullies.

Bridger got a lead on Beatrice—her code name was plucked from Dante's *Divine Comedy*—through a talent agency friend in New York. She was a talented actress who turned her mind to the paralegal profession to pay the bills. She was twenty-eight and could be described by the term "*a knock-out.*" Short Audrey Hepburn dark hair. Dark wide eyes. A great smile and the nicest person on the team, they all knew. Bridger rescued her from a life in law so she could use her many talents in makeup, acting, and research for the Spy Devil's benefit.

Some Newtonian force of nature he did not understand had bound Milton and Beatrice together. The thought of the combination—the beauty and the nerd—made Bridger smile. Milton, as Bridger reminded him, had out-kicked his coverage when it came to Beatrice.

"Excuse me. Sorry to interrupt your humorous banter, but can someone tell me where the Chinese assassins are?" Bridger asked.

"Alright," Imp started as he raised his iPhone. It was controlling the Milton-modified DJI Mavic 2 Pro Quadcopter hovering at five hundred feet above the building. "I see three teams of two.

Approaching from south, north, and west, as expected. Fifty yards out and closing. One team of two across the lane hiding in the grass. Two vans. Parked along the road at each end. One idiot each in the driver's seat. Funny, isn't it?"

"What?" Milton asked.

"The drones we are using to whack their asses are made in China."

"Poetic-fucking justice." The deep baritone voice of Beast joined the conversation.

"It is nice to know just how close they are. We are a little distracted and in the dark in here. The Devilbots are ready?" Bridger said.

"We have all four in the air targeting each of their teams. We don't have a clear shot at the guys across the lane. Trees are in the way. We will have to get a little closer. We will send up one right after to help Snake if he has issues."

"I ain't having any issues," Snake said.

Devilbots, as Milton named them, were customized off-the-shelf DJI Spark Quad Portable Mini Drones, and with his tinkering, he thought were pretty damned impressive. Compact. About the size of an open paperback book with four propellers coming out of it at forty-five-degree angles. 2-axis stabilized gimbal camera. Infra-red. 12MP still photos. 1080P/30 video. Gesture control. Flight autonomy. HD Wi-Fi video transmission. Obstacle detection. Subject tracking. GPS. Vision position-based navigation. Tactical sensors. Face recognition and tracking.

Milton was in love.

However, the improvement that gave Milton mini-orgasms and turned the ordinary drone into a Devilbot was the precision auto-firing gun mounts attached under the mini-drone chassis. From these, the Devilbot could target, site, and fire two 9mm rounds out to three hundred yards with near one hundred percent lethal accuracy.

If all else failed, each Devilbot had a shape charge on its top. It could be put in kamikaze mode, dive, and flip to slam the explosive into the target. The result was a quarter-sized hole into whatever it hit.

They were silent. They were invisible in the sky. They were deadly.

"Snake? You ready to play cowboy?"

"Yippee-ki-yah," Snake replied in an exaggerated southern accent.

Snake's solid tree-stump frame counted thirty-three years of rings. He looked like a cop. Acted like a cop. Talked like a cop. That made sense since he had spent ten years on the NYPD. The last few in the Intel and Counterterrorism Bureau—until he got shot. The seasoned street-wise investigator turned into a spy. He had the permanent look of mischief on his face under neat black hair. He wore blue jeans and a gray V-neck short sleeve t-shirt that was straining hard to hold in his biceps.

He was a block away, idling on a dented orange-and-white 150cc Kymco scooter.

"Alright. We go in thirty seconds," Bridger told his team. "Tape them," he said to Demon.

With a *rrrippp rrrippp* two pieces of duct tape covered their captives' mouths.

Bridger bent over and put his face inches from Bai's, who, for the first time, looked back with panic in his eyes. Beads of sweat on his face. His nostrils were sucking in air. His cheeks were billowing like gills on a fish.

Bai saw the instant change of expression on Bridger's face—from nice guy to devil.

"If you would have talked, maybe you could have saved your buddies. More people are going to die. Hope you said good-bye to your family." Bridger straightened and looked at his Shinola watch. "You didn't think I would see this was a set-up? I don't think you could have made it more obvious. What do they teach you at Dragon Fire school? Anything? Hell, the pimple-faced clerk at the 7-Eleven probably saw it coming."

Bai rattled in his chair, straining to break free.

"No, sorry. You can't warn your pals." Bridger felt the anger rolling in his body. He didn't try to stop it. Now, he didn't want to. "You can watch and listen."

"Um, guys." Imp's voice came over the comm. "They are coming out of the brush. Twenty yards and closing. I'm zooming on pistols and

his ear like a thousand bees were stinging his face. Blood seemed to be everywhere. His body was on fire. He was certain he was going to faint.

But the adrenalin kicked in, as did his warrior senses. He didn't have time to contemplate what happened to his team. Instead, he willed his body to move. His hands clawed at the grass. His feet propelled him forward in short hops like a rabbit. Blood filled his eyes. The ringing in his ear brought on dizziness. He was moments away from vomiting and passing out.

Li Chu thought he heard a motorcycle and then buzzing. When he realized the buzzing was closing in on him, he got up. He ran through the trees and bushes, his arms lashing out in front of him against the obstacles like he was holding invisible machetes.

When the sound was over his head, Li Chu planted his feet and jumped into the muddy water of the irrigation canal. The water on his skin and wounds gave him a moment of peace. It was four feet deep, his mind calculated. Deep enough for him to keep under the surface. Then his lungs started burning. He stuck his feet and hands into the muck on the bottom of the canal, clawing to find rocks and debris as handholds to help him stay under and move with the current.

After a minute, begging to pass out to stop the pain, he raised his head out of the brown water to eye level. Nothing was following him. He raised a few more inches and took in a lungful of air. Then let the current float him away.

Milton and Beatrice flipped the Devilbots into auto mode. In seconds, the drones fired on the Dragon Fire men. They had no chance to save themselves. Seven were dead within eight seconds. Mostly center mass shots—a few to the head.

The scooter screeched to a stop next to the door of the first van. Snake put four bullets from his Glock-19 through the window and into the Dragon Fire man's head. Snake hit the throttle on the scooter. The back wheel smoked and fish-tailed as he rounded the slight curve. He drove straight at the other van.

At ten yards, he swung his leg over and dismounted the moving scooter on the run—like a movie cowboy jumping off their horse in a hurry. The scooter kept going. It exploded into the front of the van, jerking it back as debris sprayed along the street.

Snake had his Glock-19 up in firing position, but his momentum made him stumble as he fired. His first shot was high and to the left. The stunned Dragon Fire man opened the side door. Snake was able to steady himself. His bullets went into one side of the man's brains and out the other.

"That's two." Snake folded his arms to cover the weapon as he walked away from the wreck. "No issues."

"We have a crawler. Southside," Imp announced.

Milton put his Devilbot into dive mode to ram the man, but he had jumped into the water by the time it arrived.

"He is in the water," Milton said. "Do you want me to follow?"

There was no answer.

Beast threw the door open—pistol up and ready. Bridger glanced out, then heard a strange clanking sound of metal breaking.

He turned to see Peng, in a full panic, running toward the open door. In total fright and still taped to the chair, he stood up with enough force to break the hinges holding the chair seat to the back. *Mmmmm-mmmm* came from his taped mouth. He stumbled toward the door on wobbly legs, which had not fully recovered from the gas. Behind him, pieces of the chair stuck to his body like Superman's cape.

What the fuck? Bridger thought as he watched the man try to run. It was a surreal moment he hadn't anticipated.

Then Demon shot Peng.

Peng was thrust forward and landed prone in the doorway. A neat hole was in the chair behind his right shoulder.

"Damn it, Demon! Damn it!" Bridger shouted as he knelt to check on Peng. "I told you not to kill him."

"He ain't dead. I put it through his shoulder joint. That arm may not work for a while, if ever, but he won't die from that. At least, I don't think so."

Bridger wasn't sure who he was more furious with—Demon for shooting Peng or Peng for running.

Bridger stood.

"Don't. Die. You. Dumb. Son. Of. A. Bitch." With each word, he raised his foot and stomped hard on Peng's chair. Peng moaned with each blow. Blood started to pool.

"See if you can stop him from bleeding out," he said to Beast. "Everyone, start your exfiltration plans."

Each Spy Devil had a process in place to quickly leave wherever they were. The logistics were set up by the many travel agencies in the Spy Devil's covert network. Each Spy Devil would move by different modes of transportation, in different directions and on different dates, in an alias, then true name.

Bridger reached toward his ankle and pulled his knife from its holder. He pointed it at Bai and stepped to him, his eyes and face filled with rage.

"Whoa there, Bridger. What are you doing? Remember Honduras," Demon said.

Bridger raised the knife, and in a swiping arc of his arm, cut Bai free from the chair. He grabbed him and yanked him to his feet, the blade now under the frightened man's chin.

"Let's go," he hissed through clenched teeth.

Bridger's fury had him dragging Bai faster than his feet could move.

"Is this Li Chu? Is this Li Chu? Is this Li Chu?" he asked, shoving Bai's face toward the mangled contorted faces of his dead colleagues. Each time Bai shook his head no.

On the last no, he spun Bai to face him. The violent left hook followed by a right uppercut to Bai's face made him bite the end of his tongue off. His broken jaw was forced up. The already unconscious man hit the ground with a thump.

Bridger felt the warm sun as he stood over the body. Bridger was shaking. He took a deep breath and looked around at the dead bodies of the Chinese assassination team.

Li Chu had escaped. That was a mistake.

Li Chu had somehow made it back to a safehouse apartment, where they had stashed a medical kit. He didn't recall how he was able to patch his wounds, but he had. When finished, red stains smeared the sink, shower, and floor of the bathroom. Dark red rags and towels littered the floor.

The mirror reflected a battered face he didn't recognize. Swollen black and blue eyes. The blood he missed was dried in his hair and speckled on his face.

What did I do wrong? How could this Bridger ruin my plan? Kill the rest of my men?

Tugging a cap loosely over his bandaged head and ear, he closed the safe house door behind him and stepped out onto the streets of Taipei.

Li Chu knew *it* was in the van—in the parking garage. He had to see it even though the dizziness had him close to fainting several times.

He opened the driver's door, and there it was. A black and red business card with an image of a three-pronged pitchfork. He didn't have to turn it over to read the white block letters printed on the other side, but he did. It had been left for him.

It read: *GREETINGS FROM THE DEVIL.*

THE 12TH AT AUGUSTA NATIONAL

West Texas Hill Country, USA

Bridger slept as well as he had in months—which meant 7 a.m., an hour later than usual. He had been moving continually for two days. Twelve hours ago, he landed his Embraer Legacy 450 at Austin-Bergstrom International Airport and piloted his Bell 505 helicopter to his west Texas Hill Country ranch.

Thirty hours before that, the Devils had snatched the Dragon Fire assassins from the parking garage.

That next morning in central Taipei, a suspicious SUV was discovered on the lawn across the street from the Presidential Office Building, the baroque-style palace built during the Japanese colonial period on the island during the early 1900s. Covered live on national television, special operations and anti-terror units from the Taiwan Military, Taipei Police, and National Security Bureau, Taiwan's principal intelligence organization surrounded the area and evacuated nearby buildings.

Two unidentified men, who appeared unconscious, were shown being removed from the SUV. Later on that day, at press briefings, Taiwan officials declared that the men found inside secured with duct tape were Chinese intelligence assassins. They showed pictures and videos as proof and called for United Nations investigations.

Now, back home for the first time in what felt like a lifetime, Bridger was ready to extinguish the last flame of Dragon Fire.

Bridger's sanctuary was once known as River Ridge Ranch, named for the river and tributaries that crisscrossed the acres of pasture, brush, woods, and flat to rolling to hilly terrain. Located somewhere between Austin and El Paso, the ranch served previously as a recreational hunting, hiking, riding, and fishing corporate retreat. Access to the location was only by a private dead-end road or by air.

Previously used as a lodge, the 6,200-square-foot main house had eight bedrooms, five baths, a workout room, a modern open kitchen, bars, vaulted ceilings, and a five-car garage all surrounded by a spectacular 360-degree view of west-central Texas. Other structures on the land included an equestrian center, stables, corral, barns, wilderness cabins, plane hangar, and runway. There were stocked ponds. River frontage. Livestock and wildlife of all kinds.

It was his 2,698 acres of *leave me the fuck alone* that he renamed Abaddon—a biblical term for "Place of Destruction."

It had been nine years since the newly-formed boutique investment bank Hubbard Park Investments of New York and its founder Trowbridge Hall bought the property. Trowbridge Hall, aka Bridger, made it his base of operations. An untraceable series of dummy and cutout corporations purchased the ranch for a little more than three million dollars. With aftermarket upgrades—communications, landscaping, security—the total came close to seven million dollars.

After some brief stretching to shock his jet-lagged muscles back to life, Bridger took a deep breath in, then slowly out. He caught the smell of eggs, beans, and tortillas.

When he walked into the huge kitchen, he saw Luciana standing in her stained Dallas Cowboys apron, looking at several steaming pots on the industrial-sized stove.

Luciana and her husband Luis were a somewhere-in-their-fifties couple. Luis worked outside and managed the large ranch staff. Luciana took care of the house and cooked. They were an honest, hard-working, courteous, and loyal couple. And once Bridger had vetted and tested them, he told them his secret. They were two of a small group of "civilians" who knew what else investment banker Trowbridge "Trow" Hall did for a living.

They were paid well for keeping the ranch functioning and his secret to themselves.

Luis and Luciana had adopted Bridger as a replacement for their seventeen-year-old son. He was lost years ago—the result of being on the wrong street in Laredo at the wrong time when some biker gangs decided to have a shoot-out. Mr. Trow, as they liked to call him, in some ways adopted the couple as a new set of parents.

"Mr. Trow! You are awake," she said with a broad smile through full lips. She dropped a towel and hugged him, and then kissed him on his cheeks.

"Yes, tha-anks, Luciana," Bridger sputtered out as she released him. "Smells good in here."

Her face wrinkled, and her lips curled. Walking to a pot, she picked up the towel, took the lid off the pot, picked up a spoon, and took a taste. Her face wrinkled more.

"No good," she declared, her head shaking.

"I am sure it is delicious," Bridger laughed. It was good to be... home. "I will be downstairs."

"I have food for you," she said with a slightly disappointed look on her face.

"Later, I promise."

He turned and walked down a hall and entered a well-equipped workout room. He moved to a panel on the wall and flipped it open. He simultaneously placed his hand on a glass pad as he let the biometric reader scan his face. A section of the wall popped open with a click.

Bridger descended a few carpeted steps and entered into his control room. The air was crisp and fresh, as air conditioning and filtration systems kept constant circulation in the space. He flipped a switch, and a dozen LCD screens attached to the two walls to his left and right powered to life. Stacked behind a glass wall opposite the door were racks of servers. In the middle of the room was a circular desk with several computer workstations on top. Recliners faced the LCD monitors mounted to the walls.

Bridger sat and logged into a secure cloud storage file-sharing server. The files from his production company, Atlas Multimedia, of Bend, Oregon, were waiting for his review.

"The Death of the Dragons" was the fifth in a series of YouTube news segments documenting the capture of the MSS assassins by the mysterious Spy Devils. It showed tired-looking men with red eyes sitting around a table confessing to being assassins and the recent footage of the Taiwanese para-military storming a vehicle outside the Presidential Palace.

The segment ended with a black graphic with red letters that displayed *"Greetings from the Spy Devils."*

Bridger sent a coded signal that the file was ready. In fifteen minutes, the material was sent to numerous secure management systems. They were posted and re-posted to the other popular Spy Devil social media outlets—Facebook, Vimeo, Reddit, Twitter, Instagram, Snapchat, WhatsApp, LINE, VKontakte, and dozens of regional networks.

Bridger sat back in his chair and put his hands behind his neck to hold up his still tired head. Soon the story would be picked up by more traditional news media—and intelligence services—worldwide. It would trend on Twitter in less than an hour.

Bridger had perfected the art of pointing the omnipresent eye of social media on foreign intel operations, drug cartels, human traffickers, and the rest of worst his Spy Devils operated against. It was crippling. Unstoppable. Viral. It caused more long-term pain than any bomb or bullet. Exposure and shame may not kill, but it was close enough for Bridger.

It worked. Dozens of targets around the world were no longer in operation.

The Spy Devils were famous and feared.

After securing the control room door, he began his workout routine with an hour of Krav Maga and hitting the Muay Thai bag.

After a shower, he fired up the UTV and drove to his shooting range. Pistol, rifle, and shotgun maneuvers on a 20-target course. Glock-19. AR-15. Remington Versa Max shotgun first, then the Benelli M4.

After an hour, he was satisfied enough with his progress to move to his *real* passion.

The reclusive Trowbridge Hall had hired the world's best golf course architects and green's keepers—under strict non-disclosure agreements—to build exact replicas of some of the most difficult par-3 holes in the world. Tucked away in the middle of Abaddon, they molded the terrain and used the river and ponds to reconstruct the 12th at Augusta National. The 17th at TPC Sawgrass. The 7th at Pebble Beach and a half dozen more.

He just wanted to have a place to go—in his rare free time—to do something *he* enjoyed. Golf provided the skill and discipline to maintain the focus and strategy he used to construct his complex espionage operations.

Bridger had hit his first tee shot on his replica 12th hole at Augusta National over the green into the azaleas. A challenging second shot was next. Too hard, and the ball would scoot across the green into another sand trap, or worse, the pond. Too short, double bogey was a definite possibility. He needed to identify, plan, and execute the precise shot immediately.

Then three electronic chirps interrupted Jimmy Buffet's "One Particular Harbor" playing on his earbuds. He ignored them.

He knew who it was. Only one person called this number.

With determination, he stood over the ball to complete this shot. He knew it was a mistake. His concentration was blown, and he rushed his swing. He topped the ball. It scalded through the trap, across the green, and into the pond.

Three more chirps. Then three more.

Sighing, he dropped the club.

His shoulders sagged in defeat as he sat down on the fresh green grass and clicked the button to connect the call with the last person on the planet he wanted to talk to.

"Am I catching you at a bad time?" May Currier asked.

"I'm on the 12th at Augusta National."

"I am glad you have time to play with your toys."

"Hello to you too, May. Can I call you back?" he said, knowing that it was hopeless.

"We *both* know the answer to that question," she said.

"Then I guess I have the time."

"You need to get to Serbia—right away."

"Serbia? You're kidding, right?"

Silence was her response.

"Serbia? Why? No, don't tell me. Serge."

"The details are in the Dropbox. Get it done. Oh, and happy birthday, son."

She terminated the connection.

He stood and stretched. Soaking in the warmth of the day, he reached into his pocket for a ball to replace the one he hit into the pond. Instead, he pulled out a worn brass stem ball marker. It was the size of a quarter. Blue block letters on a white background surrounded a blue crest. *OLD COURSE AT ST ANDREWS.* Bridger rubbed the smooth metal between his fingers like he had done a thousand times.

The marker was a gift from his father. He died suddenly a few weeks later. Bridger was seven.

He stuffed it deep into his pocket.

stairs. Caged industrial lighting dotted the ceiling. Dozens of closed steel doors were on both sides, spaced every ten feet.

Li Chu saw a guardroom and security cameras fixed above the guardroom door pointing in his direction on the far end of the hall. The room, normally occupied by three heavily armed National Police officers, was empty. The cameras were turned off.

His steps clicked off the concrete walls like a metronome. The sounds kept rhythm with his slightly elevated pulse. At the bottom of his tense stomach was the faint churning of acid like he hadn't eaten in a week. Despite his steady temperament and tendency to demand perfection, he refused to be viewed as a robotic killer following chronically under-qualified and corrupt Chinese leadership orders.

He was a professional.

It had been three years since his Colonel summoned Captain Zhen Jingping to his office for the brief meeting that would change the purpose of his life. He worked in the Second Department of the PLA General Staff Headquarters, the Military Intelligence Department, the MID. When Captain Zhen entered the office, his Colonel left, closing the door behind him. Zhen stood rigid at attention in front of a man sitting at the Colonel's desk.

"I am Deputy Minister Chen," he announced. "Your superiors have nominated you to lead a special assignment for the Ministry."

"I am gratified by their confidence." Zhen kept his eyes focused on the wall above the man's head.

"As a result of the new National Intelligence Law, an initiative has been approved by the Standing Committee of the State Council for the creation, by the Ministry of State Security, of a capability to exert our foreign policy in a more strategic fashion."

"I am glad to hear that, sir," Zhen kept his breathing steady.

"It will be designated Bureau X within the Ministry of State Security. Only a select number of the highest officials of the government know of the existence of Bureau X," Chen started cryptically. "You are interested?"

"Interested, sir?

"In creating and leading Bureau X," Chen said as if it was obvious what he was asking.

"Yes, Minister," Zhen said sharply.

"Then you are reassigned."

"Thank you."

Chen stood and moved in front of the man. He gave the soldier a close examination.

"You are to assemble the most qualified officers to track and remove individuals overseas who stand in opposition to our policies. They should be eliminated with no attribution to the Mainland. Do you understand?"

"Yes, sir."

After the meeting with the mysterious Deputy Minister Chen, Captain Zhen Jinping of the PLA vanished. He became Li Chu, the leader of a new covert assassination team approved at the highest levels of the government. Bureau X was born.

Bureau X went operational six months later, adopting the code-name *Dragon Fire*. Li Chu implemented a kidnap and kill strategy. Death would appear as accidental—a fall, an overdose, an accident. Dragon Fire operated without incident and one hundred percent effectiveness for over a year, clearing away regional detractors of China's South China Sea expansion military.

Then nine months ago, two of his men were captured and exposed publicly in Hong Kong. What made the exposure devastating were the videos and internet postings showing his team confessing their actions. The social media posts and videos were disastrous.

When Li Chu showed Deputy Minister Chen the black card with the red pitchfork he found in Hong Kong, where his men were seized, Chen's body went stiff.

"*Wode ma ya!* Oh, my mother! The Spy Devils are the cause of this?" he said in a low, anxious voice.

"The Spy Devils," Li Chu repeated.

Then he regained his focus.

"Yes, but they will not find us."

"They already have found you" Chen shook his head and sighed. "This is very disconcerting."

Chen shook his head in doubt and said in a whisper, "The Spy Devils."

The same thing happened twice in Australia, Thailand, Malaysia, the Philippines, and again in Hong Kong. Now in Taiwan. Each time, a flood of videos, tweets, and posts on social media followed a few days after the capture.

"I am to relay that the Standing Committee is dissatisfied with your recent failures," Deputy Minister Chen told Li Chu after the last incident in Hong Kong. "They are being queried by uninformed Politburo members about your existence. It is the same with the letters from foreign governments and the United Nations. So far, we have denied everything."

"I pledge that it will not happen again. I will find these Spy Devils."

His steps echoed when he reached a steel cell door a quarter of the way down the corridor on the left side. Next to the door, an electronic keypad glowed lime-green. When Li Chu pushed several numbers, metallic clicks of the unlocking cylinders were followed by a long buzz. The door released and opened a few inches into the hall.

When the two captured Dragon Fire team members saw Li Chu walk into their cramped cell, they jumped to their feet and stood at attention in the narrow space between the two bunks placed along the walls. The eight-feet-wide and ten-feet-deep cell was windowless. A single bright safety light was attached flush to the ceiling. A metal toilet and sink were behind the men between the bunks on the far wall.

Li Chu looked from one man to the other, then back again, communicating with a slight nodding motion of his head as he took a step closer. They wore baggy blue short-sleeved pullover tops, elastic-waist blue pants, and slippers.

He noted the feeling of the acid growing in his stomach with both a mix of aggravation—for feeling anything—and comfort. These were men he had handpicked. He trained with them and executed dozens of successful active measures with them. He led, and they followed. Good men. Strong and courageous men dedicated to doing what needed to be done for the future of their country.

Now, they were as useless as a spent brass shell casing.

Li Chu saw the expression of confidence and pride in the Dragon Fire men's faces, which were now known to every intelligence and security organization. What he was about to do was not totally their fault—not totally. It was the fault of the Spy Devils.

Li Chu turned to his left. Bai stood as tall and powerful as always, despite deep purple-yellow bruises and swelling that ran along his jaw. His lips were split and purple. When Li Chu was ordered to create the team, he immediately pulled Bai out of his counterespionage position in the Beijing State Security Bureau. Now, it was over.

"What can you tell me of Bridger?" Li Chu asked.

"Very little, I am afraid. Blonde hair and tattoos," Bai said between clenched teeth as saliva rolled from the corners of his mouth.

Li Chu looked at the other man, who had a large bandage on his shoulder. His arm was in a sling.

"You, Peng?"

Trying to stand at attention, Peng nervously answered, "I do not remember much. They used gas. And shot me."

Li Chu nodded. Without any external signs of emotion, he reached toward the small of his back and pulled out a suppressed Taiwan T75 pistol. Without hesitation, he aimed and shot Peng in his chest four times. Peng fell back against his bed, bounced off the wall, and landed sprawled across the bed. Li Chu aimed and shot the already dead Bureau X man in the back of his head, sending much of its contents onto the wall.

Li Chu was pleased to see his friend Bai was still standing at attention. Li Chu raised the weapon and shot his friend between his eyes.

"Bridger," he said with a smile and handshake. "It has been too long, and you are looking too thin, but well."

"Thanks, Goran." Bridger returned the handshake. "You look like a bureaucrat now."

"I run a department now. I get into the field, just to remind all the youngsters who they are working for."

Goran was a little older than Bridger, putting him in closer to fifty. Despite the receding dark hair on top, he was a handsome man with bright eyes and a friendly smile. He wore a dark blue tailored suit. A blue shirt open at the collar. He ran the counter-intelligence section of the *Bezbednosno-informativna agencija*, known as the BIA—The State Security Service of Serbia.

Charging a reasonable rate at the low end of the scale for a dishonest government official, Goran had proven useful to Bridger. He was corrupt, but Bridger appreciated Goran was less corrupt than many others on his payroll.

Bridger and Goran had teamed up a few years ago when the Spy Devils were on an operation to curtail the flow of illegal Balkan arms trafficking. Bridger made a deal with the largest private arms merchant, Serge Taube. He agreed to eliminate his competition in exchange for him accepting U.S. and U.N. sanctions afterward.

It worked. The Spy Devils exposed and shuttered a half-dozen dealers and their networks. Many others decided to change businesses and disappear.

Serge lived up to his end of the deal—except ignoring the sanctions. Bridger knew he wouldn't. He didn't blame him.

"Goran. My team is watching your team watching us. And I am sure your team doesn't know that. So let's back them off and talk."

Goran paused, smiled a toothy white smile, and flicked his hand in the air. A half-dozen people dressed as tourists moved away.

Bridger leaned on the cool stones. He looked out over the rivers.

"You are having issues with Serge?"

"Serge?" Goran folded his arms and leaned against the stone wall. "That is why you are here? Serge?" Goran looked at him. Bridger didn't answer. "We are always having issues with Serge." Goran sighed.

"Recently?" Bridger asked.

Goran kept his gaze on Bridger, who was looking out over the rivers.

"Ah. I did not think you were here to tell war stories. You are here about the deal with China," Goran said.

"I *might* be here about the deal with China. Tell me about it," Bridger said without answering directly.

"To put it simply, our intelligence says Serge is about to sign an agreement worth maybe five-hundred million dollars, maybe a billion when all the shipments and equity are exchanged."

"Wow," Bridger whistled low, "that is a big one. Between the Chinese and Serbia?

"It is more complicated than that, Bridger. China and Serbia are good brothers, partners, friends, and comrades. An 'unbreakable partnership,' our president said. Of course, he would say that. Serge has the full backing of the president—the Chinese met his price. Serbia needs China. They are everywhere. China's investments and trading are running the business in our country. Telecommunications. Railways. Medical—"

"So, what are they buying?"

"Small arms ammunition, heavy artillery ammunition, sniper rifles, demolition equipment, mortars, antiaircraft guns, a few helicopters, and a fucking mini-submarine. A submarine! What is Serbia going to do with a submarine? We are a land-locked country. But that is the small stuff. It is the Ukrainian part that makes it big and bigger."

"What about Ukraine? What's the connection?" Bridger asked as he watched three kids sprint too fast down the Big Staircase's long stone steps. A man and woman frantically followed.

"Ukraine? Ukraine is not so simple. China has rushed in to fill the economic vacuum after Russia invaded the Donbass. China has strengthened its connections in Ukraine. Billions are being invested in infrastructure as normal economic cooperation under the cover of China's Balkan Silk Road Initiative. The Oligarch elite is secretly selling large portions of the military industry business to the Chinese. Helicopter and jet engines."

"I know some of them. The oligarchs never miss an opportunity to make some money. But no one cares?"

"I care," Goran shot back, then recovered. "Sure, there is the press and whistleblowers. You know who gets arrested? The whistleblowers."

"And there is nothing you can do about it?"

"That is the situation. Why? You have a way to do something?"

Bridger looked at Goran and smiled.

"Maybe."

9

THE OLD TIMERS AND THE NEW KIDS

Kirkwood Headquarters

Peter Schaeffer's eyebrows raised as he checked the caller ID. He picked up the receiver of his desk phone.

"Hello," Peter said.

"Pe-ter?" The woman's voice sounded tired.

It took a few seconds to recognize it as Marilyn, the administrative assistant to his boss, Tom MacBride, the Senior Vice President of Corporate Strategy, Kirkwood International Industries.

"Yes? Marilyn?" Peter asked.

"There is a meeting. In the boardroom. In one hour. They want you there."

"Who—"

"Please hurry." She hung up, cutting off his next questions.

Peter replaced the receiver, then immediately picked it up and punched a button.

"What's up?" the female voice of Peter's chief researcher asked.

"Anything in the news this morning I should know about?" he asked as he rested his elbows on his desk.

"Nothing unusual," she said.

sign with gold lettering on a black background that declared it *"The Jacob Kirkwood Boardroom."*

"Schaeffer." The deep voice came from behind Peter, causing him to jump.

He turned to see Benton, Senior Director, Personal and Facilities Security, Office of Security, Kirkwood International Industries. Everything about Benton said retired Chicago cop—the notoriously dishonest kind of Chicago cop. Which is what he was before retiring and coming to Kirkwood as security chief. Chia Pet gray hair and a face that only a mother could love. Gray pants. Gray jacket. Gray skin. An over-sized badge on the breast pocket that just said, "Benton." No one was sure if it was his first or last name.

"Oh. Hi, Benton. On your nightly vampire leftover donut prowl?"

"I should shut that smart mouth of yours, Schaeffer," he said in a low and menacing rasp.

Peter felt Benton needed to take counter-intelligence and the threat from competitors seriously. If Peter was trying to get information on the competition, the competition was trying to do the same to Kirkwood. Those companies could count on help from their home intelligence services to steal secrets. Not Peter.

Economic espionage had infected corporate America. Business leaders would rather ignore it for the sake of profits and market share. Even worse, many were *willingly* handing over trade secrets and intellectual property as terms for doing business in their countries.

Benton *hated* Peter for sticking his nose into his business.

"They are waiting." Benton jerked his thumb toward the boardroom door.

Tom MacBride was sitting one chair from the end along the far side of a massive wood Board of Director's table. "Peter. Come here. Sit." He indicated the chair to his left.

MacBride was a New Kid who did not care if he fit the corporate executive slicked-backed image. A rare combination of brilliant scientific mind and entrepreneur. Corporate executive and nearly nice guy. A tangled mop of red hair hung from his head, stopping just above his shoulders. His hair framed a ruddy face, large eyes, large bushy eyebrows, and a large nose balancing large black-rimmed glasses. He looked a little flabby under his loose-fitting wrinkled shirt and jacket.

"Can you tell me—" Peter started.

MacBride cut him off as he raised his hand like he was being sworn to testify under oath. He punched a button on the phone on the table.

"He is here."

The Jacob Kirkwood Boardroom was a monument to the Old Timers. A rectangular and windowless space. A massive mahogany table dominated the middle of the room, accented by Kirkwood black and gold. A dozen huge black leather executive chairs surrounded it. Twelve black and gold leather desk blotters, notepads, pens, and golden mugs were uniformly positioned at each seat. Everything prominently displayed the renowned Kirkwood block "Golden K" corporate symbol made famous through various iterations for over a hundred years.

To their right, another oak door at the end of the room opened. Peter tried not to look surprised when Kirkwood International Industries' Chief Executive Officer Samuel Kirkwood, and Walter Jessup, Chief Legal Officer, walked into the boardroom.

MacBride stood. Peter followed his lead and did the same, feeling his pulse thump in the arteries of his neck.

Kirkwood reached out his hand and walked toward them.

"Hello, Tom," he said, shaking his hand. Then he turned. "Peter, it is wonderful to see you again. I am glad you could make it," Kirkwood said with a weak smile. They shook hands. "Please sit."

Peter laughed a little to himself. Among employees, Kirkwood was nicknamed "Mr. Wonderful" for his constant use of his favorite word. The CEO treated everyone with respect. Peter knew Kirkwood genuinely appreciated the work of the competitive intelligence group.

Kirkwood took his birthright location in the larger executive chair at the end of the table. Jessup sat across from MacBride to Kirkwood's right.

Samuel Kirkwood was small and round and pink. To Peter, he looked like what Charlie Brown would look like if he ever grew up to reach his late sixties. The new employee indoctrination to Kirkwood

International Industries required a lesson on the founding of the company. Peter took it over a decade ago, but the room reminded him of the key facts.

Wilbur Kirkwood, Samuel's great-grandfather, was an engineering visionary who started Kirkwood Equipment Manufacturing, as it was called then, in Chicago, in 1897. It was created to supply railroads with automated block signaling and train operation controllers. Wilbur Kirkwood expanded his manufacturing operations to build automated systems for the massive oil and transport monopolies run by JD Rockefeller. A few years later, JD introduced Wilbur to steel magnate Andrew Carnegie who bought Kirkwood Equipment Manufacturing products by the Rockefeller-controlled trainload to support Carnegie's new enterprise—United States Steel Corporation.

In less than a decade, Wilbur Kirkwood shared brandy and cigars with the wealthiest men in American history. Wilbur passed the company to his son, Benjamin, who passed it to his son, Jacob, who passed it to his son Samuel, who changed the name to Kirkwood International Industries, KII.

"First things first," Jessup said, lowering his voice as if someone was listening at the door. "Peter, what we are about to discuss should not be shared outside this room. Understand?

"Yes." Peter nodded in agreement.

Walter Jessup was in his mid-sixties. An Old Timer. The lean and athletic lawyer seeped an aura of old-money Ivy League wisdom and prudence. His expertly cut hair was graying at the temples. His accent was eastern New England, and his sentences were delivered as if he were giving a final summation to a jury.

"Time is of the essence, so let's get started," Kirkwood started.

"We hope you can use your CIA intelligence skills and connections," Tom said.

"How can I help?" Peter asked, swiveling his head to look at each man.

"You recall the contract we signed with Ukraine for our new Kirk-Comm2400 line of equipment?" MacBride continued.

"Yes, sir. We were asked to do some research on it at the time."

"Yes, I told Walt and Sam that. Maybe you can do a quick summary."

"Well, if I remember correctly," Peter's eyes looked up as he went into recall mode, "we did a profile examining their customers, product lines, and legal issues hoping to find the company's strategy and tactics. We mined their social media. We constructed a profile on Viktor Bondar, his daughter and, I think, his son—"

"And what did you conclude?"

"I wish I had time to re-read it. I could go to my office and pull it out of my files."

"Do your best," Tom said.

Peter sat forward. "The Bondar family is rich, powerful, and as corrupt as they come, even by Ukrainian standards. One thing was clear."

"What was that?" Kirkwood asked.

"It's hard to figure out why we would work with a guy who is the equivalent of John Gotti."

"They are a strange assortment of people," Kirkwood said, as he slowly rotated his leather commander chair toward the oil painting of his father on the wall above and behind him.

"You have hit upon the issue, Peter," MacBride confided.

"There is a significant issue we would need you to help us with related to this," Jessup said. He picked up his pen and absent-mindedly tapped it on his coffee cup.

Jessup straightened his back. His neck seemed to extend his head a few inches higher like a turtle. "It is, beyond a doubt, a critical issue."

"What is it?" Peter asked. His hands started to shake with stress. He hid them under the table, but he saw they were more stressed than he was.

Suddenly, the boardroom door opened. A man with gray hair and a bright tie walked in. Peter was stunned. He knew exactly who it was.

"Danny! I am glad you are here. Just in time," Kirkwood said as he stood, arm extended.

"Gentlemen. I sincerely apologize for my tardiness. Samuel. Don't get up. Please sit."

"Danny, you are right on time, as usual. This is Peter Schaeffer. He runs our intelligence function. We were just explaining the Ukraine situation to him," Jessup said.

"Peter. This is Danny Chapel," MacBride said, nodding his head in the direction of the distinguished guest. "Peter, Danny happens to know Viktor Bondar well. He will be a great asset."

"Mr. Chapel," Peter stood up as Chapel walked toward him. Peter's hand immediately got wet and shaky. Peter was sure his heart was about to explode.

I'm in the same room with Danforth Chapel. Holy fuck.

"Peter, I have heard great things about you," he reached out with his perfectly manicured hand and shook Peter's. "And call me Danny."

"Of course, Danny, sorry."

Danforth Chapel has heard of me? Did he just walk over to shake MY hand? Holy fuck.

He wore expensive Gieves & Hawkes bespoke suits. A four-hundred-dollar cut for his full head of gray hair. Tinted Dolce and Gabbana twenty-five-thousand-dollar glasses covered money-green eyes. Testoni goat-skinned shoes. A Rolex Submariner clipped to his wrist. He completed the look with his famous flamboyant, colorful silk ties.

The Danforth Chapel Company was the world's leading private intelligence agency. It should be, since Chapel created the industry. Discreet, successful, and expensive. Thirty-five offices, thousands of specialized employees, and connections spread across all regions of the world were the vanguard of his reach, but at its nexus was Danforth Chapel.

Danny solved problems. The kinds of problems that fit into categories such as embarrassing, scandal, blackmail, espionage, fraud, asset recovery, kidnapping, or top secret.

His problem-solving acumen had become a truism in business. If someone had been bad, they would *be sent to Chapel.* To the private intelligence industry, he had become a verb: "*Get this company Chapeled.*"

Chapel sat next to Jessup and across from Peter. He pushed back from the table and crossed one leg over the other—hands folded in his lap.

"Tell Peter and me about this case. As I understand it, George had a briefcase with him? And the loss of that case is a threat and could be used against your company?" Chapel asked.

"We need that case," Kirkwood added.

Peter nodded that he understood, but he didn't.

"What was in it? Why is it so important?" Peter asked.

Peter saw Chapel smile, as the others just sat looking at each other.

Wow, the silence in here just got deafening, Peter thought.

10

SERGE TAUBE

Belgrade, Serbia

"Serge Taube. You have been a bad boy," Bridger said as he sat on the seat across from the man.

Taube looked up to see who had made the mistake of sitting uninvited at his table. When he saw Bridger, he set his knife and fork down, paused, then carefully scanned the Tavern room of the Dva Jelena—The Two Deer Restaurant. At just after 3:30 p.m., the frontend of lunchtime, the rectangular room was filling with diners. It was a medium-sized rectangular room with tables lining the wooden walls. The light from bright lamps shone off the polished walls and framed mirrors.

The sound of the conversations echoed off the low ceiling, as did the traditional Serbian music that came down the wide staircase from the larger restaurant above.

A few tables away from Taube's reserved corner table, three men jumped to their feet and took steps in the table's direction. Bridger saw Taube wave them off with a flick of his fingers.

"Bridger," Taube said with a sigh.

Taube was small. Thin. Frail-looking. Skin the same color as spent chewing gum. His gray hair was oiled and combed back from a receding hairline. His eyes were set so deep into their sockets it was hard to see what color they were. Gray goatee. A voice like a Gatling gun. He wore a thick knit wool tan sweater.

"It is good to see you again, Serge. You look well."

"I look like shit. What are you doing here?"

"You know why I am here. I would have thought the man once labeled the biggest bad guy dealer of arms and munitions in the Balkans would be smarter than that. Especially after the U.S. and U.N. listed you as a human rights abuser a few years ago. That was after the U.N. blacklisted you and added you to the travel ban list after that nasty affair in Liberia. And after the U.S. froze your assets and barred anyone from doing business with you. Did I miss anything?"

Bridger looked eagerly at the plates of traditional Serbian food on the table.

"And because of all those illegal actions taken by your government, I have retired. It is what we *bad guys* are supposed to say in this situation, right?" Taube said. His blue lips curled with a smile as he speared a minute piece of beef cevapi sausage and slowly placed it in his mouth.

Bridger picked up the wine bottle off the lime green table cloth, checked the label, and nodded his head in approval. He raised the bottle up with a questioning look at Taube, who exaggerated his own nod of approval. Bridger poured, sipped, and smiled.

"Well, that is not what I hear. I *hear* you are still in the arms biz. Let me get this right."

Bridger took a crumpled piece of paper out of his pocket and put it on the table. Holding it down with one hand, he wiped his hand over it to smooth out the wrinkles. He looked at it and read.

"You are a silent partner in a boatload of companies you indirectly own and manage. You are up to your skinny neck in all aspects of your private company's daily operations."

"Not true," Taube said, still chewing on the same small piece of meat.

"Oh, come on, Serge. I thought we agreed long ago we wouldn't try to BS each other."

"Go on. What else do you think you know, Bridger?"

"Well, I know you are brokering and soliciting new illegal arms deals." Bridger looked up at Taube and stared into his eyes with the look a parent gives to a naughty child. "You have friends and family signing the deals for you. By the way, how is your nephew Jovan? Still hiding in Armenia? I *am* sorry about that."

When Taube didn't answer, Bridger continued as he casually placed his hand over his ear.

"You have at least three companies, here and in Cyprus, through which you negotiate your contracts and international sales. I think they are—"

In his ear, he could hear Imp stammering, "Geez, these names suck. Something like *Parrrr-mesan-iki Tech. Moon-pie-ski-nov Limited. Advil-aspirin-deet Technologies*...or something like that."

Bridger sighed and dropped his hand.

"Well, you know who they are. The point is, your big three-billion-dollar bottle of Rakija comes from your new number one client—the People's Republic of China."

Taube sat back. He pulled a battered and tarnished silver cigarette case from his pocket, flipped it open, took out a thin brown cigarette, and placed it between his lips. He lit it with a small lighter.

"China has been a good friend to Serbia and the Balkans."

"As I understand it," Bridger said, as he re-filled his glass, "and correct me if I am wrong, you are about to put into motion—without the usual public procurement regulations and procedures—a state to state agreement that Serbia and China signed years ago." Bridger plucked a sausage from the plate and ate it in two bites. "Damn, these are the best cevapi anywhere. It is why I knew you would be here."

"Why is my business any business of yours?"

"Excellent question. Sharp as ever, Serge. Nothing is ever done for nothing, especially in governments known for corruption. Everyone needs that little extra off the top. They are making lots of secondary and sub-contractor supplier agreements, also without public oversight. Millions. Maybe billions."

"As you say, corruption is normal. Why bother with me now?"

"Damn fine wine," Bridger said, as he reached again for the bottle. The remaining wine filled Bridger's glass only halfway. He shook it over the glass to get the last drops, then set it down.

"Do the people of Serbia know that their president, minister of the interior, and others are paying triple for some of the goods, so their elected officials can get just that much richer?"

Bridger reached into the pocket of his black leather jacket. He looked back over at the table with the three guards. Each was leaning forward, ready to jump on Bridger and beat him to death at the slightest threat to their boss. One looked more noticeably upset. The leader of the team, Bridger surmised.

He pulled out his phone and waved it mockingly at the man. After a few swipes of his screen, he found what he was looking for.

"Do they know that their country is selling off control of the mining and construction industries? Or that you are acting as a go-between for Ukrainian oligarchs and arms dealers, not only to procure small arms and mortar deals but in exchange for positions in Ukrainian munitions and helicopter companies?"

The lack of movement in Taube's eyelids told Bridger he had surprised the old man with his knowledge of the deal.

"No?" Bridger continued. "How about the Russians?"

Taube leaned forward and raised a thin hand to take the phone. Bridger sat back, keeping it out of range of the man's reach.

"A video detailing the transaction, the corruption, documents, and all the names will hit the Spy Devils' YouTube channel before I walk out the door. I just need to hit send and boom!" Bridger held his thumb over his keypad. "As you might expect, the CIA and other international entities will make certain it gets the exposure it deserves. By the morning, the president of Serbia will awake to a new reality."

"And your world-famous Spy Devils, of course," Taube said.

"Well, I wasn't going to boast, but, well, yes," Bridger said,

11

ASAP

Jacob Kirkwood Boardroom

J essup rolled the fingers on his right hand into a fist. MacBride sat perfectly still. Kirkwood's face went from raspberry to brick as he looked directly at Jessup. Chapel was smiling and brushing his tie with his hand.

"Walter, why not give Peter here all the details? It is why we are here. Isn't that right?" Chapel said after the silence lingered a few more uncomfortable beats.

"Yes, Danny. Of course," Jessup began, with the tone of the law professor.

"That would be great, thanks," Peter said, picking up the Kirkwood pen and holding it over the Kirkwood notepad.

"I would prefer that no notes be taken," Jessup told Peter, motioning with his head in a slight nod to Peter's notepad.

"Oh. Sure." Chills spiked through Peter's body at the rebuke. He set the pen down and sat back.

Jessup continued.

"Let me explain. It is somewhat complex. LeonidOre, Bondar's mining and steel operation, is a new client. We anticipated it would provide a new opening into the lucrative Eastern European and potentially Russian markets. The contract calls for us to upgrade their entire command and control data networks integrating their mining and metallurgical factories. To secure the contract, we agreed to vendor-finance a large percentage of the one billion dollars for the infrastructure and service."

"It was the largest contract for Kirkwood in many years. It came at a critical moment," Kirkwood interjected. "Critical."

Peter saw the cheeks of the CEO's round face flush to a shade of pink.

"The financing went from Kirkwood Credit Corporation to Ukraine Standard Bank, which is owned by the Viktor Bondar family."

Jessup paused and then took over again.

"As collateral on our one billion dollars, Bondar pledged stock in LeonidOre and some of his other commodities assets. We sent them half, five hundred million dollars. As of today, Ukraine Standard Bank has failed to repay KCC on the loans as agreed. The whole deal was consummated in bad faith on their part. They have ceased payment on the loan. They are not responding to our inquiries."

"The case Walt, get to the case," MacBride said.

Peter saw Jessup try to conceal his growing annoyance at MacBride. Peter wasn't surprised. It was no secret in Kirkwood's rank and file that the two men were often at odds over the company's future. Jessup, the lawyer and risk-averse. MacBride, the entrepreneur and willing to take the risk for the reward.

"George was in Ukraine to try to, um, clear things up with them," Kirkwood said, as he gently rubbed his face with his hands as if to wake up from a bad dream. When he lowered his hands, his cheeks had moved from pink to raspberry. "Why did he go?"

Peter sat forward and picked up the pen. Jessup twitched, preparing another warning, but stopped when Peter started only to lightly tap it on the Kirkwood notepad.

"The case, Peter," Chapel said, "contains sensitive proprietary information for Kirkwood. Fortunately, the case is the type that requires certain biometric keys to open. It is hoped that this will give you time to locate it before they do so."

"Why did he have it?"

Everyone but Jessup let out a sound that told Peter he had asked the big question.

"Excellent and astute question, Peter!" Chapel said, which to Peter sounded like he was Sherlock Holmes on a new case.

"Sensitive documents are all I will say, and it doesn't matter. Retrieving it is your primary focus." MacBride patted Peter on the arm as he gave him his mission.

"Are you saying Bondar killed him to avoid paying or to get the case? He was murdered?" Peter asked.

"We do not know. I hope to heavens not," Kirkwood said.

"We will let the local authorities tell us what happened," Jessup said, staring oddly at Kirkwood when he spoke. "We are not exactly certain where the case is at this moment, but you must find it. That is the priority," he added in the tone of a lawyer telling a jury they can only decide the case in his favor.

"I have all the confidence in the world in your abilities," Kirkwood said. He gestured with both hands toward MacBride and Jessup. "We all do."

The lawyer and the strategist smiled and concurred with their CEO.

"I most wholeheartedly agree," Chapel said, running his hand along his tie.

Peter sat, absorbing their comments. Peter wouldn't say no. He couldn't and wasn't sure he wanted to, anyway.

"Wonderful. Thank you, Peter," Kirkwood said, declaring the meeting was over. He walked over and shook Peter's hand. His face had returned to its usual light fleshy pink. "The company is counting on you."

"How much time do I have?" Peter asked.

The men once again looked at each other. Their faces grew more severe as they seemed to be communicating and deciding how to answer with only the expressions in their eyes.

Peter knew what was coming. He waited in the silence for the answer.

Kirkwood stood and looked at the painting of his father hanging over the door the CEO had walked through moments ago.

"We need it as soon as possible. ASAP," Kirkwood said.

As soon as possible. Peter hated ASAP.

"Can you give me an idea of when, exactly, you'd like to have this?"

"Two weeks. We announce our results in three weeks," MacBride replied.

"We would like this resolved in advance of that," Jessup clarified.

Peter remained silent, looking as if he was making some secret spy calculations in his head.

Peter stood and returned the handshake. "I will do my best."

Jessup picked up the folio and looked once more across the table at Peter. "I want it clear. This has priority over anything you are doing. It is highly confidential, do not tell anyone. Find that briefcase." He turned and stepped away from the table.

"And what about the money? Peter added.

"What?" Jessup turned back. "The money? Yes. Find the funds, of course."

Peter nodded as Jessup joined the other executives and walked out the door that led to the CEO's office. His bullshit meter had spiked into the red.

He stood alone, looking around the boardroom and wondering why he had to remind Jessup of the money. *What the hell could possibly be in that briefcase that is more important than a billion dollars?*

Resting in the back of his Lincoln Town Car, Chapel pushed a speed dial number on his phone and put it to his ear.

"I am happy to report you may proceed as you have planned."

He waited and listened.

"Yes. It is good news," he replied, watching the lights pass through the tinted windows of the armored sedan. Chapel brushed his hand down his flowery-patterned tie and nodded as the caller spoke, then he cut in.

"Will he be an issue?" Chapel laughed. "Does it make a difference?"

12

THE STREETS OF BELGRADE

Belgrade, Serbia

E ven a day later, Nikola was still upset that his six surveillance cars had lost Bridger so soon after the American left the Dva Jelena restaurant. The man had managed to evade his team within the crowds of Bajloni market on Dzordza Vasingtona. Nikola assumed the Spy Devil had found a taxi and changed cars before Nikola could call his contacts at the taxi companies to track him down.

He hadn't told Taube what had happened.

Nikola was not a novice. Formerly a professional soldier, he became, as he called it, a babysitter for a very—very—rich old man. Nikola sometimes lamented that he was once as close to a special forces soldier as Serbia could have—trained in special operations by both the Russians and NATO. He fought in Kosovo. Like many of his peers, he took advantage of the lucrative market in the Balkans and other warzones by becoming a mercenary for hire.

Now, he had his own security company but only one customer—a ruthless and powerful old man. A man who had spent decades selling weapons to all bidders—sometimes to both sides of a conflict. A well-paying man.

Nikola jammed the earbud into his ear.

As he waited with his driver in a black Volvo outside the Hotel Moscow, Nikola pulled out this throwaway pistol—a semi-automatic Zastava CZ 99 with the identifying serial numbers rubbed off. It was a reliable weapon for the purpose. No reason to use his Glock. After he shoots the man in the head, he will drop the Zastava by the body. No reason to risk getting caught with it before he could toss it in the Danube.

"He is sitting in the Pastry Shop," his man in the hotel lobby said through the radio.

"It is a good choice," Nikola replied as he looked down Terazije Street at the impressive façade of the historic hotel. "It has windows looking out to a wide square and streets. It would be hard to approach him without being seen. Multiple exits."

After his men lost Bridger, Nikola called down his list of hotel sources last night, hoping that the man was not hiding in a safe house somewhere in Belgrade. After three hours, he got lucky. A man fitting Bridger's description had checked in several days ago under the name Bobby Jones.

Using a public hotel was poor tradecraft. Nikola expected better from the famous Spy Devil.

"He is leaving. Heading for the front door," the sentry in the lobby said.

"Walking out the front door. Going left on Terazije," another voice announced.

"I will follow him on foot," Nikola informed the teams.

"What if he gets into a cab?" his driver asked.

"Stay in your positions near the hotel. I will radio my location as he moves. Team 6?"

"No counter-surveillance detected."

Nikola stepped out of the car into the crisp morning air of Belgrade. He moved across the street in quick strides. From a block away, he saw Bridger suddenly turn around and walk directly toward him. Nikola had no choice but to pull an amateur move and join some strangers looking in a jewelry shop window. He let Bridger pass behind him and let him go halfway down the incredibly long block before he turned to follow. The road became narrower and the foot traffic less heavy as they approached Andrićev Venac promenade.

Bridger cut left by the gardens and into the walking area. Nikola followed. For the next forty-five minutes, he continued to follow as Bridger walked the busy streets. Stopping. Crossing. Doubling back. Nikola marveled and felt fortunate to witness the smooth and deliberate moves of the man he had heard so much about. It took all his own skills to avoid detection.

Several times, Bridger moved through narrow choke points to funnel anyone who might be following. And each time, Nikola was forced to wait. He lost Bridger twice but fortunately caught a glimpse of a figure walking the street after a frantic search. Nikola checked his watch. It had been two hours since they had left the Hotel Moscow. Nikola realized he was drenched in sweat.

He noticed Bridger's pace slow slightly as he veered onto Lomina Street, a narrow canyon side street lined on both sides with cars, apartments, shops, and graffiti-decorated abandoned buildings. Nikola moved slowly from one recessed doorway to another, keeping the cars and few people on the sidewalk between him and Bridger. He saw Bridger move down one side of Lomina, cross, then walk back in Nikola's direction on the other side.

Bridger stopped about thirty feet away in front of a graffiti-covered corrugated steel door. Above it was a semi-circular awning frame—missing the glass—with a broken yellow sign declaring "Hostel 40" hanging from it.

As Bridger unlocked the door, Nikola pulled his Zastava CZ 99 from his belt and sprinted across the street, closing the thirty-foot gap in just a few seconds. He moved in behind Bridger as he stepped inside.

Nikola saw that Bridger seemed oblivious to the assassin behind him. Nikola raised his pistol and pointed it at the back of Bridger's head.

Then he felt the cold metal of a gun press against his temple.

Taube sat in a cushioned chair much too large for his small frame drawing hard on a thin cigarette glowing red with each inhale. He was tired, and it was late, but he was expecting the call.

When his phone beeped, he still flinched. He looked at his screen and saw two text messages from Nikola. He smiled.

The first text contained a picture taken from behind and to the left and clearly showed a man on the floor in a pool of glistening liquid. The body seemed to be wearing a dark leather jacket—the same one, Taube was sure, that Bridger had on at dinner.

The second text also contained a photo—this time from the side and closer. Taube recognized Bridger's face. Blood streaks had run down from his forehead over his pale cheeks and chin. He could clearly see an entrance hole in the side of Bridger's head behind his left ear. Blank death was the expression in his eyes.

There was no doubt in his mind Bridger was dead.

13

CHAOS IS GOOD FOR BUSINESS

Novi Petrivtsi, North of Kyiv, Ukraine

Viktor Bondar always enjoyed killing.

This attitude made him one of the richest, most powerful, and feared men in Ukraine.

Ordinarily, he displayed his keepsake Tula TOZ-8 Bolt Action .22 caliber rifle in a special walnut case behind his desk. He brought his lucky Tula with him from his Kyiv apartment office to get some pleasure shooting in before the morning meeting—shooting sharpened his focus.

Standing in a firing lane of his ultra-modern underground shooting range, Bondar chambered a cartridge, pointed, and fired at a target in the total containment collection area one hundred meters away.

The climate-controlled shooting range was located in the lower level of his compound, secluded along the Dnieper River north of Kyiv. Containing a brick mansion, stables, and dock, the area was surrounded by walls and members of his personal mercenary army, the black-clad Bondar Battalion-1. Ira, his daughter and advisor, convinced him to purchase it for more money than it was worth as a symbol to his peers and enemies of his status.

He hated the place, except for the shooting range. Bondar preferred his spacious apartment on the top floors of his flagship bank building in central Kyiv. Recent events dictated that he come to the country for the enhanced protection and wait for the calls.

The first one had come several nights ago, just after the Kirkwood executive fell to his death.

"Any problems?" he asked.

"None," said the voice.

"Then deliver the package as planned."

As Bondar anticipated, the second call came soon after. That conversation scheduled the "urgent" meeting that was to take place in a few minutes.

Without looking where the bullet struck the target, he turned, took off his protective earmuffs, and set the Tula down. He made a mental note that the rifle needed to be cleaned—a task he would do himself. No one touched that rifle but him.

He tucked his rare Makarov 59 EG, the classic Soviet Cold War Pistol M, into his belt in the small of his back, walked up winding steps, and through French doors leading to the dining room.

The smell of warm fruit-filled *varenyky* dumplings wafted through the air. Ira was sitting in one of eight metal and wood chairs that surrounded a long oval glass table. Plates of breads and pastries were spaced among other cereals, fruit, pitchers of fruit juice, and carafes of coffee. A crystal vase of fresh-cut flowers sat on the center of the table.

Bondar had not eaten that morning. He picked up a warm *varenyky* and popped it in his mouth.

He looked the part of the powerful oligarch. A suit and tie in public. For variety, he sometimes went with an open collar. Average height. American-style crew cut of dark auburn hair. Black eyes above a nose made crooked by one too many fistfights. He wore his trade-mark three day's growth of rusty-colored beard.

"They just passed the guard station," Ira said, placing her spoon into an empty bowl.

"Are you prepared?" he asked.

At thirty-three years old, Ira Bondar was known by her business

associates and the general public as gorgeous and ruthless. Ira used her blonde hair, sky-blue eyes, accentuating attire, and rapier brain to her complete advantage. She favored blood-red lipstick and nail polish as an accent color.

Bondar sat at the end of the table, picked up another dumpling, and stuck it in his mouth.

"Do not worry. They are coming to us because they are in a weak position." He smiled.

Out of the large windows, he saw a hazy central European late spring sky. Thick granite-colored clouds backlit by the sun flowed above in waves as the trees bent with punches of wind. A light drizzle began to spray.

Ira's phone rang. She answered and listened. "Escort them to the dining room." She set the phone down. "They are coming to us."

They both stood as two men, one old, the other Asian, entered the room behind a muscular man dressed in black military tactical pants and a black pullover long-sleeved shirt—the casual uniform of the Bondar Battalion-1.

Anton Vlasenko was well beyond old age. His baggy wool overcoat hung on speckled crooked limbs branching out from the core. Thin white hair over eyes that once made men shrink with fear. His life-long defining feature, pointy protruding ears, now looked like two large dinner plates embedded on each side of his head.

Age was shrinking his mentor, Bondar thought. But he was not fooled by Vlasenko's appearance. This oligarch was still mentally sharp and dangerous.

"*Dobryden*, Anton Vlasenko," Bondar welcomed the man with a hug and a pat on the back.

"*Pryvit*, Viktor Bondar," the man said in a nasal-tone scratchy voice. He turned to Ira. "Ira, you are as lovely as ever." He took her hand and kissed it.

"Thank you, Uncle Anton." Vlasenko was not her uncle, but the man and her father had been business partners and friends most of her life. He brought her gifts and gave advice when she needed it. She loved him like an uncle.

"May I introduce Deputy Minister Chen, of China."

Chen's suit was dark. His shirt was white. His tie was striped. Round cheeks framed small lips. Behind nearly invisible wire-rim glasses were deep dark eyes.

They exchanged introductions, handshakes, and bows. Ira offered seats at the table and some breakfast. No one accepted. Anton sat next to Ira, close enough to pat her on her leg. Chen sat across from him.

Vlasenko had no equal in Ukraine and most of central Europe. He was already a millionaire many times over before Ukrainian independence. Over the decades, his empire rose to gain access or control over many of the country's coal and steel resources, energy, telecommunications, transport systems, engineering, finance, real estate, and retail. If something was sold in Ukraine, Vlasenko had a piece of the profits. If it was sold to China, he had most of it. And if it was sold to Russia, Vlasenko was the one selling it.

Now, he was a billionaire many times over.

Vlasenko pulled a small orange out of his overcoat pocket, bit it through the skin, and started to chew.

They sat in silence and listened to the wind drive the large raindrops against the windows. The only other sound was Vlasenko as he bit into the orange, sucked the pulp and juice out of his teeth, and chewed the fibrous snack.

"No doubt you heard of the recent incident," Vlasenko said, still chewing, showing orange pulp stuck between his jagged gray teeth.

"I am not certain what you mean," Bondar replied. He knew precisely what Anton meant.

"Two of our men were killed retrieving the case the American brought with him. They were ambushed. The case is gone. I was wondering if you have any knowledge of where it might be," Chen said in a pleasantly soft voice.

"It?" Bondar tilted his head in a gesture of mock recollection. He leaned forward and gazed from one man to the other. The dance had begun. They each wanted to lead and they all knew the steps.

"Give the man the case, Viktor!" Vlasenko said in a stronger voice than his appearance would deem possible. "This is bigger than you."

"Are you referring to the case I was expecting the American businessman George MacLean to hand to me? The case I was told that MacLean was bringing to Kyiv that I could use as leverage against them on the debt I owe them? The case that I was to exchange," he looked at Chen "for guarantees of payment of my obligations to the Kirkwood company? That case?"

The room was silent again. Bondar looked at Vlasenko, who stared into space, chewing on the last piece of the orange as if he hadn't heard a word.

"What is in it?" Ira asked.

Chen and Vlasenko did not answer.

"I don't know. It doesn't matter," Vlasenko answered. "Let's stop all of this." His nasal voice pronounced each syllable with deliberate effort. "Viktor, I know how you think and why you think that." He flashed a pulp-filled grin. "Let me tell you what you are thinking."

Vlasenko started to pat his coat with the palms of his hands. "I know you better than you know yourself. I saw the smart, aggressive young man in 1991 looking to make his mark when the Soviet Union dissolved." He inhaled a deep wheezing breath. "We eliminated any rivals, or with the right amount of persuasion, made them our allies. Remember what I said?"

"Chaos is good for business."

"Precisely."

Vlasenko released a strain of phlegm-filled coughs. Orange debris projected from his mouth. He wiped it with the sleeve of his coat. The rest he let bead on the glass tabletop. Then he smiled as if nothing happened. "I gave you steel and coal. We all profited from the military manufacturing factories. We have done well—together."

That was true. Bondar also knew Vlasenko as well as Vlasenko thought he knew Bondar. He saw the past from an entirely different perspective.

Through years of a prosperous partnership, whether legitimate—coal and steel—or more illegitimate—selling surplus arms—Bondar was the thug to Vlasenko's master entrepreneur and capitalist. Bondar's image was that of a killer in a suit. A mobster. A nobody who became someone *only* because he was lucky enough to be in the shadow of Vlasenko.

Bondar knew one other truth. Both would not hesitate to obliterate the other if it was good for business.

And it was time to unleash some chaos.

14

WARNING SIGNALS

Novi Petrivtsi, North of Kyiv, Ukraine

Vlasenko reached his hands deep into his coat pockets and rummaged around.

"It is not a secret the war has weakened you, significantly. As a result, the government is interested in seizing your assets. I called you in good faith, offering a way to salvage your reputation." He tapped a crooked finger on the glass table. "Yes, you were worried that the Americans would still want their money, or the Chinese might not provide the new business they offered. They are businessmen also, correct Minister?"

They all looked at Chen, who remained silent as Vlasenko continued.

"You have received over two hundred fifty million dollars from the Americans on your debt. Minister Chen has promised new contracts and business. I consider that good business."

"Helping to obtain the case is a token of goodwill," Chen said, breaking his silence. Chen's eyes looked at Bondar with purpose.

"What about the Russians? I could go to the Russians." Bondar said, looking at Chen. He thought for a moment, then continued. "You think the Russians are too focused on causing havoc in Crimea and eastern Ukraine? That China will solidify its economic position in Ukraine and surrounding countries for the Silk Road while no one is looking?"

"We all have our role to play," Vlasenko said.

"I want guarantees of more contracts with the Chinese," Bondar glared.

Vlasenko waved his hand in the air, dismissing Bondar's comment. He glanced over the table. Bondar reached into his pocket and came out with a small orange. He smiled and handed it to the old man.

"Thank you, my boy." He took a big bite and started his noisy chewing process.

Ira finally spoke. "May I ask, Minister Chen, why was the American killed?"

Chen pondered his answer for a moment, then said, "He was becoming a problem and needed to be removed."

"But you didn't have to drop him ten stories. You could have killed him in a less public way," Ira countered.

"No, they needed to make it public." It was Bondar. He turned to Chen. "It was a warning sign—to us. We shouldn't cause any problems —or we will be *removed* too."

Vlasenko coughed, then coughed again as an orange river of saliva and foam rolled from his mouth.

"Uncle Anton! Are you choking?" Ira screamed as she turned and beat his back with her hand.

Vlasenko's body started to jerk forward, hitting the table. His mouth tried to suck in air, but his rapid short gasps signaled he was suffocating. His eyes were wide and glazed. His face turned a deep reddish-purple. His boney wrinkled hands clutched his chest. He started to shake. Ira tried to get her arms around the man, but his small body seized so violently she could not get a grip.

"Father, do something!"

She looked up to see her father putting the last bit of pastry in his mouth, disinterested in what was happening a few feet away. She shot a look at the man from China who also made no move to help. His face revealed no emotion.

Vlasenko suddenly went still. His hands dug into his chest over his heart. He seemed to rise from his chair for an instant. He toppled over to his right and hit the floor, curled in a ball at Bondar's feet.

With tears in her eyes, Ira knelt by the body, looking from the dead man to her father in disbelief.

"Get up, Ira. Take your seat," Bondar said in a tone as calm as if he was asking her to pass the salt.

"You killed him!"

"Get a hold of yourself and take your seat," he commanded.

She fought to regain her composure. She stood, straightened her skirt and blouse, wiped the tears from her mascara-smudged eyes, and sat.

"I have seen the effects of a high dosage of cyanide many times," Chen said.

"You see," Bondar said, "I can send warning signals too." He pointed to Vlasenko. "This man was my friend. My mentor for decades. You can do your business with me now. Only me."

Chen nodded, pushed his chair back, and stood up.

"I believe we have completed as much business this morning as possible."

"I will walk you to the car."

Bondar and Ira also rose and escorted Chen through the house to the front entrance. Bondar nodded to the two uniformed Bondar Battalion-1 security men, who nodded back. They grabbed the handles of the massive mahogany double hung doors and swung them open. Chen, Bondar, then Ira stepped out to the wide V-shaped brick paver area that flared out from the entrance to the driveway twenty feet away.

Chen didn't stop when he saw six crumpled bodies that were once Vlasenko's security detail dead on the ground. The rain had ceased. Through the thinning clouds, a glare reflected off pools of blood under the bodies.

"I am afraid Anton's driver will not be able to drive you back to Kyiv," Bondar said, indicating the large black SUV. A torso was hanging partially out of the open passenger door, trickling blood from what was left of his head like a tipped over champagne glass—the result of a point-blank shotgun blast.

"I will have my driver take you."

He pointed to another identical SUV parked behind the one containing the body. As they walked to it, the driver opened the door.

Chen stopped before he sat and turned back to Bondar and Ira.

"That is greatly appreciated," Chen said emotionlessly, as if seeing death was second nature to him. "It was a pleasure meeting you." He bowed to Ira. Then he turned to Bondar. His tone was as casual as if he was discussing the weather. It had a chilling effect.

"I was wondering if the people who took that case also retrieved the biometric passcode device? You see, it is an extraordinary case. Without George MacLean alive, or the proper and specific passkey authentication, the case cannot be opened safely. You should tell that to whoever has it—*if* you know them. Good-bye. *Zai jian.*"

Chen got in. The driver closed the door.

"*Do pobachennya.*" Bondar said goodbye and closed the door.

Bondar and Ira stood and watched the car drive away.

He spun to Ira, his eyes about to erupt with anger. "Do we have that? That device he is talking about?"

"They only gave me the case," she said.

"Absolute incompetence." Bondar balled his hands into fists. "Find a way to open it."

"I will." She stepped closer to her father. Her eyes darkened and turned cold as a deep cave. "You killed Anton! Why? Why?"

Bondar released his curled fingers and waved his hands through the air in the same dismissive manner Vlasenko had a few moments before he poisoned the old man.

"He would have done the same to me."

Her high heels ground into the brick pavers as she turned and marched away.

Bondar glared at the two guards who had escorted them out of the house. Standing four feet away, they froze in terror when they saw the absolute look of death in his eyes. He reached around his back, grabbed the grip of the Makarov 59 EG, and put two bullets into each man's chest before they could take their next breath. At that range, the 9x18mm bullets went entirely through their bodies. The already dead men fell back and hit the wet bricks with a splat.

He walked between the bodies and fired the last rounds from the magazine into each man.

"Get rid of Anton's security men, the cars, and get Anton out of my dining room." He shouted to no one in particular. "Get rid of those two. Make them all disappear—and clean the blood off my bricks."

He walked through the front door and slammed it closed behind him.

15

LOMINA STREET

Belgrade, Serbia

R eds and blues flashed in the darkness against the buildings of Lomina Street. A dozen white-and-blue Serbian Police cars crammed into the street soon after 2 a.m. when the calls came into the police station about gunshots and a body lying in the street. Blinding floodlights burned into the darkness like a welder's torch below, illuminating a yellow 'Hostel 40' sign. Police guarded the barricades on both ends, where curious citizens strained to see what was going on.

Goran made certain that was as close as anyone got.

"National security. BIA authority," Goran told the furious police officers who instantly complained up their chain of command. They protested to their Deputy Minister Assistant, who woke up and informed *the* Minister of Internal Affairs. He called down to his other direct report, the Director of the BIA, and told him to take care of whatever was going on.

Bridger's plan was simple. It required Goran to perform a few easy tasks.

Bridger told Goran to expect his call about securing the area around feet to a back wall and door to a service hall and storage. Fresh cut chains and broken locks were on the floor near a rusty metal exit door.

"Beast?"

"All clear on the street. A few people walking by. I see Snake down the block."

"Bad tradecraft, Nikola," Bridger said, as he wiped a makeup removing cloth over his faux bullet hole. He dropped it into a baggie as Beatrice handed him another. "I was hoping for that."

"Do we need him? Can I kill him?" Demon asked.

Nikola's eyes widened slightly as Bridger seemed to contemplate the question. "You know the plan. We still need him."

"Son of a bitch," Demon grumbled, as he removed the gun from Nikola's head. Nikola's body released tension just as Demon landed a left hook flush into his face. Nikola fell to the floor like a bowling pin. His face splatted and bounced into the pool of fake theatrical blood that had passed as the contents of Bridger's head a few moments before.

"What? He ain't dead," Demon said to Bridger in his defense. He holstered his Kimber and picked up his Devil Stick. Flipping the dial, he held the end to the groaning Nikola's face and released a thick dose of the Milton Gas. His body trembled, stiffened, then went limp.

"This guy is made of concrete," Beast said, as he grabbed the man's feet. Demon curled his arms under Nikola's shoulders. As they shuffled backward, Demon let his arms go limp. Nikola's head hit the thin indoor carpeting with a *thump*.

"Oops," Demon said.

"You are a bad person," Beast said with a smile.

"Takes one to know one," Demon replied, as he grabbed the man by the wrists. They carried him to the center of the abandoned shop and dropped him on the floor.

Beatrice took a brush from her large solid-sided bag and handed it to Bridger. He combed his damp blonde-brown hair.

"How long do you need to make him look dead?" he asked as he handed her the brush. "Remember, it doesn't have to be perfect. No one should be getting too close to him. We are dumping him in the street. Goran will keep the area clear."

Beatrice looked incredulously at Bridger. "Not perfect?"

He shrugged.

"Sorry."

"Now that I have seen him up close, he will be a deader-than-dead corpse in a little over an hour. Especially since jackass has already started the process," she said.

"I heard that," Demon said.

The mysterious events on Lomina Street led the news stories the next day, as Bridger and Beast discovered as they watched the coverage. It was front-page news in the papers they had scattered on the table.

The internet and social media piled on with conspiracy theories and rumors. It was an important person from the Serbian mafia. A clan. Arms dealers. Drug deal. A government official, or a relative of the president. No one knew.

On the morning of the second day, photographs and videos appeared on digital bulletin boards from anonymous sources. One image clearly showed a sheet over a body in the street. A video recorded a body being put into an ambulance. Press sources revealed that a Zastava CZ 99 pistol with its identifying markings rubbed off was found at the scene.

The Serbian Police deflected inquiries to the BIA. The BIA did not comment. The U.S. Embassy stated it had no knowledge of a U.S. citizen involved in any incident.

From his home, Taube knew the identities of both men. It was evident that once Nikola had killed Bridger, his Spy Devils killed his man in retaliation. Losing his security team leader was a slight inconvenience, but one of Nikola's men was ambitious. He had already volunteered to take his place.

What bothered him to sleeplessness was not knowing who had Bridger's phone. Would Bridger's alleged incriminating video suddenly appear in the press? If someone had it and planned to black-mail him, it hadn't happened yet—but it could at any time.

Taube had tapped his sources inside the police department. They knew nothing. His BIA contacts were clueless, too. That was some comfort. Perhaps Nikola was able to destroy the phone. Or he had somehow gotten rid of it. It had vanished nonetheless—as had the immediate threat posed by Bridger.

He felt the pressure of the clock ticking. He had to proceed with his plans.

He picked up his phone and dialed his first call. When it was answered, he spoke immediately.

"We are on schedule," he said confidently.

"Are you sure?" the voice asked with a note of caution, "The Lomina—"

"There is no connection. I have no knowledge of that. Do you have any information?"

"No. I made discreet inquiries, but no one in government knows anything," the brother of the President of Serbia answered.

"If you want to complete what has been agreed to by all parties, then we need to meet—as arranged. It would look very bad if the president backed out now."

"We are not changing our position. My brother is committed to this —activity."

"Good. Tomorrow night."

Taube cut the connection before the man could reply.

The second call was short and all business. They would be at the meeting.

The third call required no effort as the Ukrainians were eager to complete the transactions. They would call in to avoid anyone noticing their presence in the country.

16

DREAM CAREER

Kirkwood International Headquarters

W*hat the hell am I going to do? How am I supposed to find a briefcase somewhere in Ukraine?*

Peter Schaeffer, Senior Director, Corporate Intelligence and Insights, Strategy Office, Kirkwood International Industries, had been continually asking himself those questions since he left the meeting in the boardroom three days ago.

He hadn't eaten or slept much since then, which worried his wife, Janelle. She kept asking if she could help. He told her there was nothing she could do—and for that matter—maybe he couldn't do anything either.

He rubbed his temples with his fingers trying to release the tension as he arrived in his office early the morning after the meeting.

Clutter was his office décor. Books. Magazines. Mounds of unopened mail. Pictures of his family. Fantasy Football championship trophies. Yellow sticky notes, charts, and PowerPoint slides of motivational quotes he liked covered his walls like fish scales, but he knew exactly where everything was.

Something felt wrong—and his feelings were never wrong. There was more to this than they were telling him. But right now, his feelings were irrelevant. He had to make some progress on this, or his ass was toast.

MacBride had already sent him a text: *Working on this? We are ALL counting on you.*

The clock was running fast. Patience on the 10th floor would run thin like it always did. The heel of his right foot started to piston up and down with anxiety. A family tick handed down through the DNA of generations to the point Peter stopped realizing he was wiggling.

He took pride in being the guy who always could find the answer, or at least get pointed in the right direction. He won a scholarship to Northwestern University. Graduated with honors and applied to the Central Intelligence Agency. He survived a lengthy interview process, and a few months later, to his joy, he was offered a position as a trainee into the CIA's Clandestine Services Career Trainee program—the spy school.

After a few four-month rotational training assignments in various departments, fate stepped in.

His dream career as a CIA employee ended before it fully started due to a series of gut-wrenching family medical crises. His mother had a stroke and died. She was the primary caregiver for his father, who was suffering from Alzheimer's. As the only child, Peter had to stay and care for his father.

The CIA understood that he needed the stability of a "job on the outside," as the personal officer told him. Luckily, for his father's entire thirty-year career, he was a well-respected engineer at Kirkwood International Industries. It took a few calls, but he found an opening at Kirkwood as the new Director, Corporate Intelligence and Insights. He sold his life-long dream of a career in intelligence for stability, a pretty good corporate salary, healthcare, and the promise of a pension.

Sitting at his desk, he wrote on a large yellow legal pad his ideas on where he might fulfill the task of finding the briefcase.

He knew he couldn't involve his staff after signing Jessup's NDA.

Kirkwood employees' brains contained eighty to ninety percent of the information he needed. The salesforce was always probing poten-

had come to *him* and sat in *his* office and offered *his* help. He needed to go home, throw the baseball with his eight-year-old son, James, then drink a bottle of red wine and have sex with Janelle.

He put his laptop into his backpack and slung the bag over his shoulder. His phone started to ring. Panic set in. He dropped his backpack to the floor and looked at the caller ID. He let out a deep breath. It read "Private." Usually, he would ignore a private call as spam, but he hoped it was someone responding to his many emails and calls.

"Hel-lo?" he answered cautiously.

"Peter Schaeffer?" It was a female voice. Strong. Not a young voice. Mature. New England accent.

"Yes?"

"Hello. Peter. I am aware you need help in retrieving a case lost in Ukraine. Please, don't ask how I know. I do," she said in a matter-of-fact tone.

"How do you know about that?"

He heard a sigh on the other end of the call.

"Please don't ask questions. I am fully aware of the details. If you would like help, then listen to what I have to say."

Peter sat— immediately, his leg started to shake.

"I am listening."

"An excellent start. On Thursday, someone will contact you. Answer his call. He is your only hope. Repeat that, back."

"Thursday…a call…answer it…my only hope," he said.

"Excellent. Goodbye, Peter."

"What?"

The call ended. Peter's eyes fixated on his phone.

Who would call him about this? Should he tell MacBride? Is this a setup by Jessup to see if he would break his NDA? Chapel?

Peter looked at the yellow legal pad with the red lines on it. He knew when that call came he was answering it on the first ring.

He stood, picked up his backpack, and thought of one more question.

What the hell was this all about?

17

RECRUITMENT

Shanghai, China

The successful recruitment of U.S. businessman George MacLean by Minister Chen of the *Zhōnghuá Rénmín Gònghéguó Guójiā Ānquánbù*, the Chinese Ministry of State Security, started when MacLean was hired by Kirkwood two years ago.

MacLean, Chief Financial Officer, Kirkwood Technologies, had been instrumental in the financial success of an alphabet soup of tech companies. AMD. HP. IBM. 3M. The fifty-seven-year-old MacLean's everlasting cherub pink face was incongruous with his deep Texas nasal twang.

And MacLean loved to eat. Specifically, McDonald's Big Macs and fries. His body shape was categorized politely as a "fat snowman." Not so politely as "Obese walrus."

But underestimating MacLean based upon his appearance was a terrible mistake. Knowing that obese stereotypes led people to think of him as just a jolly fat man, MacLean used his size as a smoke screen to hide a shrewd and brilliant business mind. During negotiations, he always found the right moment. When his counterpart misjudged him, he would strike. He won. They lost.

What he *had* managed to keep hidden was his all-consuming penchant for gambling. Stud poker, to be precise. It was a habit he started early in life. A few dollars during weekend-long marathon games with high school friends. His skills were honed during his undergraduate and graduate years at the University of Texas-Austin.

He moved on, riding the humpback of his salary and stock options, win or lose, to the luxury tables in The Bellagio in Las Vegas, Monaco's Hotel de Paris and Casino de Monte, The Venetian Macao Resort Hotel, among some.

MacLean was a "whale," both figuratively and literally—a category above those known as a "high roller." A whale wagered large amounts of money, win or lose, and was treated lavishly by the ultra-competitive casinos. MacLean liked swimming with whales. The lifestyle. The attention.

But he was drowning.

He was unaware that his financial issues had placed him on an MSS watchlist of corporate targets of interest. The list of names included those with access to U.S. trade secrets or employed at MSS-targeted U.S. companies. If recruited, they could be leveraged to obtain proprietary corporate information, government plans, or classified technologies.

The more common name for it was economic espionage.

Penetrating Kirkwood, the American technology giant had been a priority for Chinese intelligence for years. They were an engineering colossus, with countless patents and secret government contracts. MacLean was an opportunity for success. He was worth the effort.

MacLean saw nothing inappropriate when he received a message in his LinkedIn account from Professor Zhan, the Distinguished Professor of Economics at the Shanghai Academy of Social Sciences, the SASS, a Chinese think tank and research institution. He was asking if the Kirkwood CFO could find space in his busy schedule to travel to Shanghai. They were eager for him to address the SASS faculty and students on corporate finance topics.

They would cover his expenses, plus an additional thirty-five thousand dollars as a speaker's fee—to start.

This request did not seem unusual. MacLean had visited China many times over his career. He felt he had a grasp of their culture and their need to remain competitive after a century of the West ruling the globe. *Wasn't a strong China a good thing? Having a closer, personally profitable relationship was a win-win, right?*

After a week of wining, dining, and prostitutes, the pitch took place on MacLean's last evening in China. Instead of large dinner parties, or receptions in his honor, Professor Zhan suggested they dine alone.

Actually, not entirely alone. After they sat at a secluded corner table in the dimly lit restaurant, Professor Zhan suddenly stood and bowed. MacLean turned to see a man about his age, dressed perfectly in a dark suit, white shirt, and striped tie. He had black-and-gray hair combed from left to right. The corners of his thin-lipped mouth briefly held a smile.

"*Nínhǎo!* Hello! It is a pleasure to make your acquaintance," the man said, at first bowing, then extending his hand.

MacLean heaved his body to a standing position as he finished chewing his piece of crispy duck.

"Hello," he replied, looking at the professor.

"George, I was asked to make time for this man to talk to you." Professor Zhan gathered up his phone and offered his seat to the man.

The man sat in the chair vacated by Professor Zhan. "Let me introduce myself. I am Deputy Minister Chen. I am very pleased to meet you at last."

"Really? That is very flattering. What did you want to meet about?" MacLean tried to find something in the face that could spark some recollection.

"I will honor you with being direct. We have several separate, but related efforts, you and I. We both want good relationships between our countries. You want to maximize the success of your company. True?"

MacLean rolled his body back against the back of his chair and considered the man.

"True. I—I can't argue with that," he agreed, stifling a burp in his throat.

"I will continue to be direct. Does your employer know of your financial situation? What would happen to you if they knew? Or if it were to appear in the media?

"What do you mean? I—that is ridiculous." MacLean started to stand.

"Mr. MacLean, please sit," Chen said politely, but firmly. "I can help you."

MacLean sat back down. The chair creaked.

"Good. Let me explain my comments. China wants to advance its manufacturing technology and be globally competitive soon. Greater access to the China market would help your firm and you. I want you to go back to America and obtain information to meet that goal. In return, we will pay you. Generously. Regularly. You can, therefore, relieve the financial burden you are currently suffering from and," Chen looked at MacLean with a thin-lipped smile, "protect your well-earned reputation."

"You want me to be a spy for China?" MacLean whispered to his lap, then raised his eyes to Chen.

Chen's thin-lipped smile revealed as much emotion as the cooked duck.

"I want us to work together to solve our problems, Mr. Maclean."

"George," MacLean said.

"Yes. George. Thank you. This means we share on a regular basis —as associates. You share some information, things you normally would see in the course of your day. Then, we will transfer our deepest and generous gratitude to a secret bank account in your name in return."

With drops of sweat beading on his forehead, MacLean reached out and grabbed the man's hand.

"How much is generous?" he asked, after a minute had passed.

"We can discuss—"

"Pay off my debt. All of it. And one hundred thousand dollars a month."

Chen's face showed that he was pleased with the way the conversation was moving.

"We can help with your debt over the next six months. I see no reason why this could not be a long and beneficial business opportunity. Let us start at fifteen thousand dollars. If the relationship develops and access is useful, we can discuss more."

The recruitment of George MacLean was complete.

ADAPT TO CIRCUMSTANCES

Belgrade, Serbia

"**N**ikola! Did you know you are dead?" Bridger laughed, turning an iPad and holding it up to the metal bars.

Nikola looked at the bright red multimedia home page of *Blic Online*, Serbia's most popular tabloid news portal. As he read, his expression stayed impassive.

"My Serbian is a little rusty, but—" Bridger tapped the screen advancing the photos. He stopped at an image of two photos side by side. One was a close-up ID photo of a stiff uniformed Nikola looking directly at the camera. The other was of a sheet over a body in the street. "I think this says you are dead. Right here." Bridger ran his finger along a capitalized banner headline. "Want me to read it?"

"No, that is not necessary." Nikola turned and sat on his cot. He was locked within a row of floor to ceiling bars that ran the safe house basement's fifteen-foot width. The stone floor and walls kept the windowless room cool. Besides steep steps to the upper level, only two wooden chairs occupied the area outside the bars.

"Ah, come on. I'll read it. Um…blah, blah…here…'the man was identified by anonymous sources as Nikola Vulin, a former member of the Serbian Armed Forces and founder of Vulin Security.'" Bridger looked at Nikola, who was sitting like a stone. "We made sure when we leaked that. Don't worry, there isn't any mention of Serge. Why complicate things?"

"You are very generous," Nikola said with obvious sarcasm.

The man in the cell impressed Bridger. This is a soldier. Loyal. Tough. Professional. He would make a good Spy Devil, Bridger thought.

Bridger put the iPad on one of the chairs. He picked up a book-sized piece of folded white butcher paper.

"There is simply no doubt that Pekara Trpkovic bakery shop has the best burek in Serbia. If not all the Balkans. Recipes handed down through the hundreds and hundreds of years." He stuck his hand between the bars and held it out to Nikola. "The lines are just brutal there, but I know Boris, the head baker. Nice fellow. He lets me slip in the back to avoid the wait." Bridger waved the package at Nikola, who stood, walked over, and took it from him. "I prefer the beef, but this is a plain cheese burek—I wasn't sure of your dietary habits."

Nikola reached out and took the paper. He unfolded it and took a bite into the flaky dough of the traditional Serbian pastry.

This was a test. Nikola had passed—so far.

Nikola accepted the breakfast pastry. He didn't pause, sniff, or examine it. This reaffirmed to Bridger that Nikola was a professional. It showed an understanding of the situation. A professional knew if Bridger wanted to drug or kill him, he would have done it already.

"It should be warm," Nikola said with a mouthful of food. He turned and sat back on his cot.

"Yes. I agree, but we all must adapt to circumstance." Bridger pulled one chair closer to the bars and sat.

"You went to much trouble to put me in here." Nikola waved his arms at his cell. "You faked your death. Sent the photos to Serge from my phone. You faked my death. I do not see the police here. Or BIA."

"Oh, my friend in Serbian intelligence wants you after I am done—bet on it. They helped get you here."

Bridger waited for Nikola to react. He didn't. He just stared straight at Bridger.

"You are the Bridger—from the famous Spy Devils?"

"That is true."

Nikola examined Bridger's face. Finally, he took his eyes off of Bridger and looked around the room.

"What do you want of me?"

"Nikola, you are a professional. I won't insult you with tricks, pain, or drugs. Serge thinks you killed me. He certainly has seen the news and thinks you are dead. I would be happy to set you free when we are done with you."

"I think that is not a good thing. You have made that very dangerous."

"Nikola, you *are* a smart man. I agree with your assessment. When Serge finds out you are alive, and we will make certain he does, he will kill you on the spot. He won't be able to trust you. Where have you been? Who have you talked to? You know the drill."

Nikola rolled the empty butcher paper into a ball and tossed it toward a bucket in the corner of his cell.

"You have alternatives for me. I tell you what you need to know, and I get to go," he said, as he brushed crumbs from his pants.

"It is a real pleasure, Nikola. You are making this easy. I suggest you leave the country. As an experienced practitioner, you certainly have a getaway kit hidden somewhere. New IDs. Money. Passports. Weapons. Your Swiss bank accounts have sufficient funds for you to live well."

Nikola didn't answer at first, then nodded.

"I thought so. So, all you need to do is tell me all about the deal Serge is about to complete. Most urgently, I want to know where the meeting is and when. You are free the moment we are done. In fact, for the trouble and inconvenience we have put you through, I have opened a Swiss account in your name for one hundred thousand dollars. All yours," Bridger brushed his hands together.

Nikola sighed and looked at him again.

"It could be many places," Nikola said. Bridger knew this was his test to see how his jailer would react. Bridger was prepared.

"I just want to do this the easy way. You get out, get richer, and that keeps us from running around listening and surveilling. Alternatively, I could keep you locked in here," Bridger sat forward and kicked an iron bar, "and let you starve to death where your body will rot away and get eaten by rats. Or, we tell Serge where you are when we are done. He comes in and shoots you. Your body will rot away and get eaten by rats right here. Maybe he saves the bullets and decides to burn the whole place down, right on top of you.

"Doesn't matter to me how he does it." Bridger shrugged his shoulders, sat back in the chair, folded his arms, and smiled at Nikola.

Nikola stood and held out his hand.

"Two hundred thousand dollars."

"Fair enough," Bridger said as he shook Nikola's hand.

cheek. She stepped back, leaving a trail of Chanel N°5 Parfum Grand Extrait in a cloud by his face.

The blood ran from his head, leaving him dizzy.

"Ah…umm…errr," was all he could force out of his lungs. As always, his hands started to quiver whenever he experienced the thrill of being in a room with Ira.

She maneuvered around the perimeter, looking at the machines, brushing her long slender fingers across a keyboard and the back of his chair. The scent of her perfume trailed behind her every step.

"I could never understand how these machines work."

"That's why you have me!" He couldn't contain his pride.

"Yes, yes, it is. We are fortunate."

"How may I help you?"

"We very much need your help with this." She walked by him and placed a large dark bag on his computer table. He hadn't even noticed it. He unzipped the bag and removed an oddly-shaped silver briefcase.

He had not seen anything like it. The briefcase had what appeared to be various unmarked security systems across the top. An alphanumeric keypad. Some sort of biometric scanner. *Or was it two? Three?*

"This is very unusual," he said.

"Can you get it open?"

"Yes," the sounds shot from his mouth before knowing if he could.

"You are always here for me." She moved to within smelling distance. "You cannot talk about this to anyone. You cannot take it out of this room. Understand, Pavlo?"

"I'm…I…no one." His mouth was dry.

She moved past and picked up a random sheet of paper and pretended to look at it. Then she stopped and looked over her shoulder at him. It felt to Pavlo like she was looking directly into his heart.

"I wanted to thank you again for taking care of the American money so expertly." Honey dripped from every word. Red lips pursed.

"You are most welcome. It was not too difficult," Pavlo said, letting some pride stick to his words.

Pavlo found the process of making hundreds of millions of dollars vanish intellectually stimulating. It required details on international banking regulations and the kinds of financial minutia that even a genius like Pavlo didn't possess.

Kirkwood Credit Corporation transferred the first five hundred million dollars of digital cash from the JPMorgan Chase New York main branch to the Bondar-owned bank in Cyprus through bank clearing systems in two equal installments. In Cyprus, the banker passed the funds through a dedicated server to a clone at the Ukraine Standard Bank in Kyiv. Once data was extracted, the network was disconnected. The computer was broken into pieces and tossed into the bank's furnace.

Pavlo knew more than most that nothing electronic was ever secure, and his ability to hide the business of the bank was a testament to that. The cyber capabilities of the American, Russian, and Chinese intelligence services, private companies, and even the basement-dwelling hacker-sphere were dangerous. No Bitcoin in "the cloud" wealth was allowed on his private networks.

From his bunker, Pavlo created multiple layers of untraceable investment accounts in offshore banks. Automated trades on global financial exchanges sold the securities and repatriated the monies as dollars and euros into Bondar family private accounts in Cyprus and Kyiv.

A significant portion, one hundred and eighty million dollars, was directed to the private cash accounts of the Bondar network of influence—judges, businessmen, politicians, and a private army. Some monies found their way to non-existent people, businesses, and organizations that were, in reality, nothing more than an address and bank account. Dry-cleaners. Florists. Bakeries. Trucking. Mobile phone stores. Charities.

Pavlo made the money disappear in less than a week.

"Wonderful," Ira said, brushing her hands slowly along her hips, seemingly to straighten her dress. "I was afraid it would be difficult."

"I will do everything I can." Pavlo began to sweat and hoped he could control the feeling in his pants.

"Tell no one, not even my father. Understand?"

Pavlo looked surprised.

"Pavlo?"

"Not your father. Not Mr. Oleksandr?"

"No. Only me."

"Good." He realized how that sounded. "I mean, I am sorry," he blurted out before he could stop himself. Pavlo did not like the son who regularly violated his bunker sanctuary, demanding he transfer money to his personal accounts. He reminded Pavlo of the bullies who tormented his youth. Oleksandr was not a worthy brother to Ms. Ira.

She just smiled.

"Thank you, Pavlo." She kissed him lightly on each cheek. Traces of red lipstick were left on his skin. She stepped back and lightly punched him on his fleshy chin. "Remember, don't tell anyone."

She was out of the room in three long strides, leaving behind invisible vapors swirling for Pavlo to savor.

Looking at his reflection in a monitor, he carefully wiped a tissue on his cheeks to capture as much of her cosmetic as possible. Convinced he had it all, he gingerly removed a tin box from his desk, set it down in front of him, and unlocked it. Neatly organized inside were a piece of ribbon, a leather glove, an empty Chanel perfume bottle he found in the trash, and dozens of crumpled, lipstick-stained tissues. Cautiously, he set the tissue inside. He re-locked the tin, placed it back in the drawer, then closed and locked the drawer.

Although he had never experienced it himself, Pavlo imagined the warm sensation that spread over his entire body when she kissed his cheek was the same sensation other people felt when they made love.

Inhaling deeply to capture the fading aroma of her visit, he looked back at the strange silver case.

He would get it open. He *had* to get it open.

He would never let her down.

20

NA COSKU

Belgrade, Serbia

"Two cars. Coming up fast on Krunska Street," Beatrice announced over their comm system. She looked at the screen displaying the infrared camera feed from the Devilbot. "One block away."

Through his night vision binoculars, Bridger watched the two black SUVs turn onto Beogradska Street and stop. At 2 a.m., the central streets of Belgrade were empty. He and Demon were half a block down from the intersection crouched behind a billboard on a sloping grass hill. It provided a good view of Na Cosku, The Corner Restaurant.

Bridger watched the light-enhanced images of two men exit the first car. Two more men got out of the second car. Bridger caught a glimpse of one man carrying a case as they walked in the restaurant.

"That's Serge and the Chinese, right on schedule," Bridger whispered. "He is always punctual, bless his soul."

Nikola had told the truth. The meeting was scheduled for the next day. He gave the place, location, and who was supposed to be in attendance. Bridger appreciated that. Nikola had earned his freedom as part of the deal—eventually. A dose of gas from a Devil Stick left him went silent. Within hours, @BBCWorld picked it up and retweeted the video. Retweets and comments by Bellingcat, the online investigative journalism site. Then the U.S.-funded Radio Free Europe/Radio Liberty. Students from Belgrade University organized on social media and began protesting in front of government buildings.

The most referenced part of the video were the still images of the men entering and leaving the meeting. One video segment with subtitles was replayed worldwide.

TAUBE: This has been a very long process, but I am glad we have made all the proper arrangements. I hope all are satisfied.

VUK: I am satisfied. I plan to eat, drink, and fuck girls. *(Video shows Vuk picking up a glass and drinking).*

TAUBE: What of the president?

VUK: He will fuck girls, too. Don't tell his wife! No, but seriously he was concerned with all the press you are getting right—"

TAUBE: There is nothing to be worried about, I told you that. I have my people in the government, so do you obviously (laughter).

VUK: Well, yes. Do you have it?

TAUBE: As we have agreed.

VUK: The three million?

TAUBE: Yes, and the same later. *(Video shows Taube handing the case to Vuk, who opens it. Bundles of paper bills are visible.)*

VUK: I'm in love. *(Video shows Vuk closing case and putting it on the floor between his feet.)* Will there be more?

CHINESE OFFICIAL (UNNAMED): There are possibilities, but let us first complete this negotiation. We are expecting no issues with the acquisition of the weapons.

TAUBE: Taken care of.

CHINESE OFFICIAL (UNNAMED): And no issues with the more legitimate infrastructure contracts?

VUK: No problems.

TAUBE: And our Ukrainian friends have received their payments. Correct?
VOICE ON PHONE: Yes.

The Chinese Embassy in Serbia did not respond to press inquiries requesting the Chinese official's identity in the video. At 11 a.m., reporters stationed at Belgrade Nikola Tesla Airport saw a car with Chinese diplomatic license plates arrive at the private plane terminal. They recorded a video of a man getting out of the car and entering the building from a distance.

In Ukraine, reporters searched for the person on the phone in the 'Serbia Video,' as it was now being called.

By noon in Serbia, leaders of the opposition party demanded the termination of the deals with China. Others called for a criminal investigation into the president's actions, administration, and brother. They also insisted on the immediate arrest of Serge Taube and the seizure of his companies.

At 1 p.m., Bridger called Taube using Nikola's phone.

"Nikola?" the confused and tired voice asked.

"So sorry, Serge. Nikola will be unable to assist you today."

There was silence for several seconds.

"Bridger. Of course," Taube sighed and paused in sudden realization of who was behind the events that exposed the deal.

"I don't have long to talk, but I wanted to know how your day is going."

"Congratulations, Bridger. The deals you were concerned with have been canceled." Bridger could sense Taube was trying to piece together the Spy Devil operation. "So, it was all a deception. You had nothing."

"Not nothing. It was invigorating to listen in on your meeting of your conspirators. Thank you very much for that. There is just nothing like the sweet sound of criminals admitting to their crimes. I felt refreshed."

"So you have Nikola."

"We are enjoying his company."

"Is he alive?"

"Alive and rather chatty," Bridger answered.

"Where is he?"

"In due time, Serge."

He could hear the rage in Taube's voice.

"I will not be arrested if that is part of your plan. The judges I have in my employment will make certain I stay free long enough. The president will be worried that I would make a deal and testify against him. I can say some unpleasant things. I will be appropriately treated."

"They probably don't want you around anyway, knowing what you know—much like your family, I am sure. Maybe this is a good time to retire, Serge. Take your old bones to someplace warm and enjoy the scenery."

"Retire? Me? Could you retire?" When Bridger didn't answer, Taube continued. "I thought so. I will go to Cyprus, or someplace away from the U.S. and the U.N.—and you."

"Cyprus. Good choice. Warm and sunny. You could take up fishing."

Taube laughed.

"Fishing? My business is just as good wherever I live. If the president stays or goes is irrelevant. They are all corrupt. They will make the deal with me."

"Probably," Bridger said.

"Oh, it is certain. The Chinese will pay, despite the current difficulties. The Russians and the Ukrainians, too. The Iranians, maybe. There are always customers. I will prosper. And it is not as if I do not have information and details on mysterious Bridger and his Spy Devils. The world should know. Think of the headlines around the world."

"That would be a mistake, Serge. Good-bye, Serge." Bridger hung up and tossed the phone into the Danube.

A few hours later, Serge arrived at Nikola Tesla airport escorted by Stanko and the security entourage. His line of four SUVs drove onto the tarmac and up to where his large private plane was waiting. Sporting dark sunglasses and a casual manner, Taube stepped out of his SUV and looked around.

It was a beautiful day, despite the ruinous events of the morning. A flight attendant waited at the top of the stairs with a drink. Ground personnel started transferring his baggage from his vehicles to the cargo hold of the plane.

Taube walked to the stairs. As he was about to ascend, something flew by him above his head. He looked up just as the Devilbot released a 9mm round into his forehead before disappearing into the sky.

21

BONDAR BATTALION-1

Kyiv, Ukraine

When he was a child, nothing gave him greater pleasure than shooting the rabbits and squirrels that made the mistake of wiggling through the wire into his family's vegetable garden. After school or work at the Cooperative, Bondar grabbed his Tula TOZ-8 Bolt Action .22 caliber rifle and went on the hunt. The rifle was a gift from his father on his seventh birthday and the only thing he kept from his childhood.

He would wait behind a small lath fence he constructed with sticks and twigs twisted horizontally across some wood. Invisible. Patient. They would come. When they did, he never missed. His mother would cook them for the family dinner.

You try to steal from me, then I will kill you.

It was a way of life in the rough coal-mining Donbas region of Ukraine. A tough industrial area of long-suffering tough people, the Donbas existed in an endless swirl of controlling entities. The Ukrainian Cossack Hetmanate and the Turkic Crimean Khanate until the mid-late 18th century. The Russian Empire. The Soviet Union.

Nazi Germany. The Soviet Union again. Ukraine after independence in 1992.

His birthplace was always fighting another war.

His father was a hard-working man, with a modicum of intelligence, whose body was trapped in a coal factory by the Soviet system. He wasn't a bad man, just weak—too weak for Bondar. His mother was a teacher and, by necessity, stronger, wiser, and much smarter.

Bondar knew as a child that he would never work in the coal factory or anyplace else where others told him what to do. He would not be weak. He was driven to be rich and powerful. He would not join others by becoming a corrupt politician working in the corrupt system. He would build his own business empire and control the corrupt politicians.

It took ruthless years of working with like-minded men like Vlasenko, but he achieved his goals. Rich. Powerful. Untouchable.

"Those Kirkwood assholes are assholes. Chapel called and left messages. Then sent me texts," Bondar proclaimed to Ira. "Deceitful. Treacherous. Untrustworthy. If I acted like them, I would be as dead as Anton by now."

He took a large drink from a crystal tumbler full of a clear liquid. On his ornate wooden desk, a three-quarters empty bottle of Beluga Gold Line vodka was within arm's reach.

Ira didn't laugh.

"*He* wants *me* to give him the case! Never! That is for the future. Our future!" he slurred as he rocked his chair from side to side.

As he leaned back in his chair it made a creak that echoed off the Ukrainian oak-paneled walls. Rotating, he looked at a cherry wood case affixed to the wall. Inside was his cherished Tula SKS rifle. Staring at the worn finish, nicks, and dings on the stock brought back memories of cold Ukrainian winters. Snow-covered fields. Chasing his prey.

Ira sat cross-legged on the corner couch. Her eyes followed his to the gun. She hated it. She was upset. The only signal of her annoyance was the *click click click* of her deep burgundy polished fingernails on her left hand.

They were safe within the walls of their residential apartments, which occupied the top floor of Bondar's five-story Ukraine Investment and Holding Company building. It was located behind and adjacent to Bondar's Ukraine Standard Bank. The building was fortified against intrusion. Armed guards patrolled 24 hours a day. Electronic detection and warning systems were installed on every door, window, and hallway.

The office was his sanctuary from the chaos outside the windows.

"We are not without problems, father," Ira proclaimed.

"Old news, Ira. The ministers inside the RADA are pressuring me to increase the already substantial monies we pay them. I expect they will move on our shipping assets. That is an annoyance at most."

Viktor's Ukraine Investment and Holding Company paid bribes to the ruling government, judges, and local officials to protect his businesses and control people. After the last presidential election, Bondar was not surprised to be the target of the anti-oligarch corruption reforms within the government—which he thought was ironic since most of the RADA was controlled by other oligarchs like himself.

Ira wasn't convinced.

"The disruption to our mining operation is a significant problem for all businesses. Several of our transactions run through the subsidiaries." She stared out the bullet-proof windows at the night glow of Kyiv. "The situation in Serbia and the cancelation of the asset sale is a disaster. We are under even more pressure. We needed those funds. We should cut their heads off."

"You only know the world I created for you," his words were slurring now. "You were born with a seat at the table, a feast in front of you. You have never had to shoot a rabbit to fill an empty stomach. Or fear getting caught when you steal bread from a starving person because you are starving more."

He picked up his glass, examined the amount of liquid inside, and took a drink that emptied the remaining contents. He set the glass down with a loud thump on his desk.

He continued, his arms gesturing in the air around him.

"You mourn for 'Uncle Anton,' but I *know* he was behind the government attacks on our businesses. His death is good for us."

She turned her face away from him to hide the pain he had inflicted on her by killing the old man. She loved Uncle Anton as much as her father—maybe more. Vlasenko showed her respect. Her father gave her lectures. Her finger-nail clicks were more rapid and louder.

"Unless we take precautions, we are vulnerable. If they pressure these businesses, they will pressure others. At least send our men to protect the shipping warehouses."

He scratched the three-day growth on his chin. Filled his glass with more Beluga Gold Line and sipped. He did not comment on her suggestion.

"Where is your brother? I have not heard from him. I suppose he is gone again and calls for money." No answer came. Bondar shook his head and sighed with the resignation reserved for a father to his son. "He is a total disappointment."

"I will find him."

She saw the sadness in her father's sagging and tired eyes. Ira spent her life protecting Olek from their father. He considered her brother a waste—she understood that. Since Oleksandr was not interested in the business, their father equated that with weakness.

Ira's mobile phone started to buzz. She picked it up, looked at the caller ID, and pushed the answer button.

"Yes?" She listened for less than a minute, then hung up without another word. "The Office of the Prosecutor General has signed the warrants. They are coming after our facilities in Odessa."

He finished his drink and poured another.

"What do you plan to do?" she asked.

"Kill them. Ignore them—it does not matter. I am Vik-tor Bondar."

He swallowed the vodka, leaned backed in his chair, and closed his eyes.

"Father? Father?" Ira stared at her father, who had already started to snore.

She shook her head in disgust as she dialed a number on her phone. It was answered on the first ring.

"Get your men ready."

22

NOM DE GUERRE

Chicago, Illinois

In his luxury suite at the Ritz-Carlton in downtown Chicago, Bridger sank into an overstuffed chair, wondering if this was going to be interesting or a pain in the ass. He munched some nuts from the complimentary gift basket provided by the hotel. Extra-large cashews. When those were gone, he would start on a large box of gourmet chocolates.

He felt pretty good about himself on the flight back from Serbia aboard his private plane. Not only because he was killing off his second fine bottle of an Italian Sangiovese, but the mission was a success. In. Out. No injuries. No exposure.

The rest of the Spy Devils had split up and departed Serbia by plane, train, and car. They would leave Europe from various locations using their true names like any other traveler.

Bridger's pretty good feeling ended when his mother sent a secure text telling him to divert to Chicago immediately. When he probed May for more info, her brief reply said he would get more details when he was in Chicago. He was flying into an operation blind. That was unusual.

Bridger looked around the expensive suite. He had been living the good life all his life—*well, adult life*. Although his mother was a secret government employee, she had married well—purposely he assumed.

He knew his father, Stanley Hall, was a successful early tech pioneer. When he suddenly died, he left his little boy a thirty-seven-million-dollar trust fund. Half was his when he turned twenty-one. The rest three years after he graduated from college.

When the time came, she told him he should only use it for operational purposes. No fancy car in college. No taking friends, especially girlfriends—she frowned upon them—on vacations to Cabo. No gambling or other vices—except golf.

"When you get operational, then you can have some toys."

He did as he was told—pretty much all of the time.

When the right time came, he used his money to establish his cover company Hubbard Park Investments, and subsequently, the Spy Devils. Hubbard gave him cover for status and action to run his Spy Devils operations. Trow Hall was free to travel. He could meet a wide variety of people. He could open international satellite offices. He could establish a network of independent companies and support resources worldwide.

He could be visible and invisible.

Over time, as the Spy Devils confiscated the spoils from the targets they eliminated, they became a self-funding enterprise.

He picked up a chocolate and looked at the legend paper that told him what each treat was. Milk chocolate. Coconut filling. He put it back in the box in the "eat as a last resort" section.

Then he looked at his phone. He knew it was going to ping.

He always had them—what May called his special *observation abilities*.

When he was young, soon after his father's death, they invented a game while walking on the busy streets in whatever country they were living in at the time. They called it "What's Their Secret?"

They would eat warmed spiced nuts from circular cones of striped paper and declare the kerchief-covered German *hausfrau* waddling into the bakeshop in Berlin was worried about her children. Chocolate dipped churros meant the man in Madrid was cheating on his wife but was less concerned about her feelings and more concerned about juggling more than one mistress. Over Nutella-covered waffles in Brussels, they would proclaim the young teacher was smuggling drugs into France.

At first a childish activity to pass the time, it got more serious as he grew. His mother took delight, in her own way, of his budding aptitude. And on it went. Year after year.

Espionage was his life's work and ingrained in half his DNA as much as the genetic code that assured him his hair was sort of blonde, or his eyes were sort of hazel. The other half of his DNA came from his father. That part, he figured, loved strategic thinking and golf.

From that point on, May brought him fully into her world. Whenever the opportunity allowed, she turned their son into an exploitable intelligence asset. Picnics in the park were enjoyable and good cover to service a dead drop. Trips through museums and back streets made him acutely aware of surveillance detection techniques. Dinner parties were perfect opportunities to practice elicitation techniques.

She made the time to enhance his game, turning it from passing fancy of youth into an exploitable adult skill. After each diplomatic dinner party at their home, trip to an embassy for a national day celebration, or wait in a train station, she queried him to report what he saw. The military general in Argentina was a sociopath. The Italian scientist was doing more than working on vaccines. The Slovakian businessman was an arms dealer. The cute Korean couple were spies.

Perhaps it was his moment of teenage defiance against his mother. A way to have his own identity. But mostly, he hated being called Trowbridge. He had eye-gouged and groin-kicked name-taunting kids in the ever-changing schools since he was eight years old. Trow was okay, and what most people called him in the real world.

He proclaimed that he was going to play spy and wanted a code name. She insisted on calling him by his given name, Trowbridge. But the nom de guerre he adopted was Bridger. He just liked the way it sounded.

Although he was expecting the phone to beep, he still jumped when the sound of three electronic chirps resonated across the room.

Bridger hesitated, then hit the answer button.

"Am I catching you at a bad time?" she asked like always.

"Would it make a difference?" he replied, as he bit his last good chocolate. Dark. With nuts. A favorite.

"No," she said.

"Well, I am here, as requested," he said, then licked the chocolate off his lips. "I don't know why I am here, and that is disconcerting."

"I know you have heard of Kirkwood International. They seem to have allowed a rather important piece of classified equipment to walk out the door. You need to help them retrieve it."

"Hold the phone. Kirkwood? The U.S. company? That Kirkwood?"

"Yes, as I have already said. And yes, they are a U.S.-based company."

"I seem to expressly remember a long conversation about not working in the U.S. *Ever.* True? It's one of our rules—Spy Devils Rule Number Four. No working in the U.S. *"*

"Yes, but—"

"That if we were ever caught working in the U.S. we don't have any cover, so we would go to prison for things like kidnapping, grand theft, breaking and entering, and half a dozen more state and federal laws…right?"

"Your operation will take place mostly in Europe. In Ukraine, specifically."

"I don't like it. This feels…off."

There was a moment of dead air.

"That doesn't matter, does it? The details are in the Dropbox. Keep me posted. Don't make me check on your progress."

Bridger's eyebrows raised. He sat forward in his chair.

"Since when do you check on my progress?"

"Goodnight, Trowbridge."

"Bridger," he said. The phone went silent.

Bridger stood and walked across the room bent. He picked up a putter. A few golf balls were at his feet. On the carpeted floor, ten feet from him, was a glass on its side acting as the target hole. Bridger lined up his putt, glancing toward the glass, then back at the ball, then once more at the glass. *Click*. The ball rolled across the carpet. *Clink*. A miss. It hit the right side of the glass rim and ricocheted away.

"This rooms breaks to the right," Bridger muttered, his mouth screwed across his face in disappointment.

He dropped the putter and sat back in the comfortable chair.

Closing his eyes, he visualized his golf ball cutting through a cloudless sky, landing safely in the middle of a green, and rolling toward the flag.

A one-foot putt for birdie.

23

ANNA MALINOV

Odessa, Ukraine

Early the next morning, Anna Malinov, the lead prosecuting attorney of the Primorsky District Court representing Sergei Pavlenko, Ukraine's new General Prosecutor in charge of anti-corruption, walked toward a row of low buildings in the Prymors'kyi District, Port of Odessa. Inside the buildings were the offices of Ukraine Bondar Shipping and Transport.

Overhead, the sky was confused if it was still winter or if it was time to become a Ukrainian spring. A mix of clouds and sun hung above them—brilliant rays broke through like a warm spotlight, then just as suddenly, thick clouds brought the gloom again.

Anna was a thirty-four-year-old rising star in the prosecutor's office. Tough. Determined. Smart. Her trendy teal overcoat was buttoned to the top against the chill of the morning. She took confident steps forward, holding out her left hand that clutched the orders signed by the General Prosecutor. Her other hand was buried in her coat pocket, clamped around her mobile phone.

Escorting her were six members of the General Directorate of the

National Police, each protected in deep blue riot uniforms, body vests, black helmets, and dark visors lowered to cover their faces.

Four heavily armed soldiers of the Bondar Battalion-1 met them. Bondar's lethal private militia was a mixture of Russian, Chechen, Serbian, Bulgarian, and Cossack mercenaries drawn to the Battalion by the Bondar family's generous pay. Bearded. Body armor and camouflage. Ammo belts over shoulders. Young and old. Chiseled emotionless faces. Hard faces.

Ukrainian television, radio, and social media were tipped off by the Prosecutor's Office of their planned anti-corruption activities against the Bondar empire. Instantaneous analysis by TV anchors welcomed the fall of the oligarchs that had dominated the politics and economics of Ukraine for decades. Transparency and openness were the policies of the day.

Anna stopped ten feet in front of the line of mercenaries.

"We...are here...to serve papers...legal papers," Anna stuttered with uneasiness. "Papers assuming possession of the facilities Ukraine Bondar Shipping and Transport." Her alto voice pitched higher with apprehension. Her hand was shaking as she kept the paper extended in front of her.

The men of the Battalion did not respond either verbally or by lowering their weapons. Their response was to disregard her with looks of contempt.

"I repeat." Her adrenaline was not helping enough as she faced the armed men. "We have legal authority, on behalf of the General Prosecutor's Office, to—"

Before she could finish her sentence, metallic clicks came from all directions. Four mercenaries to her left and four more to her right appeared from behind trees and parked cars. They were sighting down the length of their weapons right at her. Her hand and the paper descended slowly to her side.

"By blocking our entry—you—I must inform you— the law—" Her teeth and tongue rattled in her mouth so violently she could no longer form words.

She jumped when her phone suddenly rang inside the pocket of her coat.

"Hello, Anna," said her boss, Sergei Pavlenko, the prosecuting attorney.

To Anna, the calmness in his voice was incompatible to the drama surrounding her.

"There are soldiers. Tell me what to do."

"Yes, I can see it on television. They will not harm you." He wasn't so sure his words were true, but he had nothing else to tell her. "They are only there to scare you. Tell them they are breaking the law."

"I tried."

"I want to talk to them. Give their leader your phone."

"I don't think—"

"Please try," he interrupted.

She pulled the phone away from her ear and looked at it with contempt. No soldier had moved a muscle. She reached her hand out and waved the phone left and right, offering it to any of the men. She mustered a false smile and took a step in their direction.

"The General Prosecutor would—like to—speak with you, please?" She ended with more of a plea than a question.

One mercenary glared directly into Anna's eyes with the cold sharpness like a knife. "Go" was all the low voice said in a non-Ukrainian accent. He pointed his AK-47 above their heads and fired three bursts in rapid succession.

Abandoning any pretext of a professional demeanor, Anna let out a high-pitched shriek, tossed her phone, turned, and ran. The National Police did not fire. Instead, they quickly walked backward, protecting her retreat.

Reaching her car in a full sprint, she slammed against it to stop her momentum. She flung the door open and dove in. In seconds the engine was gunned, the wheels burned in black clouds, and the car sped away. The National Police piled into their vehicle and followed her.

Sergei Pavlenko's voice came from Anna's phone lying on the

ground at the mercenary's feet. The mercenary looked down and stomped on the device until it was shattered into pieces.

At 3 a.m., the point man picked the lock while two other men oiled the hinges on the gate at the corner of Pushkinska and Zukovskoho streets in Odessa. On the far side of the gate was the fortress that covered an entire rectangular block in the center of the city. It was the headquarters of the General Directorate of the National Police.

The compound was considered one of the more secure buildings in the city, given its occupants. By day, security managed access to the area they had just accessed. By night, there was nothing.

The thirty members of the Bondar Battalion-1 Assault Team huddled in the arched service passageway built through the mustard-colored façade of an adjacent building.

The leader knew thirty was twice as many as was needed, which was still twice too many. His men were fighters, and they were all eager to kill the government soldiers—more for practice than ideology. So when he asked for volunteers they all stepped forward.

Each carried a Fort-221 bullpup assault rifle and a Fort-17 9mm semi-automatic pistol. They were equipped with night-vision goggles on their helmets, various explosives, communication gear, and body armor.

Inside the compound was the pale-yellow training and barrack building that housed the elite members of the National Police of Ukraine. It was a Tetris-tile puzzle of L-shaped, square, and rectangular buildings—courtyards inside tree-lined courtyards.

A one-story building contained an operations center and classrooms. Attached was the two-story structure. The first floor contained the equipment and weapons of the special unit. Upstairs were twenty-four cots for the Gold and Blue Teams—eleven were currently occupied, including six who accompanied Anna Malinov to the Bondar facility the previous day.

When the gate swung open, six teams of five men crouched and moved quietly and quickly in the darkness of a row of trees lining the Pushkinska Street wall. One team spread out in sentry positions, as two teams broke off to their right, went up the steps to the lower-level training wing, picked the lock, and went in to secure the floor.

Around back, three teams entered the back door and moved up a narrow set of stairs to the sleeping area. Once in position, they moved into the room and shot each man in the head while sleeping. Men carrying twenty-liter jerry cans poured gas on the bodies and throughout the rest of the room.

A moan came from the darkness.

"This one is still alive. Tough fucker," a man reported, raising a pistol to finish the job.

"Wait. Leave him," the team leader said. When his team was clear, he took out a flare, lit it, and tossed it on one of the gas-soaked beds.

They disappeared into the darkness of the streets as flames illuminated the night sky behind them.

The moment she entered her apartment, Anna Malinov went to her kitchen, found a bottle opener in the back of a drawer, grabbed one of three bottles of wine from her cupboard, a locally produced sparkling white, and started to drink.

Two hours later, she tilted her head back as far as it would go, opened her mouth wide, tipped the glass, and in one swallow finished the last drops from the third bottle. She stood up, wobbled, then fell to the floor, where she passed out. The empty wine glass was still in her hand when she hit the floor. It shattered in her palm. Blood spread from under her fingers.

Still unconscious hours later, she didn't hear the lock on her door being unlatched, hear the door open slowly, or see two people, a man and a woman, quietly slip inside her dark apartment. They each pulled a mini red LED flashlight from their pockets and clicked them on. The rays flashed around the room. Expecting her to be in bed, when the beams found her on the floor, they stood shocked and motionless for several seconds over the body.

The woman reached down and felt for a pulse. She looked at the pool of dried blood under her hand.

"She's alive."

The man pointed his light on the empty wine bottles.

"She is drunk. Passed out drunk," he said with a chuckle.

"At least she enjoyed herself."

They each reached under an arm, lifted her, and dragged her toward the balcony. Her feet caught the rug, and they gave a little extra effort to free her. They stood briefly on the balcony and looked at a fire burning in the distance. They eyed each other and smiled.

The pair of intruders grabbed her legs and tipped Anna over the edge like they were dumping out the garbage. They heard a soft thud a few seconds later.

They calmly walked out of the apartment, took the elevator to the third floor, then used the stairs the rest of the way.

Exiting by the back door, they heard shouts echoing down the street.

Reclining on a sofa in her bedroom lounge, Ira received the call telling her both missions were successful. She leaned over to a side table and picked up a champagne flute. She raised the glass in the air and thought of an appropriate toast.

She took a sip, enjoyed the taste and pleasant feeling of the bubbles in her mouth, and set the glass down back on the table. Traces of blood-red lipstick remained on the rim of the crystal.

Here is to me, the only real Bondar left.

24

THE CAPITAL GRILLE

Lombard, Illinois

At 11:45 a.m., Bridger sat at one of four tables in the private State Room dining area in the Capital Grille restaurant, located in the western Chicago suburb of Lombard. The decor included English riding club mahogany, accented by hues of reds and greens, oil paintings, and racks of wine bottles behind glass doors. Bobby Darin's *Beyond the Sea* filled the air, mixing with whiffs of meat, bread, and money.

Patrons huddled in hushed discussions in dimly lit rooms. Leather chairs and couches were on top of plush carpets. It offered discreet three martini dining surrounded by small lamps on cloth-covered tables —and Bridger was craving a genuine medium-rare slab of American corn-fed beef.

Movement in this peripheral vision distracted him.

"I'm Peter Schaeffer. Are you...Mr. Palmer? Arnold Palmer?" Bridger looked up to see a man who looked a few years younger than himself. Bridger chuckled inside when he saw him wearing a blue blazer, striped blue button-down, and khaki pants. Bridger felt a genuine friendliness radiating from his eyes and manner. Bridger also sensed concern and skepticism.

"Peter, so good to finally meet you. Glad you could make it. Call me Arnie." Bridger stood and shook his hand like they were old friends.

Firm. Confident.

"Okay...*Ar-nie*," Peter said in a skeptical voice.

"Here is my card." Peter reached in his pocket, pulled out his Kirkwood business card, and handed it to Bridger. Bridger glanced at it. There wasn't any information he didn't already know.

"As for me," he reached into his coat pocket and pulled out a black card with a red pitchfork and slid it across the table, "have you ever heard of the Spy Devils?"

Peter raised his eyebrows in total shock as he stared at the card.

"Spy Devils? You are with *THE* Spy Devils? *Greetings from the Devil.* That's you?"

Bridger turned and nodded his chin to his chest like a Shakespearean actor acknowledging adoring fans.

"You're telling me you are associated with the Spy Devils? The gang on social media who exposes all the criminals and spies?"

"We are not a *gang*, thank you very much, but I grasp your meaning and respect." Bridger stopped, wiped his mouth with a napkin, and looked at Peter with deadly seriousness. "I lead them as we journey down into the lowest realms where the worst of mankind think they can act unabated."

"Tell me—," Peter looked around at the empty room, his voice lower, "—who are you? CIA?"

"There is a member of my team—you may meet him. He summed up who we are and what we do in a succinctly crude but surprisingly accurate way. We are the fuckers who fuck with the people who fuck with other people."

"Catchy."

"He thinks so." Bridger sat back, keeping his eyes on the company man. "For the sake of some transparency, I will say we don't usually help U.S. companies. Never, actually. This is an unwelcomed exception, in all honesty."

Peter absorbed the comments. "Why me?"

"I don't know. Your good looks and charm?"

Charles, their waiter, appeared at the table, introduced himself, explained the specials, and took their order. Streak for Bridger. Salad for Peter. Both declined desserts. Charles nodded and retreated.

"Say, Peter. I was wondering. Has anyone mentioned China or the word Hillcrest?" Bridger grabbed a flat bread from a basket and took a bite.

"China? Hillcrest?" Peter was confused. "No. Nothing like that."

"Figures. Ask about it. See what happens." Bridger sat back and folded his arms across his chest. "Now, tell me everything that has happened so far. Who asked you to do this, etc.?"

Peter took ten minutes to explain the events of the last few days. He listed off the Kirkwood executives and what they asked him to do.

"Danforth Chapel is involved, also," he added.

"Chapel?" Bridger asked.

Peter flinched at a ding signaling he had received a text message. He reached into the breast pocket of his jacket and checked. It was from Sandy Boyd.

"It is from an internal Kirkwood source I have on the executive floor," Peter said to Bridger. "She is looking for any messages and documents that might be useful."

"Good job, Peter! What does it say?" Bridger happily rapped the top of the table with his fingers.

Peter squinted at the screen. He read out loud.

Peter: I recalled something. Not sure if interesting. George was desperate to see Gilbert Street before he left. He had me call and tell him to get the case ready. He was taking it to Ukraine. They met before he left. Will send more soon."

Peter set his phone on the table. With his elbows on the arms of the chair, he interlocked his fingers in front of his chest. Bridger could tell he was thinking—he was biting the inside of his lip.

"Well, I know where I need to go next," Peter said, as he slid his phone back into his pocket.

"Where?"

"A group inside Kirkwood. KRT stands for Kirkwood Research Technologies. It is a classified, limited access, Applied Research team. It means MacLean stopped there before he left. I want to know why."

"Sounds like my kind of place. Let's get going. Time is fleeting."

"But you can't get in. As I said, it is a secure facility."

Bridger laughed. "No problem. I make a living getting into secure facilities. It is a trademark of the Spy Devils."

25

THE MOLE HOLE

Kirkwood Headquarters

C linton, the thick-necked security guard, was dressed in a black shirt with the familiar Kirkwood gold "K" on his chest and a Smith and Wesson M&P 9 in a black leather holster around his waist. He checked the flat screen to make certain Peter's name was on the limited access employee list.

"Here you go, Mr. Schaeffer. Good to see you again," Clinton said, handing Peter his badge.

"Thanks, Clinton." Peter took the badge and concentrated on keeping his hand from shaking. He felt sick to his stomach and was sure his face was as white as a wedding dress.

He could not believe the man with him looked calm—almost bored.

"Identification?" Clinton asked the stranger in his imposing security voice.

The man handed over his license and government identification. The guard took it and looked at the screen. Then he looked at the document—then the screen again. He handed them back.

"Thank you, Mr. Palmer. Have a nice day."

Peter didn't realize he had been holding his breath. He let it out slowly as the metallic sound of a lock releasing granted access through the secure door. It opened quickly and closed behind them just as fast.

Their feet clicked on the pale green tile floor, but acoustic foam tiles covering the walls and ceiling quickly swallowed the sound. They reached an identical set of stairs and secure door on the other end in less than a minute—the secret entrance to *The Mole Hole*.

"How the hell did you do that?" a shocked Peter whispered, feeling the blood rush back to his face.

"I told you. I am cleared. Relax, will you? You were so pale, I thought you had died. Just do whatever you do. I will do the rest," Bridger said.

"But—"

"Stick with the plan."

During the ride over, Peter was adamant Bridger would not get into KRT. Peter was sure he would be discovered trying to bring in an unauthorized person. He would be detained, arrested, fired, or all of the above.

"I can't be the first visitor to this place," Bridger said, when they pulled into the parking lot.

"No, but they are pre-approved. The first guard will catch you."

"No, he won't. I *have* been pre-approved. Have some faith."

"What about security cameras? They record everything."

"I think they will discover a malfunction about the time we are there."

As they approached the next door, he had to admit Bridger was correct on all counts, so far.

"Could you have picked a worse alias?" Peter said, holding his right hand on a biometric pad attached to the wall by the door.

"It is perfect. Who would use such a known name if they wanted to avoid attention? And what? You don't like Arnie?"

A warm red glow turned calm blue on the display under Peter's palm.

"*Access granted*" appeared in block letters across the top of the screen. In a few seconds, there was a sustained *buzzzz* on their side of the door, followed by a hard, metallic *click*. Peter pushed the door open and waved at the armed security guard eyeing him and his guest. They walked into a division few within the company knew existed—Kirkwood Research Technologies or KRT.

Kirkwood Research Technologies was born in 1938 during the simmering days leading up to World War II. Twentieth-century industrialist and visionary founder Jacob Kirkwood clandestinely assembled engineers from all disciplines—electrical, mechanical, and chemical. KRT had complete autonomy to experiment, develop, build, succeed, and fail.

KRT was hidden below an unremarkable two-story building fifty yards to the east of the Kirkwood headquarters. Since the group worked in a windowless subterranean home, where they rarely came up for air, those that knew about their existence christened their workspace *The Mole Hole*. The engineers were understandably referred to as "Moles."

The present-day interior of KRT was unlike any other unit at Kirkwood. They had a sleeping room, video games, fake plants, and a full kitchen. There was a guard station to the left and a wall of lockboxes next to that. Another imposing cipher-locked door covered in red warning signs was across from the guard station.

NO ELECTRONICS BEYOND THIS POINT.
NO CLASSIFIED CONVERSATIONS IN THE BREAK AREA.

Peter walked up to the guard and entered his name and social security number into the computer, which tagged the time and date. The guard gave him a look and handed him a label with his name and picture on it.

"Here you go, Mr. Schaeffer. Please wear this at all times."

Bridger gave the guard the same info.

"Welcome to KRT, Mr. Palmer. Please wear this at all times."

"Thank you." Bridger took the label, peeled off the back, and slapped it on his chest over his heart.

"And please remove all electronics and place them in the lockboxes."

They nodded, turned, and took the few steps to the small numbered boxes lining the wall. The boxes had a key with an orange grip with an elastic band in them. Peter opened one door and tossed in his cellphone and car remote. Bridger set his phone next to Peter's. Peter slammed the box shut, twisted the key in the lock, pulled it out, and wrapped the elastic band around his wrist.

Peter heard a click and turned to see the secure door to his left start to open.

"Hey, hey, hey." Gilbert Street, Vice President, Kirkwood Research Technology, shouted the words with excitement. *The King of the Moles.* The cheery triple "Hey" was Gilbert's signature greeting and part of the charm that drew and kept a loyal staff of engineering geniuses. They had a motto: *A day without three "heys" is a day without sunshine.*

"Hello, Gilbert." Peter walked toward him, hand extended, preparing for the energetic pumping that was certain to come when you were greeted by Gilbert.

"This is Mr. Arnold Palmer. He is from—the government." He pointed to Bridger with his free hand.

"Which one?"

"No comment!" Bridger laughed as he shook Gilbert's hand. "Call me Arnie."

"Hey, if you don't tell me you don't have to kill me! Right, Arnie? A friend of Peter is a friend of mine. Come on in."

Peter saw an irritating *'I told you so, why were you worrying?'* look in Bridger's expression.

Gilbert held the heavy metal door open, and they walked into the most secure area in Kirkwood. Just inside the door, a red warning light rotated from the ceiling, casting a strobe firework effect across the area. It was an alert—*uncleared personnel in the area.*

Peter was sure Gilbert's parents never had to buy him a Halloween costume. He was a human-sized owl, but still half a foot shorter than Peter. His perfectly round head was accented by pointed tufts of fading black hair above each ear. Gilbert's sharp beak-like nose separated puffy smooth cheeks. Thin lips formed a line below the beak. A head angled out of slightly stooped shoulders as if the owl was sitting in a tree scanning the forest for his next mouse dinner.

They walked down a long beige hallway lined with a few doors, discarded or broken chairs, desks, metal filing cabinets, and trash.

"I like what you have done with the place, Gilbert. It looks like a Goodwill Store barfed in here," Bridger said as they closed ranks to dodge the debris.

"I have been meaning to complain to the front desk about the maid service. Just haven't gotten around to it." Gilbert rapidly snorted air in and out like a donkey's hee-haw, as his head bobbed with each blurt.

Gilbert opened a door on the right near the end of the hallway. They walked into his office.

It was small—much smaller than a vice president was entitled at Kirkwood. It barely fit a recycled metal desk, two torn hand-me-down guest chairs, a few overstuffed bookcases, and two cabinets with combination locks on each drawer. Any free surface was covered with space memorabilia. Detailed models of a timeline of NASA rockets. Mercury. Gemini. Apollo. Space shuttle. Lunar landers and Mars rovers. A two-foot-long model of the International Space Station hung from the ceiling tiles by paperclip and string tethers.

Diplomas on the wall showed he held Master's Degrees in Electrical and Computer Engineering and Mechanical Engineering. He was as smart as they come at Kirkwood.

"So, what can I do you for you, gentlemen?"

"We don't have a lot of time, so tell us about Hillcrest," Bridger said.

Peter saw that just mentioning Hillcrest struck a nerve. Silence, followed by more silence.

"Hillcrest? What do you mean?" Gilbert asked.

He was talking too fast, Peter thought.

"Gilbert. I need you to answer some questions Right now," Bridger said with all seriousness. "Hillcrest."

Peter knew a little about interview techniques. He learned them during his brief time in CIA training. He had adapted them to use in his intelligence collection at Kirkwood. It was exciting to see them put into play by an expert like Bridger.

Control was necessary, he knew. There were a few dozen methods with unique names—*bracketing, flattery, confidential bait, assumed knowledge, and denial of the obvious*—that were meant to appear like any normal conversation between two people. In actuality, they were there to manipulate.

"I know about it, Gilbert. Hillcrest. I know it is important, but I am not sure I have all the details, exactly," Bridger started.

Feigned ignorance.

"Where did you hear about that? I'm not saying—"

"I heard it might be related to the death of the CFO. Any ideas?"

The leading question technique.

Peter felt the air chill to the level he could imagine the model airplanes needing to have their wings de-iced. Gilbert leaned further back in his chair.

"Now where did you hear that? This is a classified KRT program. Limited access and distribution."

Bridger leaned forward and put his elbows on top of the desk clutter.

"So, there is a product named Hillcrest. Tell us."

"I did not say that—I—I didn't say that. Who are you?"

"Just looking for answers. The kind of answers I need answered." Bridger's friendly smile didn't hide the seriousness of the need for an answer.

Gilbert nervously looked at Peter. His chair squeaked as he shifted his body weight.

Peter could tell Gilbert was not prepared for Bridger. *Who could be?*

"What's going on, Gilbert?" Peter asked calmly.

"Your bosses seem to be pretty worried about it. I'm trying to help everyone solve the puzzle. It's all about Kirkwood in the end."

Mutual interest.

Peter could tell Gilbert was thinking. Bridger was silent, then he did another switch. Steady. Non-threatening.

"*You* made Hillcrest. We know it is your creation." *A definitive statement of fact.*

Gilbert was visibly shifting in his seat. He rubbed his palms together like he was crushing a walnut between them.

"No. What? I cannot say anything about this without approval from above. The whole thing has become…become…complex…but it is NOT my invention…if there was one. I can't talk about it." Gilbert let his eyes roam around his office.

"It is simple," Peter joined in, calmly. "I was asked by Jessup, MacBride, and Kirkwood to look into the death of MacLean."

"Even Chapel green-lighted Peter's task, right, Peter?" Bridger said, keeping his eyes on Gilbert.

"Yes, he did. He was particularly interested in helping to get the briefcase back. Worried, really."

Gilbert's shoulders started to slump in surrender to the questioning.

"If you need to call someone to verify it, go ahead. Call Chapel." Bridger pointed to the phone.

Gilbert's furrowed brow and puffy lips told Peter he was deciding whether to let them in on whatever Hillcrest was.

He is near the finish line.

"Maybe I will call Benton in security," Gilbert said. He leaned forward like he was going for the phone.

"No—," Peter started.

"No, go ahead. Let's call him," Bridger interrupted. "You can verify all of this. What's his number?" Bridger pointed to the desk phone. Gilbert hesitated, then pulled his trembling hand back.

"The 10th floor asked you to find it?" he asked, looking beaten.

"Yes." Peter and Bridger said together.

Gilbert sighed and shook his head as he exhaled the air slowing through his nose.

"What is going on, Gilbert?" Bridger asked.

26

LATIN FOR GUARD

Kirkwood Research Technologies

"Come with me."

They followed Gilbert out the door and to the right. He led them to another door at the end of the corridor. It took a few seconds for Gilbert to navigate the fingerprint, voice, and retinal biometric systems. He punched in one final authentication code. The door clicked open. Once inside, they started down a long set of steps. At the bottom were bright walls of white and glass accented with the low hum of machinery.

There were two rooms across from each other—each about the size of a tennis court. The left room was filled with metal racks of equipment, workstations, wires, tools, and a half dozen casually dressed men and women. Desks, conference tables, and chairs were lined in a T-pattern, forming narrow aisles like a maze.

The room to the right was opposite in appearance. It was so bright it looked as if was on fire. It was white from the tile floor to the high air circulating ceiling pipes. The room was empty except for long tables with computers and workstations spaced every few feet.

"This area has the best security in the world," Gilbert said. "We have gone back to the Stone Age, or pre-1980, which is mostly the same thing. This floor is totally off the grid. No wireless. No internet. Nothing connected. We communicate by courier. I have a dedicated STU-3 secure phone in my office down here. No darned hackers can hack something that isn't linked to anything. It may not be efficient, but it is secure." He looked around the room with satisfaction. "No one is getting anything from my shop unless they dig a hole from China."

"Gilbert. Tell us. What is Hillcrest?" Bridger said, suddenly standing so close to Gilbert their shoulders were touching. Startled, Gilbert put a few inches between them. Bridger stayed awkwardly close.

"For me, it isn't important what Hillcrest *is*. That, I will not divulge. What is neat is what it's *in*."

"What?" Peter snorted with a confused laugh.

"Explain yourself, Gilbert," Bridger said.

"Yes." Gilbert scurried with excitement to a door. When he walked in, Peter saw a marginally cleaner clone of Gilbert's office upstairs. Gilbert went behind the desk and sat in a beat-up wooden chair that squeaked when weight was applied.

Gilbert sat forward, chattering with excitement.

"We are developing some exquisite technology—beautiful research with neat stuff. Well ahead of the Russians and Chinese combined." He stopped. "The government asked for KRT to help in making it harder to steal."

"Who in the government?" Bridger asked. "What is *it*?"

"I don't know, but I thought it was spooks. CIA-types. NSA. DoD. Others?" He looked at Bridger with a *"which are you?"* expression.

Gilbert reached under his desk, unlocked a cabinet, and set an odd-shaped silver briefcase on top of the desk. He sat back with the look of a proud father. They waited for him to explain. Nothing.

"*This* is Hillcrest?" Peter asked.

Gilbert sighed. "Hillcrest, the thing I will never tell you about, goes IN the case. For me, it is the case that is the unique tech." Gilbert ran his fingers on the case like he was caressing his child. "I call it Custos. That's—"

"—Latin for *guard*," Bridger said, walking around the desk, forcing Gilbert to slide his chair away a few inches.

Peter looked at Bridger, who looked at Gilbert.

"Yes, that is correct," Gilbert said.

"This case—which I am going to call Hillcrest for simplicity—this is the same case George took to Ukraine?" Bridger asked.

"Yes, but it is Cu—"

"I know," Bridger cut him off, "but whatever we call it, Hillcrest is inside?" Bridger added quickly.

"Yes, sure, but what's inside is irrelevant."

"Irrelevant? How can it be irrelevant? Isn't that the whole point?" Peter said, too loud for the small room.

"Yes, well, sort of. Hillcrest is impressive, blah, blah, sure. The case is a masterpiece." Gilbert caressed the case with his hands. "The exterior is chromium, the hardest metal on the Mohs scale, plated over titanium. Strong. Light. Its interior is entirely RF-shielded with copper, steel, and aluminum. You can't see in with x-rays, CT scans, MRIs...any of them. It is basically a built-in Faraday Cage. Access is through a unique combination of biometric and authentication controls. Even more advanced than into this room. See this panel?" Gilbert pointed to the raised panel on the side of the case. "It controls multimodal biometrics—face, iris, palm vein, voice. Big deal, you say?"

"Is it a big deal?" Bridger asked to keep Gilbert on his roll.

"Of course it is. The miniaturization and mobility of the technology are Nobel-worthy. The FAR/FRR numbers, the false acceptance rate, false rejection rate, are near zero. Zero! In any environment. It is spoof proof against unauthorized intruder attacks. A unique authentication code must be entered within a certain time limit. In the commercial world," he pointed to the case, "this is a multimillion-dollar product. Multi. Multi." Gilbert paused. "I know what you're thinking."

"Oh?" Peter looked at Bridger, who was looking at the case.

"You're thinking, forget the biometric stuff. Steal it. Take it to the shop and cut it open with a laser or plasma torch. Boom! You have what is inside."

"Well, that had crossed my mind," Bridger reached to touch it. Gilbert slid it away.

"Unauthorized access triggers an internal self-destruct mechanism. There is a thin layer of C-4 with a detonator in the lining."

"Well, *boom,* that is explosive information. Dynamite!" Bridger said with a chuckle, pulling his hand away.

"Yes, that is a good one, Arnie!" Gilbert laughed. "I appreciate a good pun. You don't want to be standing nearby when this goes off. Oh, it has GPS inside that cannot be shut off. If someone steals it, we have a locator signal."

"It has GPS?" Bridger asked, glancing at Peter.

"Yes, with a boosted signal, accelerometers, barometers, magnetometers, and a few more secret sauces I won't discuss."

"Then where is it?" Peter asked.

Gilbert sighed and bit his pink lips in a look of embarrassment.

"I don't know. It disappeared in Kyiv. The GPS could not be turned off, so it is either destroyed, or it is in a very, very, *very*, RF-proof location. If it comes out, we can pick it up. I hope."

"So, let's recreate this. MacLean took a case just like this?" Bridger asked.

"Yes, exactly."

"And a complex combination of biometrics is pre-set to one singular user?"

"Correct."

"And he took a case only he could open?"

"Yes."

"And you helped him program it for his biometrics?"

"Naturally."

"Of course." Bridger moved over toward the case, forcing Gilbert to step back against the wall. "He is dead. Are you telling me it can't be opened, ever?"

"No. I didn't say that." Gilbert's head turned to keep his eyes on the visitor.

"That means you built a backdoor into the access protocols or secure token access."

Gilbert sat in stunned silence. He put his hands on the case and slid it to his lap.

"Who are you, Arnie?"

Bridger smiled at the question. It was the question asked by every target of the Spy Devils.

"How does that work?" Bridger answered the question with one of his own.

"That's one of my trade secrets." Gilbert took the case and locked it back in the cabinet.

Bridger looked at Peter. "Hey, do you mind if I get a private word with Gil here? I just need a minute."

"Sure."

Bridger closed the door behind Peter.

A few minutes later, it opened and the men came out. Gilbert looked like he wanted to get into one of the space models in his office and disappear.

"Everything okay?" Peter said as the men climbed the stairs.

"Never better," Bridger answered.

Gilbert didn't.

They climbed the stairs in silence and moved through the door onto the main floor. The silence continued as Gilbert escorted them to the exterior door. Bridger stopped and turned to Gilbert.

"What's the difference between an introverted and an extroverted engineer? An introverted engineer looks at *his* shoes when he's talking to you, an extroverted engineer looks at *your* shoes when he's talking to you."

Gilbert's cackling laughter echoed down the hall until the security door slammed shut behind them.

Later that night, Bridger sank exhausted into the overstuffed chair in his luxury suite at the Ritz. He was happy to see the hotel staff had replenished his supply of nuts and chocolates in his complimentary gift basket. He grabbed a handful of nuts and tossed a few into his mouth.

It had been a good day. The time with Peter was well-spent. He looked to be an okay guy. Dependable. Skeptical of authority—which made him smart. Gilbert had been very forth-coming. He got all he needed from him.

There *was* one loose end that Peter dropped at lunch that he needed to address. Letting out a sigh, he picked up his phone and dialed.

"Why Chapel, May?" he asked before she could say a greeting.

"Hello, Trowbridge. It is always good to hear your voice." May Currier blew on her tea. She was sitting on her patio, enjoying the night air of her large backyard. The Potomac rushed by just on the other side of the tree line.

"May?"

"Oh, yes. Danny is an integral part of this operation."

"How integral?"

"Very." She took a sip. Still too hot.

Bridger let silence be his answer.

"You are exasperating. He is assisting the Kirkwood company with their issues with the Ukrainians."

"Which issues?" Bridger knew she wouldn't say, but by asking he might get some inkling of what she was thinking. If not, at least he knew it pissed her off.

"All of them." She tried her tea one more time. It was just the right temperature. "Danny will call *if* it comes to the point you are retrieving the Hillcrest material, he will be the one you will give it to. He will take it to Kirkwood."

"Well, then. That is nice to know." Bridger closed his eyes and absorbed the tone of her voice, the cadence of her words, and the words she was using.

"Goodbye, Trowbridge."

Lovely, he thought. *This is already messed up and it hasn't even begun for real.*

27

KILL THE DEVIL

Taipei, Taiwan

L i Chu, the covert MSS Bureau X assassination team leader, remained bunkered in his Shida/Guting neighborhood apartment safe house eating pineapple cakes and drinking Long Dong Lagers. Before he sequestered himself in this section of Taipei, he told his few remaining men to stay concealed.

For the last two days, he searched the internet and monitored the media for any coverage of his men's deaths.

Aided by the exposure from the Spy Devils, Taiwan media were pushing conspiracy theories so fast on the captured men's identities and intentions that they were causing a traffic jam on Taiwan's internet superhighway. Comparing the similarities to other incidents in countries in the region during the last year, Chinese assassins were at the top of the list.

Li Chu noticed the Taiwan government had not released anything on the two men found dead in the Taiwan National Police headquarters' basement cells. *That would be a scandal.*

Dressed comfortably in jeans, AC/DC t-shirt, and sporting a new black beard, Li Chu looked out the large window. He waited for the inevitable encrypted communication from Deputy Minister Chen. It would undoubtedly read something like: *Your mission is over. Return to Beijing. You will be reassigned.* Li Chu knew what that meant: *You are a political embarrassment. Come back to Beijing so we can shoot you in the head.*

Going back was not an option.

Killing the leader of the Spy Devils was his only mission.

A buzz on his encrypted phone brought him back to his current situation.

"Yes?" he answered.

"Where are you?"

Li Chu stood out of view and scanned out the large window to the street activity five stories below. Students with backpacks and shoppers with bags were moving along the crowded sidewalks. Cars. Trucks. Scooters. Regular people going about their business. No hit-team. No rifles on roofs across the street. No apparent threats.

"I am safe," was all he said.

"I understand," Chen replied. "I will be knocking on your door in ten seconds. I have two of my security men with me. You are not in danger. Please do not shoot me."

Li Chu tossed the phone and snapped away from the window like he had been hit by lightning. He pulled his T75 out of the waist of his jeans. He pointed it down a short hallway across the room at the door. Crouching low, he stepped to one side to avoid being directly in the way of any bullets that would come from the direction of the door. With his eyes focused and gun leveled, he stuffed an extra magazine of ammo into one pocket. He felt his knife folded in the other.

A soft knock came. Then again.

Li Chu regulated his breathing and calmed his nerves. He would kill anyone that came through the door if they had a gun in their hand.

Another knock. The knob wiggled with a slow metal squeak.

"I am unarmed. Please unlock the door." When Li Chu didn't answer, Chen whispered again. "I will have my men move away." Li Chu heard some voices and footsteps. A few seconds later, he heard, "They are gone."

Li Chu kept his weapon ready as he walked across the room, unlocked the multiple door locks, and stepped to the side.

It opened a few inches. A set of hands came through the crack. Raised. Empty.

When Chen's head appeared, Li Chu put the gun to his temple, grabbed his shoulder, and pulled him in. Chen glanced at Li Chu with a look of impatience.

Li Chu kept the gun against Chen's head like it was glued on.

"Wait." Li Chu locked the door with his free hand. Chen ignored him and walked into the living area. "Stop!" Li Chu shouted.

Chen stopped in the middle of the room next to the coffee table. His demeanor was all business in his black suit, white shirt, and narrow, striped tie. A thin smile was on his lips.

"If you shoot me, you will not hear the good news," Chen said, making sure his jacket was on straight.

Good news? Li Chu moved so his back was against the wall keeping his body away from the window.

"What good news?"

Chen sighed and shook his head. He looked around the room, then turned toward Li Chu.

"I will get directly to the issue. The Standing Committee of the State Council has terminated Bureau X. The global exposure of your failures has been too great. There are too many considerations in jeopardy with the scrutiny. It is their consideration that the risk is not worth the reward. I am to recall you to Beijing. You and your remaining associates are to be reassigned within their original organizations, but, truthfully—much like your missions—you will be arrested for causing embarrassment to the CCP and then disappear."

"That is the good news?" Li Chu said, applying a little more pressure on the trigger.

"Not at all, but you had to expect this, of course." He kept his eyes on Li Chu. "You can lower your weapon."

Chen saw the box of cake and made an approving face. He reached down, picked up the last piece, and took a bite. He nodded, then waved the cake in front of him. "A little dry, but still delicious." He set the remaining cake back in the box.

Li Chu kept his face calm, and his gun raised.

"I still have not heard the good news."

"Oh, yes. I spoke personally with the president, who agreed with me that you should not be recalled to Beijing. He continues to see value in your work silencing the enemies of China, as I do. The Standing Committee is not aware of it, but he has overruled their decision. He and I have other plans for you and the remaining members of your group."

"I have my own mission."

"The Spy Devils. Yes, I spoke to the president about that. He would also like them eliminated. Teach the American CIA a lesson, too."

Li Chu lowered his gun, but he didn't tuck it back in his waistband. He walked toward the table, picked up the beer, finished off the contents, and wiped his lips with the back of his hand. His facial expressions changed as his mind ran the thought process.

Is this real? He could be lying, but why? I need to get the Spy Devils. This might be my only chance. If he is lying, I will kill him.

"What do you need?"

"I need you in Ukraine."

"Ukraine? Why would we go to Ukraine?"

"There has been an incident. Two MSS officers have been killed. They were retrieving an important piece of equipment—a case—from an American business asset. They were successful, we believe, but they were ambushed and killed. The equipment is lost."

"It is not my concern." He walked to the window and stood to one side. The sky was turning to dusk. The lights of the city and night market were beginning to glow.

"The Silk Road Belt relationship between China and Ukraine is very important to the president. We must establish the trade and infrastructure networks connecting Asia with Europe and Africa to offset Russian aggression. Retrieving the case increases the goodwill between our governments. It will help China."

"I do not care," Li Chu said, his face emotionless, as he casually waved his gun in his hand like a baton.

"I have reason to believe the Spy Devils are also looking for this device."

Li Chu pushed away from the wall and took a quick step toward Chen.

"The Spy Devils are in Ukraine?"

"Are, or soon will be. That is what my intelligence sources have reported. More information will be waiting for you in Kyiv." Chen stood. He knew the discussion was over. "The emergency account remains open. And remember, you report to me. Only me." Chen pulled an envelope from his inside suit pocket. "Here are the logistics. Get to Ukraine immediately."

Li Chu's mind was utterly fixated on revenge against the Devils. He would get his vengeance.

"I will need more men," Li Chu said.

"I can arrange that." Chen extended his arm. They shook hands.

"Yes, thank you, sir." Li Chu bowed and helped the man unlock the doors.

"Good luck with this mission," Chen said as Li Chu closed and re-latched the door.

This is for me. My mission, not yours. I will kill the Devil.

Two cars pulled up on the street outside the apartment. A guard opened the back door of the second car. Chen got in.

Chen understood why Li Chu didn't care about China's initiatives. He didn't care either. Helping China had never interested Chen. In fact, he joined the MSS specifically to do the opposite.

It started as a youth in the 1960s during the last horrible days of Mao's Cultural Revolution. In 1989, when the army cracked down on the Tiananmen pro-democracy protests, he was a low-level officer in the MSS. That was when his eyes fully opened to a country built for the suppression of political and religious freedom.

It took planning, perseverance, and two anxious years of frustration, but Chen finally convinced an American intelligence officer that he wanted to spy against his country. Then another year of vetting and polygraphs followed. Finally, Chen became a double agent on behalf of the United States.

More years followed as he rose through the hierarchy of the MSS.

Now, as Deputy Minister, Chen was one major intelligence achievement and political maneuver away from being appointed *The* Minister of State Security. He needed Li Chu operational to complete *his* part of the deal to get the case. If it cost Li Chu and the rest of Bureau X their lives, that was acceptable. The other side was risking more—much more.

He dialed his mobile phone and waited.

"Yes?" answered a voice with a New England accent.

"He is going."

"Good. Does he know they are there?" May Currier asked.

"Yes."

"Excellent. Move to the next phase."

"You know he is very upset," Chen said. "This could be very hazardous for all involved—and you agree?"

"Yes," she answered after a millisecond of hesitation. "Yes, I do."

28

QUADRANGLE INVESTMENT GROUP, LLC

Kirkwood Industries

Over the months, George MacLean convinced himself he would stop spying for Chen and the Chinese.

The core of his successful espionage for China was built upon MacLean introducing Kirkwood officials to Mourning Dove Investments as a means to help Kirkwood with new business. Mourning Dove was one in a matrix of Chinese government-backed entities that used seed money, startup, early-stage, buyouts, and growth capital investments to penetrate markets worldwide.

Kirkwood International Industries became a valued customer.

Mourning Dove Investment's direct connection to the Chinese government was an open secret. By extension, that meant Chinese intelligence services were active in its business operations as well— and the business of its partners.

Sam Kirkwood and the senior leadership liked the idea of Mourning Dove playing a lead role in Kirkwood's business expansion. It immediately paid dividends to the corporate bottom line. With Mourning Dove acting as lead investor, the company made inroads into the African and South American markets. New revenues quickly flowed into Kirkwood.

The stress and guilt of being a traitor kept building in his substantial gut. Six months in a white-collar prison started to look better than a lifetime of spying. But the money issue could not be ignored. With two expensive ex-wives to pay off monthly to finance their wish to never see him again, mounting debt, and razor-thin credit lines, he was up against the wall. MacLean tried more than once to kick his gambling habit, but it never worked. Not even close.

He was trying to also kick the habit of the payments from Chen, which, if he included some extras provided for good work, were totaling nearly half a million dollars. Tax-free. On top of his real salary and perks, it had been a good deal. He was as addicted to the Chinese money as he was to the poker tables.

When the chance to cut ties with the Chinese landed on his desk, he couldn't believe his luck.

It was almost too easy.

"We have been approached by a company for the purchase of a nationwide KirkComm2400 secure industrial communication system. Top-end stuff," Jessup, the Chief Legal Officer, started with all the excitement of someone reading the instructions on the side of a shampoo bottle. Lather. Rinse. Repeat. "It would be the largest single contract in Kirkwood history. We need you to look it over and bring it home."

"Really? Who? Where?" MacLean asked.

Tom MacBride, Chief Strategy Officer, spoke up. "LeonidOre, a mining and steel operation in Ukraine. It is owned by Viktor Bondar. They are a new client. It gives us an opening into the growing Eastern European market."

"I have dealt in that area a few times over the years," MacLean said. "Russians. The *stans*. Ukraine."

"Good. That will help," Jessup said.

"We need you to make the deal. I reiterate this is a large, actually *the* largest contract of our new product line and is coming at a critical time. Perhaps more accurately, it is just in time," Jessup said with a tone of candor. "George. We need this deal. You know that better than any of us."

He did. To ensure success, MacLean personally led the negotiations. In a move rare for deals of this size, he agreed to vendor-finance the entire one-billion-dollar contract to secure it. Expecting the usual negotiation give and take, he was surprised and delighted when Bondar accepted his terms. MacLean completed the deal in a lightning-fast two weeks. It was a stunning victory.

MacLean was hailed as a winner.

As he had agreed since Chen's recruitment, he provided the Chinese every piece of information. That included the technical specifications and trade secret information of the proprietary KirkComm2400 secure communication system. He received a nice two hundred fifty thousand dollars bonus from Chen.

What made MacLean proud was not only the completion of the deal. Or the adulation. Or personal satisfaction. Or even the big one-time bonus. No. He was smiling because a sentence written deep into the contract, added after Walter signed-off, declared that Ukraine Standard Bank would transfer a monthly "finders and facilitation fee" of one hundred fifty thousand dollars to Quadrangle Investment Group of Delaware.

MacLean was certain no one would discover that Quadrangle Investment Group, LLC, was a shell company he formed over a year ago. Sam A. Rothstein was identified as Chair and CEO. Someone might investigate that name and discover, quite curiously, that Sam A. Rothstein was the name of Robert DeNiro's character from the 1995 gambling crime drama *Casino*. If they asked him, they would learn that *Casino* was his favorite movie. An original poster, signed by the three stars of the film—DeNiro, Joe Pesci, Sharon Stone—hung on his office wall.

The dark money would be transferred to Quadrangle and passed through to his personal bank account. Hidden money into a fake hidden company into his real pockets. It was a sweet deal.

MacLean made one rare miscalculation. He did not foresee the Bondar deal immediately going sideways when LeonidOre failed to pay on Kirkwood Credit Corporation's loan. As bad as that was for Kirkwood's financials, to MacLean, it was a disaster. It meant no monthly payment to Quadrangle Investment Group.

His escape plan money lifeboat was sunk before it sailed.

Then one night, Chen showed up on his doorstep. MacLean was busy resting in his lounge chair finishing off his second extra-large Big Mac meal.

"I have a most important mission for you," Chen said.

MacLean wanted to barf up his dinner, but instead, he took a suck through the straw of his empty McDonald's drink and asked, "What is it?"

"Have you heard of a project code named Hillcrest? In your KRT division."

"No." The large beverage was empty, but he kept shaking the ice as if that would free up some liquid.

"We know very little, also. That is why we would like you to obtain the technology and bring it to us."

"Are you kidding? I just can't walk in and say, 'can I borrow that top-secret technology. I promise to bring it back.'" He sucked air through the straw again, sending a scratching plastic noise into the room.

"Yes, you can," Chen reminded him.

MacLean knew Chen was right. He had the keys to the store. But Chen kept asking him to unlock more of Kirkwood's secrets with every demand. It wasn't the turning over of the secrets that bothered him. He just didn't want to be ordered around anymore by the smiling little man who controlled his very existence.

By virtue of his position, MacLean was placed on the small list of executives with access to information about Kirkwood Research Technologies. The man leading KRT, Gilbert Street, seemed amiable enough when he requested updates on contracts.

"I suppose I can, but—"

"Plans are in motion for you to access and deliver Hillcrest."

"What plans?"

Chen explained MacLean's role in getting and delivering Hillcrest.

With each minute, the greasy hamburgers in his stomach rose, as did his resolve.

"Those are the plans," Chen said when he was done. "Any questions?"

"No," he said, jumping up and tossing the empty drink on the floor by his chair, "but this is my last job for you. I am done. Get it? Last one!"

"As you wish." Chen smiled, turned, and left MacLean standing alone in his house.

29

THE HINT OF CORIANDER

Off the coast of Cyprus

"Wake-up."

Oleksandr Bondar did not stir when the words were whispered into his ear. He couldn't see, then he felt cloth against his face. He couldn't move his hands, then he felt the tape pinning them uncomfortably behind him.

"Get up!" The words sounded louder this time. They felt like they were inside his head. They were accompanied by a sharp kick in the ass.

Oleksandr jerked, then felt a gentle rumble on the side of his face when it bounced on the floor. The rumble wasn't the spinning, disorienting sensation that he regarded as normal after a night of partying. His head was still heavy with constant reggae and salsa beats. Even with his head covered, and his eyes closed, bright flashes of light seared into his brain.

Since he had taken ownership of the yacht three days ago, his new possession had not left the marina. Most of his time was spent on a combination of drinking, taking drugs, and indulging in the Limassol nightlife pleasures with Katya. This particular day started and ended at the Guaba Beach Bar, just a few miles up highway B1 east of the marina.

Oleksandr was in heaven. The beach bar was where the chic and wannabe chic went to party from early morning to the next early morning. Oleksandr did precisely that, paying out thousands a day for the fun that fueled his otherwise boring life.

"I said, get the hell up!" Demon grabbed the listless Oleksandr and, with little effort, lifted him off the wooden floor of the main lounge and tossed him four feet onto a trash-covered white L-shaped couch. Oleksandr bounced off the overstuffed cushions and landed on the floor between the couch and a low teak rectangular coffee table.

"Who—" A sharp sting of electricity on his shoulder made him jerk straight up, landing him back on the couch.

"What—" Another shock sent his body rotating along the couch like a top until he hit the other arm of the furniture. His breath was short, his skin was covered in sweat, and he felt nausea in this throat. He tugged his hands, but they would not give.

"Stop. Please." It was a different voice. Calmer, with a tone of authority similar to the way his father always spoke to him. "Sorry about that, Oleksandr. I promise he won't do that again. Understand?"

Bridger directed the command over his shoulder to Demon, who was holding the long black tube of the Devil Stick tightly in his right hand.

"Mr. Nice Guy. Mr. Pussy," Demon said under his breath, as he positioned himself against the bulkhead. His muscles and Devil Stick were primed to strike.

Bridger watched the rhythm of Olek's hood billow in and out with each hyperventilating breath. Bridger decided, for no particular reason, that he didn't like Olek.

The feeling started after they arrived on the boat and talked to Captain Andre and the crew an hour before. They didn't like their new boss, either.

Bridger found Olek already unconscious and lying motionless on the floor. His shoulders were rolled forward, turning him into a human comma. He was dressed in white linen pants stained with the night's activity. No shirt. No shoes. His face was chalky white with gray and red rings circling his eyes. Dark veins in his neck and arms stuck out in jagged patterns.

To his utter disappointment, Bridger was dressed somewhat the same—beach bum style baggy white pants, sun-bleached blonde hair under a yellow sun visor, and Tommy Bahama flowery shirt.

"Sorry about the hood and securing your hands like that. I know it is disorienting, especially in your diminished state, but it is necessary. Now Olek, can I call you Olek?" He didn't skip a beat waiting for an answer. "Olek, we don't have much time." He used his *nice* voice. "It's late and we have a busy day. We need to have a little chat," Bridger said with a short tone of compassion like a father explaining to a child why it was necessary to obey and take out the trash.

Bridger wished he could use the gas to interrogate this kid, but he couldn't wait for it to take effect. This worried him. Speed was an enemy as dangerous as many of their targets. Speed caused hazardous patterns. Speed led to shortcuts. But the lack of time necessitated getting the intel he needed from the body crumpled in front of him right now.

Demon had begged to stuff the kid in a shoebox and ship it to Bondar, who Bridger figured would appreciate the schooling his son received. Lucky for Oleksandr, Bridger needed him in one piece —for now.

Bridger started wandering around the lounge. The kid had turned it into a dump. It smelled of cigarette smoke, sweat, food, and saltwater.

"This is a nice boat you have here. The design and decorating are spectacular. It must have cost you millions. I figure fifty for the toy. Add a few more for the crew, registration, and the marina."

"Fuck you," the words were slurred with contempt. Olek was trying to reposition his body on the couch.

"Captain Andre was nice enough to provide a tour when we came on board," Bridger continued in an informative tone. "By the way, just between you and me, the Captain is *not* your biggest fan. Neither is his crew. They were more than happy to help us and are nice enough to take us out on this pleasant cruise."

"Fuck you," he repeated.

"This is quite a feast." Bridger was leaning over the dining table.

A small dish buffet was mixed among a forest of empty champagne bottles, cigarette butts, drugs, and Cyprus brandy. Two dozen traditional Cypriot delicacies—air-dried cured beef pastirma, meat cubes of souvlaki, halloumi cheese, olives, and breads covered the table. Bridger reached down toward a plate, picked up a sausage, and flicked the meat into his mouth. His head tilted back as his face radiated a smile of pleasure.

"This Loukanika is fantastic! I love the hint of coriander. Don't you?" He waited for an answer as he licked his fingers and smacked his lips. With a smirk, he strolled by Demon, who impatiently leaned against the polished wood of the bulkhead.

"Who are you?" Oleksandr said, his voice rough from smoke and fear.

Bridger turned quickly. Demon started to move toward the boy with the Stick poised to strike.

"No!" Bridger shouted.

Oleksandr panicked and blindly wiggled his body into the cushions as far as he could.

Demon stopped, shrugged, and returned to his position along the wall—the Stick still in striking position.

"Sorry, don't worry about him." Bridger patted Olek on top of his hooded head like a puppy. Olek flinched and turned away. "I won't let anything happen to you. To answer your question—a good question— we have been retained to find a lost or stolen article believed to be in the possession of your father. Since we have no idea where to look, we thought you could help us."

"I don't know anything, and I won't help you." The mask puffed in and out, outlining Olek's mouth. Bridger smiled.

"You will, soon enough."

He heard Olek whine like a fearful puppy.

Bridger stopped to look out the windows that made up the top half of the suite's curved sides. The blinds were raised, offering a panoramic night view of the Cypriot coast off Limassol that glowed a few kilometers in the distance. The lights cast streaks of color on the dark surface of the Med.

"What a view. You have found something here, Oleksandr. I mean, this is paradise. I had forgotten how lovely Cyprus is."

Cyprus may be lovely, but it was also a problem for Bridger. The Cyprus Chief of Police, who had assisted him on many mutually beneficial covert deals over the years, died of a massive heart attack one year ago. To do anything, he needed the complete cooperation of the local police.

His friend in Cyprus was dead—but he did have a friend in Greece.

30

DRUNK, ON DRUGS, AND DANCING

Off the coast of Cyprus

Even in his mid-seventies, Yannis Taskas was a large man in stature, personality, opinion, thirst for red wine, and appetite. He also was an expert craftsman in intelligence as a retired forty-year spy in the Greek National Intelligence Service, the Ethniki Ypiresia Pliroforion. Upon retirement, in the shadows of the Acropolis, he became an expert craftsman in his family's small jewelry shop tucked down one of the narrow streets in the Plaka neighborhood.

When he learned he was going to run an operation in Cyprus, Bridger immediately called his old friend.

Bridger liked Yannis, and Yannis felt the same about the young man. "You will make a great spy someday—like your mother," he would often prophesy when he left their apartment each night. Years later, one call to him that included the phrase "I need a favor" was enough.

"*Yassou*, hello to you, and you always need a favor. I am always glad to help my old friend. What can I do for you?" The voice was deep and sincere.

Bridger explained in general terms what he needed in Cyprus.

Specifics were not necessary or expected. Yannis knew better, and even if he asked, the answer would be silence. It was enough that they had trust and the knowledge they would assist each other without question.

Money was a different matter.

"It just so happens that I am distantly related through my blessed mother to many people, even in Cyprus—including the new Chief of the Cyprus Police. He is a third cousin, or fourth, I forget. Oh, and he is a *malaka*. Quite a *dick*, as you might say."

A loud snort resembling a laugh came through the phone. Bridger smiled on his end of the conversation. In the decades he had known Yannis, he ended up being related to just about everyone who had a drop of Greek blood in their veins.

"Can you make the call?"

"In the area of…compensation?" Yannis asked.

"Fifteen thousand dollars," Bridger offered.

"Thirty thousand," Yannis countered.

"Twenty-five," Bridger countered the counter. Yannis would have been offended if he didn't. Yannis was a former spy, but he was also a good businessman.

"You are a good friend, but cheap. I accept your meager offer."

They said farewell as the transaction was completed.

When Bridger, Demon, Snake, and Beast landed at Nicosia International Airport, Cristos Zacharias, the new Chief of the Cyprus Police, had a car waiting for them in a secure area away from the main passenger terminals.

"Hello, I am Chief of Police Cristos Zacharias," he said in lightly accented English. He bowed from the shoulders.

The clean-shaven man was wearing a neatly pressed official blue uniform and collar insignia of the police chief. Freshly cut black hair with gray temples sat under his saucer-shaped blue police chief hat. A row of service ribbons ran across his chest on the upper left side of his uniform. Shiny silver buttons ran along the front and on his sleeves.

Chief Zacharias listened carefully as Bridger explained what was needed.

"We shall go. All is ready. Yannis speaks highly of you. May we discuss my fee?" They settled on thirty-five thousand dollars. It was too much, but Bridger needed to pay for the Chief's immediate help, complete silence, and a down payment on a possible long-term relationship.

In the car, Zacharias explained to Bridger that Oleksandr Bondar was easy to find. He was a frequent visitor to the Guaba Beach Bar in Limassol. When they arrived at the location, Olek was right where the Chief of Police said he would be—in the bar, drunk, on drugs, and dancing. A few hours later, Olek led them straight to his boat.

"I want to talk to my father," Olek whimpered through the mask. "You don't know who you are dealing with." The hood was plastered to his head from his sweat. "He will send men to come here and chop you up and use your bones as firewood." He was shouting now.

Bridger walked over and lowered his mouth next to where Olek's left ear should be.

"Yes, Olek, I do know who I am dealing with," he whispered. Olek shot to his right, losing his orientation, which caused him to tip over onto the floor with a thud. Bridger stood. "I will share a secret with you. I actually know something about your father. I am not certain you want to call him. You might not like what you hear." Bridger stretched his arms over his head and arched his back.

"He will hunt you and kill you. He is my father." His comments lacked conviction. The puffing inside the hood grew quicker.

Bridger walked aft to the open glass doors that separated the enclosed lounge from the open-air sun deck. He took in a deep breath of the salty air. "I never was much for the sea, but this is relaxing."

"Go fuck yourself. When my father finds out—"

"There you go again with what your father will do to me," said Bridger, cutting him off. "I have an idea! Why don't we call him? What do you say? The Wi-Fi booster signal is great. It is picking up the coastal network surprisingly well. Where is your phone?"

Oleksandr's hooded head was still and signaled to Bridger the puzzled feeling of a child who unexpectedly got exactly what he asked for.

Bridger pulled an iPhone from his pocket. "Could this be it? You should use a passcode. Let me look at your contact list. Ah, I see one here that says *FATHER*. I will assume this is it."

He held down a number releasing the electronic speed dial beep. He pushed the speaker button, leaned forward, and placed it between the debris on the coffee table.

"It is on speaker. Oh, I speak Ukrainian—*chudovo*—perfectly. So, if you are thinking about saying something inappropriate, don't."

Demon grunted in response.

Clicks and ringing came from the phone. After a few seconds, a sleepy voice answered. It was also just after 1 a.m. in Kyiv.

"Who is this?" said a muffled, sleepy voice.

"Father! It is Oleksandr."

"What?"

"It's Oleksandr. I—I am in trouble."

There was an uncomfortable pause. Then the voice continued—its words spoken methodically. "You are in trouble? You are always in trouble. Or drunk. Or on drugs."

"Father!" Oleksandr pleaded in a shocked voice.

"You will have to deal with whatever it is. I am going back to sleep."

"There are men. They have come aboard the boat and taken me hostage."

"Boat? You have a boat?"

"I...well...I," Olek knew he had made a mistake mentioning the boat.

"What do they want?"

"I am not sure. They want to talk to me."

"So, you called me to tell me you are talking to some men?

"Yes, but—"

"No more money. And don't go crying to Ira. She isn't your mother. Don't call me again until you become a man."

There was a click, then a double peep, and then silence. Oleksandr sat motionless. Slowly, his hood sunk to rest on his chest. Bridger heard a slight sniffle, then he saw Oleksandr's shoulders start to quiver.

Bridger walked over, sat on the couch's arm, rested his hands on his thighs, and leaned toward the boy.

"Do you want to talk now?"

The hood nodded. The sound of sobbing came through the hood. His shoulders were bent over and shaking.

Bridger circled back to the food, picked up an olive, and popped it in his mouth. "I want to know everything," he said, a look of satisfaction on his face. "Right. Now."

Sitting in the safe house apartment on Baseinaya Street located in the center of Kyiv, Milton powered off his phone and disconnected it from his laptop. Beatrice filled three glasses with a few inches of red wine.

Exhaling a deep breath, Milton took a glass and sat back against the fake leather couch.

"What's the matter, Milton?" Imp asked with weary sarcasm. He also took a glass. "It worked just like I said it would."

"Like *I* said it would," Milton replied.

"It went very well. You both did well," Beatrice spoke up, acting as mediator.

"It did, didn't it?" Milton reached for the bottle and poured the remainder of the wine into the empty glass. "It worked perfectly. That kid is crapping his pants now that daddy has rejected him."

Under the auspices of a software engineering company owned and operated within the Spy Devils' cover network, Milton worked with third-party tech vendors to develop an artificial intelligence program that could learn any voice and mimic it perfectly in seconds. Milton inputted into software algorithms videos of dozens of Viktor Bondar's Ukrainian and English language interviews, speeches, and sound bites. The computer program analyzed his speech for idiosyncrasies, pronunciation, phonations, articulation, or any other characteristics of the spoken word.

When Bridger called from Olek's boat, Milton spoke Bondar's fake responses into the computer. The program immediately created near-perfect sentences in Bondar's voice.

"It helps that the idiot on the other end of the conversation is, well, an idiot. If he wasn't, we wouldn't be here. He is crying like a baby," Imp said, sitting back and resting his feet on the coffee table. "Now, quiet, we have to listen to this."

31

SHARKS IN THE MED

Off the coast of Cyprus

On the yacht, a devastated Oleksandr sat on the couch. His bound hands still made sitting awkward. Muffled short breaths escaped as he swayed his stooped shoulders a few inches to the left, then back to the right. Bridger sat to his right with his hand resting on the shaking shoulder.

"Olek. Now is the right time to start talking. I will listen."

When Oleksandr finally spoke, he explained the boat was purchased with Kirkwood monies. He provided the name of Theo Giannokis as the family banker in Cyprus. He explained that the Bondar family owned the bank to hide any business transactions his father wanted hidden.

"This is all very interesting, Olek, but it isn't near enough," Bridger said scornfully.

Bridger knew that his Kyiv-based team would be listening through a secure audio channel Bridger had opened using the ship's Wi-Fi. In less than fifteen seconds, a "got him" squawked through his secure communications earpiece. Olek was telling the truth.

"I need you to tell me the connection between Theo and his main counterpart in Kyiv. Second, as I said earlier, I need to find this case. Have you ever heard of Hillcrest?"

"No. I don't know anything about any of that," he said defiantly.

Oleksandr's defiant reply did not sit well with Bridger. Oleksandr was regaining his senses. He had stopped his swaying. His posture was more erect.

"Olek, how come I don't believe you? I think you know more than you are telling me."

"Talk to my sister, Ira. She knows everything. Ask her."

"Oh, I plan to. Right now, I am talking to you and trying hard to believe you. I am. But I don't."

"I don't care what you think. I have told you everything." His defiance was a mistake.

"This is bullshit. If he doesn't answer, I am going to toss him overboard," Demon said, still leaning on the wall directly across from Olek.

"Relax." Bridger looked over at Demon and gave him a nod. He turned back to Oleksandr.

"One more chance, Olek. Tell me about the banker, his contacts in Kyiv, and where the case is."

"You can go fuck your one more cha—"

Oleksandr did not have time to scream. Demon was on him in a blink. He picked Olek up and bounced him on the floor like a basketball with enough force to knock the air out of the young man's lungs. A few seconds later, Oleksandr felt the Mediterranean night air against his damp skin. Something was wrapped around his waist, and then, in a few more seconds, he was weightless.

In a hood, disoriented, and his hands still secured behind him, Olek tumbled like a coin tossed in a wishing well. He hit the water and began to sink.

Oleksandr gulped mouthfuls of the warm Mediterranean water, desperate for air. Water poured into his nostrils. The only sounds were the bubbling of the sea in his ears and the panicked choking of him drowning. Kicking his legs and thrashing his body in complete terror, he managed briefly to find the surface.

The hood stuck to his mouth and nose. He couldn't breathe.

Although he had only been in the water for five seconds, terror made it seem as though he was close to death.

Olek's body jerked like a fish on a hook. Then he realized he was being pulled through the water.

"Hey, are there sharks in the Med?" Demon asked, as he kept his finger on the switch that activated the electronic winch. It controlled a cable that ran from the yacht's side to a harness that he had secured around Oleksandr's body.

"I'm not sure. I didn't think about it. Maybe?" Bridger shrugged.

"I hope so," Demon said.

The sling dug deep into Olek's armpits as he slammed against the side of the boat and was dragged along the hull at the waterline. He clawed at the slick hull with his feet, hoping to catch something to get back on the yacht.

Demon released the switch, stopping the rope with a sudden jerk. Oleksandr hung suspended just overboard of the rear sun deck, shivering with terror, like a fresh catch on a sportfishing boat. His shorts were lost in the darkness of the Med. His linen white shirt was ripped open and sticking to his skin.

Olek's momentum caused him to swing out from the hull and slam back against the side with a thump and a groan.

"So, where were we?" Bridger yelled over the side at the kid.

Oleg looked pathetic. Blood was flowing over his shoulders from cuts somewhere under the hood.

"I—I—" Oleksandr stammered through chattering teeth.

"Drop him," Bridger ordered.

"No!" he screamed.

"What is the name of the person in Ukraine? How do we contact him? Where is Hillcrest?" Bridger waited. "I guess you enjoyed your drop into the water. Fine."

Bridger looked at Demon and made a motion for him to activate the winch. As Demon moved his hand, he was interrupted by screams.

"Don't. Don't. Don't!" Olek screamed. Then he whimpered through his hood. "Please?"

"Either tell me, or you'd better grow some gills because I'm cutting the cable."

"Pav-lo! His name is Pavlo! In Kyiv! In the basement of the bank. He is Ira's person. That is all I know. I swear. The banker—the banker will know everything. Believe me. PLEASE!" With each pleading word, his head ricocheted off the rocking hull.

"I believe you now, Oleksandr," Bridger said loud enough so Olek could hear him over the rushing water.

"Tha-nk...you." Oleksandr's sporadic sounds were barely audible as he lowered his head in relief.

"Lucky for you, I also believe in catch and release."

"What?" Olek screamed.

Demon reached into his pocket, pulled out a knife, flipped open the blade, and started cutting the tape binding Olek's wrists. Bridger pulled the ring that inflated a fluorescent orange flotation tube around Olek's waist and hit the cable release. Olek's shrill scream turned to a gurgle when he hit the water. Bridger saw the safety tube's reflection in the glow of the aft lights, then Olek disappeared as the boat crawled away.

With a last look in Olek's general direction, Bridger picked a radio out of his cargo pants pocket and keyed the talk switch.

"All yours," he announced.

He replaced the radio, then flipped open a box on the wall between the sundeck and lounge. He reached in and put an on-board phone to his ear. "Captain Andre? Yes. You can return to the marina. Thank you."

The engines increased power. The bow of the yacht turned to point in the direction of the lights of Cyprus.

Behind the yacht, another set of engines roared from the darkness. An oval circle of light hit the surface of the sea, swinging back and forth in quick searching arcs until it found an inflated orange tube supporting a hooded head.

"Help! Help!" The weak voice pleaded against the sound of the engines.

The grey SAB-12 Class patrol boat, marked by the blue-and-white sign identifying it as Marine Police, followed the beam and maneuvered near the floating man. Beast, dressed in a police uniform, extended a hook, caught Olek under the armpits, and hauled him up onto the deck like a tuna. His skin was pale, and he shook uncontrollably.

Beast untied the mask and yanked it off. Olek vomited water, dinner, and drugs across the deck. He wretched and gasped, then vomited again. This repeated three more times until he was empty.

"Greetings, my friend. I am Chief of Police Cristos Zacharias, and you are under arrest for possession of narcotics," he said politely, as he steadied himself in the swaying boat. "You will be pleased to know you will be spending much time as a guest of the people of Limassol in our modern facilities."

The boat turned and followed the distant lights of a yacht that was cutting through the water in the direction of the marina's lights—in the direction of Bridger's next victim.

32

100% SILK PAJAMAS

Nicosia, Cyprus

He felt the playful tug on his ear. He wiggled a little and sighed.

"Go to sleep, Spiros. Tomorrow is a busy day," Theo said, just above a whisper as he rolled over, his eyes still closed. The sensation of the silk pajamas sliding on his skin made him sigh another contented breath.

Another tug on the ear. This time a little firmer.

"Ouch. Spiros, that hurt. Stop it!" he said, this time swatting at his ear. As he did, a hand clamped his wrist and twisted it just enough to stop his arm in mid-air like a petrified flamenco dancer.

"Ouch! What are you doing?"

Theo opened his eyes, expecting to see Spiros' tussled blonde hair, Mediterranean suntanned skin, and blue eyes. Instead, his arm was frozen in place by the gloved tentacles of a monster dressed in black. A cap on his head, tinted glasses, and a dark cloth over the lower part of his face. In his other hand was something that, in the moonlit room, looked like a club.

Theo gasped in panic.

He saw Spiros sitting up on the other side of the king-sized bed, terror in his wide eyes. Theo looked at a black menace holding his lover by his silky curls with one gloved hand while the other was pressed against his smooth bare chest.

"Take what you want. Leave us alone."

"Mr. Giannokis. Theo. May I call you Theo? I am so sorry to wake you," said the American-accented demon whose death grip sent lightning bolts of pain through the soft tissues of the banker's arm.

He tried to break free of the grip, but the fingers held tight onto his wrist. He was sure the bones would break if this monster closed his claw. He whimpered in pain.

"Does this hurt? Let's make a deal. I will let go of you if you promise to sit still and listen to my proposition. Agreed?"

"Who are you? What–" Theo felt his wrist turn, forcing his elbow and shoulder into a position like a broken chicken wing.

"Let's try this again because I think you might not be all the way awake yet, and I don't want there to be any miscommunication. I am sure in your banking business, clarity plays a tremendous part in a successful transaction. So, let's aim for clarity, shall we? Should we ask your friend here? Spiros. What do you say?" Bridger looked at Spiros. "Think Theo should listen?"

Spiros was shaking like a bowl of pudding. Demon, dressed in black like Bridger, pulled Spiros' hair and, as he started to scream, his other hand clapped over his mouth and nose, cutting off the shrieking completely. His face started to go beet red.

"Stop. Stop!" Theo begged. "I understand."

With a nod from Bridger, Demon took his gloved hand off the skinny man's face, who immediately sucked air through his nose and mouth. Bridger let go of Theo's arm, who rubbed and shook his fat flipper as if to make sure it was still attached.

"So, we have a deal?" Bridger waited until the man nodded. "Good news for all." Bridger reached down and rubbed the bright floral-patterned material of the man's pajamas between his gloved fingers.

"These are nice pajamas. Italian?" The man nodded. "100% silk?" A few more quizzical nods. Bridger looked at the large "G" ornately embroidered in white thread on the pocket. "And a stylish monogram. Nice. I'm more of a sleep in the buff kind of guy. Occasionally gym shorts and the odd shirt, but if I was into pajamas, by golly, I am going to have to get the name of your tailor."

"What—what do you want?" Theo asked, bewildered on how to react to the man who had invaded his house.

Bridger inspected the pajamas once more.

"I'm sorry. That's fair. I wake you up from a good night's slumber, and I have not explained why. My mistake," Bridger said with a realistic amount of sincerity in his voice. "Down to business. I want all the information on the holdings of the bank of the Viktor Bondar estate. Account numbers. Bank statements." Bridger said as he stuck a finger in his ear, cocked his head. "Hold on." He concentrated on listening to the voice on the other end. "Yes, sorry, thanks, almost forgot. My associate says we need IP addresses, routing numbers, server locations. All that techie stuff."

Bridger waved his hand in the direction of the door, signaling Theo to move.

"I can't do that. The Bondars own this bank."

"Oh, Theo, we both know you can. You have the reputation of a quite capable financial mastermind. Let's give it a try, shall we?" Bridger gestured again.

Imp's quick research had revealed that Theo Giannokis, President, Private Credit Bank of Cyprus, was more capable than most and less scrupulous than the rest of the Cypriot financial community. His knowledge of the banking system's mechanism and, more importantly, ways to avoid any pesky regulations in the system, made him quite popular among the Russians, Ukrainians, and other groups partial to using Cyprus for illegal transactions.

The Bondars acquired the pieces of the shattered Cyprus bank in the fire sale aftermath of the European debt crisis. With the collapse of the Cyprus banking sector, the Bank of Cyprus was more than happy to sell off the "bad" asset. This coincided with the revelations of Cyprus' role in the money laundering of Russian and other international assets, forcing a series of new laws to combat the issue. The bank was poison.

Through "loans" secretly channeled from their Ukraine Standard Bank system, Bondar brought in the capital, deleveraged and disposed of non-core assets, and turned the bank into a functioning financial institution. The re-branded Private Credit Bank of Cyprus rose from the ashes.

It was the Bondars' private, secure, money laundering black hole.

"Viktor Bondar—" Theo said again.

"Yes, I know it is Bondar's bank," Bridger said, as if everyone already knew the secret. "Oleksandr Bondar told us. Quite a nice young man, once you wash away the disagreeable outer layers of an obnoxious spoiled brat."

"Mr. Oleksandr Bondar? You spoke with him?" Theo looked up at Bridger's covered face.

Bridger looked at Demon, who immediately grabbed Spiros by the back of his bare neck, pulled the naked man halfway out of bed with one arm, made a fist, and cocked his arm, ready to punch him.

"Should we make Spiros less pretty? That would be a shame."

"No, don't," Theo screamed.

"Then you need to pick between Spiros or Bondar. Now! Five. Four. Three—"

Sweat rolled down Theo's pudgy face, making wet spots on his pajamas.

"Spiros! Yes, Spiros. Stop!" Theo shouted.

"Son of a bitch!" Demon growled with a mix of frustration and disappointment. He dropped Spiros on the bed like a rock.

"Good choice. You don't want to upset him," Bridger said, looking from Theo to Spiros to Demon. "Let's go."

Theo got out of bed one leg at a time, adjusted his floral pajamas, glided his feet into slippers, and walked out of the room into the dark. Bridger followed.

"Get up!" Demon commanded. Spiros stood immediately. Naked. "Ah, Jesus. Cover up, will you? I don't want to see that. No one should." Spiros put on a silk thigh-length robe—decorated with multi-colored seashells—and tied it around his waist. Demon grabbed Spiros by the ear and twisted it like a parent scolding an unruly child. "Move it, or I will snap you."

The banker lived in a two-story villa in the Souni district of Limassol. In the dark, the moonlight detailed an interior of modern European designs and furnishings. They walked single file on the cold wood floors down the stairs and into a large living room. Theo's slippers flapped on the hardwood floor, sending *thwap* sounds echoing off the walls.

"This is a nice place. You are doing well, Theo."

Bridger and Theo walked to a cherry wood desk supported by thin aluminum tube legs. On the desk was a computer. Picture windows ran across one entire wall, providing a night view of the mountains and the sea. Around a glass table in the center of the room were a couch and two lounge chairs. Modern paintings of random circles and broad dark lines hung on the walls.

Demon tugged Spiros' now purple ear and pointed him to the couch. Spiros understood the command and obeyed immediately.

"Let's get this done," Bridger said.

He was standing over Theo, who sat at his computer now. From the glowing screen, he could see Theo's pink fleshy hands were shaking over the keyboard.

"Please wait, I have to—"

Without warning, Bridger touched the Devil Stick on the silk between Theo's shoulder blades. The shock forced the banker to squeal like a castrated pig. When he tried to stand, Bridger put his palm on the top of Theo's head and guided him back to the chair.

"Sorry about that. I really am. But come on, *that* was nothing—the lowest setting. A mosquito bite is more painful. I can make it much worse." He paused for effect. "Now, take a deep breath and get started." He leaned down and whispered in Theo's ear. "If not, I will have my friend beat Spiro's gorgeous face as raw as tartare—in about ten seconds."

Theo instantly started clicking the mouse.

"I am in the system. All the files are here. Not everything, but most are all right here," he panted after a few seconds, as he pointed to the glowing screen.

Bridger handed a USB stick to Theo. "Copy all of them and write down your passwords and access information. Open a document. I want to see it." Bridger took a picture of the screen with his phone. "Go on, finish."

Bone tired, Bridger turned and looked out the window. The slightest sliver of light was visible on the far horizon. Then he turned, checked out Theo's progress, walked to the couch, and sat down next to Spiros. Demon rotated his position and stood by the banker, who was still tapping furiously on the keyboard.

Bridger crossed his legs, put the Stick across his lap, and put his arm on the back of the couch, resting it behind Spiros' head. Bridger tapped the frightened man on the knee. With a squeal, he jerked away with Bridger's touch. Theo's head twisted in the direction of the noise. The pace of the clicking increased.

"Spiros. What I know about computers and software you could fit inside a golf ball. Hacking into this system would have taken way too much time. But I do know about people. Do you like computers?"

Confused, Spiros mumbled in a tenor voice, "Yes, I do."

"People are a weak link, Spiros. People don't have security software or applications, and if they *are* weak, you can't upload a software patch. You can't fix people." Bridger stood and walked back to Theo and put his hand on his shoulder. The banker flinched. "So, Theo is the malware in the system they not only can't fix, they don't even see."

"Let's delete them when we are done," Demon said.

Theo stopped typing and looked over his shoulder at Bridger.

"No. I said we would not harm you." Bridger pointed a finger at Demon that read, *shut your mouth.* "Theo, do you have anything to eat? I am *starving*." Bridger asked.

"What? No."

"Beast is here," Demon said, his hand at his ear.

The front door opened, and Beast walked in, no longer dressed as a Cypriot police officer, but with his face covered in a mask and glasses like his fellow Spy Devils.

"How's our baby?" Bridger asked.

"Wet and babbling like a baby in the basement of the police station," Beast said. "You guys really messed him up."

"He deserved it."

"Anything to eat here? I'm starving." Beast looked around the room, then moved toward what he figured was a kitchen.

"If you find anything, bring me some," Bridger said.

"I am done." Theo let out a sigh as he sat back in his chair. He looked from Bridger to Spiros.

"Excellent." Bridger took the USB drive from Theo and handed him another. "We are almost done. Who is Pavlo?"

"How do you know of Pavlo? I mean, I—" It was too late, he'd already messed up, and he knew it. Bridger knew it too. He looked at Theo with a smile.

"Now, Theo. Please," Bridger started to point at Demon, who rose in anticipation until Theo interrupted.

"No, wait! Yes, I know of Pavlo. He is my contact in Kyiv for all Bondar transactions, but I have never met him! Only emails. Not even on the phone. He is a stranger. I can't help you. That is all I know."

"This is where you are wrong, Theo, my friend." He slapped his hand down on Theo's silk pajama-covered shoulders and squeezed his neck. Theo cringed.

"I want to know everything you know about Pavlo. Every. Little. Thing." Bridger's hand grew tighter with each word.

Bridger looked out the window. The thin line of light had grown broader and brighter over the eastern Mediterranean. He looked at his watch, his other hand still firmly attached to Theo's soft neck.

"Then I need you to send him an email, with the document on that USB attached. And after that, I promise I will not ask you another favor." His fingers dug further into Theo's neck. His shoulders curled to get away from the pain. He maxed out his grip in the soft flesh, then let go. Theo sighed with relief.

One minute later, the message was sent.

"Excellent, Theo! I do have to admit. I lied. I have one more favor to ask of you. I think this would be a wonderful time for you and

Spiros to take a vacation for two weeks. No, make that a month. Start-ing," Bridger looked at his watch, "right now."

"But I—"

Instantly, there was the sound of fist meeting flesh and a high-pitched scream. Theo turned to see Spiros on his knees with his hands covering his face, spouting blood through his fingers onto the carpet. His screams were matched by Theo, who tried to get out of his chair to attend to his companion. A hand on the silk pajamas stopped him.

"The-o?" Bridger said with a malevolent smile.

"We will leave today!" the banker said.

At 5. a.m., on the drive to the airport, Bridger sent a Signal secure email with the attachment of the document picture to Peter.

"Some ammo for the bosses. Prepare to come to Kyiv. I will send the details. It is time for the barbarians to storm the gate."

He hit send.

"You are on your own from now on," Bridger said to Beast, who, as usual, was driving.

"Yep. I have my flight and hotel reservation."

"Okay. The rest are in the Baseinaya Street safe house. We will be at the other site. You know to keep away. Contact the Olegs and spin up the logistics for the remote location. Then you are on your own for the surveillance."

"No worries."

But Bridger was worried. They were moving fast, without his typical preparation and control of the variables. He didn't like it, but his choices were limited.

"Keep your head down and send me your updates as usual."

"Okay, mommy," Beast answered.

Then three electronic beeps from his phone filled the car. He knew May had sent a text message. Bridger didn't want to, but he checked it anyway.

Status?

He didn't answer.

Then more beeps and a text.

Status?

Bridger turned his phone off and closed his eyes.

He wasn't in the mood to be nagged. He was in the mood to raise some hell.

33

PLAUSIBLE DENIABILITY

Great Falls, Virginia

"He isn't answering," May said, tossing the phone on the end table next to her couch. She picked up her half-empty second glass of wine and took a sip.

She looked around the library of her home outside Washington, D.C., along the Potomac River. She loved the beautiful view through bullet-proof glass. There was no place else she needed to be. She could do all her work from this room. She had secure communications to the Agency and a security detail patrolling the perimeter of the grounds.

"Are you surprised?" Danforth Chapel replied from the guest chair on the other side of a solid oak coffee table.

"I think he could give me the courtesy of an update. I am his boss."

"I am not sure Bridger sees it that way all the time. I think he sees you mostly as the interfering elderly mother."

Her eyes narrowed with real anger.

Call her a *senior,* and she would retort with the cliché, '*you are only as old as feel.*' Call her *elderly,* and only self-control would keep her from playing darts with her perfectly manicured and razor-sharp fingernails into the unsuspecting offender's eyes.

"Shut up, Danny."

"It is just an observation, May."

"If you think that—then leave." Her voice was ice cold.

"No, I—"

"Shut up, Danny."

She was looking over Chapel's shoulder at her signed Norman Rockwell lithograph collection.

May loved Norman Rockwell. He was a New Englander, like May. She appreciated the irony that she had sacrificed her life and her family to protect ideals and people represented in his paintings. Plus, her father liked Rockwell. The memories of being with her father appreciating the covers of *The Saturday Evening Post* when she was younger were vivid and comforting. She found she needed comforting more often as she got older.

Her eyes focused back on Chapel when he subconsciously ran his hands over his trademark bright tie.

"Where are we with Kirkwood?" she said, glancing back at the wall.

"Mr. Schaeffer is proving to be quite adept at collecting information. He has obtained some materials that, if analyzed correctly, could prove embarrassing to our friends at Kirkwood." He ran his fingertips along the outside edge of his glass.

"It was Kirkwood who wanted to have one of their people involved for some crazy notion of plausible deniability—god, I hate that Cold War phrase," she said. "Does anyone know how hard it is to create an operational plan that is successful at *plausible deniability*? They are reading and watching too much espionage fiction crap. It takes planning and experience. Not an MBA."

"I have an MBA," Chapel said in an expressionless voice.

"You are proving my point."

"You are one of a kind, May. A sexy, cold-hearted—*aging*—spy."

She curled her fingers tight around her wine glass.

"Kirkwood wants Schaeffer to be the *plausible deniability* fallback —if needed?" she asked.

"Yes, and that is in motion, if needed. I am leaving in the morning to meet them for a meeting to discuss that very topic."

"Focus. Everything has to come together, and soon."

"It will."

She turned her body on the couch to look at the darkness of the outside world. The room was night-time quiet. The sounds of the outside filled the inside. The wind rushing through the trees. The faint sound of water in the distance. The occasional cricket.

"Are you sure you want to do this?" Chapel said, his voice breaking the silence with a layer of compassion.

"What?"

"You know what. You have a tactical weapon that you use as an instrument to execute on broad, long-term, strategic initiatives that may come in conflict with another strategic, operational consideration. Bridger, as you know, can be unpredictable and—" he pointed to her phone on the nightstand "—as he just showed, disobedient. He can cause this all to come tumbling down, and that will not benefit either of us."

"You are thinking too much like a strategic consultant. Bridger will do the right thing. I programmed him that way."

"Maybe, but there is a cost. Bridger is a wild card. I said that when you decided to bring him into this." Chapel caught a glimpse of himself reflected in the window behind May. He ran his fingers through his hair like a comb. "You don't have complete control of this anymore. Things are moving and you can't guarantee he will move in the direction you want."

"Shut up, Danny, and I *can* guarantee things will move in the right direction. I am his mother."

She picked up her phone and sent another text to Bridger.

It went unanswered.

34

THE BANK OF VIKTOR BONDAR

Kyiv, Ukraine

Two murmuring women passed by, shaking their scarf-covered heads, as Li Chu examined the burn spots on the road. The spots looked like two massive birthmarks on the skin of the street.

Two days earlier, Li Chu, under the alias Yi Wang, a journalist for the Xinhua News Agency, checked into the Dnipro Hotel—a middle-of-the-pack, older hotel where a traveling Chinese businessman could reside without suspicion. Li Chu had never been to Kyiv, and his first impression was he hated it. It was old. Dim. Brown. Gray. Cramped. There may be a nightlife, he had read about it on Travelocity, but he wouldn't see it.

He was not there for that. He had one purpose in mind.

"There is a package for you, Mr. Wang," the Dnipro Hotel front desk manager said.

Li Chu did not open the DHL envelope until he arrived in his room. Inside was a note from Chen:

. . .

Here are safe house locations, where you may find weapons, comput-ers, maps, money, and cars. Also, the most recent intelligence on the situation. Attached is the list of names and contacts of your new team. You are reminded that you must avoid contact with anyone in the Chinese delegation in the country.

The package contained limited intelligence—a few news articles about the American's death had been translated into Mandarin. There was a brief MSS assessment of an oligarch named Viktor Bondar. There were a bio and photo of his daughter Ira, who helped run his empire. A shorter biography of his less accomplished son Oleksandr. There was a cryptic reference to a secret employee named Pavlo, a technical person, who might know about the device.

In a few hours, Li Chu planned to leave the hotel and check into another, where Chen could not locate him. He would visit a safe house and take the weapons, communication equipment, clothes, and any other gear he would need. Li Chu would trash his phone and spend the day collecting a bag of burner phones. When he rendezvoused with the new team—men he didn't know, or care to know—he would pass them the phones, weapons, and his instructions.

Do what I say. Do it correctly. Do not talk to Chen.

Chen was not the reason he had agreed to travel to the depressing browns and grays of Ukraine. It wasn't for some mystery case. It wasn't for the corrupt Standing Committee. It certainly wasn't for China.

Li Chu was there to kill Bridger.

Li Chu tossed the file on his bed. He reached unconsciously to his right hip looking for a weapon that was not there. He would get it tomorrow when he visited the safe house for supplies.

He rarely wasted his time watching television, but at the moment, he felt he needed a distraction. The set was modern—a mid-sized Japanese flat screen—and it worked.

Li Chu instantly recognized the female's face. He grabbed the folder to confirm it. Ira Bondar. She was talking in a steady, forceful voice to another woman who was asking her questions.

He did not speak Ukrainian, but he liked what he saw—willpower and determination in her face and mannerisms. The characteristics of a person who got what she wanted. He knew what they looked like. He saw the same traits every time he looked into a mirror.

Now he knew for certain his path to completing the mission. It ran right through Ira Bondar.

The TV program looked like it was being broadcast live—or he hoped it was. He copied down the channel and network name and rushed to a taxi stand outside the hotel. It was a dreary night, but he didn't notice.

He communicated in broken English with the driver on where he wanted to go. When the taxi arrived outside the broadcast studios of 1+1 TV Channel ten minutes later, Li Chu stayed in the car watching the building's front entrance. To his annoyance, the driver liked to make small talk.

The weather is normal for this time of year. 1+1 was very popular. The Television Service of News program was on now. He had to drive to feed his wife and six children.

Li Chu let the driver rattle on as he scanned the darkened streets, hoping he was lucky and that she would come out this door. He was lucky. She came out forty minutes later. A car pulled up. She got in the back.

"Follow them," he told his chatty driver.

The driver was good at his craft, Li Chu observed, as the man weaved in and out of Kyiv traffic to keep sight of the car. The driver assumed the role of a tour guide as he announced the history of the areas as they passed. *"That is from the time of Stalin. That too."*

"We are heading toward the stadiums," he said as the car ahead of them turned down a street, then quickly turned left down an alley. "I cannot go there. This is private property. Bank property. Dangerous bank."

"Dangerous bank?"

"The bank of Viktor Bondar."

The bank was a four-story white and glass structure of a more modern design than the rest of the office and residential buildings on Dilova Street.

Li Chu motioned for the driver to pull over. He drove a block past the bank and pulled the car to the side of the narrow street.

"Stay, I will be back." He started to get out.

"Do not go," the taxi driver warned, pointing to the bank. Li Chu closed the door behind him.

He walked along the sidewalk opposite the bank, keeping in the shadows. He went to the corner, crossed the street, and walked back toward the bank, which was now ahead and on his left. His pace slowed as he reached an open courtyard with a big tree in front of the bank's entrance.

As he approached, two dark figures, each the size of his taxi, came out of the shadows to make their presence known. In the dim area, Li Chu could see the weapons slung over their broad shoulders. He walked on, making a note of the small hotel, storefronts, and offices nearby.

In a few moments, he was safely inside his taxi. His plan was complete. Watch the bank. Follow Ira. Identify Pavlo. Wait for Bridger to do the same, as he knew he would.

Then I will take the case. And then I will kill the devil.

If Li Chu could have gone inside, he would have seen Ira enter the residence apartments that constituted the top floors of the imposing brick building behind and adjacent to the bank. He would have heard a brief conversation with her father.

"Your interview was a disappointment. You made us look weak," Bondar slurred his words as he sat in the low light of his private office.

"I am sorry you thought that. I think it went well." She saw a mostly empty bottle of vodka on a table within his reach.

"I want the case." His fists pounded on his desk. He tried to stand, but the alcohol wouldn't let him.

"Pavlo is still working on it."

His hands waved in the air like he was swatting flies.

"I don't care. I am calling Chen. The case will—we will get more business with them—fucking Kirkwood."

"We discussed this. We should—"

"I want it. Two days. You have *two* days." His fist slammed the top of his desk, causing the near-empty bottle of vodka to spill over. He ignored it.

"You are drinking too much. Get some sleep, father."

His rage vanished as quickly as it had arrived. He sat in his chair with half-opened eyes.

She shook her head as she walked across the office, opened the huge wooden doors, and left.

Her father was changing for the worse. He was not managing the businesses as he had in the past—the debacle like the one that just happened in Serbia would never have happened. They were losing deals and being pushed around by the Chinese.

And he killed Uncle Anton.

She took an elevator down to the lowest floors, then walked through a long white hallway lit with bright safety lights every twenty feet. She punched codes into electronic locks on several doors and stepped into the subfloors of the bank.

"Ms. Ira," Pavlo spurted out with surprise and pleasure when he opened his door.

"I was not sure you would be here, being that it is so late," she said as she walked into Pavlo's basement hideaway. She knew he would be there. "I believe you have an apartment?"

"Yes. Yes, I do! Nearby." He was thrilled she knew about that. "But I have work to do on your case. I have been working on it, as you asked. I did stop to watch you tonight. On TNS. You were *very* wonderful. It was obvious they are envious of you."

"Thank you, Pavlo. You are most kind," she said with a certain amount of sincerity.

She had agreed to appear on the popular evening news program to show that the Bondar family, and herself in particular, would not hide or be harassed into seclusion. She had become the face of the Bondar empire, so appearing on the most popular news program, and answering tough questions, served a purpose.

But Pavlo was wrong. They were not envious of her. They feared her.

The next day, she was confident the press would describe her as beautiful, poised, knowledgeable, and ruthless. People on the street would call her a "kholodna suka," *a cold bitch,* and other less flattering insults. She was pleased that they would all be correct.

A beeping sound came from one of Pavlo's computers on the desk behind him. He scampered over and sat. After a few pecks at the keyboard and glances up and down from the screen to his fingers, he turned to Ira with a smile.

"I have found him! I have found Mr. Oleksandr."

35

TASTE OF BLOOD

Kirkwood Headquarters

P*repare to come to Kyiv.*
As Peter Schaeffer slowly ascended the stairs to the 10th floor of Kirkwood headquarters, he wondered what he should think, if anything, about the messages from Bridger.

Was Bridger getting close to finding the case?

Earlier that morning, he called MacBride to update him and get the approval to travel to Kyiv. Before he could call, his phone rang. It was Marilyn, MacBride's administrative assistant. Peter was needed in a meeting on the 10th floor at 10 a.m.

Last time I heard that was when this whole mess started. But this time, I know more, a lot more.

Jessup and MacBride were standing outside Jessup's office when Peter opened the stairway door and entered onto the 10th floor. He saw Danforth Chapel shaking hands with two Asian men. As usual, Benton sat in a chair in the waiting area outside the office. Peter stopped several feet away and waited. They locked eyes.

"Hey Benton, sorry. I don't have any donuts on me," Peter said, making sure his mockery was unmistakable.

"Thank you, gentlemen. We will be in contact with Mourning Dove shortly." Jessup escorted them to the elevator.

Benton opened his mouth to reply, but he was cut off.

"Come in, Peter." MacBride motioned him inside Jessup's office. Peter grinned and gave Benton an exaggerated wink as he walked. Peter heard a growl as the door closed behind him.

The men were already on the couch in Jessup's sitting area.

"Peter, sit, please." Jessup pointed to a chair across from the couch. "We are all eager to know about your progress."

Peter cleared his throat.

"Well, we *have* made progress." Peter felt their reactions. Mostly doubt. "The money was siphoned through a bank in Cyprus. We are working on getting the data."

The men all looked at each other.

"That is amazing, Peter, just amazing," MacBride said with an expression that Peter could not decide was good or bad.

"Well done, Peter, but I am a little skeptical." Chapel's voice was friendly with a hint of condescending.

Peter pulled a sheet of paper out of his pocket—a printout of the screenshot Bridger sent the night before.

"Here is a partial screenshot of a spreadsheet." He handed it to Jessup, who looked at it, then passed to MacBride, then Chapel, who studied it carefully.

"This is fabulous, Peter." Chapel folded the paper and gently placed it in his suit pocket.

"What about the case? The case was a priority, too." Jessup sounded like the case was an afterthought, not the main target of the operation. Peter was beginning to know better.

Peter flicked his eyebrows up in excitement. He knew he had to keep the Spy Devils out of the conversation. He leaned forward, rested his elbows on his knees, and flicked his eyebrows again.

"You mean Hillcrest?"

Peter's senses flared red from MacBride and Jessup's direction. MacBride swiveled to face Peter just a little too quickly. Then he looked at Jessup, who was absentmindedly picking at an invisible speck on the sleeve of his pristine white shirt. His eyes glanced up at Chapel.

"It is still in Kyiv as far as we can tell," Peter answered.

"Can you provide some insight?" Jessup asked with his best reassuring lawyer voice.

"I'd rather not. I have some sources working now."

Peter looked at Chapel, who looked both amused and stoic.

"Gentlemen, Peter here is doing the right thing by protecting his sources and methods, as it is called. I can tell you they are highly trained in these types of situations. I trust them." Chapel smiled at Peter.

Peter was shocked by Chapel's comment. *How did he know about the Spy Devils? Bridger did say they knew each other. Are they working together?*

Jessup was in full lawyer mode as he stood like Atticus Finch in *To Kill a Mockingbird.* He looked at his Kirkwood colleagues. Then he turned to Peter.

"You have done an outstanding, miraculous job finding the funds *and* what appears to be the location of the case." Then his supportive tone went dead serious. "However, I think we should bring your efforts to an end."

Peter was stunned. He sat forward on the edge of his chair as if getting inches closer to the source would help him understand if he heard Jessup clearly.

"Why? Don't you want…the case…the money?" He had trouble putting his thoughts together. His hands were moving in circles in front of him.

"You are disappointed," continued Jessup, ignoring Peter's direct questions. "I can see the look of a hunter in your eyes, the taste of blood is in your mouth. You are close to the goal, but we just can't allow you to continue. Thank you again for all your hard work."

"I don't understand this. Can you explain why?" Peter said. He looked at MacBride, who quickly looked away toward Jessup.

"There is not much to explain. There are larger considerations that are best handled by Danny going forward. You can resume your normal duties," Jessup said.

"Larger considerations? What—"

"I think we might be too hasty here." All eyes turned to Chapel when he cut Peter off. "Perhaps we should allow Peter and…his *sources*…to continue."

"I don't think that is wise," Jessup said.

"We don't want him—it is too risky—like Walter said." MacBride was rotating a few inches left and right in his chair. His fingers tapped on the arms of the chair.

"I understand. To allay your fears, I volunteer to be on the ground in Kyiv and act as a sort of mentor, if needed. I would make sure nothing happens that could hurt Kirkwood. If they can retrieve the case, I could act as an intermediary and return it. You did ask for Peter's help in this for a *reason*."

Peter was waiting for someone to ask for his input, but they talked about what he could or could not do, like he was invisible. He was getting upset, and when his foot started to wiggle, he crossed one leg over the other and held it.

"True. But, are you sure, Danny?" Jessup looked at MacBride. "Can this be done without unintended consequences to the company?"

"No harm, right, Peter?" Chapel ran his hand down his tie.

"Of course not. That is the last thing I want to happen," Peter said, but he knew his face betrayed his confusion. Finding the case was all-important a few seconds ago, now he was being taken off the task.

"Okay, Danny. Peter, you may continue," Jessup announced.

They stood in unison. Dismayed, Peter shook their hands and left.

Peter was waiting outside for Chapel. "Thank you, Mr. Chapel. But I have to ask—"

"Call me Danny, remember?" he cut in. "Glad to help. This is important."

"What is their problem? The comment about harming the compa—"

"Forget them." He waved his hand like swatting away a fly. "What do you need?'

"I need to get to Kyiv."

"Then you can join me on my plane, as my guest."

The meeting stunned Peter, and he carried the feeling with him as he drove home.

He was zombie-driving—moving by habit with glazed eyes focused straight ahead. Because of that, he didn't notice the car that pulled out behind him when he left Kirkwood. He didn't check his mirrors to see if it was still there when he pulled off I-88 at the Naperville exit. He paid no attention when it parked on his street a block away.

An hour later, he didn't see it pull behind his Uber and follow him to O'Hare.

Peter had made several mistakes.

36

THUNDERLOVER

Kyiv, Ukraine

The pounding beat of the electro-dance music in Pavlo's ears wasn't as distracting as the tube-dressed blondes and brunettes shaking their way to any man who looked like he had money in his pocket. Clouds of perfume, hairspray, estrogen, and testosterone hung in the air. Like cats, they meowed their way along the crowded bar, lounges, and dance floor, looking for a treat.

"Buy me champagne. We need to have fun tonight. Drinks, and then you will take me to the private clubs," they purred through red, or aqua, or green painted lips. They wiggled and giggled their way up to one man after another, rubbing their skin-tight dress all over the leg a horny tourist—who didn't know what was happening—or a local—who was hoping something would.

Some were local girls legitimately out for a good time. Some were local girls legitimately looking for the drunken stooge to declare his love, marry her, and take her away to America, where she would leave him and start a new life. Most were 'house whores,' who were paid a few hryvnias for the number of champagne bottles they rung up on the guest's bar tab.

Pavlo was there for none of that. A year ago, a girl looked at him with what he thought was lust, only to find out she wanted him to move so she could get to the women's restroom. Tonight was different. Standing near the bar, he raised on his tiptoes trying in vain to look over the top of the hundreds of taller, gyrating people.

Pavlo had met her only two days ago during his regular nighttime troll through his array of X-rated web chat rooms, adult live porn sites, and dating and singles sites. Pavlo, AKA *Thunderlover*, was a premium member to them all. Thunderlover never paid or gave any sign-up information that could be stored in any centralized system. He just hacked into the sites and set up his own accounts.

Every night, either in his basement bunker or like tonight, from his own small apartment down the street from the bank, Pavlo would start his Thunderlover routine. First, he would rotate from one web chat site to another, looking for interesting conversations. At the dating sites, the pages were loaded with statuesque women in tight dresses, or less, bending into their idea of a seductive pose.

Around 3 a.m., he would log into the Ukraine singles sites. He liked the anonymity. He could have conversations without being seen. His fingers were Cyrano De Bergerac. The rest of him was a tree frog.

She popped up on Ukraine Omegle, saying she spoke German and English. The username, NEWGIRL, didn't provide much detail for Thunderlover to decide whether to click the connect button.

NEW: Hi. (smiley emoji)
TL: Hi.
NEW: I (Heart emoji) UR name!
TL: (astonished face emoji) THX. Made it up.
NEW: I (heart) it. I'm German. New in Kyiv. I don't speak Ukrainian—YET!
TL: I guessed that. LOL (laughing emoji). English is fine. (prayer hands)
NEW: R U in Kyiv?
TL: Yes. (thumbs up emoji) Born here (frowning emoji)
NEW: What do you do?

TL: (Computer emoji) U?
NEW: (Artist, palette paintbrush, framed picture emojis)
TL: (thumbs up)
NEW: ATM I'm looking for a job.
TL: Maybe I can help?
NEW: OMG that would be Gr8t. But I have to go. Talk L8R. (2 heart emojis)

Then she was gone. An apparition that Pavlo couldn't believe was real. She was talking to him! She wanted to talk to him again! He had no idea what she looked like, and he didn't care. He was sure she was different.

NEWGIRL.

It was such a beautiful name.

By mid-day, Pavlo dedicated one of his monitors exclusively to the chatroom—in case NEWGIRL logged in early. Every few seconds, for the next eight hours, he glanced at the screen. No NEWGIRL. The feeling of hope in his chest tensed like a kite string straining not to break. By 11 p.m., his hands shook so much with anxiety he had difficulty hitting the keyboard. By 1 a.m., the tears started to roll down his chubby cheeks.

At 1:35 a.m., his computer let out a ping. The quivers started in his hair, traveled through his body to his toes. Pavlo couldn't contain the tremors. His heart was beating faster when he saw the name *NEWGIRL* on the screen.

NEW: Uthere?
NEW: Hello?
NEW: (teary-eyed emoji)
TL: Yes!!!!
NEW: HI!! (two thumbs up emojis)
TL: I have been waiting for you. I was worried.
NEW: Busy day. (walking person emoji). Getting settled. Sore (feet emoji).
TL: Any luck?

NEW: Yes, slow. I could use some help! Show me the nightlife!
(beer, wine, martini, champagne bottle emojis)

During the next day, they typed progressively longer messages back and forth. The emojis became less frequent, except those that might coax an answer—prayer hands, winking yellow faces. Pavlo learned a lot.

NEWGIRL was in her mid-twenties and had moved a few weeks before from Berlin. NEWGIRL needed a new, fresh start after a bad relationship. She didn't want to talk about it, and he didn't ask. She was an artist. Oils and pencils.

She finally revealed that her name was Katinka, *"but my friends call me Tinka."* Her parents were from Finland. Her father was in sales *—computers, or something like that and always gone.* Her mother *was a bitch.* Tinka was an only child. Lonely.

He told her he was too. *Why did I say that?*

It wasn't all awkward. They shared jokes and their favorite things —Tinka liked chocolate. He said he liked it too, although that was a lie. Lots of LOLs and LMAOs. She turned her camera on without warning. There she was on his screen. A smile inside a perfect face. She was prettier than Ms. Ira.

Ms. Ira! I need to work on her case...later.

NEW: Well? Turn on UR (camera emoji)!

Pavlo closed his eyes, raised his hand over the key, and pushed. When he opened his eyes, she was still there.

She waved.

"Hello, Thunderlover," she said in a voice that sounded like vanilla.

He waved back.

Tinka's smile seemed even broader.

Her hair was a mixture of red, blonde, and brown, resembling the color of a country road. It hung into her turquoise eyes and down the sides of her round face to her shoulders. She wore a sheer white blouse that buttoned down the front with small shiny buttons. The outline of a black bra was barely visible. Pavlo could not help but look at her chest, where the button was open on the shirt at the convergence of her breasts. He could see the lace of the bra and a small red bow.

They kept talking until they agreed to meet at midnight at The Caribbean Club for drinks and dancing *and fun.*

She saw him in the crowded club before he saw her. There was a tug on the sleeve of his shirt, and he felt a peck on his cheek. He turned too defensively and pushed her without seeing who it was. Pavlo was terrified as he watched her fall back and bump into a group of people who yelled and pushed her back. He caught her.

She wore the same white blouse with shiny buttons. Below was a black thigh-length pleated skirt. Her hair was pulled back in a ponytail and alternated colors with the disco lights.

"I'm...I'm sorry. I should go," Pavlo spluttered, his words faltering as tears filled his eyes.

"Don't be silly!" Tinka grabbed him and gave him a bear hug. Her arms barely reaching halfway around his sweat-soaked midsection. "I am so happy to meet you."

In shock, Pavlo reached around and reciprocated with a hug of his own. He could feel the contours of her body against his. Her hair was in his face. She smelled like fresh rain.

After they separated, Pavlo bought beers. He hadn't had a beer in as long as he could remember. He didn't like the taste, but this evening, in the heat and noise of the nightclub, it was wonderful.

"I don't want any more beer," she screamed into his ear over the noise twenty minutes later. "This round is on me."

She headed off in the direction of the bar. When he lost sight of her in the crowd, he knew what was happening. Tinka was escaping him now that she saw him in person. The tears started to form in his eyes. He waited a few minutes, just in case. But when she didn't return, he turned toward the exit. He felt a tug on his arm.

"Try this!" Her smiling face was inches from his. She thrust a large glass filled with a clear liquid and lime into his hand. "A delicious drink. Vodka tonic! Drink. Drink!"

She used her beautiful hand to help him raise the glass. He took a few sips, then a few more. Tinka was right. The refreshing drink did feel good in the steaming dance club.

"Come on, Pavlo. Have some fun!" Tinka was smiling and laughing as she dragged him onto the dance floor.

He thought that maybe it was the constant strobing of the lights and booming of the dance music making him nauseous and drowsy.

"I am hot." Pavlo was rubbing his hand on his head.

She bit his earlobe, then screamed into Pavlo's ear.

"Me too. Let's go to my place."

"I…um…well," he mumbled in shock.

A light drizzle was falling when they stepped into the heavy 3 a.m. Kyiv air. A short walk through a courtyard brought them to Symona Petlyury Street. Pavlo staggered and grabbed Tinka to lean on her for support.

"It is a beautiful spring rain." She locked her arm around his and dragged him along the damp street. She guided him right, then left, then straight down the narrow Nazarivska Street. It ran along one side of the Botanical Gardens. The van was idling in the darkness down the block under the overhanging trees of the gardens.

She had to hurry. The Rohypnol she had dumped into his drink was close to taking full effect, and he was too fat and heavy for her to carry alone.

37

WHERE IS TINKA?

Kyiv, Ukraine

Pavlo was not sure if his memories were real or just drunken delusions.

He recalled rain. Drinks. Laughter. A car. A person in a black hood. Screams. Breaking glass. The smack of fist on flesh. Again. A woman screamed. A fist in his stomach. Then another. Gasping for air. Darkness. Silence.

A bag was covering his head.

Something sharp dug into his shoulders and chest securing him to whatever he was sitting on. His hands were cuffed tightly to what felt like a ring bolt on top of a table. His fingers swollen and numb. The panic set in. He was hyperventilating, and the resulting dizziness made him sick.

Then he remembered Tinka.

"Tinka!" he shouted, as he jerked and twisted. "Tinka, are you here?"

His words echoed from one wall to the other, then he heard the metal on metal grind of a latch opening.

With a click, bright light burned into his eyelids through the hood.

Pavlo turned his head away, rocked from side to side, and squeezed his lids as tight as he could. It didn't help. With the light came heat, sweat, and fear.

Then, as quickly as it arrived, the light dimmed to a tolerable level. The hood was ripped off Pavlo's head. With some effort, Pavlo opened his eyes. He blinked away tears and bright spots as the space around him came into focus. The room was small, maybe ten feet square, with cinder block walls and concrete floors. No windows. He was sitting at a metal table. Two empty chairs were on the other side. Between the lights was a metal door.

The air smelled like dust, rats, and decay.

Two men walked out of the glare and loomed over Pavlo. They were identical, except Oleg Koval had a ragged scar running along his jawline and down the side of his neck. Oleg Rudenko had a goatee that came to a point like an ice pick a few inches under his chin.

They were tall and muscular. Their bald bullet-shaped heads sat on tattooed necks that rippled with each breath. They wore black boots, jeans, and gray short-sleeved shirts under black leather vests. Tattoos of crosses, skulls, and knives covered their arms.

Pavlo didn't know who they were, but he knew that body art of skulls and knives meant these men were mobsters—Russian or Ukrainian—and that they were killers.

"Where. What?" He couldn't form a sentence through a mouth so dry he was sure they plastered his tongue to the top of his mouth.

"Please. Quiet." Koval said with a thick Ukrainian accent. He dropped his paw on Pavlo's shoulder, left it there, and squeezed. "You worry about the girl? You are a nice man."

Pavlo's head crushed into his neck as the pain rolled through his body. "Where…is…Tinka?" he gasped each word.

Rudenko sat down in his chair. "Let him go."

"Little fat fucker," Koval said disappointedly, as he raised his hands in the air spreading his fingers wide.

He walked behind Pavlo, slapped him on his sweat-drenched scalp, sending a snapping sound and grunt ricocheting around the room. Rudenko took his time moving toward the empty chair—the one to

Pavlo's left. He grunted as he sat, leaned back, and rested his shiny black leather boots on the tables' edge. He stretched his hands behind his head like it was nap time. He rested a boot on the table top. Pavlo saw the shape of a knife carved in the sole of his shoe.

"Wh-why?" Pavlo said.

"We will explain," Koval said. He leaned forward and interlocked his fingers as he rested his elbows on the table. Each knuckle had diamond "ring of thieves" tattoos on them.

"It is simple. Your boss is scum. Bondar. And his whore daughter. They killed our boss. Vlasenko. Now they plan to—," Koval looked at Rudenko and shrugged, "—I don't know what he plans to do? You?"

"No fucking idea. But I would like to fuck that daughter. She is sweet," Rudenko said, looking disinterested in the conversation. He pulled out a knife from his belt and started to clean his fingernails.

"We want that case as payment for killing our boss, and—" Koval said as a matter of fact, "—to keep us from killing you and the cute bitch in the other room."

"I know nothing of killing…or any case." Pavlo added the lie in a moment of courage. "Where is she?"

Rudenko dropped his boot to the floor with a loud thud.

"What?" Rudenko shouted in his face.

"I…don't…know…I…don't…know—" he whimpered. Snot ran out of his nose and stuck to his lips.

With surprising agility, Rudenko wheeled forward, arching his hand high in the air. The knife hit the table with a metallic *thwap* a quarter of an inch from Pavlo's right hand.

Pavlo began to shake, then felt a warm stream of urine running down his leg.

"Shit, he is wetting himself!" Rudenko stood up and looked at Koval, then over the table. "Shit." He pulled his knife out of the table and wiped it on Pavlo's shoulder.

Pavlo began to cry. "Tin-ka. Tin-ka."

"Is that the pretty bitch? A fine bitch…well, not now," Koval and Rudenko laughed together in unison.

"What have you done? Is she—" Pavlo screamed.

"Dead? No, she is not dead. Do you think we are animals?" Koval chuckled. "Want to see her?" Koval reached into his vest and pulled out his mobile phone. He swiped a few times with his thumb. "There."

Pavlo squinted at an image that showed Tinka wired to a chair. Her head was bent forward. The angle revealed a bruised and bloodied face. Her eyes were swollen closed. Her chin rested on her chest. Her hair was matted to her face. Dark brownish-red lines came from her nostrils, over her split lips, and pooled into a darker stain against her blouse.

"She can take a punch. I will give her credit for that. Tough bitch," Rudenko said, laughing too loud for the room.

Pavlo glared at him.

"Do not look at me, fat fucker." Koval slapped Pavlo hard across the cheek. Blood began to drip from his nose.

"We should visit her again. Tinka? Finnish girl—" Rudenko said.

"I like Finnish girls," said the other man, laughing.

"No!" Pavlo shouted, as he tried to break his restraints.

"Go show 'wet pants' that we are serious," Koval said to Rudenko.

Pavlo watched Rudenko get up and turn toward the door.

"No. No!" Pavlo screamed. His hands jerked frantically. Sweat rained off his face, and his urine splashed under his feet as he struggled to stand.

Rudenko opened the door, stopped, and turned. "I'll be back," he said in a bad Arnold Schwarzenegger impersonation. He laughed again and closed the door behind him.

Koval showed Pavlo the screen. Tinka looked up in total terror when Rudenko walked into view. He glanced over his shoulder at the camera with the look of absolute evil. He raised his hand and swung it down. She jerked, then was still. Rudenko smiled back at the camera and walked out of view.

Pavlo sat fossilized. Nothing moved. His eyes were wide. His upper teeth had bitten into his lower lip, causing a small line of blood to run down his chin. Koval put the phone in his pocket and walked to avoid the puddle on the floor. He leaned against the wall to Pavlo's right.

"That's enough," a voice said with authority.

Pavlo startled when he heard the words. His head swiveled, looking to see where they had come from.

"Pavlo. I know you are a little upset, and I want to help." He saw a silhouetted shape hidden within the glare of the floodlights. "Understand? But I need you to help make that possible, Pavlo. Can you do that?" the voice asked.

The lights increased to a blinding brightness. Pavlo flopped his head to his chest. Snot and drops of blood trickled from his nose onto his shirt.

Rudenko came into the room and grinned at Koval.

"These men are serious. I want them to stop, so you and Tinka can leave. I can only hold them off for so long. And then I can't stop what they do to Tinka, or you. Now is the time. Not a minute from now. Not ten seconds. Now."

"The bank. In the basement," Pavlo whispered immediately.

The lights dimmed more.

"We need to go get it. Can you help with that?"

Pavlo nodded.

"Excellent. Don't worry about Tinka."

"I...I want...to see her...see Tinka," Pavlo panted each word with heavy breaths.

"She will be fine, as long as you help me." The voice was closer. Pavlo looked up to see a man in a cap standing over him. "Tell me all about the case and the bank."

Pavlo nodded again. He was broken.

38

TRUTH IS STRANGER THAN FICTION

Over the Atlantic

W hen Peter opened his eyes, he felt like he had fallen asleep in the boring black-and-white corporate intelligence world and awoke in the magically colorful world of espionage.

It was right out of a Daniel Silva novel.

The future of his company and perhaps his career rested on his assignment to locate some mystery case from an evil oligarch in Kyiv. He was working with an even more mysterious bunch of spies named the Spy Devils. The man who created the private intelligence consulting industry—and in some spheres was considered one of the most powerful men in the world—was treating him like a colleague.

"My home in the sky," Chapel told Peter, as he glanced around the tans, browns, and polished wood accents of his Bombardier Global 7500 private plane.

"Quite a home. It is bigger than my split-level hovel in the Chicago suburbs," Peter quipped. "Saying 'this is nice' is an understatement."

"It does serve a purpose. My life can be somewhat hectic."

Chapel smiled, then picked up an already open bottle of red wine, filled a glass, and handed it to Peter. He filled one for himself and set the bottle down.

"Never too early," Chapel declared. "It is a simple Louis Jadot Pommard 2010. A full-bodied red. Look for the hint of raspberries, spices, and mint. Cheers."

Chapel swirled his wine, looked at it, stuck his nose inside the glass. He inhaled, sipped, sucked it around his mouth, then swallowed. His face showed his satisfaction.

"This won't take long—a quick hop over the Atlantic. A stop at Heathrow to refuel, then on to Ukraine. From there, I will let you proceed with your plans. Until then, make yourself at home. Ms. Stead will take care of you. If you will excuse me, I need to take care of a little business."

Chapel turned toward the rear of the plane, opened a door, and disappeared.

"May I get you something?" a pleasant voice said. Peter turned and was face to face with a smiling woman wearing a white shirt with *Danforth Chapel Company* sewn over her left breast. She was in her twenties and wore the look of someone who enjoyed her life flying the world with powerful people.

"Maybe some peanuts?" Peter replied, trying to appear as if he was a regular on private jets.

"Certainly." Ms. Stead turned and walked to the galley.

Peter sat in the most comfortable seat he had ever sat in on a plane. Moments later, Ms. Stead re-appeared with a white ceramic bowl filled with warm mixed nuts.

"Anything else, Mr. Schaeffer?"

"Um, no, thanks." He didn't know why he was surprised she knew his name, but he was.

Peter found a card that described the jet and looked it over.

Maybe I will get one of these someday.

The interior was divided into four sections. The flight deck and crew suite were in the front. Next was a lounge and dining area where

Peter was sitting. Eight leather seats facing each other in two sections of four. The third section—where Chapel was now, he figured—was an office and lounge with couches and desks. In the rear was a private master bedroom suite. The air smelled like a new car.

Dinner was prime rib. Vegetables. Baked potato. Chocolate cake.

The ride was so smooth he had to remind himself he was in a plane over the Atlantic Ocean and not sitting in front of his TV at home. Chapel spent most of his time in the office section and in his master bedroom. From what Peter could tell, he was on the phone talking, yelling, cajoling, and laughing. Peter figured lots of people needed the help of the world's best fixer.

Peter was impressed with Chapel's stamina as he heard him on one call after another. Peter just wanted to sleep.

The sounds inside the plane and interior design made it hard for Peter to eavesdrop on Chapel's side of the conversation, but he still tried. There was a Hollywood star whose phone was hacked, resulting in sex videos being posted online. A senator was caught in an airport restroom doing something Peter couldn't make out, but Chapel convinced the person not to jump off a ledge. A world leader was checking on his fortune before fleeing the angry populace of his country.

Peter was a little jealous. His conversations with Chapel were mostly brief and causal. Chapel did the asking. Peter did the answering. Work. Family. Career. As much as he hoped he would, Chapel never mentioned Bridger or the Spy Devils.

There was one exception.

After the refueling in London and during the shorter hop to Kyiv, Peter realized he must have fallen asleep. It took a moment for the fog in his brain to comprehend where he was. Then he saw Chapel sitting in the chair facing him. His legs were crossed. His manicured hands were in his lap. His eyes were fixed on Peter.

Peter quickly pushed the button on his chair to bring it from recline to a normal sitting position.

"Mr. Chapel."

Chapel eyed Peter for a few more seconds.

"Peter. Danny, please." He flashed his mesmerizing smile.

"Yes, Danny, sorry." Peter cursed himself for making the same embarrassing mistake.

"Peter, sometimes, truth is stranger than fiction—and riskier. You are involved in a very serious situation. I am certain you are aware of that. You should be cautious." Chapel's face morphed from a look of trusting best friend to the scolding school principal.

"Um. I don't—? Cautious? Of what?"

"Very cautious. People's lives and livelihoods depend on your professionalism," Chapel said, one hand coming up to brush his bright orange and yellow tie. Without another word or change of expression, Chapel stood and walked back to his office.

Peter searched his brain for any idea of what Chapel meant. Peter was wide awake for the rest of the flight until they landed at Boryspil Airport in Kyiv. When the plane finished its taxi to the private jet terminal, Chapel came out of his office. Peter stood, not knowing what to expect.

"Here we are, Peter! I don't believe you have been to Kyiv before, right?" Chapel said all bright and happy. His demeanor gave no indication of the dire warning he issued just a few hours ago.

"No, I haven't."

"Then I hope you have the opportunity to get a chance to enjoy this historic city." Chapel led Peter to the open door and the steps.

"I hope so, too."

Peter descended the steps into the Kyiv night. A blue-and-yellow carpet led from the jet to the entrance of the building. Chapel followed him down.

"Peter. I shall leave you here, as I have an urgent meeting at the Ministry of Defense. My staff will see you through the immigration process."

"Oh, okay. Thank you for the ride."

"Anytime, Peter. Anytime." Peter watched Chapel walk a few steps toward a waiting black SUV, where a security guard held the door open. The engine was running. Chapel turned and looked back. "Say hello to the boys and happy hunting."

He smiled and entered the car. The guard closed the door and ran around to the other side. In three seconds, it sped away.

Peter was alone—but not for long.

39

IT SUCKS TO BE PAVLO

Kyiv, Ukraine

Based on a photo provided by Imp taken from Peter's Facebook page, Snake intercepted Peter when he walked in the main hall of Boryspil Airport.

"Bridger," was all Snake said.

Peter nodded and followed. Traffic was light, so it was easy for Snake to check for surveillance on the drive to the warehouse. Peter dozed.

The interrogation of Pavlo was over when Peter arrived. The Spy Devils were sitting around a cluttered industrial-sized rectangular table in the middle of a windowless room. Wires from a table full of electronics ran out the door in the direction of humming generators.

The Spy Devils had taken over a deteriorating building near the port. Discarded boxes and fading labels revealed it had once been a canning and shipping facility for fruits and vegetables. Graffiti covered the walls. Mounds of trash and discarded drug paraphernalia covered the floor.

"Come over. How was the trip?" Bridger asked Peter.

"Chapel's plane is pretty nice," Peter said as they shook hands.

"Yes, I know. It's a Bombardier Global 7500. Nice ride. What I meant was, what did you best friends talk about?"

"Not much. Just warned me to be cautious. Like my life depended on it. He says hello, by the way. He liked your info from Cyprus. Said nice things."

"He is such a sweetheart." Bridger was still not thrilled Chapel was involved. "I assume he stuffed it into his pocket."

"Yes," Peter nodded.

"Like always. He will take credit for it. He always does."

"He is the new point of contact," Peter said, rubbing his tired eyes.

"Yeah. I heard." Bridger said, making sure the sarcasm was obvious. "We are on a tight schedule, so this has to be quick." Bridger waved his arm around the room. "You met Snake. These are most of the famous Spy Devils. Everyone. This is Peter. He works for Kirkwood."

Peter nodded at the people around the table. It felt surreal to Peter. They looked like normal people. A man. Woman. A kid. The Snake. Only one not normal-looking was the older mean-looking guy who was pacing. He looked scary. It was hard to fathom that they were a celebrated group of spies he had been following on social media for years.

They looked tired and showed it in their posture and red eyes.

"How's business?" Bridger asked Peter. "Tell us. Anything more from your sources?"

"Not much." Peter briefed them regarding his conversations with Kirkwood management. How they wanted to take him off the assignment. Chapel offering to act as a point of contact.

"Interesting," Bridger said. "They tried to drop the whole thing, did they? I need to think about that. Anyway, we have been busy, too."

Bridger gave Peter a quick sketch of Pavlo's interrogation. As he did, they watched a split-screen monitor showing Pavlo getting dressed on one side and Tinka's now empty room on the other.

"Aren't you excited? We are almost there," Bridger said, clapping his hands and looking at Peter with a smile.

Peter was horrified by what he saw and concentrated on keeping a neutral face.

"I'll believe you. I feel sorry for him," Peter said, as he watched a trembling man struggle to tie his sweatpants.

"Why?"

"He looks—abused."

"Abused? Not at all," Bridger said, without displaying any remorse. "He works for a mob thug who, in some way, killed *your* CFO. He helped them steal money from *your* company. I don't care about him at all."

Peter kept his eyes on the man struggling to put on some shoes. "What happens when they find out he gave us the case?"

"They can cook him," Imp said from the other end of the table. "They can cut him up and barbeque him for all I care. It sucks to be Pavlo."

"You want him cooked just because you are jealous," Snake said.

"Jealous?" Imp said, his voice rising in disbelief. He pointed to the screen. "Of that?"

"Him!" Milton pointed to the screen.

"It worked like a charm, fool," Imp said indignantly.

Peter looked at Bridger. "That's Imp. Whiz-kid geek. Touchy. The other is Milton. Engineering genius."

Imp's trojan virus buried in Theo's email should have granted immediate access to the Bondar network, but Imp was surprised. Pavlo's network, he discovered, was an impressive display of computer expertise. Imp encountered a sophisticated ring of security partitions. After a few hours, he was finally inside the files and retrieved the information they needed.

The other Spy Devils noticed Imp's struggles and quickly used it as a way to mock the self-absorbed kid.

"You can all eat shit," Imp said. They let out an exhausted laugh.

"This is going to take forever. This clay will never come off," Beatrice said, rubbing spirit gum remover across her forehead.

"Beatrice. Disguise. Technical. She has had a long couple of days," Bridger said to Peter.

Beatrice was at the table looking into a mirror, vigorously wiping her face with tissues and creams. A dozen bottles, jars, puffs, tissues, and towels were spread out in front of her. A wet brownish wig was in a bag on the floor. Milton was next to her, making sure all the trash was collected for disposal.

"Would you rather be tackling the makeup right now or spend some more time kissing our pal here?" Imp jerked his thumb toward the screen. Beatrice looked at him, flipped him the finger, then turned back to the mirror. Milton grinned.

The door opened, and Peter saw two large men walk into the room.

"Olegs! Bridger said.

"Spy Devils?" Peter asked.

"Friends of the Devil."

Bridger exchanged a handshake with each man. "You guys were great."

"It is not too hard, as you saw, Mr. Bridger," said Oleg Koval.

"We thought he might shit his pants," Oleg Rudenko added.

"I thought he had," Imp said, as he tapped on his electronics.

"We are available for you any time," Rudenko said.

"Great. The money is already in your accounts. Once we are gone, you can scrub this area and pack up the equipment and put it back in storage."

"Yes, sir, and thank you. We appreciate your generosity," Koval said. "You are a valued customer."

"Make sure you tell Lana and Anna hello. And those kids of yours."

"Thank you," they said in unison, as they walked out the door.

"I love Oleg," Imp said.

"Which one?" Milton asked.

"*Oleg*," Imp said with emphasis.

"He's the good one," Milton agreed.

"Time to check on another one of us," Bridger said, as he took out his mobile phone and launched the Signal app.

As it connected, he hit the speaker button and put the phone on the table.

"Beast? We are about ready here. What's your status?"

"Status? It is still dark if you can't tell. I'm in my room. The street lights are on. I can see cars parked everywhere. The usual Kyiv parking chaos. Same cars and scooters as before, generally. I will head for the restaurant when it opens at six—in about forty-five minutes. I will have a better view of the sidewalks and the street."

Since they departed Cyprus, Beast had worked solo gathering intel on the Bondars and their facilities. Traveling as a businessman, he stayed in a boutique hotel next to the Ukraine Standard Bank, a prime location to surveil the bank and adjacent residence location. He noted the times and which doors they used to enter and exit the buildings. Beast observed the cars and drivers that parked or passed by the bank more than twice. He memorized who was on the streets each day and at what times, looking for patterns of plain-clothed security. He reported his intel back to Bridger three times each day.

"Okay. We will leave when you are in position. See you soon."

"Roger. I will enjoy my morning coffee."

Imp looked up. "Can I put in an order?"

The phone was silent.

"Jesus, what does it take to get a little coffee around here?" Imp let his complaint be heard as he turned back to look at his glowing laptop screen.

"Snake, I want you on a scooter," Bridger said.

"How about the Devilbots?" Milton asked, his face lighting with the hope that he could release his toys.

"Keep one over the bank and the other one handy, just in case. I don't know where the safe house is yet. When I do, I will let you know."

Beatrice patted Milton's arm as he wiggled in his chair, unable to hide his delight in hearing the positive response.

Not knowing the safe house location irritated Bridger.

"Demon, you take the Toyota and run counter-surveillance to the bank. Imp, you ride with Demon. Find a spot on Dilova Street and get your eyes and ears on that bank. We will take the Skoda. Milton and Beatrice. You load the bots into the van and leave. Where are you setting up?"

"There is a parking lot for a skate park south of the nearby sports stadium secluded in some trees," Milton reported. "We scouted it out yesterday. There wasn't much pedestrian or car traffic. I am sure there is nothing at this hour."

"Good. Get a Devilbot in the air right when you arrive. There won't be much time."

"Got it," Milton said.

"Beast should be nearby in support if anything happens. Imp, you have Pavlo's information on the bank security and layout?"

"Yes, but getting surveillance into his little RF-protected ferret den will take a few minutes. He has disabled all computer cameras and sound. I am blind there."

"Pavlo stump you again, Imp?" Milton asked.

Imp ignored the comment. He hit his keys hard like the finale of a Beethoven piano concerto. Then he slammed his laptop closed and tossed his hands in the air. "Done."

"I want everyone alert. This is ripe for mistakes. Peter, Pavlo, and I will get the case. I call Chapel, get the address, and head to the safe house. When I get the address, I want you on your horses checking it out. We hand over the case to Chapel. Then we get the hell out of here and go on vacation.

"Everyone ready? Beast, we are on our way." Bridger disconnected the call and pocketed his phone. He put on a baseball cap, some glasses, and darkened three days of stubble he had grown.

"Put these on." He tossed Peter a floppy worker's cap and a pair of tinted sunglasses. "Not great, but should be enough for this."

Bridger picked up his backpack and slung it over his shoulder. "Just your average spy disguise."

"Why him?" Demon asked. He pointed his finger at Peter like a gun.

"Relax. Peter is the client, sort of, so he can be in on this. And barring any problems, we are home tomorrow morning."

40

THE DAY

Kyiv, Ukraine

At 5 a.m., Li Chu's driver backed the Renault Logan onto the sidewalk and wedged it between a tree and some scooters. Across the street was the Ukraine Standard Bank—the bank of Viktor Bondar.

He told his man to turn the car off. The heat would have been nice, but idling exhaust and dashboard lights could give away their position. His Chen-supplied rookie Dragon Fire men had lost Pavlo and the woman hours ago at the bar—inexperience, coupled with the rain and darkness—worked to his opponent's advantage.

Today is the day I will get him, he thought.

Li Chu knew the Spy Devils would arrive soon with Pavlo in tow. It was what he would have done, but he knew the Spy Devils *were* CIA —and the CIA always make their plans too elaborate and challenging. It was what Americans did. Make things hard.

His goal was simple—capture and kill the leader of the Spy Devils. He decided to retrieve the mysterious case that everyone seemed to be seeking. Why not take advantage of it? He wondered what was in it. He would use whatever it was for whatever he decided whenever he decided. Or, maybe he would sell it and go independent and provide his services to those in need of a Chinese assassin.

His plan was fluid. Surprise and violence were the best tools at his disposal. The other, more palpable tool, was vengeance. Vengeance for destroying Dragon Fire. Vengeance for forcing him to kill members of his team.

Three of the new men were on scooters positioned at the main intersections around the bank. Two were on foot, strolling separately along the streets. Two were in a car, waiting for a signal to use the vehicle to block the north exit onto the street. One was next to him in the driver's seat. He wanted snipers on the building's roofs but feared another encounter with the drones that killed his men and chased him in Taiwan.

Whatever happened, whoever came out of the bank with a case, would be attacked. Li Chu wanted to take Bridger alive. He wanted to interrogate him—before he killed him.

Li Chu couldn't suppress the nervous tension he felt throughout his body. His men were unproven, but they were still MSS officers for what it was worth in these days of incompetence and self-preservation. He had never used the 9mm Makarov PM Chen had left for them. When he distributed the favored weapon of the Russian Spetsnaz units to the men, he wished they could spend a few days practicing at a range. Instead, they had a few hours before they went operational.

Totally unacceptable were the portable Motorola 2-way digital radios Chen left for their communications system. But his options were limited. He had distributed burner mobile phones to the men, but texting and calling were awkward in the middle of an ambush. He reset the frequency and privacy codes to reduce the odds of someone listening to any conversations. He ordered them to use phones first and radios only as needed. His radio was powered on and rested in the cup holder of the center console.

"Mr. Li Chu, are you there?" said the American-accented voice.

Li Chu couldn't help but flinch at the unexpected words cutting the silence within the car. Momentarily staring at each other with perplexed expressions on their faces, Li Chu and the other MSS officer in the car quickly regained their composure. Raising their Makarovs to the windows, they flipped off the safeties and slid down in the seats. The Chinese assassins turned their bodies to scan in all directions for movement. In the dim light of the street lamps, the only shapes visible were the nearby buildings, cars, and scooters.

"Mr. Li Chu. Are you there? My name is Danforth Chapel. Perhaps you have heard of me? I would like to make a proposal. Please respond." The voice paused. "I would like to provide you some information to assist with your planned action this morning. Please respond. We need to discuss this before they arrive. Which will be soon."

Li Chu looked at the driver, then turned his head to look at the bank. Lights came on in the restaurant across the street. He used the added light to look for any threats. People were in the building, but nothing seemed out of place.

He knew the name Chapel. Everyone in the world did. The fact he was calling on a radio at this time was incomprehensible—almost. There was only one answer. Li Chu picked up the radio with his left hand. His right hand still held the Makarov pointed toward the window.

He depressed the push to talk button.

"Yes?"

"Good. Good. I know these radios are not very secure, so I suggest you provide me a number of a disposable phone, and we can discuss my proposal. Deal?"

Li Chu gave his phone number and set the radio back in the console. It rang two seconds later.

He pushed the answer button.

"Yes?" He said slowly. He listened, then replied to each question. "Yes, I do. Why?" More silence. "Text me the address."

He stared at the blank mobile screen for a moment, set down his phone, and keyed his radio.

"Cease surveillance immediately. Meet at the address I will send." He put the radio on the car seat. The Makarov went back into its holster. A moment later, after sending a group text to his team, the Renault Logan rolled off the sidewalk onto Dilova Street.

Today is still the day.

Danforth Capel slid his phone into the breast pocket of his Gieves & Hawkes suit. He felt at ease in the familiar communications center on the lower floor of The Danforth Chapel Company, Ukraine headquarters. He looked over at Chen, whose faced displayed a rare moment of worry.

"Are you concerned, Minister? I think that went quite well. The frequency, channel scanning, and location software enhancement worked to perfection. Our message has been delivered, and all elements of the situation are under control." Chapel sat back in his chair, brushed his hand over his tie, and smiled.

"Yes, but now we are at the moment when we do not control much of the next events as they occur. Li Chu is a motivated and intelligent man. It will not take him long to conclude who assisted in his being located," Chen said.

"Today is a busy day. I could use a drink." Chapel stood. He patted Chen reassuringly on the shoulder as he walked by. Chapel opened the door, stood back, motioned with a slight bow of his shoulders, and waved, indicating that Chen should go first.

"Yes, thank you." Chen stood and walked toward the open door.

"Minister Chen," Chapel said in a soft voice. The man stopped, and Chapel saw his face had regained its traditional expressionless appearance. "No matter which direction destiny takes us, it will not matter. For us, our position is secure, and we will prevail either way. *You* are safe. For others, sad to say, this is their last day on this earth."

Chapel followed Chen out the door.

41

FADE TO BLACK

Kyiv, Ukraine

Olek had spotted Beast the previous day. He had just returned from Cyprus after Ira arranged for Olek's release. When Olek's driver turned off Dilova Street heading to the Bondar residence behind the bank, he had just enough time to do a quick glance—then another. He spotted a familiar face sitting on a bench under a tree in the small brick plaza outside the bank entrance.

"I saw him," he told Ira.

"You are sure?" Ira held up a grainy photo taken by the Cyprus National Police captain of a bearded man in a police uniform. "Him?"

"Yes, but now he has no beard. But he *is* one of them. He was there when…I was tossed into…"

A clean-shaven Beast checked into the cramped three-story hotel using his alias as a U.S. salesman for an abrasives company. Given the hotel's location near several businesses and financial institutions, and with the added benefit of being away from central Kyiv's congestion, it was a popular hotel for foreign visitors. It was also adjacent to the Ukraine Standard Bank and the Bondar residence building behind it.

He requested a third-floor room with a street view. The enclosed restaurant that was literally built on the sideway provided a perfect spot for static surveillance.

At 5:50 a.m., Beast gathered up some newspapers he purchased the day before, stuffed them under his arm, and headed to the restaurant that would open in ten minutes. Imp's plea for coffee did not fall upon deaf ears. Beast was exhausted and could use a pot of anything black to clear his head. Plus, he was starving, and the desk staff promised a pretty good morning buffet of breads, cheeses, fruits, cereals, and meats.

The buffet was to Beast's left as he entered the rectangular dining area. Three rows of two- and four-seat white tables and chairs ran the length of the room. Windows covered the three sides facing the street in front and the sidewalk to the left and right.

When he arrived, there were already a few men in suits sitting at tables drinking coffee. Beast plopped his papers on a table next to the windows facing the street and sat, making sure the spot had the right sightlines to the entrance of the bank. The dim light of dawn started creeping up the horizon.

Before he stood to get his coffee, he felt the unmistakable metal of a gun pressed against the back of his neck.

"Do not move," a deep, heavily accented voice said. Beast placed it in central Europe. *Not Ukraine. Maybe Serbian.* He saw the reflection in the windows of two other men standing in sentry positions. Suppressed pistols were pointing at him. "Keep your hands raised, or we will just shoot your head off."

"This must be a mistake," Beast said. He felt the gun press harder.

Beast could tell that all three were some sort of soldier. Fit and hard men. It figured to be a pretty even fight.

The Serbian reached under Beast's jacket. He took the Sig Sauer P226 from his Kydex holster. He pulled Beast's pager-sized secure radio transmitter and receiver off his belt. The man tucked the P226 in against the small of his back, powered the radio system off, and shoved it in his pocket.

He sure knows a lot.

"Follow him." The Serbian waved toward a smaller man who had a tough, weathered face. The Serbian was behaving like the leader, and to Beast, that made him the most dangerous of the three.

He will be the hardest to kill.

Beast was slow to move and felt the push in the middle of his back from the third man. Beast kept his hands up at chest level like he was doing push-ups against a wall. He turned and stared into the blank, empty eyes of a person who killed automatically—like a robot.

They led him to a narrow set of stairs at the end of the ground floor hallway—Tough Face. Beast. Robot. The Serbian.

"Up," the Serbian commanded.

Beast complied. He didn't see any other guests in the halls or on the stairs. No staff or other people coming in or out.

They took control of the hotel just to get me.

As they reached the top of the stairs, they exited on the third floor and started down the narrow hall. Carpets and walls were decorated in beiges and gold. Beast's room was halfway down on the right.

Advantage me.

Beast made it a habit to memorize his surroundings.

His room was long and narrow with slightly outdated European-style laminate furniture. A rectangular shape—maybe fifteen by twenty. Two twin-sized beds were pushed together on the wall to the right. Along the wall to the left of the door was a tall dresser—a place to hang clothes. Six feet from the foot of the bed was a wooden desk with a chair. The bathroom door was between the desk and the wall opposite the door, which had two windows that looked over Dilova Street.

Some hazy light of dawn crept into the room.

At the door, Tough Face stopped and held out his hand. Beast looked at him. Tough Face shook his hand.

"Ah, I get it." Beast took his plastic key card from his front pocket with his right hand. When the man took it with a quick grab, Beast hooked his thumb in his nylon belt.

Tough Face grumbled something unintelligible, turned, and slid the key into the slot. A green light blinked as the latch clicked. The door swung into the room to the right. He put the card in the slot on the wall to the left. The lights kicked on. Beast felt Robot shove the gun in his back again.

This is it.

Beast moved his right hand to his buckle and, with a short unseen upward motion, grabbed the black rectangular buckle from the belt, exposing a four-inch blade. He thrust it into the kidney of Tough Face and twisted. The man screamed and tried to jerk away, but Beast grabbed the man's jacket with his left hand and tossed Tough Face into the dresser to their left. Beast spun left and down with the momentum to get out of the line of Robot's fire.

Robot hesitated for less than a second, but it was enough. Robot managed to fire off two rounds with a suppressed *thwomp thwomp.* He missed Beast. Two holes appeared in the far wall.

Beast reached up and grabbed the front of the man's jacket with his left hand. With his right, he brought the razor-sharp knife up and, with all his strength, jammed it into the man's groin. The razor-sharp blade easily cut into the soft tissue of the scrotum. Sliced through his testicles and punctured his penis like shish-kabob. He screamed and dropped his gun as his hands automatically reached to his damaged crotch.

Blood exploded onto the floor, covering Beast's hand. Twisting the knife deeper into Robot, Beast launched into the howling man, driving him backward into the Serbian, pinning him against the wall. Beast landed two solid left hooks to the jaw of the Serbian before he could get his Glock aimed at Beast.

Beast jumped back into the room and landed on his back by the bed. The knife ripped out of Robot's body, effectively castrating him. The dazed Serbian ricocheted off the wall and tripped over the crying Robot.

Beast heard a *thwomp,* and his right quad immediately started to burn. He looked to his right. Tough Face was kneeling four feet away in a small puddle of blood—his gun in his wavering hand pointed at Beast.

He hoped to find Robot's dropped Glock, but he couldn't see it.

Beast instinctively tossed his knife at Tough Face. The metal buckle knife was coated with blood, causing his hand to slip off as he threw it. The blade struck Tough Face sideways in the forehead. It wasn't lethal, but it was enough of a distraction.

Tough Face recoiled, sending his next shot into the ceiling. Beast rolled and jumped toward Tough Face as best he could through the pain in his leg. They smashed into the desk, and Beast dropped his weight on top of him. He reached for the gun, jerked it up, twisted, and pointed the end of the suppresser under Tough Face's chin. Beast jammed his finger into the trigger guard and pressed.

Tough Face lost parts of his tough face as the 9mm bullet traveled through his chin, jaw, tongue, teeth, the roof of his mouth, nasal cavities, and left eye. It exited out his forehead, sending his head back with a violent jerk. Blood, bone, and tissue splattered over the wall and Beast's face. He felt the bits of goo in his eyes and mouth and started to spit them out as he gripped the gun and rolled onto his side to face the door.

The Serbian had recovered and was stepping into the room over the moaning Robot. He turned and fired blindly in Beast's direction. Beast felt pain in his left arm and shoulder. He grasped the handle of the Glock in his blood-soaked right hand. Through blurred vision and still spitting Tough Face's face out of his mouth, he fired off four shots into the Serbian's head and chest. He fell dead against the bed.

Beast pointed the gun into what was left of Tough Face's skull and fired a safety shot. He saw the shape of Robot curled in a massive pool of blood by the door—dead. Beast pointed the weapon in his direction, then decided to save the round.

Beast sat sweating, bleeding, and sucking in air as he leaned against the desk. Setting his gun in his lap, he tried to wipe the debris from his eyes so he could see the damage caused by three 9mm rounds that ripped into his body. Then, he recognized the symptoms of shock. Dizzy. Sweating. Shallow breath. It was coming.

Confusion was another symptom of shock, and that is what he thought was happening when he saw another shape enter the room. *A blonde-haired woman in a red dress? Did she pick up a gun? Is she pointing it at me?* He was even more confused when he looked down and saw his chest exploding with a series of red holes. He looked up as his vision started to tunnel shades of gray around the edges.

The last confusing moment was when he thought he heard the word "devil" before everything faded to black.

42

A PROPOSAL

Kyiv, Ukraine

At 6:00 a.m., Bridger backed the rusty Skoda into a parking space by a courtyard adjacent and northwest of the Ukraine Standard Bank. It gave them some level of invisibility from three directions protected by trees. A review of Google Earth indicated the space also gave Bridger, Peter, and Pavlo a clear view of a rear door into the bank.

The light of dawn was starting to define the shape of the bank.

A narrow drive passed by the plaza connecting Dilova Street to a parking area in the rear. On the other side of the alley was a six-story building that took up the entire corner of Dilova and Velyka Vasylkivska Streets. A low building was attached to the Ukraine Standard Bank in the rear, which led to Bondar's five-story Ukraine Investment and Holding Company building.

"This, ladies and gentlemen, is a poor place to run an operation. Cramped. Limited access. Security guards not too far away," Bridger said. "In espionage parlance, this location sucks.

"Demon?" Bridger asked.

"We are in a don't park zone a block down the street. Can't see shit," Demon said, with more gravel in his voice than usual. "Should we proceed on foot?"

"Imp, tell me what you see."

"I don't see anything on the cameras I can access," Imp added. "You are in the blind where you are parked. I will blink the cameras as you move. I don't hear radio chatter…and I could use some coffee."

"Milton?"

"Beatrice has it in the air. Nothing on IR. The closest images of guards are to your north, near the building in the back. They seem to be stationary. This is a good time."

"Snake?"

"Yeah, I'm scootin' not shootin'," Snake answered.

"Beast?" Bridger said into his comm system. "Beast?" he repeated louder a few seconds after he didn't receive an answer. "Beast, are you there?"

Still no answer.

"If he is asleep, I am going to kill him," Demon barked.

"Maybe his comms are out," Snake said.

"Or in the can," Imp suggested.

"Our comms, don't 'go out,'" Milton said with slight irritation.

"Demon. You see him in the restaurant?"

"I don't have a good angle to see anything. Want me to check?"

Mistakes were in the air—Bridger could feel them. Lack of time forced compromises to his normal planning process. His senses were hyper-alert as his eyes swept the windows of the surrounding buildings —cars in the lot, pedestrians, and the entrances to the area. His ears listened for sirens, revving engines, or Imp yelling a warning. Even his sense of smell was checking for strange odors.

"No. Let's get this case, then figure it out where the hell Beast is." He was worried about Beast, but they had a mission and time was short. "Gotta love espionage," he said with confidence. He took one more look out the window. "I'm going inside. Stay here," Bridger told Peter.

"But—?" Peter started to protest.

"*You* are staying," Bridger said. He looked over his shoulder at

Pavlo. "Pavlo. *You* are coming with me. Do you see anything out of the ordinary?"

"No, but there will be guards soon. We should get inside," Pavlo said quickly, like he was running out of air.

"Yeah. I agree. I don't want to sit here. Here we go," Bridger announced.

With his Devil Stick in one hand, Bridger got out of the car, walked to the rear passenger door, and let Pavlo out. He took a firm grip on Pavlo's arm with the other hand and started toward the back entrance to the bank.

The rear door was forty feet away, about ten feet in from the alley. Above the white metal safety door was an industrial light that was still on and a security camera that Bridger hoped was off. Next to the door attached to the wall was a silver metal box.

"Okay, get us in," Bridger told Pavlo.

Pavlo flipped up a lid on the box to reveal an alphanumeric pad. His hands were shaking so much he missed the numbers and had to start over twice.

"Relax, Pavlo. Open the door," Bridger said with a friendly pat on the back.

Pavlo steadied his hand and pushed five buttons. A click signaled his success. Bridger pulled the door open, and they stepped inside.

Bridger poised his Devil Stick for a possible attack. He kept Pavlo in front of him as Pavlo led them downstairs to an unmarked subterranean door. A small yellow bulb in a metal cage cast dim patterns of light and shadows along the walls and across the door.

"Where are the bank security guards?" He could feel Pavlo shaking.

"Normally, upstairs sleeping off the *salo* and *kovbasa* they stuff themselves with every night. This is off-limits to them, by order of Ms. Ira. This is my space," he said. Bridger appreciated the mixture of pride and vanity in the little man's voice.

"This is my door. The room is RF-protected. No radio signals."

"Yeah. Imp was thrilled to hear that. Open it."

With quivering hands, Pavlo keyed a code into another security lock.

As they stepped into the room, Bridger saw motion and instinctively grabbed Pavlo by the collar and pulled him closer. He raised the Devil Stick, prepping for a fight. Bridger waited. He swiveled to look behind him, then to each side.

Then he saw her. A gorgeous woman with blonde hair and azure eyes sitting in a padded desk chair rotating slightly right and left. She was in a red dress that did not reach her knees. On her feet were black leather boots that did. On the floor next to her, Bridger saw a silver case—just like the one Gilbert had shown to them in KRT.

Pavlo gasped and sank to his knees. The collar of his sweatshirt tore away, leaving a handful of material in Bridger's hand.

"Ms. Ira! I am…I am…they took me…I am sorry!" He gasped out each word, then started to cry even harder. He brought his hands to his face and bent over at the waist like he was prostrated in prayer.

"It is fine, Pavlo. You have done nothing wrong. Do not worry. Please stand up," she commanded, like he was her pet dog.

He stayed on the floor—the buzz of computers, air conditioners, and Pavlo's sobs filled the air. She took in a breath and let out a sigh, shaking her head at Bridger in a *'what can I do?'* look.

"Hello, Mr. Bridger. I am Ira Bondar. I would like to discuss a proposal with you." She stood and held out her hand. He didn't move any closer to her. She dropped her arm and sat.

Bridger looked at her, then looked around the room. She was the only one inside. The room was exactly as Pavlo described in his debriefing. Lots of computers and racks of equipment. Monitors and workstations. The air conditioners hummed, but it was still warm in the room.

"Yes. Ms. Bondar. I have heard of you. And Pavlo here speaks *very highly* of you," he said, trying not to react to her calling him by his name.

How the hell do you know so much, Ms. Ira?

"Yes, I am sure. Please call me Ira. And my apologies, as time is short and we need to discuss some important matters—however, I would like this conversation to be only for our ears. Perhaps—" Her voice trailed off as her pupils zeroed in on Pavlo—still in the same position and sobbing softly.

"Ah, I get it."

Bridger raised and extended his Devil Stick. He flipped the thumb controls.

"Pavlo, get up." The man didn't move. "Get up, please. Pavlo, I've got chocolate!" Still no movement.

Bridger shrugged and touched the end of the Stick against Pavlo's back. The stun gun setting let out a staccato electric pulse. Pavlo's arms and legs flapped on the floor. Bridger moved his thumb one more time. He turned his head away, pointed it at the defenseless man's snot, sweat, and drool-covered face. He pressed the activator switch. A fine mist shot out of the end into Pavlo's face. In seconds, the man went limp—his relaxed neck muscles dropped his head to the concrete floor.

"That is amazing," Ira said, uncrossing her legs and leaning forward to get a closer look at the unconscious man. "I had heard of this, but to see it used. Amazing." Bridger could not help but notice the tips of a black lace garter clipped to the tops of her stockings.

When was the last time I had sex....?

He scolded himself for the lapse in his concentration.

"You have *heard* of *this*." He waved the Devil Stick in the air as he asked her the question. "May I ask how that is?"

"Yes, but please sit. I will explain."

She gracefully flicked her hand to another padded desk chair a few feet in front of her.

When Bridger didn't move, she smiled in understanding. "Please. You are safe, since you are here and not dead. I ordered my security teams to allow you to enter. Our time is short. I would like to negotiate a deal with you."

Instead of asking about the deal, he raised his nose into the air. *Sniff. Sniff.*

"I am catching a slight scent of a bouquet of flowers in the room." His face took on the look of a man in full concentration. *Sniff.* "Let me think." He sniffed once more. Then he slapped his free hand on his knee—the other still held the Stick—and said, "Ah-ha! I have it. Chanel No. 5!"

"Quite right!" Ira said with a laugh.

"I have a good nose." Bridger raised his eyebrows and smiled. "I can sniff out scents that smell sweet, just as well as I can when I come across the odor of something that stinks."

Your face tells me you got my meaning, too. Red is your color, Ira.

"How? I know what is in the public domain. How do you know so much detail about—?" he paused for a moment. At first his face showed concentration—then understanding.

"Oh, yes. Of course. I know of you from your presence on social media. I am a fan."

"Thank you. We are coming out with a line of clothing soon."

She paused for a moment with a bewildered look on her face. Then she smiled. "Yes. I see. I became aware you were searching for the case in Kyiv through a consultant who works for us. His name is Danforth Chapel. He seemed quite well versed in your professional skills and expertise. He highly recommends you."

"Yep. Chapel. A recommendation from on high, but why not just give him the case?"

"Then I would not get what *I* want."

"And what is that?" he asked, as he leaned his tired body back in the comfortable chair.

"I want you to rid me of my father."

43

TAKE IT TO THE BANK

Kyiv, Ukraine

Her words were spoken so calmly it actually made Bridger uncomfortable.

"Rid you of your father?" He repeated in a slight accent. "Rid? Do you mean to *kill* him?"

"I didn't state I wanted you to kill him." Ira corrected him.

"Okay. Explain it to me, then. I like hearing the ideas that roll around in the minds of the rich, powerful, and sociopathic."

"Oh, Mr. Bridger. Please, it is a business matter. I am disappointed with how my father has been handling our businesses—poor planning and partnerships leading to the loss of assets. The American company is a problem only because he took their money to cover our losses. He never intends to pay on our debt. A recent setback in Serbia is his fault."

"Serbia? What happened in Serbia?"

"He trusted the Chinese," Ira continued. "A catastrophe that has caused more issues with our finances and stress with our relationship with the government."

"You were working with Serge?"

Ira was shocked. "Serge? Yes. You know Serge? You know of the issues in Serbia?"

Bridger let a few seconds of silence be his answer as he fixed his unblinking eyes on her.

"What's the real reason you want him gone, Ira?" Bridger finally asked.

"He—" she paused and swallowed as her eyes looked down, "— killed a man very close and dear to me—very dear to me."

"Ah, well, so not only about business." He faked a frowning face. "Everyone has a story, Ira."

"Excuse me?" She was puzzled.

"What do you want me to do?"

She leaned in slightly, rested her white hand and red nails on her knee, and squeezed. Her face momentarily turned red. "As I said, I cannot kill him. He is my father." She sat back. "I would like you to ruin and humiliate him, such as you do on social media. Pressure and embarrass him, so he must step down and leave the country. That will give me enough to convince him I should take over the businesses."

"You think so? How I am suppose to do that."

"I have all the materials you will need here." She indicated a leather satchel by her chair. "Implications of illegal arms trading. Murders and extortions. There are videos and audio files. More than enough."

"Won't that hurt your business? Having him exposed like that?"

"Mr. Bridger," she said, with a look of amusement, "this is Ukraine. The people know the government and oligarch class are corrupt. It is expected. But when a global high-profile and respected group such as your Spy Devils tells the world, it will have much more credibility. It will be hard for him. Even his judges and politicians will abandon him quickly. After all, he will no longer be able to pay them bribes to control them—unless I do. He will need me."

Bridger gave her a look of approval. "Nice plan. What's in it for me?"

"You will receive this case as payment for your efforts," she said, pointing to the Hillcrest case at her feet. "I never wanted it. It was my father who wanted to take it from the Americans. He stole it before he could give it to a Chinese government official."

"Chinese government official? Which Chinese government official?"

"Minister Chen, I believe. The American was bringing the case to him. Did you not know?"

"No, I didn't know." Bridger narrowed his eyes. "Minister Chen?"

"Yes." She crossed one black boot over the other at the ankle. "I would forever be in your debt."

Bridger's eyes did the involuntary glance at her legs.

"I supposed if I just take the case and walk out that door, the security guys waiting outside would be a hindrance."

"Of course. What is in it?" She asked. "Pavlo was unable to open it. Do you know?"

"Nope."

Bridger rubbed his hands through his greasy hair. He got a whiff of his armpit. He smelled like a lab experiment gone wrong.

"Okay," he finally answered.

"Thank you." She picked up the satchel, walked to Bridger, and handed it and the folder to him. "I will take you on your word."

"You can take it to the bank!" Bridger laughed, as he looked around. Ira also laughed, placing her hand on his shoulder. He felt a tingle.

"There should be a bag for this. Have you seen it?" Bridger asked.

"I do not know."

Bridger found it in a corner. He slid the case into the bag and zipped it shut. He turned and started for the door. He stepped around Pavlo, who was still lying unconscious, then stopped.

"Oh, Olek is in jail in Cyprus. We got a little—creative—with him. We didn't hurt him, too bad, I hope. Tell him we are truly sorry. Nothing personal. I apologize. Oh, but we aren't giving the boat back!"

She hesitated, then said, "Well...thank you."

"See ya, Pavlo. Thanks for the help. Maybe we will meet again under different circumstances."

Bridger walked through the door wondering if they could get through the day without any additional surprises.

44

BEAST IS DEAD

Kyiv, Ukraine

When he reached the Skoda, Bridger got in and handed the bulky bag to Peter.

"You got it!" Peter bear-hugged the bag that contained Hillcrest. "I can't believe it. This is great!"

Then Peter realized the car wasn't moving. Bridger wasn't giving orders to the Spy Devils. "What's going on?" Peter asked after nervously waiting alone in the car.

"Nothing," was Bridger's one-word *leave me the fuck alone* answer.

Within seconds, he pulled the Skoda into the early morning traffic to start his surveillance detection route.

Bridger checked his phone for messages. Nothing from Chapel. No safe house location. No message from Beast. His senses were firing on all cylinders.

He opened his Signal secure application and sent a message to Chapel: *Have it. Where are we meeting?*

Bridger then launched a group voice call and selected the speaker on his phone's audio controls.

"Any word from Beast?" Bridger asked. He felt his pulse rise when no one answered. "Demon, find him."

"Right," Demon replied.

"Be careful, okay?" Bridger said with genuine concern. The fatigue was getting to him. His mind was not focused, and his emotions were too close to the surface. He looked at Peter, who was still clutching the bag, his eyes half-closed and his head resting against the window.

"Have you heard where the meeting is?" Snake asked.

"I don't know. We are on an SDR. I'm contacting Chapel. I'll send a message when I know. Get someplace and be ready to move."

Bridger did not like the idea of going anywhere blind. Operationally, he would always have the team check the location in advance. A Devilbot would be in the air. They would know the in and out. He had none of that.

"Can I get some coffee while he is Beast hunting? I saw a place near here," Imp asked.

"I want some, too," Beatrice said.

"I could use a bagel…with a schmear," Milton added.

"You all suck," was Imp's response.

"Get to work. Demon, let me know," Bridger said, then cut off the call.

"Your team is insane and irritating at times," Peter said, lifting his head off the window.

Bridger's phone gave out three electronic beeps. He let out a tired sigh when he saw the 'M' caller ID.

Reluctantly, he hit the answer and speakerphone buttons.

"I'm a little busy, May. Can I call you back?"

"No, and can you ever be polite?" she asked.

"That was polite." He checked his mirror for any familiar cars. He took the next right turn, looking to see if any followed.

"You have it?"

"Yes."

"Good," she answered, then said nothing else.

"What do you want, May?" He checked his mirror and did a quick lane change—which drew angry honks from several cars. He turned the car down a side street.

"I just wanted the update—" she paused, "—and to see how you are doing."

Bridger's face creased with a look of confusion.

"How am I *doing*? You are calling at this moment to ask me how I am *doing*? Well, I have a headache. Probably because I've only eaten protein bars for the past two days. I need some sleep. I smell. That's how I am doing. Thanks for asking."

"Well, that was quite informative," she said tersely.

Bridger could tell she was annoyed. He felt better.

"What is actually going on, May?"

"Call me later." She ended the call without another word.

Bridger didn't know what to make of May calling, and he was way too tired to think about it. The long day had turned into two long days. Knowing there was a chance it might be ending soon invigorated him.

His Signal phone application identified a secure group call. He punched the speaker button.

"Beast is dead! Beast is dead!" Demon's voice yelled out of the phone. "Shot dead in his room."

There was a pause, then gasps and shouts as the other Spy Devils reacted to the news.

"Quiet!" Bridger shouted and shook his head. "How?"

Bridger jerked the Skoda across a lane of traffic and stomped on the brakes. It lurched to a stop. He jammed the transmission into park.

The Hillcrest case bounced off the dash and hit Peter in the face. He felt a trickle of blood roll from his right nostril.

"What the hell, Bridger?"

"What did you say? Say that again!" Bridger shouted.

"Dead. He must have six holes in his chest. It is hard to tell—it is a fucking mess. There's blood everywhere, but—I don't think it is all his. There is too much. Looks like some guy's brains are splattered on the wall. Not his. Spent brass. Beast's knife is covered in blood. I think he took out—three of them."

Demon saw a small pulpy clump of flesh at his feet. He bent over, picked it up, took a close look, and rubbed it between his fingers. "I think he cut some guy's balls off." Demon flipped the mass on the floor like he was tossing a used tissue.

"No other bodies?" Bridger asked.

"Nope, and I don't think any of them walked away. Hang on. I see something in Beast's mouth. Hang on. There is a note. In his mouth."

"A note? What does it say?"

"What the fuck?" Demon said.

"What does it say, Demon?" Bridger barked.

"It says *'A gift for the Devil.'*"

Bridger's hands gripped and twisted on the steering wheel, causing a squeaking sound of flesh on plastic. He turned his head and looked out the side window.

"What?" Peter looked at Bridger.

Bridger waved his arm to silence him.

"Execute your exfiltration plans."

"What about Beast?" Demon asked.

Bridger hesitated this time. Thinking was a struggle. He blinked hard once and let out a breath.

"I have to get rid of this case and talk to Chapel. Call the Olegs. They can help with Beast's...body. And get out of here. I will contact you when we are moving."

"We need to watch you! Let's get the bots in the air. We can pull off and have them over the location in twenty minutes," Beatrice shouted through her sobbing.

"No. Execute your plans. I want you out of here."

"Fuck that," Snake said, just before he hit the off button.

Bridger shifted the transmission into drive and pulled the car back into traffic. Peter wedged the case between his legs and grabbed the door handle.

Bridger had lost a Spy Devil, something he had never experienced before. They were built to be invisible. He had failed and didn't know how or why. He wanted to get this over with as soon as possible.

The card in Beast's mouth was meant for him as a warning.

Payback for some operation, perhaps. But who knew the Spy Devils were there? Who knew anything about Beast *being* a Spy Devil?

It is a short list. A very short list.

The ding of Bridger's phone interrupted his internal dialogue. He saw the bright letters D.C. contrasted against the black screen.

"It's Chapel, finally." The message contained only an address. "Look this up," he told Peter, showing him the screen.

Peter punched the address into the navigation system on his phone.

"It's in Lebedevka Village. Across and along the river. Looks like a thirty-minute zigzagging drive through mid-morning Kyiv traffic."

Peter's directions led to a narrow tree-lined road that paralleled the river. The address was the last house on the road—a three-story brick mansion with large windows on a wooded lot. A driveway, bound by low stone walls, snaked through the trees and came to an end at a set of red brick steps leading to the front door.

"Nice digs," Peter said.

Bridger didn't answer.

"I missed it," he whispered, "I can't believe I missed it."

"What?" Peter asked. "Missed what?"

"Damn it! I was distracted by—. I lost my fucking focus," Bridger said, with a pound of his fist against the steering wheel.

"What?" Peter shouted.

"This is an ambush."

Bridger slammed his foot on the accelerator, causing the vehicle to fishtail on its worn tires. Suddenly, the road came to an abrupt dead-end at piles of tree stumps, dead brush, and construction debris.

A cloud of gravel and dust rose as Bridger hit the brakes, reversed, and backed into the driveway. He gunned it forward back on the road, finally pointing the Skoda in the right direction.

They didn't see the car until it was too late, so they had no time to brace themselves.

The Renault Logan came out of the brush on the left side of the road. It smashed the Skoda like a javelin hitting right behind the driver's seat. The car went airborne. The right-side back quarter-panel crushed into a tree on the other side of the road. It spun to the left and pivoted slowly on its nose like a ballerina on pointe until it keeled over and started a rapid slide on its left side down the hill toward the river. The momentum slowed as it pinballed off tree trunks and stumps until it stopped.

It was a total wreck. Steam hissed from the awkwardly bent radiator angling out of the engine. Fluids leaked. The familiar smell of gas mixed with the scent of pine needles. The wheels slowly rotated with creaking sounds.

Bridger couldn't tell what was worse. The ringing in his ears? The pressure behind his eyes? The dizziness? The tacky sweat all over his body? Or the feeling he was about to barf? Glancing down, it looked like his left wrist was completely fucked up. A blurry image entered his head of his hand jamming into the steering wheel.

His hazy vision picked up the outlines of bodies moving toward him.

He stood but fell before he could take a step—then it was dark.

When Bridger woke up, his ears were ringing like a bell choir. He shook his head and squeezed his eyes tight. He saw his hands were zip-tied to the arms of a chair. His feet, which he couldn't see, and couldn't move, must have been bound the same way. His left wrist looked like a bruised eggplant.

"Peter?"

He looked up and squinted his eyes, hoping it would help bring things into focus. No Peter to the right. He twisted back to the left and saw Peter slumped in a chair. He looked bruised and maybe had blood seeping from a large cut across his forehead.

A shape in front of him started talking.

"He is alive," a voice said in Chinese.

Bridger concentrated his eyes on a Chinese male of average height. Dark straight hair. Dark eyes. Wide cheekbones.

"I know you speak Chinese," the shape said.

Bridger did his best to focus. It was hard enough to form a thought in English. Now he tried to formulate a reply in Chinese.

"Yes, I do. A lovely language," Bridger said in Mandarin.

"I understand you are Bridger. The leader of the Spy Devils. And this is the spy from the American company," the voice said.

Bridger remained silent. Then it came to him—through the pain and the fog of a possible concussion.

They had been captured by Dragon Fire.

45

WHAT IS IN THE CASE?

Lebedevka Village, Ukraine

"What? Who am I?" Bridger asked, using English this time. "I will call you Bridger unless you want to tell me your real name." Li Chu switched to English, too.

"I know who you are, too, Li Chu."

Li Chu was just as described by the Dragon Fire men as Bridger was interrogating them. A military presence and the familiar look of an assassin. Bridger thought the man needed a shave and looked as tired as Bridger felt. He wore jeans and a tight leather jacket with—*a Springsteen t-shirt underneath?*

"My name is Jack. Jack Nicklaus," Bridger said.

"Jack. Your name is Jack? Right…Jack," Li Chu said with a scoff. He held up the Devil Stick and examined it. "We found this in the vehicle. I am not sure how it works. Like this, *Jack?*"

He touched it to Bridger's chest. Pain exploded through a body already in pain as a crackling sound echoed in the room.

"Ouch! That hurts!" Bridger said, forcing a mocking grin.

Li Chu seemed perplexed by Bridger's reaction. He touched Bridger again.

"You need practice," Bridger said, immediately after the shock stopped. Then he looked at Li Chu and puckered his lips into a kiss shape. He pantomimed blowing a couple of kisses.

Bridger could see Li Chu was totally mystified by his reaction.

"Tell me the nature of your organization, the names of the members of your team, and where we can find them. Who do you work for in the CIA?"

"Are you still employed by the MSS? I thought they would have lined you up and shot you by now."

Answering a question with a question. An annoying tactic. And it pissed off Li Chu.

Where are we? How long was I out?

Li Chu knocked Bridger's chair over with a shove of his foot. Unable to cushion his fall, Bridger hit the floor hard on his right side. Li Chu kicked Bridger in his stomach. Bridger gasped in pain and worked to suck air back into his lungs. The man behind Bridger put him upright. It allowed Bridger to analyze the room.

It was a massive rectangular living area with a vaulted ceiling. He guessed thirty by forty feet. The wall he faced was mostly all glass. Sheer white curtains covering floor to ceiling windows. A sliding glass door. On the other side of the glass doors and windows were a large brick patio, trees, and glimpses of a river reflecting sunlight.

On his left was a carpeted sitting area. Two large couches. A table with a few magazines on it. A large flat-screen television was anchored to the wall. On his right was a fireplace surrounded by bookshelves. He faced a dining table that was turned the long way to the wall. One chair was on the other side. Two were moved out of the way. Two were occupied by Peter and Bridger.

Peter was still unconscious to his left. His chin was down. Saliva dripping from his mouth. Blood drying on his face. In the window's reflection, he counted two men behind them and one over by the door.

Then he saw the Hillcrest bag on the dining table a few feet away. That's when he got the idea.

Although it might hurt a little.

"Your strategy to expose us in the media was brilliant—and a death sentence, as you knew," Li Chu said

"Thanks, buddy. Hey. How does it feel to blow the brains out of your elite team? What was it? Seven? No, eight times, wasn't it? And thanks for the positive and constructive feedback. It is always welcomed."

"Who do you work for?" Li Chu shouted through clenched jaws.

The yelling made the front of Bridger's head throb.

He is getting pissed off. Let's see how far I can take this. I need him to make a mistake.

"Who do I work for? Myself." Bridger painfully rolled his neck. "No, really. I made you an international star. It *has* been my pleasure to ruin your life in doing so."

Li Chu walked behind Bridger. He leaned down to whisper into his ear. A sign of control.

"You were able to locate us. How?" Li Chu asked in a hissing tone.

Bridger typically would have ignored the obvious interrogation technique, but he decided to go along with it. Bantering about spy tradecraft could be fun, plus it stretched the clock.

"Actually, that is a good question."

Bridger knew the intel came from May. It was good information that led to them tracking air and hotel reservations, car rentals, and movements of the enemies the Chinese had targeted for assassination. Without it, finding the Dragon Fire team would have been impossible —as impossible as trying to find the Spy Devils.

So how did Li Chu find us? Why did he kill Beast?

Beast. The physical pain caused by the ambush had temporarily made him forget the mental pain caused by the news that someone had killed his man. The chance that *the* someone was a few feet from him re-energized Bridger and refocused his plan. He had to keep control.

The moment will come. It always does. Usually just once, and only for an instant. I have to recognize it and be ready.

Bridger ran his tongue along his teeth and felt blood stuck to some of them.

"How did we locate you? I call it good old fashioned espionage by us and bad tradecraft by you. You were sloppy."

Li Chu pondered the appraisal of his tradecraft. He started a small pattern of pacing a few steps, then turning. Repeat. Repeat. He shook his head.

"No. No. We were not."

"Okay. To be fair, we had some good intel. Great intel. You didn't stand a chance. The MSS has been penetrated, and they have been reporting on you like a 24-hour news channel."

Li Chu walked to the patio door. He thought about this as he looked over the patio and yard. "That is more likely. Who?"

Bridger was peering out the window, too. The midday sun was glaring off the glass. Bridger had an idea—a guess. If he said the name and was wrong, no harm to him. The problem he had at this moment, zip-tied to a chair, being interrogated by a Chinese assassin in Kyiv, was if he was right, and he was reasonably confident he was, he wasn't sure of the ramifications. Right now, it was best to say nothing.

I will deal with that later. I have to kill this guy first.

Li Chu grabbed the bag.

"What is in this case?"

"I got no problem telling you. It's called Hillcrest," Bridger said.

Do it.

"What is it? Bio-weapon? Gold? A suitcase nuclear weapon?"

Open it and find out.

"Open it and find out."

Li Chu unzipped the bag, reached in, pulled out the case, and set it on the table.

You just made the mistake.

46

THE STUFF DREAMS ARE MADE OF

Lebedevka Village, Ukraine

"Say, I might have missed it. Who gave you this address?" Bridger cocked his head and painfully raised his eyebrow. "We both know you couldn't find out for yourself. So, who helped you?"

Li Chu jammed the Devil Stick into Bridger's chest. He spasmed and gripped the chair with his purple left wrist, sending even more pain through him. The sweat rolled off his face as his eyes leered at the man.

"Admit it, you made too many mistakes. As we say, you sucked," Bridger poked Li Chu with a laugh.

Li Chu waved the weapon in Bridger's face. The glare of anger in his eyes.

"I am not the one tied in the chair."

"I can't argue with *that*."

It was Li Chu's turn to laugh. "You will soon be ruined, and we will be gone, with this."

Good. Good. The case. Keep going, idiot.

"Jack, I must thank you for one thing. You have shown me the value of social media as a powerful weapon." Li Chu stood in front of Bridger with his mobile phone camera pointed at Bridger's face. "I planned on killing you, but I think you value your anonymity more than life. The secret and mysterious Spy Devils." His voice was filled with sarcasm. "When we are done here, I will send your image to the world and make you as famous as you made us. So, I will kill you, so to speak, as you killed us."

"Now that is bad news." By sending Bridger's image to the world, he would seriously harm Bridger's entire life and the Spy Devils' operational activities—maybe permanently.

"That would be disappointing," Bridger said a few seconds later, with the pain still pulsating in his chest. When he recovered, he fixed his eyes on the Chinese assassin. "Why did you kill my person?"

Li Chu looked genuinely confused.

"What? I haven't killed anyone. As I said, I do not plan to kill you either, Jack."

His spinning head didn't help him sort out the confusion caused by Li Chu's comment. Would there be a reason for the leader of the Dragon Fire to lie to him? Spite. Hatred. Okay, that he would accept. But he didn't show any of that.

"Right. You didn't touch him. Is that what you are saying?"

"I am not a liar. I would not deceive you. I hate you as an enemy, but I can respect you as an opponent. Let's not be petty."

"I appreciate that, buddy. I'll send you a card for your birthday." Bridger tried to wiggle his numb fingers.

Li Chu gave him a quizzical look, not exactly sure what to make of this man secured to a chair. He continued with his interrogation.

"Where am I?" A weak voice. Peter. His face was pale and damp. Blood dripped from a cut over his left eye.

"Peter. You are alive." Bridger winced in pain as he turned his head.

"What have I missed?" Peter spit some blood from his mouth, then he looked around the room.

I just need to keep delaying. When the time comes, we make our move.

"Well. The Chinese are about to kill us. No, he isn't going to kill me. I am not sure what he plans for you. I think that sums it up." Bridger's tone was between mocking and serious as he stared at Li Chu. "Does that about cover it?"

"I'm...well...that is...not good." Peter struggled against the restraints. Then he stopped and straightened his body in a moment of recall. "Hillcrest?"

All eyes turned to the sunlight-splattered silver case lying on the table.

"What is in it?" Li Chu said to Peter.

"I hope it is lunch. I am hungry." Bridger shrugged his shoulders as much as he could. "He would know better than I. He works there. But if you are asking my thoughts, I would hazard a guess it's '*the stuff that dreams are made of.*'" Bridger let his Humphrey Bogart impression, one he always thought was pretty good, bounce inside Li Chu's head.

He could see by the blank expression Li Chu did not recognize the voice or the famous line from *The Maltese Falcon*.

"What is that...stuff of dreams?" Li Chu stepped away from the table.

Bridger shook his head, amused. "It was a bird. A movie. Forget it." He waited for the next jolt. It didn't come. Instead, he enjoyed the stupid look on Li Chu's face.

Li Chu pointed to the table.

"Isn't it curious that all of this is about getting something we know nothing about?" He held it up in front of Bridger.

Be alert, Peter.

"Isn't that the definition of espionage?" Bridger asked. "How often do we ever know what it is about, or more interestingly, what will be the result of all our work? You think your side is right. I know my side is right. So what? We deceive and plot and target and act, then move on to the next more important thing. Like this case. What were *you* doing —what, a few days ago—before you even knew this existed?"

"Jack. Open it."

Li Chu moved the case back in front of Peter.

"Jack?" Peter was confused. "I don't know how, either."

Peter seemed to be more in control. Bridger could see some *fuck you* in his attitude.

"I have been told it cannot be opened, or the contents will be destroyed. But I have been told there is a way." Li Chu swung the case in front of Peter, then Bridger, then Peter again, as if it would magically give him the solution to the puzzle. "Open it!"

"I don't know how. I don't!" Peter said.

Li Chu reached for the Devil Stick. Peter recoiled as much as he could in the chair.

Bridger looked at the irate man, then at Peter.

Perfect. Now is the time.

"I do," Bridger announced in a matter-of-fact tone.

Peter and Li Chu stopped immediately, like their batteries had suddenly run out.

"What?" They said simultaneously, looking at him with disbelief.

"I can open it. What else do you want to know?" He said it with a sigh like he was bored talking about the subject.

"How can you open the case without harming the contents?" Li Chu asked.

"Yeah. How can you open the case without harming the contents?" Peter was shocked. "Since when?"

"Since whenever." Bridger stared into Peter's eyes, hoping he could comprehend his role in Bridger's plan.

Come on, corporate spy.

"I am not a fool," Li Chu said.

"Well, I disagree, but that still doesn't mean I can't open the case." Bridger smiled.

Li Chu looked at Peter disbelievingly. "Can he get in?"

Peter met Bridger's gaze.

Back me up. We can get out of this.

"If Jack says he can, he can," Peter said, with a shrug.

Then Bridger saw it— behind Li Chu–a few feet on the other side of the glass door. The Devilbot was hovering and pointed straight at Bridger.

It's time to fuck with this fucker.

47

A THIN METAL DEVICE

Lebedevka Village, Ukraine

"It is in my backpack, which was in the car."

Li Chu motioned to his man by the door, who turned and left the room.

"Is there a reason why you didn't tell *me* about this?" Peter still had his eyes turned to Bridger.

He's a little miffed.

"Nope. Just never thought about it."

The guard returned a few minutes later, holding a backpack. He handed it to Li Chu, who impatiently dumped the contents on the table. A plastic bag containing a ball of tangled power cords. Power adaptors. USB sticks. Pads of paper. Loose change. A few open rolls of antacids —each half gone. An assortment of pens. Golf balls.

Frustrated, he held it out to Bridger.

"Where is it?"

Bridger looked at his wrists. Then at Peter. Then back at Li Chu. Then he saw the Devilbot pull away from the windows and out of his sight.

"Don't we all want to see what this has been about? We have been chasing, dodging, and whatever else for days, and for what? You won. You got us. You got him. Way to go!" He flinched toward Peter. "If you want my help, cut us loose."

"No. Tell me where it is and how to use it." Li Chu snapped his fingers in the air. Bridger felt the cold metal of a gun on the back of his neck. He didn't react at all. In fact, to Li Chu's surprise, Bridger showed more annoyance than anything.

"Really?"

This was *the* critical moment. Bridger had to irritate the hell out of his captor one more time. If not, the chance of getting out was slim and none, and slim just left town.

Bridger continued.

"It goes like this. If you kill me, you still can't open it, because I am the only one who can, and so on and so forth. Then you will realize I am right and threaten to shoot him," Bridger nodded toward Peter, "and I say fine. You were going to kill corporate spy boy anyway, and if you do, I am definitely *not* going to help you open it. And, to be totally transparent, which is all the rage these days, he doesn't mean anything to me. You will be doing me a favor." Bridger gave no indication he was lying as he ended with a broad smile.

"Thanks. I love you, too." Peter frowned.

"Then, as poor Peter here bleeds out on the floor, you will threaten to beat me up and torture me, which you know won't work, at least not for many hours, or days. So why not cut us loose? We can all work together to look inside this pain-in-the-ass case."

There was a moment of silence as Li Chu considered the logic of Bridger's argument. He gestured to the guard, who cut the zip-ties from the arms and legs of both men.

Each man immediately rubbed their sore muscles and checked their wounds. Peter rose slowly from his chair, grasping the back to steady himself and get his balance. He touched the wound above his eye with his fingers. They came back stained with blood.

Bridger winced as he pulled his left arm up with his right and tucked it into his shirt for support. He rubbed his right hand through his wet hair. After a few seconds, he shuffled around the table to face the room. He saw the guards were still close, their guns out and pointed in their direction.

"It's here." He picked up an eleven-inch-long travel power strip. It had space for three plugs on each side and four USB ports on the end. An eighteen-inch cord extended from one end. Then, he dropped it. "I need some help." Bridger looked up at Peter.

Peter looked at Li Chu, who nodded approval. Peter walked around to stand next to Bridger. That gave Bridger time to get a better view of the room.

The couch is six feet away. Two big steps. One chair in the way.

"Pull the cord out of the end of the adaptor," Bridger instructed Peter. "Grab each side of the power strip and pull in opposite directions." Peter did as he was told. "Good. Slide it open and separate it into two halves. Drop the lighter half. Shake the other one upside down. Catch what comes out."

Peter caught a thin metal device that looked like a small television remote. It had a screen, some buttons of various sizes and colors, and a touch biometric pad.

"Here," he handed it to Li Chu.

Li Chu looked it over, holding it the long way, turning it in his hands cautiously. Front. Back. Sides. He stopped on the side with an alphanumeric pad under a display panel, which ran the silver device's length. In the lower-left corner was a larger red button with the universal circle and line symbol signifying an on/off switch. Li's Chu's thumb hesitated over the red button. He thought, then moved his thumb to the side.

"How does it work?" Li Chu stepped closer, his head twitched from the device to Bridger and back. He handed the passkey to Bridger.

Bridger seared his eyes at Peter with a '*here it comes, be ready*' expression.

"I like you, Li Chu. We are a lot alike, I think. Perhaps under different circumstances, we could be friends. Do you play golf?" No answer. "Ah well. Say, I want to make certain of one point. You did not kill any of my people or leave a little message for me to find. Correct?"

"What? I told you. No."

"Thanks for that." Bridger smiled back.

Bridger shoved the contents of his backpack on the floor with his right hand and moved the passkey device. Li Chu was to his left side. Peter on his right. The three Dragon Fire men were across the table at various distances.

"Once it is powered on, a timer starts to count down. Something called a…bypass authentication code…appears, and we have ten seconds to input it perfectly—no mistakes, none—or it shuts down. Permanently. Then it self-destructs. Then boom!"

"How?" Li Chu looked at the device like it was going to bite him.

"Yeah, how do you know this?" Peter asked.

"Later." He said to Peter. He looked at Li Chu. "That's all I know. I didn't get the manual. You want to do it?" Li Chu stepped back. "Yeah, I figured."

Bridger turned to Peter, who shook his head. "No way."

"Cowards." Bridger leaned his legs against the table to steady himself. "Peter, when I say so, count down the time." Bridger took a deep breath. "Well, if we want to see this, here we go. Now."

He pushed the red button. The screen blinked to life and glowed amber. A quick beep from the case startled them. The keypad and display on the case also lit up. On the token, a 12-digit random alphanumeric bypass code appeared.

"Holy shit," Bridger said.

"Ten. Nine. Eight—" Peter counted.

A digital tone filled the room as Bridger pushed each key.

"Crap. Crap." Bridger's hand trembled.

"Seven. Six. Five."

"Crappy crap."

"Four. Three. Two."

He pushed the last three keys as fast as a woodpecker.

"One."

With the push of the last symbol, each device released the same tone. Silence followed. The case access panel lights glowed green, which was followed by a few soft clicks.

Relief hung in the air as they stood for a few seconds looking at each other. For the moment, curiosity had overcome animosity. Together, they were going to see Hillcrest.

Bridger saw the three Dragon Fire men move toward the table.

Li Chu glanced at the others. He reached his hands to either side of the case. His thumb and forefinger gripped the corner as he slowly lifted the silver top.

The room was silent.

The case contained dark gray impact foam with the center cut out in the shape of a square—nothing else.

"It's empty." Li Chu's eyes went from the case to Bridger, then to Peter.

Peter reached his hands into the case and tried to pull the foam out. It was attached. "How can—what is going on? Where is Hillcrest? What is it?" He couldn't take his stunned eyes off the empty case.

"Empty!" Bridger broke out in a loud laugh. "That Gilbert is something else."

He kept his eye on the token as his right hand grabbed Peter hard around the elbow. The display blinked and a digital count down appeared.

Five...four...

Bridger turned and pushed Peter as hard as he could toward the couch. Li Chu and his men hesitated.

*Three...two...*Bridger wrapped Peter in a bear hug and jumped. The momentum carried them over the couch, landing on the carpet between the couch and coffee table. The Dragon Fire men raised their guns, wildly firing at the diving men.

Li Chu saw the countdown on the passkey and leaped away.

One.

48

CHAPEL AND CHEN

Lebedevka Village, Ukraine

W hen the detonator was triggered inside Hillcrest, it set off a small charge within six ounces of C-4 explosive material lining the metal case. That charge set off the chemical reaction decomposing the C-4. Gases expanding at over twenty-six thousand feet per second sent a force through the metal case. The destruction was instantaneous.

Bridger's ears were ringing so bad he thought his head had exploded. It took a few shakes of his head to get enough of his senses back so he could scan the situation in the room.

Most of the glass wall was gone. The ceiling over the explosion had partially collapsed into the four-inch deep, circular hole in the floor. The force of the exploding C-4 had blown the couch against Bridger and Peter, scooping them to the wall like a shovel, the burning and splintered furniture slamming them against the far wall. The cracked television fell off its mountings onto the floor by their heads.

Peter was next to him on the floor, coughing and covered in white dust. All the glass windows and doors leading to the patio were shattered. Broken tables, chairs, and debris were scattered around the room. Dust and smoke from small fires swirled in the air. He grunted as he used his body to tip it back and leaned against it to steady himself as he stood on wobbly legs.

The metal Hillcrest case had become red hot shrapnel and sliced into the men like porcupine quills. The smoke was too thick to his left, so he couldn't see what happened to Li Chu. The Dragon Fire man nearest to the explosion, the one who liked to stick a gun against his neck, was dead. What was left of his front was red and pulpy, looking more like a well-tenderized steak at the meat counter.

The man who stood behind Peter was alive. He was about five feet in front of Bridger, on his hands and knees, groaning, full of holes that were dripping blood and pieces of his head onto the floor like melting candle wax. He was missing most of his scalp, and it looked like a chunk of his right arm was gone and a few fingers on his left hand.

Through the smoke to his right, Bridger saw the sentry by the door bent over at the waist, looking at the floor, shaking his head. He was bleeding like a fountain from gashes in his neck, chest, and legs, but Bridger considered him as operational.

Bridger had to decide who to kill first. Should he risk turning his back on the nearby Scalpless as he goes for Bleeder as the more imminent threat? Does he have time to take out Bleeder and get to Scalpless before he recovers and shoots Bridger in the back?

Bridger flashed his eyes down to look at Peter's face. It was white with shock. Blood was flowing from another cut on his head. He was still coughing as he inhaled the smoked-filled air.

"Get out of here," Bridger yelled into Peter's ear. Bridger grabbed Peter's arm, dragged him over the smoldering couch, and shoved him toward the shattered wall of glass. He stumbled over the wreckage and fell. "Get the hell out!" Bridger yelled again. Peter stood and stumbled through the opening onto the patio.

Bridger picked up the broken leg of a wooden chair and took a step toward Scalpless, who was trying to stand. He swung the wood up like an uppercut, slicing Scalpless across the face. When he hit the floor groaning, Bridger raised the chunk over his head like a knife and swung down hard, jamming it deep into Scalp's right eye socket.

Without waiting, he turned to the man by the door.

Bleeder was upright and looking at what Bridger had done to his colleague. He reached for the Makarov on the floor at his feet. Bridger took three large steps to close the distance between them. As Bleeder raised his weapon with his right hand, Bridger threw his right arm up, grabbed the Makarov by the muzzle, and twisted it outward to stay out of the line of fire and loosen Bleeder's grip.

He hit Bleeder with a left across his jaw. That was when he was reminded of the earlier trauma to his left wrist. The rush of adrenalin and numbness was not enough to cover the paralyzing waves of pain that rolled up his arm and through his body. His eyes filled with tears, and he felt his knees go weak.

With Bridger's punch, Bleeder fell back against the wall as more blood pumped from the cuts. He recovered quickly. When Bleeder saw Bridger immobilized in pain, his swollen left arm at his side, he torqued up his right leg and hit Bridger in the left arm and side with a powerful roundhouse kick. Bridger saw it coming at the last instant and slipped his body on an angle to lessen the blow.

Bridger grunted as the air was forced from his lungs. He saw Bleeder pull his arms back to set up strikes to his head. Bridger was still holding Bleeder's gun by the muzzle in his right hand. When Bleeder came in for the kill, Bridger swung his hand up, hitting Bleeder under the chin with the butt of the gun. When he fell back against the wall, Bridger stepped in and speared Bleeder in the throat twice with the gun grip. Bleeder grabbed his throat, wheezing as he slid to the floor.

Bridger figured he had about ten seconds before any Dragon Fire re-enforcements arrived. He checked the gun to make sure it was working and loaded. He flattened his chest against the wall, crouched, and held the gun out with his right hand toward the lower part of the door. In a few seconds, he heard the quick steps of a man approaching.

The MSS man ran through the door holding his gun chest-high with both hands. Bridger shot him in the right knee as he passed, sending bone and blood flying. The man screamed, spun forward, and fell to the floor. He rolled onto his back, reaching for his missing knee. Bridger stood above him, aimed, and mechanically fired one round into the man's face.

Bridger turned, slid left, pointed the Makarov through the door, and emptied the magazine down the hallway. When the slide locked back, he dropped it, picked up and checked the dead man's weapon, and turned toward the opening Peter stumbled through thirty seconds ago. As he walked by Bleeder, he fired three 9mm bullets into his chest.

Passing from the dim smoke-filled room to the bright sunshine nearly made Bridger's concussed head feel like it wanted to explode off his shoulders. He managed to keep one eyelid open enough to make his way across the debris-covered brick patio. At the edge, he fell over a knee-high brick wall onto the grass and rolled a few feet down a slight incline.

Peter was there. He was flanked on one side by Demon, a 1911 in one hand, a large knife in the other. Snake was on the other side. He had a Devil Stick and a Sig Sauer P226. Beast's Sig, Bridger noticed.

"You look like a bad night in Tijuana," Snake said.

"I've had worse," Bridger gasped. He turned to Peter, who was crouched low beside him. Tears were rolling down his red cheeks. "You okay?"

Peter nodded.

"You did good, Peter."

Suddenly the soft whirl of two Devilbots flew over their heads. At about twenty feet above the ground, they held stationary at the corner of the house.

"Beatrice says we have visitors heading our way," Snake said. "She says we should duck."

As they lowered behind the wall, they glimpsed four men moving cautiously around each side of the corner of the house with weapons raised. Then they heard the two *cracks*. Followed a few seconds later by two more. The Devilbots whirled straight up like they were pulled on a string.

They looked over the wall and saw four men lying on the patio.

Three looked dead. One was crawling in the last desperation of a dying person trying to hold onto life.

Demon looked at Bridger. "Rule Number One is suspended until further notice," Bridger said, malice in his voice.

Demon smiled. He stood up and stepped over the wall. His 1911 aimed at the man, he walked over and stood over the dying Dragon Fire.

"No!" the man shouted, holding out his hand like it could block a bullet.

Demon stopped and lowered his pistol. "

Xie xie!" The thankful man dropped to the ground gasping for breath. "Xie xie."

Demon raised his arm and fired twice into the top of the man's head.

"That's for Beast." He turned and walked back to the wall.

"Would you have let him shoot me?" Peter was trying to wipe his face as he held his hand over his cuts. Blood leaked from between his fingers.

"You want to discuss that now?" Bridger looked at the pained face of the corporate spy. "To be honest, I hadn't thought that far ahead." He paused, then smiled. "Yes, I think I would have."

"Milton says more cars are heading this way," Snake said, as he lifted his Stick. They turned to try to see the road through the trees. Two black SUVs and a van were moving fast up the road toward the house.

"Should we go?" Snake asked, his eyes scanning the area around them.

Bridger's attention was on the vehicles.

Eight large and well-armed security guards flew out of the van and took up protective positions from the SUV's doors to the house. One opened a door, and a distinguished-looking man with gray hair and a bright tie stepped out. Danforth Chapel spoke a few words to another person in the car. The second man, an intense, professional-looking Chinese man, stepped out.

The man looked around, then he and Chapel turned and walked toward the front of the house and out of sight. In a few seconds, they could see the men walking through the debris of the destroyed room.

"Chapel. And that must be Chen." Bridger said through gritted teeth.

49

WHERE IS THE CASE?

Lebedevka Village, Ukraine

W hen Chapel walked into the mess left behind at the safe house, it was more than what he expected, but he was not concerned.

He considered himself an optimist, but he was also a pragmatist. Random chance. Holes in preparation and planning. Blind luck. Bad luck. Bad faith. Those and more were sure to rear their ugly heads without warning. He knew regular intelligence officers dealt with the uncertainty as part of a life working in espionage.

But this was *his* world. Corporate intelligence. Risk management. His reputation was continually on the line on a global scale. Chapel was worried whenever he spoke to a client in distress of losing their business. Losing business was not acceptable. He would manipulate them until they agreed to remain with his firm and even expand his service offering.

He would not lose anything today.

It had to be done, he knew. Chapel actually felt some sympathy for Bridger and his Spy Devils. Chapel had to make sure Li Chu was at the safe house when Bridger arrived. There was a risk. It was a messy ad hoc plan to begin with—help Chen by using the Spy Devils and the case as bait to draw out the renegade Li Chu and his Dragon Fire team. Get Hillcrest to Chen so he could get it to China. The variable of Bridger's survival was factored in—and the calculation didn't hold out much hope for him.

Chapel was impressed with May's motherly intuition. It was much more powerful than his calculations. She said they could rely on Bridger's ingenuity to survive. His body was not in the room, as he expected. It seemed she was right.

Dead MSS officers were everywhere. A hunk of wood jutting from the eye of one man. Bullet holes in others. He was looking for Peter, but he must have escaped with Bridger. That damaged one of their potential spin scenarios.

Kirkwood Employee Killed While Selling American Secrets to China.

The files left in Peter's office and downloaded to his computer should be enough to back that up. Kirkwood would pay Chapel Communications for support to push that narrative. It could still work if he was alive. A win-win.

"Where is the case?" Chen was kicking the rubble, spreading dust all over his black shoes and suit.

Chapel surveyed chunks of scorched metal and mutilated bodies scattered around the room.

"There." He pointed at a dead man. "There." He turned again and waved his hands in semi-circles around the room toward another dead MSS officer. "There. I think there. No engineer was good enough to Humpty Dumpty these men back together again." He patted Chen on the back.

"But the case is not here. It is supposed to be here," Chen proclaimed.

"It is here. Just in little pieces. Don't worry. We will take care of you, but it will take a few days. Agreed?"

Chen nodded.

Bridger and Peter sat on the ground across the Dnieper River with their backs against one of the rental cars. Using a military first-aid kit, Snake was tending to his boss's wounds. He had already closed up and bandaged the corporate intel officer's injuries. Standing next to them, Imp held an iPad showing the Devilbot feed. Milton and Beatrice had positioned the drones on an angle to see into the room.

When they were paddled across the river in a small fishing boat, Bridger gave a brief account of the meeting, the deal he struck with Ira Bondar, and the events that led to them being ambushed.

"You royally fucked up," Demon said in disbelief. "*You.*"

"I was distracted," he confessed to them.

"*You?* Distracted? That—" Imp's voice set up for one of his juvenile snarky comments. Bridger looked up and gave Imp the *do not fuck with me at all* look. Imp went back to his monitoring activity.

"Thanks for the rescue," Bridger said.

"You are lucky we never listen to a word you say," Demon said.

"I was counting on it. And you picked up the GPS location of the Hillcrest case?"

"The Imp did," Snake replied.

"You are welcome," Imp said.

"We had bots in the air searching when we picked up the signal," Beatrice added, keeping track of her Devilbot controller.

Milton was doing the same but added with his Alabama drawl, "We had them there in about fifteen minutes."

"The rest is Spy Devils history—including your fuck up," Demon said to complete the story.

"I appreciate that."

Bridger pulled his bandaged wrist away from Snake. He motioned Imp to give him the iPad showing the camera feed from the drone. Resting it in his lap, he saw a perfect view across the river into the house. Bridger hit a key on his phone and put it to his ear. On the screen, he saw Chapel reach into his pocket and take out his phone.

"Hello, Bridger."

"Are you enjoying the view?"

"A little messy." Chapel replied, walking to the opening in the wall. "It is good to know you are not dead. So, how are you?"

"I'm unhappy, to be perfectly honest, thanks for asking. I probably have a broken wrist, but I am confident my golf game won't suffer."

"You seem to have survived. I don't think I can say the same for Hillcrest."

"No, sorry, if that was your plan. Blowing it up seemed like the thing to do at the time. Especially after Li Chu and his goons ambushed us at the same safe house you sent us to—the safe house where we were supposed to meet *you*."

Bridger saw Chapel scan his eyes across the river. He was uncharacteristically silent.

"Sorry if I ruined your plans," Bridger said.

"There are always alternatives, as you have proven today."

"Oh. Hey. Thanks for the recommendation to Ira Bondar. She has significant daddy issues."

"Viktor has been a disappointment—for everyone. Mistrust is such a toxic feeling, especially within families."

"How about mistrust with the MSS guy next to you?"

Chapel kept up his scanning.

"George lost trust with all of us. He made it even more toxic with his threats of exposing his Chinese activities. If he would have left it alone, none of this would have happened. He would have gotten his share for his efforts, and my friend Anton would not have been poisoned—by Viktor."

"Did you know the case was *empty*?"

"What? No? *Empty*?" Bridger could sense and see Chapel was surprised at this new information. No deception. "No, I did not. Makes the effort to retrieve this case not worth it."

"Wish I knew." Bridger saw Chen looking around the room behind Chapel. "Beast is dead. Did you know *that*?"

Bridger heard silence and watched Chapel walk further onto the patio. Chen followed. He looked at the four dead Dragon Fire men.

"Beast? Dead? I am sorry to hear that. I truly am."

Bridger paused and absorbed Chapel's response. He saw the same tone and look of surprise as he had with the empty case—shock, mixed with sincerity.

"Did you have anything to do with it?"

On the screen, Bridger saw a slight shift of Chapel's shoulders. He scratched the back of his neck as he walked in short, slow strides.

"No, not at all. Never. I have no idea what happened to him, whatsoever. Believe me, Bridger. I did not," Chapel added with a quiet, remorseful sound.

Is he lying?

"I am about to raise holy hell and release the Devils on whoever *was* responsible."

"Do you need me to do anything? Arrange transport of the—his remains?"

"No, I appreciate that. We have it taken care of," Bridger said.

"I promise I will look into Beast."

"You do that. You look into it. It won't make a difference whether they know we are coming or not."

Bridger read the tone of resignation as he witnessed a slow nod of Chapel's head.

"My only mission is to find out who killed Beast—and kill them."

Bridger disconnected the call.

"Let's go."

Chapel looked at his phone. Seeing the call was over, he dialed his pilot.

"I will be there within the hour."

Chen walked over and stood in front of him.

"Yes? Minister Chen, how can I help you?" Chapel asked.

"Where is Li Chu?"

50

RESEARCH

Jacob Kirkwood Boardroom

"We're busy. *Very* busy." Jessup was irritated and checked his watch once. Then twice. "You have five minutes."

Peter was wondering why he wasn't fired on the spot for not having Hillcrest with him. He expected Benton to laugh all the way to escorting Peter out the door.

"Peter, your head. It is injured." MacBride looked at the bandages and bruises over his eye.

"Are you alright?" Kirkwood asked.

"Yes, just something I picked up in Ukraine." Peter flashed a quick look at each of the senior executives.

Peter had landed in Chicago aboard Bridger's plane at 4 a.m.

After a shower and some fresh clothes, Peter took one last look at his notes. During the flight back, he used his analytic skills to dissect the MacLean and Kirkwood documents he received from Sandy Boyd. Combining his own research, financial, and news reports, he culled through every bit of information, looking for the patterns.

Once Peter figured it all out—or as much as he could with what he had—he debated whether he should inform the FBI and SEC. Should he raise his suspicions of economic espionage by the Chinese, or the falsification of Kirkwood's earnings? Or should he wait and see what happened? Essentially, keep quiet and do nothing.

His conclusions were rock solid—Peter had no doubt of that. If he went through with his presentation, he knew the shit was going to hit the fan. He didn't want the company to lay off any of his colleagues due to a scandal he exposed.

He called Marilyn at 8 a.m., telling her he needed to meet immediately with MacBride, Jessup, and Kirkwood "regarding the Ukraine assignment."

The executives were sitting around the boardroom table in the exact locations where, two weeks ago, Peter had been given this assignment by the same men. Peter gave them his report, ending with the news that Hillcrest was destroyed.

"Well, that is certainly quite a story," MacBride said.

"Yes, it is. The case being destroyed makes its recovery moot," Jessup said.

"And the funds?" Kirkwood inquired.

"I do not know," Peter answered.

"Well, that is *very* disappointing. I was counting on you," Kirkwood said.

"Well, thank you, Peter. We need to discuss our next course of action, so if you will excuse us," Jessup said in a completely condescending way, dismissing Peter like a child.

Decision time had come.

"I looked into Kirkwood regarding Ukraine and other issues."

"Why?" MacBride seemed surprised.

"It's not unusual to do an analysis of your own company." Peter's answer was professional, not defensive. "I do it from the perspective of the competition. You see, then we can see how the competition views *us*. Maybe make some assumptions on what they think we might do and in reverse, what they might do. So—," Peter leaned over and read from his prepared notes, "—I used the same process for all the activity since George MacLean arrived. I wanted to know."

Peter picked up on their nervousness. Kirkwood's cheeks were lava red. Jessup pursed his lower lip out and in. MacBride was rubbing his thumb and middle finger together as fast as a hummingbird's wings.

"Does this have a point?" Peter saw Jessup put on his lawyer's face.

Peter flipped open a folder and read from his notes.

"Kirkwood was part of Nigeria's supply contracts for Abuja's massive metro rail public transport system. Kenya. Senegal. Ghana. Oil and infrastructure deals." Peter's head hurt, and he pulled the paper closer to his face to read it better in the dim light.

"In Latin America, we won deals for the oil refineries in Costa Rica, the hydro projects in Argentina, roads, ports, and railroads in Peru, Brazil, Venezuela, and hell, pretty much across the continent. Quite a run. A firm named Mourning Dove Investments was not involved in any contracts before George MacLean's arrival. Can't find them anywhere. Now, Mourning Dove is a factor in—well—everything."

"That is not a secret," Kirkwood said, as his hue stabilized at stop sign red.

Jessup was ready to pounce.

"George introduced us to Mourning Dove. They've been a valuable partner. We are very busy, Peter, and I am sorry to say you are not helpful here."

Peter forged on.

"I noticed a company called—" Peter paused while he checked his notes, "Quadrangle Investment Group, LLC, buried deep in every Mourning Dove contract. I traced the ownership, but it ended before it began. The company was consistently included in our business and it makes me wonder." He stopped short of adding, "...and was obvious MacLean was funneling funds through inflated revenues in those contracts and taking a cut with each deal. He was committing a crime..."

"Anyone ever heard of Quadrangle?" Peter asked.

"Poor George. Few knew he was in such a terrible predicament," a voice said from the direction of the door.

Peter involuntarily flinched. Before he turned, he knew it was a man in a nice bespoke worsted wool suit and floral tie.

"Hello, everyone." Ever the consultant, Chapel sauntered around the table, shaking hands. He sat opposite Peter, to Kirkwood's left. He reached out and patted Kirkwood's arm.

"Hello, Danny. Wonderful to see you," Kirkwood replied with a sound of relief. Having Chapel in the room seemed to be the crutch Kirkwood needed to offset the red-checked look of dread that had taken over his face since Peter started laying out the facts.

"Peter, if I had known you were coming back so quickly, I would have invited you to join me." He pointed at Peter. "Gentlemen, you should be very proud of your employee here. He did all he could to bring a complex situation in Ukraine to a favorable end for Kirkwood. And he seems worse for the wear. Are you alright, Peter?"

"Yes, thank you," Peter answered, knowing he wanted to strangle the smug smile off Chapel's face with his floral tie. Peter was amazed at how fresh he looked.

"It there anything else, Peter?" Kirkwood asked.

"Well, I'm just confused. Things are rattling around my head on how the different events were connected—if they are. MacLean. Hillcrest. Bondar. Kirkwood. Mourning Dove." He left out Hillcrest plus Chapel plus Chen plus The Spy Devils. The equation was too complicated.

Peter's head throbbed, but he needed to finish what he had started. There wasn't another option.

"Do you mind if I ask a couple of questions?"

"Time—" Jessup said as he abruptly stood.

Peter got the message.

"Thank you, Peter. Another job well done."

The executives exited the boardroom through the far door that led to the CEO's office.

"Peter. A moment." Chapel stopped him with a grab of his arm. "I believe you left out many details that you have come to know. True?"

"Yes. I did," he said, nodding. "I just wonder how much technology we have given to China in return for new business deals? How much have we been inflating revenue to strengthen the stock of the company?"

"Peter, you should be very careful about what you *think* you know and *to whom* you convey your feelings."

Chapel put his hand on Peter's shoulder. This time it wasn't friendly pats. He felt the fingers tighten deep into his skin. Then he let go. Peter's heart was beating through his chest as he watched Chapel stride through the door on the other end of the room.

"Remember, the comment about truth being stranger than fiction? On the plane?"

"Yes, I do," Peter answered.

"You should have listened better." Chapel turned and walked across the boardroom. He exited through the door to the CEO's office.

Peter stood. Chapel's warning was clear.

Peter knew too much.

51

WRATH OF THE DEVIL

Kyiv, Ukraine

The two Mercedes' luxury sedans' license plates indicated they were diplomatic vehicles registered to China's Embassy in Ukraine. They were parked mid-block, half on the sidewalk and half on Pavla Skoropads'koho Street. Their flashers blinked red in the dark Kyiv night. The meaning was clear: *stay away*.

The drivers leaned on the hood of the second car, chain-smoking cigarettes. A pile of butts collected at their feet on the red bricks. Street kids knew enough to stay away from the pair but had no fear of hassling the well-dressed people walking up the sidewalk. It was only midnight, so there was plenty of darkness left to hassle unsuspecting tourists.

They were on the street outside Skybar—one of the more elite and trendy nightclubs in a city known for elite and trendy nightclubs. Situated atop a building in the fashionable Arena City area, Skybar's panoramic view, dance floor, music, drinks, and food attracted crowds of tourists, locals, and VIPs.

Bridger was ready. No more Peter Schaeffer. Kirkwood, secret cases, or corporate intrigue. He didn't need May to give him a mission.

He had one, and that mission was to find out who killed Beast and kill them. He was ready to unleash the wrath of the Devil on those responsible.

The Spy Devils are the ones who fuck with people. Not the other way around.

No Spy Devil had ever been killed. The risk was inherent in covert operations. It's hard to avoid a few scrapes when combating the most dangerous and corrupt humans or organizations on Earth. The Spy Devils didn't know it, but Bridger always calculated the risk versus reward equation to avoid a dead Devil. This mission from May had forced him to rush.

It had killed Beast.

Every member of the Spy Devils had a 'Death Folder' containing contact info and a series of potential cover stories depending on where they worked in Bridger's covert business network. Bridger knew Beast had some family in New York. A mother and sister. An ex-wife and daughter. It was Bridger's duty to inform them—something he had never done before.

He was providing personal security for a client that can't be named, sorry. You should be proud. A brave man.

Seared in his brain was a list of people who might have killed Beast. Tonight, he was going to make that list shorter.

Neither Chinese driver felt the danger coming. However, they simultaneously felt the fifty thousand volts of the Taser prongs when they hit them at the base of their skulls. They rattled on their feet for three seconds, then collapsed straight down to the sidewalk. Demon and Snake slid off of the Mercedes' roof and landed next to the men.

Releasing the wires, they jammed the weapon into each man's eye and pushed the stun gun trigger. The electronic clicking kept time with the bodies quaking. To make certain the Chinese guards were obedient, they rotated the handle to the switches that controlled the aerosols. They stuck the end under each man's nose and released an airborne fentanyl and pepper spray mix. Their bodies arched as their heads rolled back. Then they stopped moving.

"Anything?" Bridger pinged Imp, who was in a stolen Toyota Camry nearby.

"Clear on all frequencies. Now I need you to plug in the doohickey I gave you into the China guy's little comm gizmo."

Bridger complied.

He was grateful that the massive doses of painkillers were finally working. In a few seconds, Bridger heard, "Okay. We own the bitches. I will knock them out of their systems as you move. Go have fun in the nightclub full of naked drunk girls. I will sit here in a car that smells like donkey piss."

As Demon and Snake locked the men in the Mercedes, Bridger walked toward a frosted glass side entrance door to the building a few feet from the cars. The door opened slightly, and a watermelon-sized head peered out.

"Hello, Yaroslav."

"Mr. Bridger. It is good to see you. I did not know you were in Kyiv." The bald-headed security guard, dressed in a black T-shirt, jacket, and pants, was as large as a city bus. He swung the door open and let the men in. They entered into a small hallway that led to a fire door ten feet away. To their left was an elevator.

"Just for the day. How is your little boy, Yaroslav?"

"Not so little anymore. He is twelve now, big as a bull."

"Twelve? My goodness. Time is an angry beast. It just keeps moving on. Here." Bridger pulled packages of American baseball cards from his black windbreaker. "Give these to him."

Yaroslav took the little packages into his massive hands. "Thank you, sir. He will enjoy these."

"There are some Chinese men here?" Bridger asked, his head flexing up to the ceiling.

Yaroslav glanced toward the frosted glass door where he knew the diplomatic cars and the drivers were on the street. "Yes. Upstairs. The important man and several others. They come often. They are very arrogant with our security men and the guests."

"Where are the others?"

"One is usually at the elevator entrance. Two with the man. One roams on the balcony. All in gray suits."

"Thank you, Yaroslav. Do you mind if we go upstairs through the employee entrance?" Bridger asked, as he pushed the button before he had an answer.

"No, sir. Of course." Yaroslav held the door open to let the men in, nodding to each as they passed.

"Thank you. And…um…keep an eye on that Mercedes, okay?" The doors closed on the service elevator.

When the door opened, the deafening music, spinning lights, intense heat, body oder, and gyrating bodies assaulted Bridger's senses. The place was packed with men trying to look tough and women who didn't need to work hard to look sexy.

The ceiling was illuminated with semi-circular rows of colored lights positioned like stars. Powerful beams of light—greens, yellows, purples, blues—hanging from spinning overhead projectors sliced the darkness, catching the fog shooting from machines at the stage.

Plush gray couches and high-backed chairs were arranged in rows facing the bar and stage. They were jammed with patrons laughing, pointing, and screaming into their friend's ears, trying to be heard over the booming music. Every table was coated with glasses, bottles, and plates. Along the far wall was a large panoramic window with a stunning night view of Kyiv.

To Bridger, it looked like something out of an Edgar Allen Poe horror story.

"Beatrice? Milton?"

"We are jammed by the windows about twenty feet away from the target."

Bridger could barely hear them in his earbud.

Dressed as tourists, Milton and Beatrice had arrived at the club two hours before—just moments after the Chinese. The couple had been dancing and drinking since then.

"Okay, wait for the clicks," he semi-shouted into his comm.

Snake broke right out of the elevator, then left. He walked between the DJ stand and stage where girls in mesh tops and short skirts whirled their arms over their heads. Snake forced his way past the bar toward the elevators that went directly from the ground floor to the club level.

Snake could see a small man in a gray suit shouting in the face of bigger men. The security men's faces were red with anger, but they let the little man shout and point at them. He pointed at the people coming off the elevator and back toward the sitting area.

Snake had his Devil Stick in his left hand along his leg. In stride, he grabbed a square appetizer plate off a table with his right hand, walked into the elevator alcove, and tapped the shorter man on his shoulder. The screaming Chinese intel officer wheeled around, exposing his neck as he tilted his face up to glare at the taller intruder.

Snake speared the man's throat with the edge of the plate. He staggered back and gurgled as he grabbed his damaged windpipe. Snake dropped the plate, grabbed him by the lapel, and shoved the Devil Stick into the man's groin.

He quickly maneuvered the guard against the wall. A pistol fell from the man's jacket and clattered on the dark floor. Using his weight to keep him in place, Snake kept up a constant Beethoven's 9th Symphony rhythm on his groin —*tap, tap, tap, taaaaaap*. After ten seconds, Snake let go. The MSS officer slid down the wall and crumbled at Snake's feet.

Skybar security guards were going about their jobs of inspecting people exiting the elevators. No one entering the club seemed to notice or care what was happening a few feet away. The security men turned as Snake walked by.

"He is all yours."

Snake heard through the earsplitting music the sound of steel-toed boots hitting a body and the crack of ribs breaking. He clicked his comm once. Over the noise, he heard two clicks come back.

Demon was on the narrow balcony that overlooked the nightclub. Five small tables and chairs were crammed along two large horizontal tubes that served as a railing. The four tables nearest Demon were crowded with partiers. At the fifth and farthest table, one man in a gray suit sat alone, looking down, mostly on the dancing girls below.

For a man many decades older than his target, Demon was agile and quick. The party-goers were oblivious to the man squeezing by them. The MSS man froze for an instant, caught off guard by the terrifying look on the face of the man who appeared like an apparition above him. Before he could retrieve the gun from his jacket, Demon was on him.

With a high thrust of the knife, he held it palm down, entering it straight into the neck near the man's Adam's apple. He rotated his hand up to maximize the damage and sever the left internal jugular vein and left common carotid artery. The space was small, so Demon kept the knife in place as he rotated his hips to bring his entire body weight to bear on the dying Chinese sentry. He held the man up, counting off the seconds. Their faces were inches apart. Demon smiled into the fading eyes, which in seconds transitioned from pain, fear, and finally, the eternal blank stare of death.

Ten seconds later, using the knife like a joystick, he guided the dead man into his chair and propped his head against the wall. Demon pulled the knife out. Blood instantly flowed down the dead man's new suit, onto the table, and then the floor. Demon wiped the bloody knife on the shoulder of the dead man's suit, turned, scanned the crowd below, and headed to the stairs. He turned and pointed his Devil Stick at the people a few feet behind him, expecting some of them to have noticed his bloody attack.

None had.

He clicked his comm once. Two clicks came back.

Bridger remained by the service elevator while Snake and Demon completed their tasks. With the confirmation clicks, it was Milton's and Beatrice's turn to move. Bridger spotted them in the far corner of the club on a direct diagonal from where he was. They were collecting their things and standing.

He looked right and saw Chen in an intimate area separated from the masses by a line of couches. Beyond them, out the huge window, was a view of the city. Seated to his right was a blonde. To his left was a red-head. Two brunettes sat across from him on a short couch. Bridger's mind wandered for a moment, thinking that the only thing the beauties had in common with the Chinese master spy was a taste for champagne. The evidence was the empty bottles covering nearby tables.

Two gray suits sat on colorful square ottomans on either side of the couch. They faced outward, their eyes scanning the crowded room.

Bridger walked along the outer wall to avoid the crowd. Snake and Demon fanned out to flank the sitting area. Beatrice and Milton weaved through the couches, tables, chairs, and people, closing the twenty feet without any suspicion from his security—until it was too late.

Milton and Beatrice each pulled out a mini-Devil Stick, extended it to its six-inch maximum length, and sprayed each MSS man in the face as they walked by. The guards froze for an instant, then fell out of their chairs to the floor. The couple walked to the line where other patrons were waiting for the elevator.

Chen reacted, but it also was too late. Demon and Snake blocked his escape.

"Ladies," Bridger said, handing each two hundred dollars, "Good-bye." They did not hesitate. They hurriedly collected purses and coats and disappeared into the crowd.

Bridger sat next to Chen.

"Hello, Minister Chen. You might not know me—"

"I know who you are," the man said calmly through thin lips.

"Good," Bridger smiled back.

Chen looked over his shoulder at Snake and Demon. When he looked back, Bridger had a Devil Stick pointed at his nose.

He released a cloud of spray into Chen's face. They let him fall to the floor.

52

MR. NICE GUY

Kyiv, Ukraine

"**M**inister Chen." He waited, then shouted, "CHEN!"

Even with administering an extremely low dosage of spray, over an hour later Chen was still under its influence. Bridger pondered how it was possible that Chen's black hair was still shiny and combed, despite being drugged, dragged from a club, and tossed in the trunk of a car. He tapped Chen on his cheeks like they do in the movies to wake someone from a coma.

"Want me to smack him?" Demon said. He and Snake were leaning against the wall behind Bridger. Bridger ignored the offer.

"What...I...am..." Chen slurred. His eyes were glassy. His head was circling like a cement mixer. His dark suit and white shirt were splotched with streaks of grime.

They were back at the same warehouse, sitting in the same chair, behind the same metal table where they had broken Pavlo. Now it was Chen's turn. Chen's hands were also shackled to the table in front of him. The lights were on—not quite as bright—but enough to get good lighting for the cameras recording the interrogation. Even at 2 a.m., the room was hot. No windows. A broken ventilation system.

Bridger needed answers. Getting those answers was complicated by several factors out of his control. First, time mattered. He did not have the luxury of interrogating the person in a friendly, casual manner.

Second, Chen was different. This was an experienced MSS master spy seated across the metal table. Chen would know how to draw out his responses, which played back into the time issue. Chen wasn't a robotic killer whose greatest skill was pointing and shooting. As an experienced espionage officer, Bridger knew Chen would resist as long as he could—perhaps totally. That was not acceptable. If he didn't cooperate and provide helpful answers right away, Bridger would be forced to resort to alternate means to extract what he wanted.

Finally, the Chinese embassy and MSS would be out searching for their diplomat. They would alert Ukrainian security, and the streets would quickly fill with law enforcement. They needed to get this over with before an army of armed men smashed through the door.

"Minister Chen. Usually, I offer snacks. I'm considerate and polite, but not today." Bridger's head shook. "Not today. Not with you."

Bridger sat down and winced when he wiggled his left arm in its sling. He wasn't sure if his wrist was broken or if it was a bad sprain. Snake, the Spy Devil's designated medic, had done his best to keep Bridger moving—mostly with painkillers.

"I would like to know if you killed my man."

"You…making…error." Chen's eyes spiraled like pinwheels as he tried to focus on Bridger.

"I would like to know if you killed our man," he repeated.

"What are you—" Chen then attempted to stand, not realizing his hands were bound to the table. Snake moved behind him. Ready. Just in case.

"Who killed my man?" Bridger said with the same tone.

"I…do not know…what you are talking about." His breathing was already irregular. He sucked in air between words.

Bridger tapped Chen with the stun gun setting on his Devil Stick. He jerked and twisted off his chair, falling to his knees—his hands kept him from getting all the way to the floor. Snake grabbed him and shoved him a little too hard back onto the metal chair. Bridger let it go.

Larger beads of sweat rolled down Chen's cheeks, soaking the collar of his shirt.

"That was the lowest setting." He held the Stick to Chen's face. "I have your attention now?

"Do what you want…I have nothing to tell you."

Bridger sighed.

Tough man.

Without a word, he reached into his pocket and pulled out a rusty pair of pliers.

"What are you…doing?" Chen sputtered as he saw what Bridger was holding.

"Hell yeah!" Demon said, walking toward Bridger to take the tool.

"Chen. There comes that time in a mission when I get pretty sick and tired. That time is right now."

Before he could react, Bridger quickly extended his arm and firmly grabbed the end of Chen's left index finger with the head with the pliers' gripping jaw. He squeezed.

Chen screamed. When he tried to pull away, Bridger squeezed harder.

"Son of a bitch!" Demon said, clapping his hands together in frustration. "That's my job."

Bridger just stared at Chen. Chen met Bridger's stare with one of his own. Sweat was bubbling off his skin, but he remained motionless.

"Tell me everything, or I crush this finger, then the next and the next, until I hear the truth," Bridger said slowly, as he tightened the pressure on the plier handles. Chen winced as his nail cracked. The end of the finger immediately started to turn red.

"You want…truth…call your…mother," Chen said, his voice a mix of pain, resolution, mocking, and anger.

Bridger released his hold on the pliers, which hit the table with a loud clang.

"What did you say?"

"Call…your mother. She will be…interested in my…well-being," Chen panted in short breaths, but sounding more to Bridger like the professional intel officer that he was.

Bridger looked at his phone, and as if she was listening, three electronic chirps filled the room. An 'M' appeared in the caller ID. He picked it up and answered.

"Just calling to see how I am doing, May?" He didn't hide the pleasure in his voice.

"You can be so insufferable. Please do not harm Mr. Chen or any more of his security guards."

"Oh. You are late to the party. Unless you have more, we are all out of security guards."

"Don't be annoying. Is Minister Chen with you?" Exasperation laced her voice.

"Yep. We were negotiating on how many fingers Chen will lose before he decides to talk."

"May I speak with him?"

"Nahhhh. I don't think so." Bridger picked up the pliers and started to tap them on the table. *Tink. Tink. Tink.* "How long has he been a source? Or is he a target—or both?" She paused. That moment confirmed it. "If I don't get the answer I want, I will return him to you in pieces, starting with one finger at a time."

Silence. Sigh.

"He is *the* most significant penetration of the MSS. Ever. Deputy Minister Chen is positioned to rise to the highest levels of the Chinese government. Procuring Hillcrest is the accomplishment he needs to ascend to the top. If that happens, the MSS would be run by a CIA asset."

Bridger sat back. He wasn't often stunned, but that news stopped him cold. He looked at Chen, who sat with a pleased thin-lipped smile on his face.

"Wow. That *is* significant. I guess he is so significant he was worth risking *my* life?" *Tink, tink, tink* went the pliers.

"Oh, don't be so melodramatic. Choices had to be made to save the operation—a very important operation that has been years in the making. The only reason you are even involved was Bondar went off schedule. You would have made the same decision."

"The Devils were years in the making, too—if that matters." He tossed the pliers on the table, sending a disturbingly loud *clang* through the small room.

"I had every confidence you would successfully extricate yourself. My confidence seems well-placed."

"But he didn't get the case. I am sure Chapel told you that. I blew it up and almost got blown up, too—thanks for asking."

"Yes, he didn't get the case." Her voice sounded as tired as Bridger felt. "But there are always alternatives in a complex operation. You know that."

"I don't know. I also know that Beast is dead." He hadn't entirely accepted that Beast was gone. He closed his eyes to lock in the emotion. Bridger's mouth turned bone dry. He sucked some saliva and swallowed. "Who killed him? Do you know?"

"I heard. That is sad news. Bridger. But I can assure you that Minister Chen had nothing to do with that."

"Maybe not. Maybe yes."

"He didn't, believe me," she said calmly.

"Believe you? That's funny coming from you."

"What are you going to do?"

"Beast is dead."

He hung up. He had his answer.

They cleaned Chen as best they could and packed him in a stolen Kia Sportage. With a bag over his head, they drove around Kyiv, then let him out on a corner outside Holosiiv Park.

When they drove away into the drizzle of the night, Bridger was confident of one thing—he knew where to find the person who killed Beast.

53

WHO KILLED BEAST?

Kyiv, Ukraine

B ridger checked his watch.

A few heartbeats before 2 a.m.—just short of twenty-four hours since they gassed and released Chen.

Twenty hours since Bridger and the Spy Devils added an important asset to the team. They had stopped by Pavlo's one-room apartment and offered the former Bondar employee a temporary position as an expert on the Bondar financial structure and building security. With very little cajoling, Pavlo accepted.

He had constructed a plan, but the borderline impromptu scheme he came up with was a little rough around the edges. He was preparing to wing it—one last time.

It would be another ninety seconds before the new Spy Devil team of Pavlo and Imp, which Milton had already begun to call 'Pimp'—to Imp's displeasure—turned on the lights in the residence.

Bridger gave the Spy Devils four hours to eat and get some sleep.

He tried to do the same, but it was difficult. It was hard to comprehend the revelation about Chen being a double agent run by May. After four hours, they went back on the attack.

Getting into the residence was simple.

The Pimp team had disabled the security systems and locked the security panic doors, effectively sealing off Bondar's security guards. Snake had placed the portable mobile phone jammer on the roof. Milton and Beatrice had the Devilbots up. One on overwatch, the other doing close-in surveillance outside the windows of the residence floor.

Bridger sat in the shadows at Bondar's wooden desk, admiring the enormity of it. It was impressive, he thought. *Bigger than the Oval Office.* He tried not to be too juvenile with the "compensating for something" cliché.

The den covered one-quarter of the top floor. The light coming through the windows illuminated deep blue carpeting. Massive wooden doors. Two deep green leather high-back guest chairs, with curved mahogany legs, were opposite him. Bookcases and tables mirrored each other. A sitting area occupied the space to the right of the door. On top of an ornate Persian rug were a long gray couch, matching chairs, and a glass table.

In the other far corner from the desk was a square black game table with four chairs around it. A fully stocked built-in bar was in the corner behind the table. A door next to the bar led to a bathroom. He had taken advantage of the facilities when he arrived an hour ago.

Somewhere in the darkness, a clock ticked.

Covering the walls were pictures of Bondar with people—some he recognized. Businessmen. Politicians. Charities. There were even two U.S. presidents. Bridger realized that nowhere in the sea of narcissism was a picture of any member of his family. Bridger noticed a worn rifle hanging on the wall behind the desk.

He checked his watch and covered his eyes just as all the lights in the rooms blazed on.

Bridger sat back in Bondar's comfortable desk chair and waited.

Twenty seconds later, Demon opened the door. Bridger watched all the Bondars—Viktor, Ira, and Olek—shuffle through it, startled and half asleep. Demon stayed inside the room. Snake closed the door and stood outside. Demon leaned his back against it, the Devil Stick in his hand. Bridger saw the large knife attached to his belt. His hand was on the handle.

"Olek! I wasn't expecting to see you." Bridger waved his good hand and smiled. "This is a surprise, a welcomed surprise. You don't look too worse for wear."

"Who? What—" Olek sputtered, dressed only in a pair of neon green boxers.

When Ira came into the den, she took a few steps toward the bar area. Perhaps, Bridger guessed, she thought she could make a break for the bathroom or out the main door.

"Ira," Bridger said warmly.

As he approached, arms out like he wanted to hug her, she looked puzzled. Even in the middle of the night, she was stunning. Her hair was pulled into a ponytail. She wore a sheer knee-length satin white robe tied around her waist. It was distracting.

"It is good to see you again. I am glad you are here. You found Olek! That was fast. Well done. Please, sit with him."

"What are you doing here?" she asked with malice in her voice.

"I will explain, but for now, please sit." This was spoken as a friendly command. She hesitated. "Sit, Ira," he said firmly.

She flinched in a way that suggested she was not used to being ordered where to go. Eventually, she walked to the sitting area and took a corner spot in the furthest part of the couch. She grasped the corners of her robe and pulled them to her lap.

Bridger turned to Bondar, whose face was red—registering a shade somewhere between seething and irrational hatred.

"Viktor. It is nice to finally meet you. I am—well, they call me Bridger—perhaps Ira, or Olek, have mentioned me? Or Danny? I lead a group called the Spy Devils. Perhaps you have heard of us?"

"Fuck you," Bondar's hands were balled into fists. His body seemed coiled and ready to strike.

"Are those silk?" Ignoring the comment, Bridger walked forward and rubbed the sleeve of Bondar's black pajamas. "Why, they are! I saw a pair like this recently—they were on a Mr. Theo Giannokis in Cyprus. Do you know him?"

Bondar's expression was now confused. The actions of the man who had invaded his private sanctum—this Bridger—made no sense to the oligarch. He sucked his cheeks in, causing wrinkles to crack across his face. He looked over his shoulder at Olek, who turned his head toward Ira, and closed his eyes.

Bridger continued.

"So, Viktor. If you would, this is your office, please." Bridger motioned to the desk chair.

"What do you want?" Bondar shouted.

"Calm, Viktor. Please. I will explain everything. I don't want to keep you up a REM cycle longer than needed. My goodness, what I wouldn't give for a good night's sleep. I once had some sheets in Cairo —well, perhaps later. Please. Sit."

He seemed confused. He hesitated, looked in Demon's direction, then went around the desk and sat.

"Wonderful."

Bridger rotated a guest chair in front of Bondar so he had a better view of the sitting area. He removed his arm from the sling and rested his throbbing left wrist on the desk.

"That is more comfortable. So, let me get to business so we can all get back to bed, as I promised. I am here to find out who murdered my man, who we affectionately called Beast. Olek, you met him. He was the person who fished you out of the Mediterranean, off the coast of Cyprus. Remember?" Bridger turned to Bondar and chuckled. "You should have seen him. Bobbing and splashing. Quite a sight."

Bondar glanced at Olek as he rolled his chair closer to his desk.

"Oh. Viktor, don't look for your very nice Makarov. I removed that and all the other weapons. Except that." Bridger pointed to the gun above Bondar's head. "Is that a Tula? I haven't seen one of those in years. Was that yours?"

His face was chiseled tight.

"I killed my father with it," he said with a threatening chill.

"May I?"

Not waiting for an answer, Bridger stood up and walked around the desk. He reached up and grabbed the rifle off its hooks with his right hand. Walking back to his chair, Bridger admired the weapon. Bridger saw the threatening look as he fondled Bondar's precious keepsake. "This is a classic." He placed the rifle on the desk next to him.

"Back to business." Bridger re-positioned his tired body in his chair and slapped his knee with his good right hand. "Oh. The panic button you are pushing under your desk will not be answered. Pavlo and my man Imp turned off all the security alarms and access. We will not be disturbed."

Bondar and Ira's heads spun to look at Bridger.

"Didn't I tell you? I *must* be tired. Pavlo has come to work with us. He was quite eager—not surprisingly—being unceremoniously fired. Such a waste of talent to dismiss him so abruptly. He is quite a unique lad. Incredible tech skills. We will take advantage of them. Hell, we already have!"

Bridger looked directly back at Ira, then Bondar. Discomfort radiated from their bodies at the news of Pavlo's defection.

"So, I pose the question. Who killed Beast? My list has grown short. All that remains," his face turned malevolent, "is the Bondar family. I am going to cross Olek off the list. The only thing he kills is his own brain cells." Chuckle and smile. "That leaves Ira and you, Viktor."

"I have no idea what you are talking about," Bondar said defiantly. "I want you out of here."

"As you might suspect, I have given this some thought." Bridger sat forward with his gaze fixed on Bondar's unblinking eyes. The silence lasted for five, then ten, then fifteen seconds. A clock clicked time as the tension grew. Bridger's stare went uninterrupted. Finally, he spoke. "No. No, I don't think you know anything."

Bridger turned to look at Ira with eyes that conveyed one meaning —vengeance.

54

YOU ARE A LIAR

Kyiv, Ukraine

"Do not look at me. I have no idea, either," Ira said matter-of-factly, as she clicked the red paint off her left index finger with her right thumb.

Bridger looked back at Bondar, then back to Ira.

"Oh, Ira…and I thought we were friends. At least business partners. I thought we had a deal. Should I tell your father about our last conversation?" Her face went pale, then flashed to red as he kept his eyes on Ira. "You see, Viktor, your daughter and I have met before, did you know that? Just a few days ago in Pavlo's room in the basement of your bank. Ira was kind enough to let us in—unharmed I might add. We had a brief but worthwhile conversation." His eyes shot to Bondar, looking for a reaction. "I enjoyed it."

Bondar looked at Ira. Bridger wondered if she was too terrified to talk. He could sense the waves of panic emitting from her. Her complexion was flusher than a poker hand.

"We discussed—," Bridger started as he looked over at Ira, "—you. It seems that she is not happy with you, Viktor, about anything. Family. Business. But she is quite riled about the killing of a man named Uncle

Anton." He turned back to Bondar. "Does that name mean anything to you?"

"What—" Bondar started.

"What were we supposed to do? She asked me to leak some very unsettling information about you. Arms dealing. Extortion. Bribery. Blackmail. Murder. An impressive list. Did I forget anything, Ira?"

"I have no idea what he is talking about. He is a liar."

"Is that right?" Bondar asked. It was a question from a cold, iron-fisted businessman. Not a father.

"No, he is a liar." It was the voice of someone feeling real fear for the first time.

"Well, she gave me the case from Kirkwood as payment. Did you know that Viktor? We went through all this effort to get it, and Ira just hands it to us. I hope you didn't have plans for it. I sort of blew it up, the reason for my sore arm here, but we don't have time to rehash that story." Chuckle and smile. "What should I do with the information you gave me, Ira?" He pointed. "Viktor, you will find copies in the folder in front of you. I hope you don't mind. I am keeping the originals."

Bondar hesitated, opened it, and flipped through the contents. Every few pages, he would glance up at Ira or Bridger. When he was done, he closed the folder and sat back.

"It isn't true, father." It was the voice of a scared daughter.

Bondar answered with a face chiseled tight in disappointment. He stood and walked around the desk.

"You want to get rid of your father so desperately you asked *him*?" He balled his hand into fists again and shook them at her. "You think you can run my businesses better than I can? You should be grateful for all I have given you and your worthless brother."

Ira exploded off the couch. Her robe fell open, exposing a small white lace nightgown. She stormed across the room to within a few feet of her father.

"You are the worthless one for what you did to Olek! You abandoned him to rot in a jail in Cyprus."

"What are you talking about? I did nothing to him in Cyprus—"

"Um. Excuse me," Bridger interrupted. "Let me clarify this point.

For the sake of our mission, we took the liberty of pretending to be you, Viktor. Olek was a little confused. It is technical stuff. I don't understand it, but it was effective. I am sorry if it caused any bad feelings."

"What? It wasn't father?" Olek stammered.

"Nope." Bridger shrugged and raised his eyebrows at Demon. "Guess it worked." Demon nodded.

Bondar grabbed Ira tightly by the arm above the elbow and pulled her close till her face was an inch from his.

"What were you thinking?" Saliva landed on her face. He pushed her away. "I would have respected you more if you had just shot me. *That* at least has some honor. Show some guts. It is how I lived my life. Kill or be killed. I am a killer."

"You killed Anton," she screamed at him.

Bondar was silent. He took his time walking back to his desk chair. He sat, crossed his arms across his silk pajamas, and leaned back to stare at the ceiling. Silence packed the room, except for the clock ticking in the corner like a time bomb.

"You," Ira turned to Bridger—her rage reappearing, "you did all this." She tried to hit him, but he grabbed her arm and wrenched it outward, then down in a ninety-degree angle. She grunted in pain as she bent over to relieve the stress in her elbow.

"So if I plot this right, you had Beast killed just before our meeting? Am I correct?"

"No." She forced the word out through clenched teeth.

Bridger flinched in actual surprise. He let go of her arm. She stood and rubbed her elbow in relief.

"Care to explain that?"

"I didn't *have* him killed. *I* killed your man, this Beast, for what you did to Olek. I do not grieve for him."

"You killed him, yourself, then met me to make a deal to destroy your father?" Bridger was genuinely shocked. "I will admit to being surprised." He looked at Bondar. "That is quite an industrious daughter you have. Tell me, Ira, how did you find him? Chapel, or Chen?"

"Neither. We did it ourselves. I recognized him sitting outside the bank," Olek bragged from his corner of the room. "Your shitty group of spies were sloppy."

"Shut up, Olek, you fool," Ira hissed at him.

Bridger looked at Olek. Then to Demon.

"Just bad luck," Demon said, from his position guarding the door. "It happens."

Bridger stood. He looked around the room and turned toward the door. "Well, our business is complete. I will leave you to resolve the family issues." He saw Demon go on alert.

Bridger turned around. Bondar had the Tula tucked under his right armpit, pointed at Bridger's chest.

"Come now, Viktor. You can't kill me," Bridger said.

"You *are* a devil."

"You don't know how much I appreciate the kind words. But, you see, you won't kill me because I have all your money, known or hidden. If you kill me, it will vanish. If we leave here unharmed, I will consider letting you have some of it back."

"You are a liar."

"There it is, Demon. I am being called a liar, and I think I am the only one here who has told the truth." Bridger shrugged his shoulders. "Let me explain. It started with that delightful gentleman, Theo Giannokis, the one with the exquisite taste in pajamas, like yourself. He provided us access to quite a lot of your financial data there. Quite a lot. Then I asked my new employee Pavlo to give us the whole enchilada, as they say. You forgot to change the access codes and techie stuff when you let him go."

Bridger tossed up his good hand in the air. He walked toward Ira and stood over her. She glared back.

"*That* was a mistake. So, I took it. I couldn't resist the temptation. Kill me, and you lose all your money. Of course, if you want some of your wealth back—you could, you know—do me a favor. Earn it, if you know what I mean."

Bridger stood looking at Ira for another moment. Bridger turned and walked to the door.

"Burn in hell," she snarled at him.

Then he stopped and looked at Bondar. The Tula was still aimed at him.

"Thank you, Ira. Consider my offer, Viktor. It is only good for—" Bridger checked his watch. "—a few more minutes."

They walked out of the room. Snake followed as they moved to the elevator.

A few seconds later they heard the sound of a rifle being fired.

"I'm glad they worked out their issues," Bridger said as they stepped into the elevator.

55

WE WIN AND THEY LOSE

Kirkwood Headquarters

Peter found it difficult to settle back into his corporate intelligence routine.

Less than a week ago, I was blown-up and running for my life. Now I'm back in my ergonomic chair staring at my computer.

His immediate task was the hundreds of unanswered emails in his inbox; each, he knew, was a person who wanted him to do something for *them*. It all seemed irrelevant after the events in Ukraine. Childish. He wanted to 'select all' the emails and just delete them.

Click. Out of inbox. Out of mind.

There *were* a few things on the bright side.

First, he had not heard from Bridger, which had only re-fueled his apprehension.

Second, he was reading all he could about Viktor Bondar's arrest for the murder of his daughter. Unfortunately, it was only superficially covered in the U.S. press. In Ukraine and many countries in Europe, it was big news. As much as the people wanted to see Bondar's fall, their hopes were dashed when he was set free by judges he had bribed for years. Bondar was rumored to have fled to Geneva.

"Hope you have secured your files." Peter jolted when Benton's mocking baritone voice reverberated around his office.

"Miss your daily dosage of donuts this morning, Benton?" Peter shot back.

"Upstairs, asshole. Boardroom. Let's go."

Peter entered the Jacob Kirkwood Corporate Boardroom a few minutes later.

Inside, painted by the lamp's glow, CEO Samuel Kirkwood stood with his hands laced behind his back. His head was tilted up toward the life-sized oil portrait of his father. Bold strokes and use of color formed the aura of strength and leadership in Jacob.

"Hello, Peter."

Ever the gentlemen, Kirkwood approached him with his hand extended. Peter did the same, and they exchanged a quick handshake. Peter felt the moisture on the palms of Kirkwood's hand. Kirkwood indicated that Peter should take the chair at the table by the CEO's seat.

Peter walked to the spot and gingerly lowered his sore body to the padded seat. The cushion let out a low rush of air. The room was warm, the lights were low, and the chair was *really* comfortable. It took all the concertation he had not to just put his head on the table and nap.

Peter expected Kirkwood to sit. Instead, he stood behind his chair, gazing across the room.

"I am glad you are back and safe. Danny has kept me informed of your exploits on behalf of the company. It was, well, um, exciting, and dangerous. It's wonderful. I greatly appreciated it."

Peter winced as he nodded his bandaged head. "Thank you."

"Peter, you know this company was built by my father, Jacob. His father Benjamin and his father, Wilbur. All the greatest minds of the time. Now, it is my time." He started to walk in measured slow steps around the room, examining all the paintings and pictures. He stopped and peered at a large watercolor of the first Kirkwood headquarters. A three-story all-brick building on a crowded Chicago neighborhood street.

Peter saw Kirkwood's head scan the picture from top to bottom.

"I spent time here with my grandfather." He moved to the next picture and looked at it. Without turning to Peter, he continued. A Kirkwood has been at the epicenter of technological developments that have made this a better world for over one hundred years. The Kirkwood name stands as a bellweather example of all that is exceptional in business and America. The finest technology genes are written into the DNA of every employee."

Before Peter could respond, Kirkwood stopped and leaned on the table across from Peter. His cheeks were glowing orange-red. He reminded Peter of a cockatiel.

"I employ tens of thousands of people. Good jobs. Good salaries. I support this company and the entire country. When we are needed, I answer the call. That is more than most can say. You agree?"

His voice was getting higher in pitch. A fine mist spewed from the round mouth of his round head.

"Yes, sir." Peter's anxiety rose. Kirkwood, the mild-mannered CEO, looked like he was either going to jump across the table and attack him, or explode.

"Big and successful global companies do big successful global company things. It is how *we* win and *they* lose. From what I understand, *you* think we have taken some improper actions. That we shouldn't share technology with our Chinese business partners to get their business and investment? How do you think we grow or make money? It is what we have to do."

Kirkwood was leaning so far over the table his sweaty palms slid and he lost his balance. He pushed back and regained his footing. The shock seemed to calm him. He continued.

"I will never allow Kirkwood to be compared to the likes of Enron. Or Waste Management. Or Worldcom. Health South. Tyco. Freddie Mac, and certainly not Lehman. No FBI. No SEC."

Then, just as suddenly, the atmosphere changed again. Kirkwood stood straight, and his eyes looked around the room. His voice was back to a soft tenor. His face was returning to its pink fleshy tone.

Kirkwood walked to him, his hand out in front, offering a handshake. Peter stood.

"I hope you understand now. These are important times for *our* company." Kirkwood led Peter toward the door. "I want to thank you for all the wonderful things you did for the company. We asked you to do the impossible in very little time, and you did that and more. Thank you."

Kirkwood opened the door for Peter, and with his hand in the small of his back, shoved Peter out of the Jacob Kirkwood Boardroom.

On the drive home, Peter decided he would let whatever happens happen. His concentration was on getting home and on when he would hear from Bridger next—not the car following him.

Peter pulled into his garage as the trailing car rolled down the street, made a loop around the block, and stopped.

Peter lugged his body through the garage door and into the mudroom off the kitchen. He expected to smell dinner or hear the TV tuned to some cartoon. He didn't. Then he noticed the door to the kitchen, which was always open, was closed.

"Janelle?" Peter whispered. "Janelle?"

He went back and looked in the garage. Her car *was* there. Panic started to set in. He grabbed a broom that was against the wall and held it in front of him like a spear. Taking in a deep breath, he opened the kitchen door.

"Peter. Finally. We have to get going," Bridger said. Bridger was sitting at the table, eating a rather large sandwich. "Janelle has shown me your files on your employer. They have been very, very bad boys." He pointed at the broom still in a spearing position. "Nice broom."

"Hi, honey." With a smile, Janelle got up and gave the stunned Peter a kiss on the cheek. "James is at Chuck's house. Give me that." She took the broom and walked to the mudroom.

The sight of Bridger being at his house, sitting at the table eating a sandwich, talking to his wife was somewhat disconcerting.

"Peter, we have to go." Bridger got up, took one more large bite of sandwich. "Yummy. Roast beef. Thanks, Janelle."

"What? Where?"

Peter had never seen Bridger so excited.

"If the mountain won't come to us, we have to blow up the mountain."

56

THE STUFF OF FICTION BOOKS AND MOVIES

Lombard, Illinois

Bridger knew Chapel wasn't the kind of guy who met in dark alleys. He didn't do recognition signals. SDRs. Disguises. Any of that espionage stuff. That was far beneath Danforth Chapel. Nope. Chapel liked the good life—the *very* good life.

In the rare instance he needed to personally obtain information, Chapel preferred to do it over a fabulous meal. His source would carry a briefcase containing the secrets into a private room in an expensive restaurant. The person would place it under the table. Then they would eat a fine meal. After dessert, the source would leave. The case remained behind. Chapel would have an after-dinner drink. Congenial and satisfying.

The stuff of fiction books and movies.

Bridger knew it was his one exploitable weakness. That was why when Bridger and Peter pulled into the lot near the Capital Grille, Lombard, the Devil knew exactly what to expect.

"He is a predictable pompous ass." Bridger laughed and slapped Peter on his shoulder. He was in a good mood. "He takes the same suite in the classic Drake Hotel in Oak Brook. Medium rare steaks at the Capital Grille. All close to Kirkwood HQ. No time wasted sitting in traffic."

Bridger looked at Peter.

"Ironic, huh? This is where we had our first date," Bridger said.

"I will mark it in my calendar and cherish the date forever," Peter replied.

Bridger laughed, then said, "Here he is."

They watched the Lincoln Town Car pull up to the valet entrance of the steak house. A mountain-sized security man got out, looked around, and opened the door. Chapel got out. He buttoned his Gieves & Hawkes, glanced left and right, then entered, followed by the guard.

The driver backed the car into the end parking space parallel to the building. He got out of the Town Car and walked toward the entrance. He stopped just outside the door and took a standing position under the green awning covering the entrance.

"I will give his security goons credit. They at least sweep the car twice a day for trackers and bugs. But it isn't enough. Not today. Not by a long shot."

The 8 p.m. twilight cast long shadows across the ground as the setting sun cleared the horizon. The darkness they needed would be upon them shortly.

"Is there any reason that we just can't pull this guy over, *whomp* him, and take the case without all this cloak and dagger stuff?" Demon asked over the comm system. He and Snake were following a few lengths behind Chapel's dinner guest.

"Yes, there *is* a reason." Bridger rolled his eyes at Peter, who was given his own comm for this op. "The answers are, I need to talk to them to get some important intel, *and* to satisfy my pure, unadulterated spite."

"Well, okay. I like the spite part of the plan. We are five minutes out. Maybe ten, the way this guy drives. If he was going any slower, it would be yesterday."

"Beatrice? Milton. Status?"

"Chapel just walked in and went into a small private dining room. The middle one on the right. His security guy is immediately outside, sitting at a table. And this steak is great." Milton said from a booth inside.

"I recommend the salmon. It is perfect." Beatrice was across from him.

"Imp? Wake up."

"Yeah, yeah. I'm ready to push the button." Imp rose from the back seat. "I like steak, too."

"We will drive through McDonald's later and get you a happy meal, brat," Beatrice said.

"We are here," Snake alerted them.

Bridger and Peter watched a white early 2000s Chrysler Minivan pull into the Capital Grille lot and park near the entrance. A few seconds behind, Demon and Snake, in a Ford Explorer, rolled by the building and parked on the opposite side.

They watched Gilbert Street, Kirkwood Research Technologies leader, the 'King of the Moles,' walk from the van, past Chapel's guard, and into the restaurant. He carried a large canvas duffel bag in his right hand.

"Oh Gilbert, let's find out what May has done to you," Bridger said, as he got out of the car and motioned for Peter to do the same. "Demon? Snake?"

"We are in position."

"Beatrice?"

"The guy with the bag went into the room with Chapel. Guard still outside. The door is closed when the waiter isn't there."

"Large wooden door. Opaque glass. Window-framed." Milton added.

"Now, Imp."

Imp pushed a series of buttons on his computer. The vehicle security system of the Lincoln activated like fireworks on July 4th. The panic alarm blared as the interior and exterior lights flashed. Chapel's driver jerked with surprise at the sight and sound. He ran toward the car, frantically pushing the control buttons on his key fob. As he reached for the front door handle, Imp cut the system off just as suddenly. The guard stopped.

He didn't see Demon wave the Devil Stick in his face. The man's body quivered and gagged as it fell against the side of the Lincoln. Unable to brace himself, he rolled like a raindrop down the side and hit the concrete curb with his face. Cracking, plinking, and grunt sounds indicated a broken nose, lost teeth, and unconsciousness.

Demon grinned at Snake. "Maybe we should have caught him?"

Snake shrugged.

They grabbed the unconscious man under his arms and locked him in the trunk.

"One in the trunk," Snake announced.

Wearing a nice patterned gray blazer, white button-up shirt, and trendy casual jeans, Bridger walked into the restaurant to the sounds of Frank Sinatra. Peter followed.

Beatrice stood and walked toward the private room. The guard stood and blocked her way.

"I'm sorry," she said, appearing startled. "I am looking for the ladies' room?"

"Over there." When he took his eyes off of her to point her in the right direction, she raised a mini-Devil Stick and let him have a small dose. She turned away as Bridger grabbed the man by the lapels— ignoring the pain in his wrist—and guided him through the swinging doors into the private dining room.

Peter held the door open, then let it swing closed. Bridger pushed the man into the room and let him fall to the carpeted floor like a tree, making sure he didn't hit any of the four tables on the way down.

Chapel sat at a table in the corner, his back to the wall. Gilbert was seated to his left.

"Hi, guys. Mind if we join you?"

57

A DELICIOUS RUFFINO CHIANTI

Lombard, Illinois

"Bridger. Peter. This *is* a surprise. I will be honest." Chapel's face remained impassive. He looked at his comatose guard on the floor, then to the door. Bridger shook his head. "The rest of my men?"

"None of your goons will be coming to your rescue."

Bridger pulled out the wood and green leather chair and sat across from Chapel. Peter took the remaining seat across from Gilbert, whose face furrowed with confusion.

"Hi Gilbert," Peter said.

"Yes, hello, Gilbert," Bridger said. "Heard any good jokes lately?"

"Peter? Arnie? Arnie Palmer?" Gilbert was confused.

Chapel looked at Bridger with a raised eyebrow. Bridger shrugged.

Gilbert was teetering between shock and panic. He gripped the armrests like he was on a rollercoaster and began to stand.

"Gilbert. Hang around for a minute." Bridger gingerly raised his hand in a *stop* sign. "We are starving." Bridger looked at Peter, then Chapel. "Did you order?"

The door swung open, and a pear-shaped waiter, carrying a bottle of red wine, walked in. He gasped and froze when he saw the body on the floor.

"Charles! Over here. It is good to see you again. What are we drinking?"

Charles stepped by the prone man and approached the table. "A beautiful red wine a—"

"—a delicious Ruffino Chianti," Chapel added, trying to regain control of the situation.

Bridger reached into his blazer pocket and handed Charles an envelope.

"Here is the rest I owe you, Charles, and twice that for any unexpected residual effects. Get something for your wife, Dolores. Please give her my regards and that I hope we can meet soon. If you could uncork that delicious wine, then leave us to complete our meeting, I would appreciate that. Make sure we are not disturbed, will you? Thank you, Charles."

"Yes, sir." Charles nodded, took the money, shoved it into his white apron, filled each glass with a good pour, and went out the door, making sure it was closed behind him.

Bridger raised his wine glass high. Chapel followed. Peter hesitated, then raised his glass in confusion. Gilbert did not move a muscle.

"A toast. To Hell. May the stay there be as enjoyable as the way there." Bridger smiled and sipped. Bridger savored his sip and nodded his approval to Chapel, then he looked at the duffel bag.

"I assume, Gilbert, being the patriot that you are and despite pressure and instructions," he continued as he picked up a cracker, "you were not pleased with giving away classified government projects. So, you didn't. Consequently, MacLean's case was empty when we opened it."

Gilbert un-coiled in elation.

"Yes. Yes. Exactly!" He was so excited he accidentally bumped his wine glass with his gesticulating hands. The white table cloth went purple. He started to sop it up with a napkin.

"A waste of fine Chianti," Chapel said. He had already finished his glass and was pouring himself another full glass.

"Go on, Gilbert," Bridger said as he picked up a warm dinner roll.

"The woman called and said it was alright. It was important government work that Kirkwood had approved. I still wasn't sure, then Mr. Chapel came."

"Gilbert. Does this actually contain—whatever it is?"

"Yes." Gilbert's eyes darted in a circuit from Bridger, Peter, the bag, Chapel, then to his lap. He took a sip of wine.

"What is in it, Gilbert?" Peter asked.

Gilbert shifted in his chair, avoiding eye contact.

"Gilbert, I think you should go now and enjoy the rest of your evening. Oh, and leave the duffel," Bridger said politely, leaning his smiling face in the man's direction.

Hesitant at first, Gilbert looked at Chapel for approval, and when he received the nod, he said his goodbyes and left as quickly as he could.

"Such a nice man, that Gilbert. Loyal. A patriot." Bridger sipped his wine. "I am sorry if losing the Bondar account cuts into your business in Ukraine."

"On the contrary! I want to thank you. Poor Olek is in way over his head and has already reached out for my support—which I happily gave with a twenty percent increase in my fee." Chapel raised his wine glass toward Bridger, took a drink of chianti, and smiled.

"Well, I didn't expect that, but congratulations, Danny." It was Bridger's turn to toast and drink.

"What is your objective, Bridger? Does this intrusion have, well, have a point?"

Bridger took a bite of a roll and relished the moment. Then he continued.

"Man, I could use a steak. I think I have most of it, but I need you to explain one thing, Chapel."

"How can I help?" Chapel finished another glass of wine.

"I understand that Chen didn't get the case because Bondar stepped in, but why not just give it to Chen in the first place? What was the need for all the Kirkwood melodrama, and getting poor Peter here caught in the cross-hairs?" Bridger looked at Peter, who was nodding.

"I'm kind of interested myself," Peter said as he twirled the stem of his wine glass between his fingers.

Chapel sat back, brushed his tie, and looked from Bridger to Peter.

"I am sorry to say, Peter, that your entire escapade was just, well, a futile act by your management. We had a confluence of semi-separate events that needed addressing. First, May had arranged for Chen to receive Hillcrest—with senior corporate approval. Next, you had Kirkwood International in some quite stressful financial situations and needed the Mourning Dove relationship to continue. Plus, they needed Viktor Bondar to make payments on the LeonidOre deal. That was a bad deal by MacLean."

"For the company. Not for him," Peter added.

"Exactly, Peter. You were exactly correct in your analysis," Chapel said.

Chapel poured the last drops of wine into his glass and set the bottle aside. He looked at the door expecting a waiter to be ready with another bottle. He looked away when he realized Charles was not returning.

"Then there is Viktor Bondar, who had his own financial situation with the Chinese and who mistakenly believed he could hold Hillcrest hostage for more contracts. On this point, Ira was correct. Viktor was past his prime. Finally, we had George McLean—who was recruited by Chen several years ago—and who was going to cause some significant disruption by exposing his connection with Chinese intelligence. That would hurt Kirkwood's businesses. Most critically, the driving force was the potential exposure of Chen by MacLean. That would destroy any chance of promotion to the head of MSS. A lot of hard work would be ruined."

"And May would not be happy," Bridger said.

"And May would not be happy," Chapel repeated.

Chapel took a drink of water and frowned.

"All those separate events were connected by Chen, you, and May, of course," Bridger concluded.

"Yes, indeed. By eliminating George and getting the case to Chen, that would solve three, as Chen could make certain the Mourning Dove deals continued without fear of exposure."

"And we take out Viktor for Ira, with some agreement brokered by you that she pays on the contracts."

"Exactly. As it has turned out, once this case gets to Chen, everything will have worked out for everyone."

"Everyone except Beast." Bridger corrected Chapel with a statement of fact.

"Yes. That was unfortunate."

Peter raised a finger to get their attention.

"So, MacBride, Kirkwood, and Jessup know about this? That Hillcrest was being taken to the Chinese? They allowed that?"

"Allowed? They were ecstatic when presented with this as a way to appease their Chinese partners and get paid. They just did not want to know all the details." Chapel took a larger sip of water. "It is most interesting to see what supposedly very intelligent people will do when faced with the ruin of their fortune, reputation, or both."

Imp spoke into Bridger and Peter's comm.

"We have something on the Chapel comm system. Cars coming. More security. Three minutes out." They looked at each other.

"Well, Danny, as fun as this has been, we need to go. And you were wrong about one thing," Bridger said as he stood. "You don't have the case to give to Chen. Peter, could you grab the duffel?"

"Peter," Chapel said with a layer of warning in his voice. "Think."

Peter hesitated as he reached his arm toward the bag. He looked at Chapel, then picked up the bag.

"I don't have to think."

"Bridger," Chapel called out, as the men reached the door. They looked back. "You *know* what you *have* to do. It is the *only* option. It's up to *her*, not *you*."

Bridger paused and glared at Chapel. He took the bag from Peter, turned, and walked out of the room.

58

CERTIFICATE OF APPRECIATION

Kirkwood Headquarters

S itting in his office the next morning, Peter assumed the call would come early, and it did. The electronic ring ricocheted off the metal walls of his small office.

"Peter, this is Tom. Could you come up?"

The voice was off. Pleasant, but forced.

When he arrived outside the office, Marilyn, his admin, was in her cubicle. She didn't look Peter in the eyes.

"Hello, Peter. Go on in."

MacBride sat behind his desk, rocking in his executive chair. Sitting to his right, on the end of the couch opposite the door, chin-up, straight-backed, was Sheila the Human Resources grim reaper, with her face expressing a mixture of false compassion and corporate duty.

Peter heard a noise come from behind him. Benton closed the door and leaned against it.

"Peter, sit down, please." MacBride indicated the guest chair opposite Sheila.

Peter sat, consciously keeping his head up, body forward, and eyes level.

"Sheila?" MacBride looked at her. She was ready.

"It has come to our attention that you have seriously violated Kirkwood policies."

"What are you talking about?"

"We were alerted, by Benton, to your unauthorized access to confidential corporate documents. Specifically, the receipt of numerous files of executive staff meeting minutes, financial documents, and details on classified technology programs. Is this true?"

Peter was as still as roadkill. It was true, but he wasn't going to say anything until he heard it all.

"Keep going."

Sheila wrinkled her face in disappointment.

"The IT data is clear," she continued. "As you know, Sandy Boyd has already been fired—dismissed, I mean. Your actions, like hers, are in direct violation of IT and corporate policies. There is also the even more serious fact of your escorting an authorized individual into the classified areas of KRT. Do you deny any of this?" She looked at Peter with an HR holier than thou smug face.

"Anything else?" He would not to admit to anything.

"However," she picked up the folder, "senior leadership has directed HR to offer a quite generous compensation package." She flipped it open and looked at the first page. "To be honest, it is much more than I would have offered, or think should be offered, but—"

"Sheila." MacBride cut her off. His rocking stopped. "Given your long history and your recent efforts, we want to show our appreciation."

Peter was confused.

"Am I being rewarded or fired?"

"Yes. We appreciate your long service and recent efforts," MacBride said. "Sheila will explain the details."

She opened the folder with a quick flip of her wrist.

"As I stated, this is quite a unique severance package. One I —"

"Sheila. We have gone over his. Please continue," was all MacBride said.

Peter enjoyed watching Sheila squirm. She was caught between her disapproval of whatever was to come and her inherent need to appear to management—at all times—as a loyal and professional employee. With a sigh, she picked up a large document-sized golden envelope and read aloud.

"For your recent efforts on behalf of Kirkwood International Industries."

She reluctantly handed him an envelope.

"That is ten thousand fully vested incentive stock options. You have ninety days to exercise them," MacBride announced.

Peter was speechless and confused.

Sheila continued.

"The current Kirkwood severance pay is one week for every year worked. Although you have only been with the company for eleven years, I have been authorized to offer you twenty-two months of pay. Plus, the company will fully cover your health insurance costs for this same period." She closed the folder and handed it to Peter. "Quite generous, as I said." She handed him the folder.

"Why?" Peter looked at MacBride, who was rocking slightly in his chair.

"Why are you being released, or the severance package?"

"No. Yes. Both."

"To receive the options, the extended severance, and health care, you must sign a binding non-disclosure agreement." MacBride stopped rocking. "Legally binding."

"Another NDA? Why? What for?"

"Walter thought you needed an NDA that contained more specific post-employment restrictions." MacBride tilted his head so his glasses could focus on a sheet of paper. "You are not allowed to discuss, write about, or present any facets of your work at Kirkwood. All your files would be sequestered by lawyers as they are property of the company. You cannot take anything concerning this operation with you. We keep your laptop and phone. They are company property."

"For how long?"

"Forever. In the event you want an exception to this NDA, you are required to get written approval, in advance, from Walter Jessup directly." MacBride paused as he sat back and started swiveling again. "Despite whatever actions taken during the recent Ukraine events, you have been an asset to the company and we want you to know that."

Peter looked at the folder with the stock options. It felt expensive. The gold embossed lettering shone in the fluorescent lights, creating a contrast to the matte black background. It told the ex-employee, *you may not have a job, but you have a nice souvenir folder to remember us by.*

"What if I don't sign?"

"Why wouldn't you sign?" Sheila was apoplectic. "There are thousands of employees who would beg for this package. Not sign? Are you kidding?"

Peter heard Benton let out a grunt. He had forgotten Benton was still in the room.

"Sheila, will you excuse us? Thank you." MacBride waved his arm to the door. "Benton, you can stay."

Slightly flustered, she did her best not to show it as the door closed behind her.

"Not signing would be a mistake. Then you will be immediately terminated with cause and without any severance. Benton. Tell him," MacBride said.

"There is that bunch of incriminating documents you already received from Boyd. If others were added to your files—and they have —when found would show you are a spy for China. Hell, you let a foreign spy into our classified area—it would be more than what we need. Twenty years in prison—minimum," Benton said, as happy as Peter had ever seen him.

"Yes, I got docs from Sandy, but you know none of the rest is true," Peter said, as his pulse raced.

"What does the truth have to do with anything?" Benton replied with a snort.

MacBride stood. He moved to Sheila's vacated spot on the couch. "Sheila is annoying, but she is right." He leaned forward, his elbows on his knees. "You should take it. Sign it, Peter. Please. We don't want this to go any further, but if we have to, we will—to protect the company."

Peter saw MacBride glance up to Benton, who was still leaning against the door. MacBride continued.

"Then we can all move on from this. You may be interested to know that Gilbert Street retired this morning."

"A loss for Kirkwood." Peter stood. "Thanks for the offer, I mean it, but I'm not signing. I quit."

"Peter!" A stunned MacBride said, as he watched Peter turn and walk to the door. Benton blocked his way out. Peter moved in close.

"Please move."

Benton waited, then stepped aside, not hiding the grin on his face.

"See ya, Schaeffer."

At 4 a.m., Peter thought he heard a soft snap, followed by a metal rumble downstairs. It sounded like the screen door to the patio was loose. James was known for not closing it all the way. If it was a windy night, Peter had to get up in the dark to stop it from rattling and banging with every gust.

He hoped he just imagined it.

He hadn't slept much after the events of the day. One moment he had a job—the next, he had nothing. It was a cover-up. He wouldn't play, but he had a family to support. But he also didn't want to go to prison.

Then he heard another sound.

Peter let Janelle sleep as he slid out of bed. He checked to see if James was asleep, closed his door, then went downstairs. As he took the last step, he heard electronic sparks. The sound was followed by a grunt and the unmistakable sound of a body free-falling and hitting a hard surface.

Peter whirled around the corner, using his elbow to flip the light switch on the wall. The front entry and hallway lit up. Laying in the hallway, face down, was Benton dressed head to toe in black. On the floor, a few inches from his hand, was a large knife.

Standing over the unconscious man was Demon, also dressed in black and holding his Devil Stick like a sword. He looked up, then down, a big smile on his face. Snake was by the sliding kitchen door.

"Full power. Went down like an anvil in a swamp." He pulled the electrodes out of Benton's back and rolled them up. "This is a pretty big hunk of meat. I had to let him have it." He clipped the Stick to his belt, reached down, and tossed Benton—who probably had fifty pounds on Demon—over his shoulder like a bag of roof shingles.

Peter was speechless.

"You should use your security alarm." Demon turned and walked toward the kitchen door.

"How? What?" Peter finally asked.

"Greetings from the Devil," he heard them say, as they disappeared into the night.

59

ANGEL

Abaddon Ranch, Texas

As he worked in the Spy Devils Ops Center below his house on Abaddon Ranch, Bridger relished the ease in which he could destroy Kirkwood International Industries.

They were a sitting duck.

In minutes, media business experts would report the company was having *"an issue."* In a few hours, stories would proclaim *"serious allegations"* surrounded the management of the company. By the end of the day, it would be described by financial news commentators as a company that required *"criminal investigation."*

Bridger just couldn't stomach Chinese intelligence ripping off technology from a U.S. company. He couldn't stomach the culpability of Kirkwood executives in their fraudulent actions. Most of all, they were going to suffer his wrath for how they treated Peter—and the attempt on his life—which was a stupid move.

When Demon called with the news that he had intercepted the intruder at Peter's house, that stoked the flames of his wrath.

"What do you want me to do with him?" Demon asked.

"I don't care," Bridger replied. "Use your imagination."

"Hell yes!"

Bridger could give a rat's ass. Chapel had called trying to convince Bridger one last time to hand over the case—which Bridger replied with a *"In all due respect, go fuck yourself."*

Chapel then informed him about Peter's decision. Bridger respected that Peter didn't cave to Kirkwood's bribe offer or NDA demand. That showed him something. A man with a family risking it all for principle. A rare commodity. Chapel understood that, too. Bridger assumed the relaying of the intel on Peter was the real reason Chapel called.

He had Imp hack into Peter's computer to retrieve all the documents he would need as proof of Kirkwood's crimes. It was there. The arrangements to significantly inflate revenue from Mourning Dove contracts in a subtly crafted exchange for trade secrets and technology.

He sent the info through back channels—not as a Spy Devils-branded investigation—but to a BBC News Business contact. The story was the lead for their 7 a.m. news program. Simultaneously, it appeared on BBC's webpage and social media. Bridger's sources at NHK in Tokyo and ChannelNewsAsia in Singapore, 4 p.m., and 3 p.m. local time, respectively, picked up and led with the BBC scoop.

The news crossed the international dateline at digital speeds, reaching all the morning business shows in New York City five hours later, 7 a.m. local.

With slight variations, all the media read or reprinted the reports from the same Bridger-supplied copy. The bright red 'Breaking News' banner blared - *Kirkwood International Suspected of Accounting Fraud.*

Before Kirkwood's communications staff could answer the tidal wave of text messages, calls, and emails looking for a comment, he released the next story: *Kirkwood CEO Linked to Chinese Intelligence.*

Later in the evening, armed with a stack of emergency search warrants, FBI agents, supported by SEC officials, raided Kirkwood headquarters. The images of FBI agents clad in dark jackets with yellow block letters across the back, were added to the developing story. They hauled out boxes and computers as anxious employees looked on.

In an emergency board meeting vote the next day, Samuel Kirkwood was removed as Chairman and CEO. Walter Jessup retired immediately. Tom MacBride was put on leave.

———

Peter received a package the next afternoon.

He ripped the tab open, pulled out the bubble wrap, and dumped the contents on the table—a white envelope and a mobile phone. He set the phone aside, opened the envelope, pulled out a few sheets of paper, and read.

Peter:

I hope you don't mind receiving a letter from the Devil. My wrist is recovering nicely, thanks for asking.

You did well in Kyiv. Unfortunately, your former employer, Kirkwood, is not doing as well. They will not be bothering you further.

As you might remember, I have an opening. If you are interested, I have a company in my network called EDR&J that needs to fill a position. It is an international political consulting firm in need of a "business development manager" with experience in the public and private sectors. You will get a package to finalize all the details.

You will find attached some invoices dated over the next year and a signing bonus totaling $2.1 million. They are made out to the company with the catchy name Peter Schaeffer and Associates, LLC.

I took the liberty of setting up a few accounts in Switzerland and the Cayman Islands on your behalf. The access codes and contact details are attached.

You might find it coincidental that $2.1 million is the exact amount I found in one of the numerous private accounts of Viktor Bondar. Viktor was not thrilled to know I took them. I told him just before he shot poor Ira.

The phone is for Spy Devils work only. Keep it on you. Be prepared.

The rest of the gang says hello. You might be pleasantly surprised to learn they have already chosen a name for you.

Welcome to the Spy Devils, Angel.

The Devil.

Peter set the letter on the table and looked at the next sheet listing bank accounts and access information. He put down that paper and smiled at the thought of being a Spy Devil.

He picked up the phone Bridger sent and powered it on.

It blinked to life.

So did he.

DON'T CALL ME

Great Falls, Virginia

S nake covered the fifty feet from the shore in a low crouch. He scooted around the trees and thick brush and stopped behind a bush where the well-kept lawn sloped gently up to the large colonial home. Light came through the windows on the lower level.

More like a colonial mansion, he thought as he flipped down his night-vision goggles.

The area was large and secluded. The magnificent two-story house had a veranda that encircled the house on all sides, framed with a white railing on all sides. Square windows with black shutters. Paths led down from the house to a stable. On the far side, a long one-lane drive circled up to the front door. A flag pole with an American flag flooded by lights was in the center of the circle.

"Milton?" Bridger asked, from his prone position behind some bushes next to the circular drive.

"Guard coming around the front—pacing along the porch," Milton's southern accent whispered through the secure comm system. He adjusted the camera of the Devilbot hovering above them. "Two guards on the west veranda, walking in overlapping patterns. Another…hang on standing far side. I think."

"You think? You think?" Demon scowled.

"Enough," Bridger interrupted. "Imp?"

"As usual, due to my incredible skills, we are all clear. They are quiet, except for a brief chat about each other's small reproductive organs. Shameful to talk about their colleagues that way."

"You should know, pencil dick," Demon cracked.

Some laughs over the comm.

"Beatrice?"

"I'm ready," she replied.

"Okay, Imp. Kill all the security systems, cameras, and alarms. Jam their communications. Let's go."

Demon crept up behind one sentry.

"Hey," he whispered.

The guard wheeled around as Demon rose from his crouched position. He coiled, then swung his Devil Stick backhanded full force across the face of the sentry.

The guard made a soft "Oooomp," followed by the crunching sound of his shattering nose and cheekbones. Demon caught the unconscious man before he hit the ground—not to be polite, but to avoid the loud noise of his body thudding to the patio.

Demon looked up to see another guard turn the corner ten feet away. The sentry instinctively crouched and raised his weapon. Demon was ready and released the Taser dart electrodes. They struck the chest of the man above his heart. Demon covered the distance in two seconds and sent a fist squarely into the shaking, defenseless man's face. His twitching, unconscious body flew back and over the rail. He crashed into some bushes, snapping branches as he sunk.

"Geez. This is what passes for security now?"

"What's your status?" Bridger whispered, exasperation and tension in his voice.

"Two down and in need of a dentist and plastic surgeon."

Beatrice stood as a guard who must have heard the branches break quickly turned the corner of the veranda on the far side of the house.

She released a full dose of gas into the face of the unsuspecting man. The capsaicin neurotoxin was so strong he didn't even react. He simply dropped to the ground like his bones had been removed.

"Three down," Beatrice reported.

Snake rose from his location and did the same to the guard in front. "Four."

"Imp, unlock the doors."

"What would you do without me?"

Bridger adjusted the soft cast on his left wrist and stepped out of the darkness onto the porch by the front door. Bridger steadied his nerves, opened the front door, and walked in. He held his Devil Stick tightly in his right hand, given the cast covering his wrist. In his other hand was the bag containing Hillcrest.

She was on the couch talking to a man sitting in one of two high back chairs across from her.

May saw him in the doorway. "Speak of…well…the Devil."

Chapel peered over the top of the chair. "Hello, Bridger. We meet again, as they say. As you can see, I have not 'fucked myself' as you suggested." Chapel waited for a snappy retort from Bridger. When it didn't come, he shrugged. "Come in and have a drink."

"Sit down, Trowbridge."

She pointed with a thin finger to the empty chair across from her. He didn't move. She signaled again. He stood with a look that he hoped betrayed nothing of what he was thinking or feeling. It was working. Bridger saw her eyebrows rise an eighth of an inch.

"Please display some common courtesy. Do what your mother asks —for once," Chapel said.

Bridger walked into the study and sat on a second chair across from her. Chapel, dressed in his usual suit and tie, was to his right, arms crossed. Calm and composed, Bridger set the Faraday Bag on the floor by the chair.

"It is nice to see you." She nodded to his injured wrist. "How are you feeling?"

"I'm fine for having to blow myself up." He let the Devil Stick rest in his lap—the end was pointed directly at May.

"I am glad." She looked at the weapon, then back to Bridger's unflinching face.

"That *was* quite an audacious idea," Chapel added with a laugh. Bridger looked at him with disdain. "And my guards? Demon did not kill them, did he?" Chapel looked over May's shoulder out the window.

"You both will find your security teams are in less than perfect operating condition." Bridger looked at Chapel. "Again."

"Disappointing," he said. "I was told these men were better."

May reached for a cup of tea on the end table. Her steady hands brought the hot beverage to her lips, sipped, then returned it to the saucer with a rattle. "It might not come as a surprise, but I was expecting you."

"No, I am not surprised. I assumed Chapel whined to you about our dinner date," Bridger said.

"I do not whine." Chapel brushed his tie as he smiled and turned in his chair.

"Shut up, Chapel. I wasn't talking to you."

Chapel ignored Bridger. "I told her she should expect you, since, as I said, you had no choice but to come here."

"Shut up, Chapel," Bridger said, keeping his eyes on May.

Chapel looked at the bag and continued with the pompous tone he used to let others know how prescient he was. "I expounded that your options are limited. And here you are."

Bridger twisted his wrist, pointed the Devil Stick at Chapel, and clicked the Taser switch. The probes hit Chapel at point-blank range in his neck, just above the knot of his tie. He gagged, stiffened, and jerked back as his feet spasmed against the floor, propelling him and the chair backward. Bridger flipped the controls, extended his arm, and let out a blast of spray into the grunting man's face.

He went silent.

Shock crossed May's face as she realized her son had just attacked one of the most powerful men in the world—and a useful tool.

She looked at Bridger. Now the Devil Stick was pointed directly at her. His hands were steady. His eyes were focused on May. Bridger rolled his thumb to the gas controls. He saw her body tense.

"What do you want?" she asked.

"Tell me everything, May. Everything."

"What don't you know?"

"Why us?" His thumb slowly rubbed across the control like he was scratching an itch.

"I made a deal," she said. Her eyes nervously flicked again at his hand.

"A deal?" He felt the sweat in his palms. He tightened his grip on the weapon.

"I had to get the case to Chen. It was the last step in a decades-long operation. You were the only option. The *last* option. Chen had supplied all the intel you used to eliminate the Dragon Fire—I assume you ascertained that."

"I'm not a fool."

"No, you are not. Chen thought it fair I do the same—as a final show of good faith. Imagine, after all these years, and the things we have done to get to this point. He wanted a show of good faith."

"I can only imagine."

"I had to figure out a way to get the case and get rid of the rest of them, and, well, the only way to do that was to use you and your team."

She started to reach over toward her tea, then stopped when she saw her hands were trembling. She clutched them together and set her hands in the lap of her dress.

"Chen had to *appear* to have acquired the case and bring it back to the MSS. We had made them think it was a vital technology. A long and steady deception op with Chen seemingly overcoming all odds. Now, acquiring it is their number one priority."

"What is inside the case?" Bridger asked.

"Nothing we can't live without and something his side will commemorate when he brings it to them."

"But, like most ops, it all went sideways. He couldn't fail."

"At the most critical moment. First, MacLean and Bondar. Then

Mr. Li Chu, who had nothing to do with Hillcrest until he went out on his own looking for you in Ukraine. I promised to give Chen the Spy Devils. He had a *small* amount of leverage. Can you believe that? Leverage on me!" She shook her head a few times. "Certainly, you can see allowing him to locate you was the only alternative left to me. Once you had your encounter, either way, Chen would be happy. Li Chu dies by your hand or his. He gets the case. I kept face."

"No matter the outcome?" Bridger asked.

For the first time, he noticed the deep creases of age around her eyes. Her shoulders were slightly stooped. The hands she still tried to hide were mostly tight skin over protruding blood veins and bones. She was getting old.

"Yes. No matter what, but you knew that before you came in," May answered.

"I knew it. I just didn't want to believe it. You picked a double-agent operation with Chen over your son and the Spy Devils. It almost cost me my life. And Peter Schaeffer, too. It cost Beast his."

"It is a hazardous profession."

"Chapel was your channel to Kirkwood and the Chinese—to us." He glanced at the motionless body crumpled on the floor to his right.

"Danny is a man with power connections in all sectors—and with me, of course."

She started to reach for her cup. This time her hands were steadier.

"Why attack Peter Schaeffer at his home?" He was tapping the Devil Stick up and down on his thigh. He saw that she noticed.

"I had nothing to do with that," May said, just a little too quickly. "That was an internal Kirkwood decision." She looked him in the eyes to show she was not deceiving him. "It was rather impulsive what you did to Kirkwood. They might not recover. Classic Bridger. You always were impulsive, no matter how much I tried to train that out of you." She forced a smile as she changed the subject.

"You can fire me."

May's face displayed slight exasperation with her son.

"I *am* sorry about Beast," she said, after a moment of silence.

He still had to notify Beast's family. He dreaded it. He planned to open an account and shift a few million to help support his family. *"He had a generous life insurance policy."* It was something.

"What's on your mind, Trowbridge?" She looked at him.

Bridger could *practically* see true maternal instincts on her face.

He wasn't exactly sure what *was* on his mind. Perhaps it was betrayal by his mother. Perhaps he was just tired of the espionage game. Maybe he could get out and live a more normal life. Get married. Have kids. The things real people do. Swap the Spy Devil life for the Peter Schaeffer life.

Live as Mr. Trowbridge Hall.

Bridger knew what was eating at him.

He knew he had to give May the case. She knew it too and that made it worse. If he analyzed the situation from her perspective, her decision was the correct one. Chen becoming the head of the MSS would be an intelligence coup of immense proportions. The intelligence would be immeasurable. Maybe change the history of the world.

Who was *he* to ruin that? *He* was expendable.

He stood, Devil Stick in hand, regarded her, and turned. He left the case by the chair. He stepped over Chapel, walked toward the door, then stopped.

"Don't call me. Deal?"

She let out a sigh and reached for her tea. Steady hands brought the cup to her mouth this time. She grimaced.

"It's cold." She set it back on the saucer. "I was just talking to—"

"Nothing for at least a month. A year would be better," Bridger interrupted with his demand.

She stood up and followed him.

"You are joking."

"Call it what you want, but don't call," he said as he reached for the front doorknob.

"I can't—" She saw her son's face. "Alright. I promise. *One month.*"

"I will hold you to that. Don't make me come back here." His face was serious—the Stick was poised in her direction.

He opened the door and started to leave. Then he stopped and turned back to her.

"Oh. And happy birthday—mother."

He disappeared into the darkness.

.

ONE MONTH

Abaddon, West Texas Hill Country, USA

B
ridger told the Spy Devils to get lost until he called and that he didn't know how long that would be.

It took two solid weeks for him to decompress. He locked his phone away in the control room. He rode around his vast property in a UTV for hours, enjoying the sun and fresh air. He watched the sun set and rise. He tried fishing—too boring. He rode horses and helped Luis and his team with some ranch maintenance.

Bridger watched as little news as possible. He saw a story about the disappearance of the Chief of the Cyprus Police. Bridger knew where at least Demon spent part of his time off.

Bridger let his arm heal enough, so by week three, he could get out on his golf course and try chipping and putting. He was awful, but it didn't matter. He was golfing.

The rest of the time, he spent sleeping, reading, and eating lots of steaks perfectly prepared by Luciana.

And by the end of week four, he was bored to death.

At precisely the one-month mark, and while he stood on the green of the 17th at TPC Sawgrass, three chirps in his earbuds cut into The Marshall Tucker Band singing "Can't You See."

"Yes, May," he said.

"It has been a month. Time to get back to work."

"I said a year."

"Bridger, try not to be disrespectful, like usual. I have a rather unique operation for you, unlike anything."

"More unique than the last one?"

"Yes, it is," she answered.

"That is hard to believe."

"I will send the details to the Dropbox," she said, just before the call ended.

He tugged his cap tighter on his head to block the blinding sun from his eyes. He bent over and placed a golf ball by a worn brass marker with blue lettering. He rubbed it between his fingers before he put it in his pocket.

"More unique than the last one," Bridger repeated.

He set his feet, lined up a putt, and tapped the ball. It curled and dropped into the cup ten feet away.

"Good," he said.

THE END

AUTHOR'S NOTE

Why so much time between books?

My first novel, *Secret Wars: An Espionage Story,* came out in 2014. That's a long time ago. Well, it isn't for lack of writing. I started a sequel to *Secret Wars,* but I was convinced to stop a quarter of the way in. Agents want contemporary action books, I was told.

Scrap the sequel? Okay, but what should I write?

How about a corporate intelligence thriller? I worked in that field for years and have lots of real-life experiences. Sounded like a plan.

After starting, stopping, starting, and finally finishing a draft, I found out something: the corporate intel world is a boring topic for fiction—no matter how I sliced it. No action. Certainly free of thrills, unless filling in travel expense spreadsheets thrills you.

I decided to merge two of my worlds—the CIA and the business arena. I still had a few experiences up my sleeve. Can I squish them together to build a realistic story?

I also had this theme running through my head, dictating my writing.

"Everyone has a story."

Readers needed to say "that could be me" about the characters when they were done reading. The characters required lives. Relationships. A basis in reality. Then I needed to place these characters into situations that were believable as they were.

I ended up with about 300,000 words searching to find the right balance of business and government—the right combination of action and reality.

Along came the Spy Devils—the first in a series. Is it real? Is it fiction? Does it matter?

As in all works of fiction, some moments push credibility, especially when it comes to the Spy Devils (as Bridger wrote in the Foreword).

As I wrote in *Secret Wars*, it isn't Hemingway, but I hope you enjoy a good story.

Thanks for reading it.

Joe
Wheaton, Il
USA

ACKNOWLEDGMENTS

"No book is an island."

Okay. That's not exactly what John Donne wrote, but it is true. It takes a community to move an idea for a book from ideation to publication. I have benefited from many visitors to my island who provided wisdom, assistance, and support.

The most important inhabitant of my island is my wife Lynda. She has endured way too many days of my often-grumpy mood-shifting process. Without her encouragement—I don't want to think about it. The rest of my family provided support all along the way. Jessica (Goldberg) Sobie, Roger Sobie, and the grandkids Elliott, Reid, and Adelie. Sarah Goldberg. Benjamin Goldberg. Thanks team.

My brothers: Stan, Mike, Gary, Alan. At various times, they pushed, pulled, and encouraged.

Within seconds after I typed "THE END" on the very first draft of *The Spy Devils* and posted a photo on Facebook, my phone rang. The incomparable Ryan Steck, of *The Real Book Spy,* was on the line. We talked. We plotted. We became friends. Ryan has provided guidance, honest, constructive comments, and so much more. His friendship is invaluable. *The Real Book Spy* is the real deal.

I would not have stayed on course without the friendship, advice, and material support of JT Patten, aka Scott Swanson (read his books). We consumed a lot of BBQ talking about plots and the profession. If you need someone in your corner, start with JT.

When I foolishly thought I had a pretty good manuscript, John Paine showed me otherwise with his incredible professional editing skills. You have read the results of his expertise. Jessica Garvin made the last thorough copy edit review. Renee Rocco for her formatting skills. Heidi Aubin for her photography. Damonza.com for the great cover.

Some outstanding writers and others have, in some way, encouraged or buttressed my efforts—Josh Hood. Simon Gervais. Mark Greaney. Kevin Mauer. KJ Howe.

Eric Bishop who has done more to market *The Spy Devils* than I have! You are a steely-eyed fiction man. I look forward to reading *The Body Man*.

James Abt, Kashif Hussain, David Dobiasek, and the rest of the team at Best Thriller Books. You are filling a very important need for authors and it is greatly appreciated.

Sean, Mike, and CE at The Crew Reviews.

Jack Murphy at The Team House.

David Darling. Cathy Helowicz. Julie-Watson. Kronos Ananth. Each volunteered to read ARCs of the book. Intel professionals Derek and Arik Johnson of Aurora WDC. Sandy Fries. Journalist. Author. Professor.

Finally, I want to thank Bridger and the Spy Devils for letting me tell their story, even as a work of fiction. Greatly appreciated.

ABOUT THE AUTHOR

Joe Goldberg has had a diverse career. He has been a CIA covert action officer, a corporate intelligence director, international political consultant, and a college instructor. He holds degrees in Political Science and Communications from the University of Iowa. He has a passion for writing, U.S. history, Jimmy Buffett, the Iowa Hawkeyes, and his family.

Joe can be found on the internet and social media at:
Joegoldbergbooks.com
Facebook: www.facebook.com/joegoldbergbooks/
Twitter: @JoeGoldbergBook
Instagram: @JoeGoldbergbooks

ALSO BY JOE GOLDBERG

Secret Wars: An Espionage Story

COMING SOON:

Rebellious Son: A Spy Devils Thriller

Made in the USA
Las Vegas, NV
05 February 2022

43167419R00193